science short stories   2,00

AT THE TRACK

AT THE TRACK

A TREASURY OF
HORSE RACING STORIES

Edited by

Richard Peyton

GRAMERCY BOOKS
NEW YORK

For
DICK FRANCIS
First past the post in anyone's book!

This 2004 edition is published by Gramercy Books, an imprint of
Random House Value Publishing, a division of Random House, Inc.,
New York, by arrangement with Souvenir Press, Ltd

Gramercy is a registered trademark and the colophon is
a trademark of Random House, Inc.

Random House
New York • Toronto • London • Sydney • Auckland
www.randomhouse.com

Printed and bound in the United States

Library of Congress Cataloging-in-Publication Data
Deadly odds.
At the track : a treasury of horse racing stories /
edited by Richard Peyton.
p. cm
Originally published as: Deadly odds.
ISBN 0-517-22387-2
1. Horse racing—Fiction. 2. Detective and mystery stories, English.
3. Detective and mystery stories, American. 4. Race horses—Fiction.
I. Peyton, Richard. II. Title.

PR1309.H64D4 2004
823'.01'08355—dc22

2004047415

10 9 8 7 6 5 4 3 2 1

AT THE TRACK

CONTENTS

INTRODUCTION

Horse racing is an integral part of British history, a vivid and colourful pageant of people, courses and, above all, great horses, stretching back over three hundred years to the reign of that great sporting monarch, Charles II. He it was who first instituted races across the glorious heath at Newmarket, which has rightly come to be known as the 'Horse Racing Capital of the World'. In Britain, too, we created the thoroughbred racehorse and saw the rise of some of the greatest jockeys ever to mount a winner—Fred Archer, Jem Mason, Steve Donoghue, Gordon Richards, John Francome and Lester Piggott, to name just half a dozen.

We can also claim to have created the mystery story of the Turf now practised with such stunning success by writers like Jon Breen, John Welcome and, of course, Dick Francis, the 'King of Sporting Thrillers'. Today's great horses and riders owe much to their forebears, but so, too, do those who deal in crime and detection in the world of horse racing acknowledge their debt to the men who pioneered this fascinating genre a hundred years ago and more: that neglected pioneer, Angus Reach; the famous creator of Sherlock Holmes, Sir Arthur Conan Doyle; and his contemporary, Guy Boothby, who created the villainous Dr Nikola, as beloved of Victorian readers as Professor Moriarty. This book has been assembled to pay tribute to them and their successors, as well as to bring together in one volume the very best and most diverse examples of their art.

The world of horse racing is one of high drama and even higher stakes, and it is no surprise to find the elements of intrigue, corruption and even murder lurking just beneath the surface. It is a world of the good and the bad, the talented and the crooked—jockeys, trainers, owners, bookmakers, punters, touts and enthusiasts of every kind —all drawn by the unique sight of man and horse in partnership and exhilarating competition. That this sport should have fascinated some highly accomplished writers is, I think, hardly to be wondered at; my only surprise has been that such a collection as this has not been assembled before.

The fascination with horse racing is worldwide, and so I have included stories from America, Australia and even India, as well as featuring some of the great races on the calendar like the Derby, Royal Ascot and the Grand National. Gathered here are writers forever associated with the sport, like Nat Gould, Edgar Wallace and Damon Runyon, rubbing shoulders with equally famous authors who were just as fascinated by the Turf—Rudyard Kipling, Ralph Straus and Lord Dunsany. Add to them such excellent modern crime writers as Anthony Gilbert, Ellery Queen, Julian Symons and Michael Innes and you have a field of undoubted winners!

The odds may be deadly, but your entertainment in such company is, I am confident, assured.

Richard Peyton

THE DAY OF THE LOSERS

by Dick Francis

The Times *recently hailed Dick Francis as 'the great thriller writer of the racing world—the only man in history capable of turning a long journey into a pleasure', and anyone who has read his twenty-four hugely successful books will surely agree with that. Dick brings to his stories all the knowledge garnered from his years in the racing world when he became famous for riding many of the Queen Mother's horses to victory. When Dick first started writing he considered himself 'just a jockey who has a story to tell', but now he is as highly regarded in the literary stakes as ever he was on the turf—and so he should be with sales in excess of twenty-two million and races named after his books!*

Dick's best remembered moment as a jockey was the extraordinary collapse of his mount, Devon Loch, in the Grand National when he was only a couple of hundred yards from the winning post. Strangely, that bizarre incident has never found its way into any of his books, and indeed the only story he has written about the National is the following one which he wrote in February 1977 for the magazine Horse and Hound. *'The Day of the Losers' is full of the atmosphere, people and the inevitable 'dirty deed', which are the hallmarks of a Dick Francis story; I am delighted that it should open this collection, at the same time making its first appearance in book form.*

*   *   *

He set off to the Grand National with £300 in his pocket and a mixture of guilt and bravado in his mind.

Austin Dartmouth Glenn knew he had vowed not to put banknotes into premature circulation.

Not for five years, he had been sternly warned. Five years would see the heat off and the multi-million pound robbery would be ancient history.

The police would be chasing more recent villains and the hot serial numbers would have faded into fly-blown obscurity on out-of-date lists.

In five years it would be safe to spend the £15,000 he had been paid for his part in springing the bank-robbery boss out of unwelcome jail.

That was all very well, Austin told himself aggrievedly, looking out of the train window. What about inflation? In five years' time £15,000 might not be worth the paper it was printed on.

Or the colour and size of fivers might be changed. He'd heard of a frantic safe-blower who'd done 12 years and gone home to a cache full of the old thin white stuff.

All that time served for a load of out-of-date, uncashable, rubbish. Austin Glenn's mouth twisted in sympathy at the thought. It wasn't going to happen to him, not ruddy well likely.

Austin had paid for his train ticket with ordinary currency, and ditto for the cans of beer, packages of cellophaned sandwiches, and copy of the *Sporting Life*.

The hot £300 was stowed safely in an inner pocket, not to be risked before he reached the bustling anonymity of the huge crowd converging on the Aintree race course.

He was no fool, of course, he thought complacently. A neat pack of 60 fivers, crisp, new, and consecutive, might catch the most incurious eyes.

But no one would look twice now that he had shuffled them and crinkled them with hands dirtied for the purpose.

He wiped beer off his mouth with the back of his hand; a scrawny fortyish man with neat, thin grey-black hair, restless eyes, and an overall air of self-importance.

A life spent on the fringes of crime had given him hundreds of dubious acquaintances, an intricate memory-bank of information and a sound knowledge of how to solicit bribes without actually cupping the palm.

No one liked him very much but Austin was not sensitive enough to notice.

Nearer the front of the same train Jerry Springwood sat and sweated on three counts. For one thing, he was an outdoor man, and found the heat excessive, and for another, owing to alcohol and sex, he had no time to spare and would very likely lose his job if he arrived late; but above all, he sweated from fear.

Jerry Springwood, at 32, had lost his nerve and was trying to carry on the trade of steeplechase jockey without anyone finding out. The old days, when he used to ride with a cool brain and discount intermittent bangs as merely a nuisance, were long gone.

For months now he had travelled with dread to the meetings, imagining sharp ends of bone protruding from his skin, imagining a smashed face or a severed spine . . . imagining pain.

For months he had been unable to take risks he would once not have seen as risks at all.

For months he had been unable to urge his mounts forward into gaps, when only such urging would win; and unable to stop himself steadying his mounts to jump, when only kicking them on would do.

The skill which had taken him to the top was now used to cover the cracks, and the soundness of his long-time reputation bolstered the explanations for defeat which he gave to owners and trainers.

Only the most discerning saw the disguised signs of disintegration, and fewer still had put private doubts into private words.

The great British public, searching the list of Grand National runners for inspiration, held good old Jerry Springwood to be a plus factor in favour of the third favourite, Haunted House.

A year ago, he reflected drearily, as he stared out at the passing fields, he would have known better than to go to a party in London on the night before the big race.

A year ago he had stayed near the course, drunk maybe a couple of beers, gone to bed early, slept alone. He wouldn't have dreamed of making a four-hour dash south after Friday's racing, or getting drunk, or going to bed at two with a girl he'd known three hours.

He hadn't needed to blot out the thought of Saturday afternoon's marathon, but had looked forward to it with zest, excitement, and unquenchable hope.

Oh God, he thought despairingly, what has happened to me?

He was small and strong, with wiry mid-brown hair, deep set eyes, and a nose flattened by too much fast contact with the ground. A farmer's son, natural with animals, and with social manners sophisticated by success. People usually liked Jerry Springwood, but he was too unassuming to notice.

The crowds poured cheerfully into Aintree race course, primed with hope, faith, and cash. Austin peeled off the first of the hot fivers at the turnstiles, and contentedly watched it being sucked into the anonymity of the gate receipts.

He safely got change for another in a crowded bar, and for a third from a stall selling form sheets.

Money for old rope, he thought sardonically. It didn't make sense, holding on to the stuff for five years.

The Tote, as usual, had opened its windows an hour before the first race to take bets on the Grand National, because there was not time after the second to sell tickets to all who wanted to buy for the big third.

There were long queues already when Austin went along to back his fancy, for like him they knew from experience that it was best to bet early if one wanted a good vantage point in the stands.

He waited in the shorter queue for the £5 window, writing his proposal on his race card.

When his turn came, he said, 'Fifty to win, number twelve,' and counted off the shuffled fivers without a qualm.

The busy woman behind the window gave him his tickets with barely a glance. 'Next?' she said, looking over his shoulder to the man behind.

Dead easy, thought Austin smugly, stuffing his tickets into his jacket pocket. Fifty on number twelve, to win. No point in messing about with place money, he always said.

Mind you, he was a pretty good judge of form: He always prided himself on that.

Nothing in the race had a better chance than the third favourite, Haunted House, and you couldn't want a better jockey than Springwood, now could you? He strolled with satisfaction back to the bar and bought another beer.

In the changing room Jerry Springwood had no difficulty in disguising either his hangover or his fear. The other jockeys were gripped with the usual pre-National tension, finding their mouths a little dry, their thoughts a little abstracted, their flow of ribald jokes silenced to a trickle.

Twice over Becher's, Jerry thought hopelessly: the Canal Turn, the Chair, how in God's name am I going to face it?

The Senior Steward of the Jockey Club was lunching a party of eminent overseas visitors in a private dining room when Chief Superintendent Crispin interrupted the roast saddle of lamb.

'I want to speak to you urgently, sir,' the policeman said, bending down to the Turf's top ear.

Sir William Westerland rested his bland gaze briefly on the amount of brass on the navy blue uniform. 'You're in charge here?'

'Yes, sir. Can we talk privately?'

'I suppose so, if it's important.' Sir William rose, glanced regretfully at his half-eaten lunch, and led the policeman to the outdoor section of his private box high in the grandstand. The two men stood hunched in the chilly air, and spoke against the background noise of the swelling crowd and the shouts of the bookmakers offering odds on the approaching first race.

Crispin said, 'It's about the Birmingham bank robbery, sir.'

'But that happened more than a year ago,' Westerland protested.

'Some of the stolen notes have turned up here, today, on the race course.'

Westerland frowned, not needing to be told details. The blasting open of the supposedly impregnable vault, the theft of more than £3½ million, the violent getaway of the thieves, all had been given wider coverage than the death of Nelson.

Four men and a small boy had been killed by the explosion outwards of the bank wall, and two housewives and two young policemen had been gunned down later.

The thieves had arrived in a fire engine before the crashing echoes died, had dived into the ruins to carry out the vault's contents for 'safekeeping', and driven clear away with the loot.

They were suspected only at the very last moment by a puzzled constable, whose order to halt had been answered by a spray of machine-gun bullets.

Only one of the gang had been recognised, caught, tried, and sentenced to 30 years; and of that he had served precisely 30 days before making a spectacular escape. Recapturing him, and catching his confederates, was a No 1 police priority.

'It's the first lead we've had for months,' Crispin said earnestly. 'If we can catch whoever came here with the hot money . . .'

Westerland looked down at the scurrying thousands. 'Pretty hopeless, I'd have thought,' he said.

'No, sir,' Crispin shook his neat greying head. 'A sharp-eyed checker in the Tote spotted one of the notes, and now they've found nine more. One of the sellers in the £5 windows remembers selling £50 worth of tickets early on to a man who paid in fivers which *felt* new, although they had been roughly creased and wrinkled.'

'But even so . . .'

'She remembers he backed only one horse to win, which is unusual on Grand National Day.'

'Which horse?'

'Haunted House, sir. And so, sir, if Haunted House wins, our fellow will bring his batch of £50 worth of winning tickets to the pay-out, and we will have him.'

'But,' Westerland objected, 'What if Haunted House DOESN'T win?'

Crispin gazed at him steadily. 'We want you to arrange that Haunted House DOES win. We want you to fix the Grand National!'

Down in Tattersall's enclosure Austin Dartmouth Glenn passed two hot fivers to a bookmaker who stuffed them busily into his satchel without looking. A tenner to win on Spotted Tulip, at eight to one.

In the noise, haste, and flurry of the last five minutes before the first race Austin elbowed his way up the stands to find the best view of his money on the hoof, smirking with satisfaction.

In the changing room Jerry Springwood reluctantly climbed into his thin white breeches and fumbled with the buttons of his shiny red and white striped colours.

His mind was filling like a well with panic, the terrible desire to cut and run growing deeper and deadlier with every passing minute. He had difficulty in concentrating and virtually did not hear when anyone spoke to him.

His hands trembled. He felt cold. There was another hour to live through before he would have to force himself out to the parade ring, onto the horse, down to the start, and right round those demanding four and a half miles and over 30 huge fences.

I can't do it, he thought numbly. I can't face it. Where can I hide?

The four Stewards in charge of the meeting sat gloomily round their large table, reacting with varying degrees of incredulity and uneasiness to the urgings of Chief Superintendent Crispin.

'There's no precedent,' said one. 'It's out of the question. There isn't time,' said another.

A third said: 'You'd never get the trainers to agree.' 'And what about the owners?' asked the fourth.

Crispin held racing in as little esteem as crooked politicians and considered that catching the Birmingham mob was of far greater social importance than any particular horse finishing first.

His inner outrage at the obstructive reaction of the Stewards seeped unmistakably into his voice.

'The Birmingham robbers murdered nine people,' he said forcefully. 'Everyone has a public duty to help the police catch them.' 'Surely not to the extent of ruining the Grand National,' insisted the Stewards.

'I understand,' Crispin said, 'that in steeple-chasing in general few stud values are involved, and in this year's National the horses are all geldings. It is not as if we were asking you to spoil the Stud Book by fixing the Derby.'

'All the same, it would be unfair on the betting public,'' said the Stewards.

'The people who died were part of the betting public. The next people to die, in the next violent bank raid, will also be the betting public.'

Sir William Westerland listened to the arguments with his bland expression unimpaired. He had gone far in life by not declaring his views before everyone else had bared their breasts, their opinions, and their weaknesses.

His mild subsequent observations had a way of being received as revealed truth, when they were basically only unemotional common sense.

He watched Crispin and his fellow Stewards heat up into emphasis and hubbub, and begin to slide towards prejudice and hostility. He sighed internally, looked at his watch, and noisily cleared his throat.

'Gentlemen,' he said calmly and distinctly. 'Before we reach a decision, I think we should consider the following points. First, possibility. Second, secrecy. Third, consequences.'

Stewards and policemen looked at him with united relief.

'Jump jockeys,' Westerland said, 'are individualists. Who do you think is going to persuade them to fix the race?'

No answer.

'Who can say that Haunted House will not fall?'

No answer.

'How long do you suppose it would be before someone told the Press? Do we want the uproar which would follow?'

No answer, but a great shaking of stewardly heads.

'But if we refuse Chief Superintendent Crispin's request, how would we feel if another bank was blown apart and more innocent people killed, knowing we took no action to prevent it?'

The meeting looked at him in silence, awaiting his lead.

Jerry Springwood's head felt like a balloon floating somewhere above his unco-ordinated body. The call of 'Jockeys out, please', had found him still unable to think of a way of escape. Too many people knew him.

How can I run? he thought; how can I scramble to the gate and find a taxi when everyone knows I should be walking out to ride Haunted House?

Can I faint? he thought. Can I say I'm ill?

He found himself going out with the others, his leaden legs trudging automatically while his spirit wilted.

He stood in the parade ring with his mouth dry and his eyes feeling like gritty holes in his skull, not hearing the nervously hearty pre-race chit-chat of owner and trainer.

I can't, he thought. I can't.

The senior steward of the Jockey Club, Sir William Westerland, walked up to him as he stood rigidly in his hopeless hell.

'A word in your ear, Jerry,' he said.

Jerry Springwood looked at him blankly, with eyes like smooth grey pebbles. Westerland, who had seen that look on other faces and knew what it foreboded, suffered severe feelings of misgiving.

In spite of Chief Superintendent Crispin's opposition, he secured the stewards' whole-hearted agreement. The National could not be fixed—even to catch murderers.

He came to the conclusion that both practically and morally, it was impossible. The police would just have to keep a sharper check on future meetings, and one day soon, perhaps, they would catch their fish as he swam again to the Tote.

All the same, Westerland had seen no harm in wishing Jerry Springwood success; but he perceived now that Crispin had no chance of catching his men today. No jockey in this state of frozen fear could win the National.

The backers of Haunted House would be fortunate if their fancy lasted half a mile before he pulled up, or ran out, or refused to jump because of the stranglehold on his reins.

'Good luck,' said Westerland lamely, with regret.

Jerry made no answer, even ordinary politeness being beyond him.

Up on his vantage point in the stands, Austin Glenn watched the long line of runners walk down the course. Ten minutes to race time, with half the bookies suffering from sore throats and the massed crowds buzzing with rising excitement.

Austin, who had lost his tenner on Spotted Tulip in the first, and fifteen more to bookmakers on the second, was biting his knuckles over Haunted House.

Jerry Springwood sat like a sack in the saddle, shoulders hunched. The horse, receptive to his rider's mood, plodded along in confusion, not able to sort out whether or not he should respond to the crowd instead.

To Austin and many others, horse and rider looked like a grade one losing combination.

William Westerland shook his head ruefully, and Crispin wondered irritably why that one horse, out of all of them, looked half asleep.

Jerry Springwood got himself lined up for the start by blotting out every thought. The well of panic was full and trying to flood over.

Jerry, white and clammily sweating, knew that in a few more minutes he would have to dismount and run.

Have to.

When the starter let them go, Haunted House was standing flat-footed. Getting no signal from the saddle, he started hesitantly after the departing field.

The horse knew his job—he was there to run and jump and get his head in front of the next.

But he was feeling rudderless, without the help and direction he was used to.

His jockey stayed on board by instinct, the long years of skill coming to his aid, the schooled muscles acting in a pattern that needed no conscious thought.

Haunted House jumped last over the first fence, and was still last five fences later, approaching Becher's.

Jerry Springwood saw the horse directly in front of him

fall, and knew remotely that if he went straight on he would land on top of him.

Almost without thinking he twitched his right hand on the rein, and Haunted House, taking fire from this tiniest sign of life, swerved a yard, bunched his quarters, and put his great equine soul into clearing the danger.

Haunted House knew the course: had won there, with Jerry Springwood up, in shorter races. His sudden surge over Becher's melted his jockey's defensive blankness and thrust him into freshly vivid fear.

Oh God, Jerry thought, as Haunted House took him inexorably towards the Canal Turn, how can I? How can I?

He sat there, fighting his panic, while Haunted House carried him surefootedly round the Turn, and over Valentine's and all the way to The Chair.

Jerry thought forever after that he'd shut his eyes as his mount took the last few strides towards the most testing steeplechase fence in the world, but Haunted House met it perfectly and cleared the huge spread without the slightest stumble.

Over the water jump in front of the stands, and out again towards Becher's, with the whole course to jump again. Jerry thought, if I pull up now, I'll have done enough.

Horses beside him tired and stopped or slid and fell but Haunted House galloped at a steady 30 miles an hour with scant regard for his fate.

Austin Glenn on the stands, and William Westerland in his private box, and Chief Superintendent Crispin tense in front of a television set, all watched with faster pulses as Haunted House made progress through the field.

By the time he reached Becher's on the second circuit he lay 10th, and seventh at the Canal Turn, and fifth after the third last fence, a mile from home.

Jerry Springwood saw a gap on the rails and didn't take it. He checked his mount before the second-last fence so they jumped it safely but lost two lengths.

On the stands William Westerland groaned aloud, but on Haunted House Jerry Springwood just shrivelled inside at his own fearful cowardice. It's useless, he thought. I'd be better off dead.

The leader of the field had sprinted a long way ahead, and Jerry saw him ride over the last fence while Haunted House was a good 40 lengths in the rear. One more, Jerry thought. Only one more fence. I'll never ride another race. Never.

He locked his jaw as Haunted House gathered his muscles and launched his half ton weight at the green-faced birch. If he rolls on me, Jerry thought . . . if I fall and he crashes on top of me . . . Oh God, he thought, take me safely over this fence.

The horse in front, well-backed and high in the handicap, took the last flat half-mile at a spanking gallop. Jerry Springwood and Haunted House, still on their feet, had left it too late to make a serious bid to catch them, but with a surge of what Jerry knew to be release from purgatory they raced past everything else in a flat-out dash to the post.

Austin Glenn watched Haunted House finish second by 20 lengths. Cursing himself a little for not bothering about place money, he took out his tickets, tore them philosophically across, and let the pieces flutter away to the four winds.

William Westerland rubbed his chin and wondered whether Jerry Springwood could have won if he'd tried sooner. Chief Superintendent bitterly cursed the 20 lengths by which his quarry would escape.

Sir William took his eminent foreign visitors down to watch the scenes of jubilation round the winner in the unsaddling enclosure, and was met by flurried officials with horrified faces.

'The winner can't pass the scales,' they said.

'What do you mean?' Westerland demanded.

'The winner didn't carry the right weight! The trainer left the weight-cloth hanging in the saddling box when he put the saddle on his horse. The winner ran all the way with 10lb less than he should have done . . . and we'll have to disqualify him.'

Forgetting the weight-cloth was done often enough; but in the National! William Westerland took a deep breath and told the aghast officials to relay the facts to the public over the tannoy system.

Jerry Springwood heard the news while he was sitting on the scales and watching the pointer swing round to the right mark. He felt, not joyful, but overwhelmingly ashamed, as if he'd won the prize by cheating.

Crispin stationed his men strategically, and alerted all the Tote pay-out windows.

Up on the stands, Austin Glenn searched for the pieces in a fury, picking up every torn and trampled scrap and peering at it anxiously.

What if someone else picked up his tickets, and claimed his winnings? The idea enraged him: and what was more, he couldn't stay on the course indefinitely because he had to catch his return train. He couldn't afford to be late; he had to work that night.

Crispin's men shifted from foot to foot as time went by, and were left there growing more and more conspicuous while the crowd thinned and trouped out through the gates.

When the Tote closed for the day the Chief Superintendent called them off in frustrated rage, and conceded that they would have to wait for another day after all.

In the weighing room Jerry Springwood bore the congratulations as best he could, and announced to surprised television millions that he would be hanging up his boots in a few weeks, at the end of the season.

Austin Dartmouth Glenn travelled home empty-handed and in a vile mood. He cursed his wife and kicked the cat, and after a hasty supper he put on his neat navy blue uniform.

Then he went off scowling to work his usual night shift as a warder in the nearby high security jail.

THE FIELD AGAINST THE FAVOURITE

by Angus Reach

Although Dick Francis is undeniably today's leading writer of racing thrillers, he would be the first to admit that he is only continuing a long-standing tradition dating back to the nineteenth century. In 1849, a Scottish journalist named Angus Reach published an episodic crime story called Clement Lorimer; or The Book with the Iron Clasps. *Reach, the son of an Inverness solicitor, had taken up newspaper work as his profession and, perhaps because of his family background, became fascinated with crime and criminals. He was also an enthusiast of the Turf and a regular visitor to several Scottish race courses where, apparently, his penchant for wild gambling often left him penniless.*

It was in an attempt to restore his finances that Reach began the serial story of the gentleman of fortune, Clement Lorimer who, like his creator, has a passionate interest in horse racing. Undoubtedly the most striking episode of this now extremely rare story concerns Lorimer's bid to win the Derby. Not only is 'The Field Against the Favourite' the earliest fictional story to feature that famous race, but also, so far as I know, the first horse racing thriller in short story form. In comparing it with Dick Francis' story, written more than a century later, you will find that both have striking elements in common . . .

* * *

In a room overlooking Hyde Park, Clement Lorimer was lounging on a combination of easy chairs. Apparently his musings were not of the agreeable sort, for his brow was clouded and his lips bore the mark of having been bitten.

'I'm a fool!' he muttered to himself, 'a thrice-sodden fool, to live the life I do! What does anyone care for me—for what do they get out of me? Bah! They're all alike, men and women. And my money—it may stop any day. There's no certainty—it may stop and leave me perhaps some forty thousand worse than a beggar!'

For a moment he was silent, and then: 'I know! I'll pull up—I'll—I'll make a grand coup on the Derby. I'll bet as man never did before. Snapdragon shall win as a horse never did before, and then I'll have the yacht and be off—off from Europe, and try to find some place where there is no civilisation to make people savages, and no religion to make them heathens.'

A footman appeared at the door, and announced laconically, 'Tim Flick.'

'Just the man I wanted,' responded Clement Lorimer. 'Up with him directly!'

Straightway Tim Flick appeared.

He was a very little man, not five feet high, and a perfect marvel of thinness. He had an old, wrinkled, meagered face, with two sharp grey eyes, and the facial muscles worked under the dry, tawny skin like sharply-tugged whipcords. His body seemed formed of nothing but skin, bone and sinew; his arms were long and wiry; and his legs, which were very bandy, were of a uniform thickness, or rather thinness, from the thigh to the ankle. This odd-looking personage wore a white cravat fastened with a huge silver horse-shoe, a tight-fitting coat, the waist of which appeared rather below the hips, and which was garnished with a vast number of outside pocket-holes; and he had encased his flute-like legs in a pair of corduroys which clung to him like a second skin, and were ornamented with half-a-dozen buttons above the ankles.

'Bravo, Flick! You're come in the nick of time!'

'Yes,' was the reply, in a harsh, dry, grating voice, 'I got the office, an' I made the running.'

'Well, sit down.'

Mr Flick deposited his grey hat upon the carpet, took a cotton handkerchief out of it, with which he appeared about to dust the chair; but, suddenly changing his purpose, he dusted the seat of his trousers instead, and then, perching himself on the extreme edge of the *fauteuil* which Lorimer pushed towards him, waited to be spoken to.

'Well, Flick, how does the horse train? All right down at Hawleyden, eh?'

Flick looked cautiously around: the door was closed, and the windows fastened. Then, leaning forward, he said in a low, hoarse whisper,

'It's a safe thing—it is! I've a-ridden seventeen Derbies and won five, and I tell you so. Inwest, Mr Lorimer, inwest!'

'He trains well, then? I'll go down tomorrow and see him gallop.'

'I was pretty nigh, as I may say, born in a stable, and I never see such a pace as that 'ere 'oss can put out. I'm proud o' him—as proud o' him as if he wor mine—every ounce of horse-flesh o' him, Mr Lorimer!'

'How about the other horses? I've heard no gossip—hav'n't been at the Corner for a week.'

'Don't tell me of other 'osses!' replied the jockey. 'We're safe. I know 'em all—saw 'em all take their gallops. There ain't the stride of our Snap in any two of them. Barring accidents, Mr Lorimer, I'll win by four lengths, and not a hair turned. I've a-ridden seventeen Derbies, Mr Lorimer, and won five; and this I'll say, there ain't a 'oss going as 'll touch Snapdragon—unless, mayhap, the ghost of Flying Childers come on the Downs, with the devil for a jock—'

'Look here, Flick,' said Lorimer, 'I believe you to be an honest fellow!'

'Thank ye, sir—thank ye! I'm no better than I ought to be in many things, but I never sold a race. I've a-ridden seventeen—'

'Yes, yes,' interrupted Lorimer, 'I know. Well, Flick, this race must be won!'

'It shall, sir. Gents may laugh at a jockey's word—'

'I laugh at the word of no man who I believe pledges it sincerely.'

'No, sir, no; but we're the dog as has an ill name, and there's a good many on us as deserves it—there's no denying that. However, sir, as I said, I never sold a race; I may have done a many things wrong, but I never sold a race to any one, and it's not likely I'd do it to you, who has been kind to me and mine, and who—'

'Well, well, you fully believe that Snapdragon can win?'

'I've laid out every penny I have in the world on it, and I'd a done so if it wor twice as much.'

'Snapdragon can win, and you ride Snapdragon; therefore Snapdragon will win.'

'Sir,' said the jockey, 'the stakes is as good as in your pocket!'

Lorimer mused.

'You should ha' felt that horse rise under you, sir! His muscles is like ropes o' steel, and his wind is as good arter a sweating gallop as though he was standing idle in the stall.'

'Of course, Flick, I need not tell you to keep a good look-out in the stable.'

'Lord bless ye, sir, I sleep in it! And there's Thor and Odin, your two Saint Bernards, chained on each side of the stall. He'll be a clever fellow, sir, that'll play tricks with Snapdragon!'

'Bravo, Flick! I'll be at Hawleyden tomorrow, and in the meantime my mind's at ease—I trust you, my man—I trust you.'

'If it wouldn't be asking over-much?' said the jockey, holding out his brown, horny hand.

Lorimer shook it heartily.

'Win this Derby, Tim Flick, and you're a made man!'

'Mr Lorimer, I've a-ridden seventeen—'

'Good—never mind that now. Have something—wine? —a thimbleful of brandy?'

'No, Mr Lorimer, with your leave, not a drop.'

'Why, man, it will do you good—with your hard exercise and sweatings.'

'After Snapdragon is placed, Mr Lorimer, but not before. You mind the Mazeppa Derby!'

'Certainly—five years ago—you rode the second horse, Firefly. It was a close thing—Mazeppa won by a neck.'

'Mazeppa won by a tumbler of champagne!' said the jockey—'a tumbler of champagne I drank in the paddock.'

'Ah?' inquired Lorimer, 'tell me how it was.'

'It needs a clear head, Mr Lorimer, to ride a Derby. There ain't no excitement in the world equal to it. I hadn't had much breakfast that day; I couldn't look at anything to eat, and I felt faint when I was on my 'oss—I suppose my backers see it, for one of them says, says he, "Take a drop of champagne, Tim," says he; so I emptied the glass, and sure enough I felt the better for it. Well, we came to the scratch, I felt the wine in my head—but it was quite comfortable and pleasant like—and I thought, "I'll win, I'm sure on it." Well, "Go!" says the starter; and go we did. Sir, a good 'oss under one is always exciting, but a racer at the pace is enough to madden one. It did me. What with the fury of the gallop, and the rush of the air, and the roar of the people, I felt as if neither heaven nor hell could hold me. I headed 'em all in the first hundred strides—I dug the spurs into the 'oss—it answered me, sir—I felt how it rose—every time I punished it. Then I looked over my shoulder, there was green turf between me and the second 'oss. I got sure of my race—we came up the rise like a whirlwind—and round the corner; and the broad course, sir, and the swarming crowd, and the carriages, and the stands, all flashed on me like a dream. It was just then I felt Firefly flag in his stride— I welted him with the whip, and dug his flanks with the spur. He swerved, but he didn't answer as before. Then my head began to swim, sir—I wasn't cool from the first, but then I lost all presence of mind. I pressed the 'oss—checked him—punished him, but I couldn't work him with hands and knees as I felt I ought. Then I hear the second 'oss close on his haunches—I had given Firefly too much to do at first, and he couldn't keep it up—I rode him as bold as ever man did—but with no judgment, sir. Mazeppa come abreast of me—I could see his rider was cool and comfortable. We glared in each other's eyes as we went stride for stride together, until, just fifty yards from the post, he lifted his 'oss—lifted it, sir, past me—and won by a neck. I had the best 'oss, but my 'oss hadn't the best rider; no one blamed me, but I made an oath then—and I kissed my mother's Bible on it—that never, s'help me God! from that day, would I touch drink for a month before the Derby day.'

'And I won't press you,' rejoined Lorimer. 'How is your son? Does he like his place in the City?'

'He does, sir, he does; and he blesses you as got it for him. He's a good boy, sir, is Dicky, and fond of his old father. I hope I'll get him kep off the turf, though—sir—'

Lorimer smiled.

'Ay, sir, I've had my share of luck in it, too. I've a-ridden seventeen Derbies, and won five; but it ain't a good trade, and I hope Dicky'll stick to his pen, and never go a calculating the odds, nor a backing either Field or Favourite.'

'What! not even Snapdragon?'

The jockey winced—smiled—blew his nose, and fidgeted uneasily. His audience was over, and presently, with a profusion of bows, he took his leave. On the stairs he met Blane, but resolutely declined that worthy's invitation to have a snack in the steward's pantry.

'But—I say,' he whispered, 'you're a true blue sort o' chap, and you belong to us. Back the Favourite. Snap is to win: it's on the books. Inwest, and no mistake.'

Blane marched slowly into his own room, sat down, and meditated.

'I wish,' pondered Blane, 'that nobody could tell lies but myself, what a world it would be then to be sure! Now, here's an honest jockey; that's at once a fool and a phenomenon; but he is honest, and he believes master's horse is going to win. Again, there's the old hunks in Abingdon Street, he's not honest, but he's deep—deep, and he believes master's horse is going to lose; what shall I do? Ah! I'll do what I've done all my life—I'll try to butter my bread on both sides—I'll hedge.'

*　　*　　*

In a dim court off Fenchurch Street is the counting-house of Messrs Shiner and Maggs. The establishment occupies the ground floor; and if you have business there you enter a large low-roofed room lighted on dark days by gas, and behold a dozen or so of clerks scribbling busily, or handing huge ledgers about from one to the other over the brass rails of the desks. From this room two doors, of frosted glass, lead to the private business apartments of the two members of the firm. On one of these portals is painted 'Mr Shiner's room', on the other 'Mr Maggs' room', and if you were suddenly to push open the first, you would probably find Mr Shiner drinking soda-water and sherry, and reading a sporting paper; while, if you were to swing open the other, you would, in all likelihood, discover Mr Maggs drinking nothing at all, but deeply absorbed in the report of the mission to Quashybungo,—a pleasant tropical coast, where the good missionaries have got possession of some twenty square miles of land and two converts, who are continually striking for more wages. People wonder what could have brought Messrs Shiner and Maggs together, but together they are, and carrying on, principally under the management of their head clerk, a very thriving business.

It is, however, with the clerks, not with the merchants, that we have now to do. Nine o'clock is striking from a neighbouring church tower, and the former-named gentlemen are dropping hurriedly in. Each, as he arrives, signs his name in a book, and a porter stands ready, after the five minutes of grace have expired, to draw a line below the last signature, and thus expose the misdeeds of the lazy and the lagging. The five minutes are nearly up when the two junior clerks arrive together. The names they inscribe are Richard Flick and Owen Dombler, and having hurriedly scribbled these appellations, they proceed to their desks, in the darkest corner of the office; and as they check off the entries of the books under their care, manage to carry on a whispered and interrupted conversation.

Flick is an open-featured, freckled, country-reared-looking lad, the expression of his face simple, ingenuous, and confiding; Dombler is a pale London boy, with long, sharp features; ugly, pinched, and bilious-looking.

'Dick,' he said to his companion, 'you're quite browned by the sun since Saturday.'

'Yes; I've been to Hawleyden to see the old boy at the stables. Oh, ain't he a good old fellow—just! He says he'll get us both into the grand stand at the Derby; and the horse he's to ride—Mr Lorimer's horse, Snapdragon—you know, is sure to win.'

'Ay, but will they let us off? Old Maggs hates races.'

'Yes, but Shiner don't; and the governor is to ask Mr Lorimer to ask Mr Shiner to give us a holiday.'

'I'd like to go. I hav'n't had a bit of fun since Spiffler left our lodgings.'

'Who was Spiffler?'

'Oh, don't you know? he was an odd sort of chap —literary they said—connected with newspapers, and theatres, and all that. He stayed in bed all day, and was out all night, and paid for his lodgings in orders for the play —little, dirty pieces of paper, with "Admit two", and "Before seven o'clock", written on them. I never get an order now.'

'Oh, I'll manage that for you, if you care about it. I can get as many as I like.'

'You!'

'Yes—orders or almost anything. Hush!—in your ear—I never told you of my new friend.'

'No, who?'

'I don't know his name, I call him—the man at the eating-house. It's an old gentleman who has taken such a fancy to me—oh, such a nice old chap, he goes every day to the eating-house at the same time that I do. We sit in the same box, so he got to speak to me, and he tells me such lots of things, and gives me treats, and I like him so—only I don't know, sometimes I'm afraid of him—he's so solemn and grave, and has such staring black eyes, that when he looks at you you somehow feel as if he was burning you.'

'What is he like? I never saw him at Boffle's.'

'No; you don't dine till after me, and by that time he's gone.'

'Well, but what is he like?'

'Oh, an old man with black sunk eyes that glare so, and grey hair, and a thin pale face, and long skinny hands, and funny marks, like threads, all along his cheeks and forehead.'

'And will you see him today?'

'Oh, I suppose so; he's got such a manner, and talks so to

one. I've told him every bit about myself, and what I am here—yes, and about you, too, and—'

'Take care, Dick; perhaps he's a cheat, and wants to get information about the house.'

This supposition staggered Richard Flick for a moment, but he speedily recovered himself, and treated the suggestion with disdain.

'A cheat—he's more like a bishop—he's as good a man as any in the world—he's as good as my father,' and then, in a lower tone, 'But even—even if he were a scamp, do you think he'd get anything out of me? Oh, you may call me countrified, but I tell you, Owey, I'm down—down as a hammer.'

Dombler gave a grin and a shrug, and at that moment the head clerk called out,

'Now then, you two, you're chattering a deal too much for work. Take care there's not an error in your books —that's all.'

And so the tasks were plied in silence until two o'clock, when Richard Flick, after interchanging meaning looks with his comrade, went out to dinner.

Now, not only that day, but for several days thereafter, it was a mighty puzzle with the *habitués* of Boffle's, who the old gentleman might be who seemed, in the vernacular of the speculators, so 'thick' with young Flick of Shiner and Maggs. His dinner—generally a plate of beef and greens —bolted down, the boy would lend a devouring ear to the whispered discourse of the old man, the pair being generally ensconced together in the furthest corner of the most deserted box; and those who stole furtive glances at the couple, and watched the eager, upturned face of the boy, and the cold, clammy, glistening eyes which were fixed upon it, and caught the low-murmured, but deeply musical tone of the voice, which the boy appeared to drink up with his very soul—the people who saw and heard all this thought of the stories they had read of fascination, and how tropical birds flutter, screaming from the branches, into the very jaws of the serpent beneath.

To be sure, it was a vulgar place for charms and enchantments that cheap city eating-house, with its steaming atmosphere, redolent of over-cooked meat and simmering watery vegetables, and crowded all day long with hungry clerks munching large and small plates of boiled and roast, and ceaselessly demanding more 'breads', and additional 'half-pints', and inquiring whether the potatoes were 'nobby mealy 'uns', and whether the waiter could, upon his credit as a gentleman, affirm that the pork was 'in prime cut'. It was a vulgar, shabby, uncomfortable, hot, steaming, greasy place; but there, nevertheless, day after day, the young clerk remained up to the very last moment he could devote to dinner, in earnest converse with his unknown friend.

And in the meantime Richard's general manner became gradually silent and preoccupied. The chief clerk of Shiner and Maggs had no longer any necessity for checking his chattering propensities. Dombler questioned him, quizzed him, threatened to quarrel with him, but could obtain nothing save the very driest answers. The lad's character seemed suddenly changed. He gave Dombler the orders he had promised him, but without any further explanations as to the old gentleman at the eating-house. In fact the conversation which we have just narrated was all that passed between them upon the subject. Dombler bored perseveringly for further information.

'What had happened?' 'Happened! Nothing had happened. What made him ask?' 'What was the matter?' 'Nothing was the matter. Why should he think that anything was the matter?' 'Had Shiner and Maggs been saying anything?' 'No, of course; what could they have to say?'

So Dombler shook his head, gave it up, and waited for the mood to change, concluding either that his friend was labouring under a tremendous fit of the sulks, or that something unpleasant, which he did not care to communicate, had occurred at home.

So stood matters when, on the Monday before the Derby, Flick repaired at his dinner hour to Boffle's. The old gentleman was there as usual; Dick ate little or nothing, which his companion observing, and attributing his want of appetite to illness, caused some hot spirits and water to be prepared, and pressed the boy to drink. We have now to let the reader into the secret of this apparently odd companionship.

'Richard,' said Michael Benosa—for that was the old gentleman's name—'you say you love your father?'

'Dearly; you know I do.'

'And to make him comfortable in his old age would be the joy of your youth and the pride of your manhood?'

'Yes—yes—a thousand times yes!'

'You know that old bones cannot bestride racers, and that the men who own racers are proverbially selfish and indifferent to the welfare of those—men or brutes—who have won for them their cups or their stakes, when the strength and the speed, or the skill which gained those trophies, have passed away?'

Richard nodded acquiescence.

'Well, your father cannot ride many more Derbies. He is past fifty.'

'How do you know that?'

'No matter, I do know; and you have seen, Richard, that I know many things besides.'

The boy half sighed.

'Well, have you considered what I said yesterday?'

'I cannot do it.'

'Reflect, Richard. Have I not your good, and your father's good, at heart? A month ago I was a stranger to you. I came accidentally to dine at this place, I was struck with your face—your air. I liked both. I am an odd, eccentric old man, I have whims, and take caprices and sudden tastes. I liked you—we soon got acquainted; we got to be friends—good friends I hope; and so you told me about yourself, and about what you are, and what you did, what you liked, and what you hoped for. I encouraged you, sympathised with you, and wished well to you, and you liked the old man's talk and the old man's stories. Is it not so?'

'Yes, until—until that day—' and Richard hesitated.

'Good—go on. You would say until the day when, becoming thoroughly acquainted with your particular position, and your particular opportunities of acquiring certain knowledge by which vast amounts of money can be gained, I laid before you a simple, harmless plan, by means of which in a week from this time you may be the possessor of a fortune.'

'Yes, but the means; it would be to do evil that good may come of it.'

'And why not? Listen, Richard. Near us is the cathedral of St Paul's. You have seen the paintings on the cupola; they were executed by Sir William Thornhill. One day, forgetful of the dizzy height whereon he stood, the artist walked backward, step by step, to watch the effect of a group he had just painted. He neared the edge of the planking—still, step by step, he unwittingly approached it. A stranger was on the scaffolding, he saw the artist's peril, he saw that another backward pace and he would be a mangled mass on the marble pavement below. To call to him would be but to hasten his fall, so he seized a brush and flung a daubed smirch over the dainty flesh tones and the pencilled draperies; the artist rushed forward to save his work; the painting was indeed injured, but the painter was preserved. Evil had been done that good might come of it. And was not the doer of the little evil the author of the great good?'

Poor Richard was no match for the subtle casuistry of his antagonist. He could only murmur some argument at once unintelligible and inaudible.

'But in this case,' resumed the tempter, 'there is not even a little evil to be done. It is only the semblance of evil. The law has rightly said, that he who shall imitate another's signature, with the intention or in the hope of obtaining another's goods, commits a crime. But the law does not say that he who imitates another's signature, without any such intention, is guilty of offence. Suppose you wished to imitate the signature of Charles the First; to imitate it without intent to deceive anybody, could that be called a crime? It would only be a feat of penmanship, like drawing a swan of flourishes. One would be just as harmless as the other.'

'But Shiner and Maggs are not dead and gone two hundred years ago, like Charles the First.'

'No; but the imitation will no more hurt them—can no more hurt them, than it would or could hurt Charles the

First. Crime consists in intent to injure, not in the act of injuring.'

'Still, what you want me to do is forgery.'

'No—it is only imitation. Suppose you go to your room, and draw a cheque for a thousand pounds, and sign it with the name of Rothschild, and then tear it up or burn it—you perform an act of imitation. But if, instead of destroying the paper, you present it at the counter of a bank as genuine, then you commit an act of forgery.'

'But in this case I am not to destroy the paper without presenting it.'

'No—but I am. You doubt me? Fie, fie, Richard! Why should I present it? I would then be the forger, because the presentation makes the uttering, and the uttering constitutes the crime. I should thus be punished, not you.'

'But why do you not commit the for— I mean, make the imitation yourself?'

'Because I am not at all acquainted with the signatures to be imitated, and because, even if I were, I am old, and my hands shake.'

He held forth his long, skinny fingers—they trembled with a palsied motion.

'You say that the reason why you wish for the imitation cheque of Shiner and Maggs is just to show it, to flash it about among people who are not intimately acquainted with the signatures of City firms—?'

'Precisely: so as to get credit, and by means of credit to get riches.'

'Is credit necessary in betting?'

'Credit is necessary whenever money transactions are concerned. Do you think a man would bet five thousand with a person who might not have the means of paying if he lost—?'

'And do you mean to bet five thousand?'

'Five thousand—ten—twenty, if I can; the more I bet the more we win.'

'But if we should lose?'

'Lose! What did your father tell you, last Sunday, when you were at Hawleyden?'

'That Snapdragon will run fourteen inches for every foot that any other horse in England can cover.'

'Good, he can win. The question then is, will he be ridden to win?'

'Sir,' exclaimed the boy, with a glowing face, 'my father never sold a race.'

'I know it; the race, so far as human calculation can go, is then already won.'

'But human calculations are not infallible.'

'Granted; but we must act on the best calculations we can make. We may die tonight, but we do not the less provide for tomorrow. See, if I have the cheque, I get the credit; if I get the credit, I make the bet; if I make the bet, I win the money.'

There was a pause.

'I—am—afraid,' murmured the boy.

Benosa, unseen by his companion, made a gesture of violent anger, and then resumed the conversation in his softest and most musical tones.

'Wednesday come and gone,' he said, as if speaking to himself, 'and fortune will have come with it—fortune destined for high and holy ends—that the poor may be enriched, and the aged pass their evening days in peace.'

Richard's face flushed, then grew deadly pale. The tempter eyed him keenly. Then the boy set his teeth, and clenched his hands, and said, 'I will do it.'

'A bold boy and a good son,' said Benosa; and then in a whisper, 'Have you the cheque?'

'Yes.'

'I knew it,' said the old man to himself. 'He kept his hand in his pocket, and I knew the precious paper was grasped there.'

Richard stole a quick glance round—no one was looking, and he rapidly passed an envelope to his companion. Benosa opened it leisurely.

'Take care—take care, for Heaven's sake!' whispered the clerk, in an agony of apprehension.

'There is no fear, Richard—no fear whatever,' replied his companion. He glanced at the contents of the packet. It was a cheque on Messrs Smith, Payne, and Smith, in Richard's writing, and purported to be for the amount of five thousand pounds. The signature was an approximation to that of Shiner and Maggs. As Benosa read it, Richard made a half snatch, as though he would recover possession of the fatal document. Benosa observed the motion.

'My dear boy,' he said, 'if you repent what you have done, you may undo it. Here is the cheque;' and he held it out to Richard, who took it, and gazed for a moment on the face of his companion. It was calm and smiling, and the eyes had their usual glassy, lustrous stare.

'No,' he muttered. 'No—I was a fool—there, take it,' and he returned the cheque.

'Would you like it to be destroyed by me or by yourself?'

'By myself,' said Richard, in a choking voice, and wiping the perspiration from his forehead.

'Good—by the time the horses start it will be on its way to you. Shall I address to Shiner and Maggs?'

'No, no—to my lodgings.'

'Then, on Wednesday evening, by the six o'clock delivery, it will be there.'

'Oh, indeed—indeed, I have done this innocently. I have done this for my father—my poor, old, good father! On you be the shame, if there be shame—and on you the guilt, if there be guilt!'

Having uttered this burst of passion, the boy flung his arms on the table, and rested his head on them.

When he raised it the old gentleman was gone.

*　　*　　*

It is the night before the Derby, and the whole of sporting London—and for that matter, a great part of London to which the term cannot in strictness be applied—is in a state of nervous restlessness, anticipating the chances of the morrow. The thousands who have risked money upon the race are on the *qui vive* for any stray information which may enable them, even at the last hour, to improve their prospects of success. Reports and rumours fly hither and thither from mouth to mouth. The last editions of the evening papers are ransacked for hints from sporting correspondents, and the latest shade of variation in the betting at the Corner. The sporting taverns are crowded with those who are knowing on the turf and those who desire to be thought so. Mysterious intimations—half-spoken, half-retracted hints of one horse, which is to be made 'safe', of another which, at the eleventh hour, will be 'scratched', of one stable which has 'declared to win', of another which boasts a wonderful 'dark horse', secret information touching one steed which, it is whispered, has mysteriously fallen lame; dark doubts flung out as to a flaw in the pedigree of another, and certain news of the style in which a third had that morning taken its sweating gallop—all this chaos of hints, nods, winks, morsels of exclusive intelligence, and scraps of secret information, is discussed, amplified, canvassed, disputed, amid the fumes of tobacco and spirits, until the young gentleman who has started a 'book', and dropped into the sporting public-house in quest of information for his hedging projects, drops out again, utterly bewildered by the mass of contradictory intelligence and diverging advice which a dozen of high authorities, each in possession of authentic and exclusive particulars, have favoured him with.

And the excitement is not confined to the more vulgar haunts of gentlemen who speculate on the turf. Wherever you go the words, 'Snapdragon', 'Odds', 'Field', 'Favourite', 'Safe to win', strike your ear. You catch them in the whispered converse of the opera-box; you distinguish them in the noisy hum of the theatre when the act-drop has fallen; even ladies catch the universal epidemic, and lay reckless wagers of gloves and flasks of eau-de-Cologne; the clubs echo with the chances of tomorrow; and the debate in the House of Commons must be exciting indeed, if groups of members, under the galleries and in the galleries, be not clustered together, eagerly discussing the merits of the line of horses which will be tomorrow drawn up before the starter on Epsom Downs.

Snugly ensconced in his well-littered stall, in the training stables of Hawleyden, stands one of the unconscious objects of all this excitement, all this anxiety. Snapdragon, as he arches his neck, tosses his head, and neighs and snorts in the flush of his rampant energies, has little idea of the noise his name is making in the world. The animal itself, muffled in warm cloths, and the padded sides of his stall, show the care of the comfort and the health of the racer.

The hour of ten can be faintly heard tolled by Epsom clock, when the door of Snapdragon's stable opens, and three gentlemen, attended by Flick the jockey, and one or two of his subordinates, emerge into the yard.

'Bring the horses out, and we'll ride over to the Spread Eagle at once,' said one of the group; 'I think, Flick, we may sleep sound upon the chances of tomorrow.'

'Yourself saw the 'oss, Mr Lorimer; he couldn't be in better condition for running,' replied the jockey.

'Mind you keep him so, my old Trojan,' said another of the party, in the hoarse voice of Sir Harrowby Trumps.

'For if you don't,' continued the third, 'my address, in twenty-four hours from this blessed moment, will be the Hôtel de Suède, Brussels—a good house that, Trumps; and if Snap's heels should not be the speedier, I would recommend you to patronise it. The air of Belgium is always my specific for complaints of the money-making organs.'

So saying, the party mounted their horses.

'I shall be over tomorrow morning by six, Flick— meantime don't leave the horse—I know your people here are honest, but they may be tampered with; and this is just the nervous night.'

'Never fear, Mr Lorimer; I slept over the stable for a month, and I shan't go for to be caught napping the last night: whoever touches Snapdragon, sir, must put me out of the way first.'

'Good, I have all trust in you. Come, gentlemen, supper waits at the Spread Eagle.' And the party rode briskly away without noticing the figure of a man, who crouched behind a cart in a dark corner of the stable-yard.

Flick watched his patron and his friends until the ring of their horses' hoofs died away in the distance. He then turned into the stable. It was a small building, containing four stalls, of which Snapdragon and another racer occupied the two centre ones, while, in each of the others, was chained an immensely powerful dog of the Saint Bernard breed. Both of these animals lay with their grim muzzles resting upon their outstretched forepaws, and their deep dark eyes twinkled suspiciously around, as Flick moved about the stable. The place was dimly lighted by a large dusty lamp suspended from the roof; and at one end a ladder, rising upwards through a trapdoor in the ceiling, led to the garret apartment above, which, as Flick had intimated, had lately been occupied by himself.

The jockey carefully locked and bolted the stable-door, and, after casting a hasty glance at the horse, took from a large chest, which stood in the far corner of the stable, a light racing-saddle, and commenced an examination of the girths and leathers—so minute that it seemed as if every particular thread in their stitching underwent an individual scrutiny.

'All right,' he murmured, as he laid the article down; he then cautiously proceeded into the stall with Snapdragon, and, stooping down, appeared to occupy himself in feeling and chafing with his hands the joints and legs of the noble animal.

'Not a bit of stiffness or swelling,' he muttered, as he rose and patted the neck of the racehorse. 'You'll do your work tomorrow; won't you, old Snap?' he continued, speaking in a caressing voice to the horse. 'You'll show 'em the blood you come of—ay, and how Tim Flick can ride you—won't you? Eh, old Snap?'

The racer, as if he understood the questions put to him, tossed his delicately-moulded head upwards, and answered by a loud shrill neigh. It had hardly subsided into silence when a low growl rose from the next stall.

'Hey, Odin!' said Flick, 'what makes you angry, old dog?'

He left the racer's stall and entered that of the Saint Bernard mastiff. The dog was on its legs, straining upon the strong chain which bound him to the manger; his outstretched muzzle sniffing anxiously in the direction of the stable-window, and his muscular tail lashing his sides with long, measured sweeps.

'The dog scents something,' said the jockey; and just at that moment, Thor, the mastiff, in the other and further stall, took up the growling concert.

'Can there be anybody lurking about the stable?' thought Flick. He went to the window and glanced out. Everything was dark and silent. He then cautiously undid the fastenings of the door, slipped out, examined narrowly all round, but saw or heard nothing to alarm him. Then, after lingering for a moment upon the threshold, he re-entered the stable and closed the door as before. As he did so, a man cautiously slipped down from the lower branches of a huge elm which overshadowed the stable, and took up his position behind its trunk.

The night waned slowly. One by one all the lights in the buildings of Hawleyden were extinguished, except that which gleamed from the window of the stable in which stood the Favourite. Eleven had long ago struck upon the distant Epsom clock. The night breeze made a moaning music over the bare Downs, and in the creaking branches of the old elm. The stars appeared and disappeared as sailing clouds passed between them and the earth. Now and then a swallow, accidentally awakened, would twitter in the eaves. Now and then, with a loud buzzing hum, a flying beetle would shoot past upon the damp night air; and now and then the rusty weathercock which surmounted the stables would creak and rattle as a gust, fresher than ordinary, caught and twisted its painted vane. With the exception of such night noises, there was the silence of midnight over Hawleyden.

It might be one hour towards the morning when the man who descended from the elm advanced cautiously to the stable-door, and looked through the keyhole. The light still burned. He stood a moment, as if undecided. Then there was heard a recommencement of the former growling. Neither Thor nor Odin had gone to sleep. This seemed to decide the lurker, for he immediately rapped, not loudly, but distinctly, at the door. The dogs replied with a volley of hoarse baying, in the midst of which Flick's voice, demanding, in startled tones, who the knocker was, could be barely distinguished.

'Are you alone?' was the answer of the applicant.

'What's that to you? What do you want?' returned the jockey. 'Be off! or I'll loose the dogs on you!'

'I am armed,' replied the stranger; 'and if you do I must shoot them, which I should be sorry for. I dare say they are fine animals.'

There was a pause.

'I must speak with you!' continued the stranger.

'About the race?' inquired the jockey.

'About that in the second place—there is a more important matter for the first.'

'But you said you was armed. How do I know you've not come here to do some mischief to the 'oss or to me?'

'Will this prove to you that my purpose is inoffensive? —see, here are my pistols.' He produced the weapons he spoke of and shoved them beneath the stable-door. 'Now I am defenceless,' he said.

Apparently the jockey was satisfied with this demonstration of confidence, for he undid the fastenings, and, partially opening the door, held up the lamp, which he had lowered from the ceiling, to the stranger's face. It was one he had never seen before—the face of an elderly man, with keen black eyes, an aquiline nose, and thin grey hair.

'What do you want with me, and at this hour of the night?'

'Admit me, shut the door, and I will tell you,' said the jockey's visitor.

'No, d— me, tell your business first!'

'It is about your son.'

'My son!' exclaimed Flick, starting backwards, and evidently alarmed. The stranger took advantage of this movement to make good his entrance.

'I trust in God, sir,' said the jockey, 'that there's nothing wrong!—nothin' turned up agin the lad! Richard is a good boy, sir! It would break my heart if there was anything wrong—'

'I know that,' said the stranger; 'that is the reason I am here. Shut the door and silence those dogs.' Thor and Odin were still growling at the intruder. The jockey hastily did as he was directed, and then, turning to his visitor, saw him seated upon the corn-chest, over which Flick had spread a small mattress, and upon which he had been dozing when disturbed as we have seen.

'Now, sir, if you please,' said the jockey, with considerable nervous anxiety—'now, sir, if you please, about my son—about Richard—'

'So that is Snapdragon—that is the Favourite!' said the unknown.

Flick's suspicions as to his mission revived at the keen glance the stranger cast upon the horse, and he flung himself between his visitor and the racer.

'You need not be afraid, Mr Flick,' observed the intruder, 'I shall not do anything to the horse without your full permission.''

''You had better not try,'' muttered the jockey.

'Nor will I—. To business.'

'Ah, to business—the sooner the better.'

'Good! You have a son in the firm of Shiner and Maggs—?'

'General agents and commission-brokers, Curney's Alley, Fenchurch Street, City,' continued the jockey, with volubility.

'A fine lad—I see him often,' replied the stranger. 'Shiner and Maggs bank with us—with Smith, Payne, and Smith, I mean—I am a cashier in that house.'

The jockey rubbed his hands nervously. He could not divine what was coming, but he feared that all was not right.

'I do a little in the sporting way, however,' continued the cashier. 'One must have some other amusement than counting sovereigns all day long which don't belong to us—eh, Mr Flick?'

The jockey assented. 'But what's all this here got to do with Richard?' he inquired.

'Oh, everything in its proper time,' replied the cashier. 'We are very methodical, we bankers.'

Flick stamped with impatience, and cast his eyes towards the dogs, who from time to time showed their teeth and snarled.

'I have invested largely in this Derby, Mr Flick,' pursued the cashier, 'and I've backed the Field against the Favourite.'

'Then, as sure as Snapdragon stands in that stall you'll lose!'

'As sure as Snapdragon stands in that stall I'll win!'

The jockey started back.

'No tricks!' he exclaimed. 'Hands off!—no tricks!—I'm awake!—I am! Oh, the d—fool I have been to let you in! But lay a finger on that 'oss, or stir a step towards him, and by the God above both of us I'll blow your brains out with your own pistols!'

And so saying, Flick presented one of the weapons at the head of the cashier. The eyes of the latter flashed, and his nostrils dilated, but he neither shrank nor quailed, but looked steadfastly into the muzzle of the pistol, which was not two feet from his forehead.

'To return to your son,' he said, with the most perfect coolness; 'one of two things will happen—either Snapdragon will lose, or your son will be hanged!'

The jockey's face grew ghastly pale, and the pistol dropped upon the ground.

'What's that you mean?' he stammered, pressing his hand forcibly upon his heart, as if to control its throbbings.

'Nothing can be clearer,' returned the cashier. 'Look at this' and he produced from a closely-clasped pocket-book a cheque.

'Do you know the hand in which this cheque is drawn?' said the cashier.

'Oh, God!—yes, it is Richard's!' gasped the father.

'Do you know the hand in which this cheque is signed —"Shiner and Maggs?"' continued his questioner.

'Yes—yes—it is the same as the other—it is Richard's!'

'So the hanging I spoke of, Mr Flick, is not quite such an improbable business as you seemed to think.'

The poor jockey staggered against the wall, hid his face in both of his hands, and sobbed convulsively.

Benosa—he must have been recognised—looked at him, his big black eyes flashing with excitement. Yet the expression of that terrible face was not a vindictive one; on the contrary, there was an undefinable look of pity in the gaze.

'Oh!' groaned the jockey—'oh, I thank God that his mother didn't live to see this day!'

'Your son, Mr Flick,' continued Benosa, in his former un-moved tones, and putting the cheque carefully away in his pocket—'your son, Mr Flick, presented the document I have shown you, this afternoon. Fortunately for him, he presented it to me. I saw the forgery at once; and I could have guessed it from the boy's manner if I did not hold the proof in my hand. But there it was—in black and white. Now, Mr Flick, I do not pretend to be better than my neighbours, and a notion came across me as I looked at that forged cheque. I told your son that the hour for paying money was past, but that he had better leave the cheque and call the first thing in the morning. He was afraid to object; so here I am, now, to await your decision.'

'My decision on what, sir?' faltered the jockey.

'On your son's life,' said the pretended cashier.

'It is in the hands of the law,' murmured Flick, wringing his hands. 'Oh Richard—Richard! that it should have come to this! You I always thought the best—the best of boys. Oh my God, but this is hard to bear!'

'Your decision!' said Benosa, sharply.

Flick looked vacantly up.

'Listen. I have told you I backed the Field against the Favourite. If the Favourite wins, your son hangs! You understand that?'

'Snapdragon must win,' murmured the jockey. 'He could do it in a canter.'

'Not if he had half-a-dozen drops from this bottle down his throat,' said Benosa, drawing from his breast a phial filled with a dark-coloured fluid.

'It is poison!' exclaimed Flick. 'You would poison the 'oss.'

Benosa uncorked the phial, and allowed a drop or two of the liquid to trickle into his own mouth.

'What is poison for horses is poison for men, Mr Flick; except for throwing him off his speed for four-and-twenty hours or so, the mixture is as harmless as mother's milk.'

'No, by G—! no! I won't do it, nor suffer you to do it. There stands the swiftest horse in Europe, and he sha'n't be doctored. Keep off, I say—keep off!' and the jockey, snatching up the pistol, stood between Benosa and the stall.

'Did you ever see a hanging?' muttered Benosa.

The jockey shrank backwards as though bitten by a reptile.

'Hinder me from giving this dose to the horse, and you'll see one that will interest you. Permit me, and by the time the news reaches London that the Favourite has disappointed her backers, the cheque will be in your son's hands; and I presume he will not again try the experiment of cashing it in a hurry.'

The jockey groaned in bitterness of spirit. Benosa's keen eye saw the inward struggle which was going on.

'A gambler's interest,' he said, 'or a son's blood—choose!'

But the jockey remained dumb.

'Oh, Mary—Mary!' he murmured at length, 'that your boy—that our boy should have done this thing!'

Benosa saw the direction of his thoughts, and skilfully availed himself of them.

'Richard is like his mother, is he not?' be inquired.

Flick writhed in mute agony at the question.

'It's hard—very hard,' muttered the false cashier—'a favourite son, and an only son, and one that reminds the father of a dear one gone.'

The jockey uttered a loud inarticulate cry of agony, and then fell on his knees.

'Spare him!—spare him!—spare Richard! Spare my son!'

'Then you consent?'

Flick bent his head in answer. His hands were stretched before his face.

'Turn the horse in his stall,' said Benosa, in as cool a tone as though he were giving an ordinary stable order.

The jockey quietly complied, undid Snapdragon's halter, and the docile animal, obeying his voice and the pressure of his hands, wheeled himself round, with his tail to the manger.

'Now fetch the lantern.'

Benosa spoke in the composed but decided tone of a man to whom command was habitual.

Again Flick mechanically obeyed, placing himself between the racer and his visitor.

Benosa uncorked the phial. 'Stand aside,' he said.

Poor Flick flung his arms round Snapdragon's neck, and then, shrinking from the piercing gaze of Benosa's eyes, staggered to the corn-chest, instinctively supporting himself upon it, while he held the lantern so as to light his companion.

'You swear it will do no lasting harm to the 'oss?' he exclaimed.

'You may enter him for the St Leger, and win it, too,' replied Benosa. 'Only you will be in the ruck tomorrow.'

The jockey groaned aloud.

'How am I to face Mr Lorimer?' he gasped.

'Are you responsible for the horse's health or the horse's humours?' answered Benosa. 'It is enough for you, that having watched all night in the stable, you know that he has not had foul play.'

During this brief conversation Snapdragon began to snort and move restively, as though his instinct told him that all was not right. Benosa stood upon the near side, soothing him with word and touch; all at once, with his left hand he grasped the nose and jaws of the horse. The animal snorted, flung aloft his head, but the long thin fingers of Benosa grasped its flesh like firmly-screwed iron bars.

'Open—brute! So—there!' he exclaimed, violently wrenching the upper jaw, and at the moment that the teeth parted, dashing between them the phial, which was rimmed with brass. The noble animal reared upwards, Benosa clinging to it, and still holding the phial between its open jaws.

The jockey stared wildly at the struggle. For a moment it was a terrific one—the horse plunging and snorting in its terror—and Benosa, with his long arms twined round its neck, and his bright black eyes flashing into those of the racer's, dashed upwards and downwards, as the animal wildly flung about his head, and struck out alternately with his fore and hind legs. But the strife only lasted a moment. All at once Snapdragon dropped down upon all fours—his ears, which were laid back, assumed their natural position. He breathed hard and quickly, and then became motionless in the stall.

In a moment Benosa slipped from its side, recorking the phial.

'The sedative does its work at once,' he said.

He took Flick's hand; it was trembling and moist with perspiration.

'I have lost the honesty,' murmured the poor jockey—'I have lost the honesty I was proud on for them twenty years—I have sold a race!'

'You have saved your son,' said Benosa, 'and you have read him a lesson. Henceforth let him count as enemies all who have not proved themselves friends.'

The jockey looked at the false cashier wonderingly.

'Richard will explain the rest. He is not so guilty as you think him. You may be a happy father yet—a happier father than I am. Farewell. God forgive you and me, and all of us.'

Turning to the door, Benosa rapidly undid its fastening and glided out. Flick followed in haste, but his mysterious visitor was gone.

'God help us,' said the jockey, turning back to the stable. 'It seems like a dream of the night.'

*　　*　　*

The great yearly festival of London is the Derby day. Christmas-tide brings its associations and its joys. Easter inaugurates the Spring, and Whitsun-tide crowns Summer on her throne. All these are festive times—times of holy-day-making and epochs in the story of the year, but the especial day on which London rouses itself, and pours itself forth beyond its bricken barriers, is undoubtedly the 25th of May, when the great race of England—of the world—is run on Epsom Downs. Describe the English, if you will, as a shopkeeping nation, as a peerage-worshipping nation, as a roast-beef-eating nation, or as a bell-ringing nation, their proper definition is a horse-racing nation. England alone worships with unbounded devotion at the shrine of the Turf. In some countries racing is a passion—in others it has become a *mode*—but in England it is at once a rage, a fashion, a science, an art, a trade. Men give up their lives to it. Men study it as they would study an abstruse branch of philosophy. Men make and lose fortunes by it. The turf furnishes at once a matter of business and a game of chance. We devote our commercial energies to it. We lavish our gambling propensities on it. We have erected it into a profession, a science, a mystery. It has its technicalities, and its outer and inner secrets. It is represented in every place and degree of our social system. It has its partisans in parliament—its representatives and its advocates in every department of public and domestic life. Developed by certain mental features in our national character, it has created new ones. It has its calendars, its journals, its hand-books, its guides. It has fostered schools of literature and art exclusively its own. Nay, more; at a period of political disorganisation it gave a party in the legislature a leader, ready cut and dry; and in the most matter-of-fact times the world has ever seen—times of stubborn facts and rigid figures—has not the turf furnished us with the only race of vaticinators who have ever found not only honour, but profit, in their own country—with those far-sighted soothsayers who, mounted on the tripods of Journalism, prophesy the fate of sweepstakes, and announce the hidden destiny of horse-flesh!

This, then, is the Derby day, and Snapdragon is still the favourite! Every bridge leading from Middlesex to Surrey is a highway of that grand procession which marches annually from London to Epsom Downs. That long jolting, rattling, glancing, glittering train of equipages, which could be poured forth by no city of the earth, save our own Island Capital—that interminable cataract of toiling, panting, perspiring pedestrians, rushing forth in endless march —pushing, hustling, swarming—blackening the broad highways of the suburbs—blackening the winding roads of the open country—straying and straggling away from the main line, across fields, and in search of soft turf and yielding grass, fresh and grateful to hot and blistered feet—that wonderful annual Pilgrimage—that great British Caravan on its annual journey to the Mecca of the Grand Stand—is in full, roaring march. We need not here stay to describe the minutiae of the procession; we need not dwell upon the upsets—the collisions—the crushed panels—the

slaughtered horses—the battles round the turnpikes—the
general engagement before the Cock at Sutton—the shout-
ings and yellings of rural charioteers—the plungings and
lashings of frightened and infuriated steeds—the gibes,
and jokes, and flying 'chaff', bandied from pedestrian to
equestrian, launched from britska and landau, and caught
up by van and donkey-cart—all this has been done, and
well done, again and again—is annually done, in fact—in
the pages or the sheets of magazines and journals, which
every year find a feature in the great racing festival of
England. It will be enough to say that, on the present
occasion, the throng, the crush, and the excitement, were
as great as ever—that the usual array of dashing equipages
smoked along the dusty road—that the usual number of
slangy four-in-hands were 'tooled' down by knowing
whips—that the usual number of creaking, lumbering vans
went jolting by—that the heterogeneous mass of wheeled
things, carts, gigs, phaetons, buggies, cabs, and masses of
vehicles to which any name, or no name at all, can be
properly applied, filled up, as usual, every interstice in the
procession—and that the whole moving mass of men,
women, horses, carriages, equestrians, and pedestrians,
rolled on together—one long column of dust, noise,
smother and excitement!

On the road to the Derby, or on the Downs, might be
found, with one exception or two, all the personages introduced in this history. Mr Maggs, of the firm of Shiner and
Maggs, had, indeed, chosen to manifest his contempt for
the great racing anniversary by presiding on that day over
the first annual meeting of the Society for Inducing the
Ashantees to wear Nankeen Breeches; but his partner, Mr
Shiner, was rattling along the road in a snug, open
phaeton, drawn by a couple of nettlesome bays, and occupied, besides himself, by one of the most dashing and
agreeable wits of the Stock Exchange—a gentleman who
had invented more lies, in the way of getting the fluctu-
ations of the funds to suit his own particular purposes, than
had been ever perpetrated by the combined efforts of the
diplomacy and the press of Europe—and a couple of young
ladies, presumed to be connected with the ballet depart-

ment of one of the theatres, of very gay and flaming exterior, and such childlike simplicity that they never blushed or fidgeted at the most self-evident *double entendre*. Mr Shiner had likewise given a holiday to several of the clerks—Richard Flick and Owen Dombler amongst the rest; but, to the intense astonishment of Owen, his friend had hung back from accompanying him. Dombler was there, however, in full fig, perched upon the top of a four-horse coach, beside his friend Spiffler who, having made a decided rise in his profession of penny-a-line litera-ture, had come out very strong in a second-rate weekly sporting paper as a Derby Prophet, and who, grounding the prediction on the information which he had received from Richard Flick through Owen, had finished his pro-phetic poem, published the Saturday before, as follows:

On none—though, like *Lavinia*, they have friends—
On none of these the laurelled crown descends,
For, pure in blood, symmetrical in bone,
The 'Favourite' claims the Derby as his own:
Yet, unless every sign and omen fail,
Jim Crow, placed second, sees Snapdragon's tail!

Not far behind the flying chariot of the Derby Prophet rolled a low, open landau whisked along by four thorough-bred greys, bestrode by the smartest of post-boys in the smartest of jackets and caps. It was occupied by three persons—Mlle Chateauroux, Mr Grogrum, and Dr Gumbey—who were proceeding in great and confidential amity together. For these three worthies could only afford to quarrel in the make-believe style—not that they did not distrust each other up to the very limits, and perhaps beyond the limits, of a good, wholesome, mutual hatred, but so long as their interests pulled in the same way, the three strands of a cable could not be more amicably unanimous.

'They say, if he loses this race, he's a gone 'coon,' said the manager; 'regular up the tree, and no mistake.'

'Let us hope that these are but the malicious rumours of the enemies of our good friend Mr Lorimer,' replied the doctor, in his castor-oiliest of tones.

'Well, I don't care, I don't hold his paper,' rejoined Mr Grogrum. 'He has had his day, like any other dog; there's people been cheating him long enough. When he's sucked dry, let him turn to and suck some one else; that's the way the thing is done: d— it! I ought to know.'

(And, to do him justice, so he ought.)

'Nay, nay, Mr Grogrum, hush now; remember our dear friend here; you are positively quite unfeeling.'

'Let him alone, *mon cher docteur*, let him alone,' said Mlle Chateauroux, in her foreign accent. 'He's a great, coarse man, who has no feelings and no *délicatesse*. Lorimer will win the race, I feel it here,' and she indicated her heart. 'I know it, he must win; or, if he loses, and what you say be true, why then—' And she stopped and touched her eyes with a handkerchief, which appeared one bundle of lace.

'Well, mademoiselle,' said the manager, winking at the doctor, and affecting a voice broken by sympathy, 'you were saying—"why then?"'

'Why then,' exclaimed the lady, briskly twitching the handkerchief from her face—'why, then—*Ventre St Gris!* —as your English proverb says, "There is as good fish in the sea as ever came out of it!"'

And the sympathising three burst into a loud laugh.

The landau had hardly assumed its position on the Downs when Clement Lorimer appeared by its side. He was deadly pale, but his manner was as quiet and composed as usual. His appearance was of course the signal for a volley of greeting.

'*Ce vieux chéri Lorimer*,' murmured the *danseuse*, leaning over the side of the vehicle, and whispering in her sweetest tones—'We shall win—*ne c'est pas?* It is what you call "safe"? Oh, I am in such a state of terrible anxiety! *Corbleu!* I did not sleep a wink these three nights.'

'It's all right, Lorimer, my boy?' said the manager. 'Gad, we'd be broken-hearted if there was a miss: but all the knowing ones say the thing is safe.'

'I hope the knowing ones may be right,' said Lorimer quietly. 'Much hangs today upon a horse's sinews,' and he began to compliment Mlle Chateauroux on the fashion of her parasol.

'He's d—d down in the mouth, Gumbey,' whispered Grogrum. 'There's a screw loose, depend upon it.'

'I hope and trust our friend Snapdragon is in full feather this morning?' said the doctor.

'I hope so, too. I see nothing wrong with the horse. But it does strike me that his eyes looked dimmer, and his motions were not quite so fiery this morning as usual.'

Gumbey and Grogum exchanged glances.

'Tell me, Lorimer,' whispered Mlle Chateauroux, 'there is nothing wrong?'

'Absolutely nothing. But one has all sorts of whims and fancies when one is jaded and excited. I took it into my head, for example, this morning that Flick, the jockey who is to ride Snapdragon, looked flurried and confused. I can hardly tell what made me think so, but I did.'

'Pshaw! You are tormenting yourself. *Sacré bleu!* Is he still as confident as ever?'

'In words: but the tone seems altered.'

'Pooh! You are nervous. There, go drink a glass of sparkling Moselle. That wicked *docteur* has stolen one out of the hamper already, on purpose to pledge to Snapdragon.'

But here the saddling bell rang, and Lorimer hastily left them to be present at that important ceremony in the paddock. In a short time the competing horses appeared one by one before the Grand Stand. The crowd pushed and hustled in their eagerness to see and criticise. Opinions and hopes were loudly bandied about. Books were reopened to enter final bets. Profound amateurs of horse-flesh discussed action, blood, and bone. Mounted jockeys received final hints and instructions from their backers, and the limbs of the competing horses were chafed, and their nostrils sponged for the last time. A loud shout proclaimed the appearance of the Favourite; and the noble animal, with its arched, glancing neck, its thin, finely-chiselled head, its widely-dilated nostrils, and sinewy, stag-like legs, paced proudly out upon the turf, becoming an immediate centre of interest and admiration. Flick was already in his saddle, bearing himself as though he were part of the animal he bestrode.

'Here, Flick,' said Lorimer, 'let me feel your hand.'

'It's steadier than most upon the Downs, sir,' replied the jockey, putting his hand within that of his employer. It did not tremble certainly, but it was clay-cold.

'You look very pale, Flick,' said Lorimer.

'Watching, sir. I haven't had over-much sleep lately, and I was werry nervous last night.'

The owner of the Favourite looked long and anxiously at his horse, felt its joints, and then, patting its neck, said,

'Do your best—man and horse.'

In half-an-hour after this the start was momentarily expected. There was the dead hush of expectation, gradually wrought up to its highest pitch, over all that vast assemblage; the course, like a bright, broad, green riband, stretched down between two masses of breathless human beings. Not a face but was either preternaturally pale or preternaturally flushed. People grasped each other's hands and strained their eyes till their heads grew dizzy. Everybody was on tiptoe—everybody pressing forward—everybody looking towards the same point, the famous Tattenham Corner. All at once a throb, like a flash of moral electricity, passed through the crowd.

'They're off!'

There was a movement—a wave, so to speak, rolled through that human ocean—those behind were pressing on to the front. Then came a moment of noisy turmoil. 'Keep steady!'—'Down in front!'—'Hats off!'—'Hurrah!' —'Hush!' and the murmur subsided.

A cluster of horsemen were seen at a full gallop dashing over the ridge of the eminence to the right.

'Here they are!'—'They're coming! they're coming!'— 'Hurrah!' and one of those indefinable, indescribable noises, which none but an excited crowd can produce, rose with a mighty murmur into the summer air.

At that moment, the point where the broad green course forms a portion of the horizon near the corner, became, as if by magic, dotted with the hurrying figures of the racers. The next moment they were careering down the course, as it seemed, in a cluster.

Then the low, universal murmur, rose and swelled into a

loud, hoarse roar, and voices, frantic with excitement, shouted and screamed their hopes and fears.

'White and Pink! White and Pink! Where's the Favourite?'—'Red is leading! Hurrah! Red! Red! Tom Tit for ever! Where's Snap? Where's White and Pink?'—'Hurrah, Red!'—'No, Blue! give it 'em, Blue! Go it, Jim Crow!'—'My G—! the Favourite's in the ruck! Red! Red! Red! Hurrah!' —'Blue does it! Blue does the trick!'—'Red! White and Pink! Blue! Here they are! Hurrah! hurrah! hurrah!'

And amid one loud, universal, roaring shout, and speeding, fleeting, impalpable as a vision of the night, there shot past hundreds of thousands of dazzled eyes a dozen of careering horses, flying at a speed which made the eye dazzle and the brain whirl, and beating the turf with their hoofs like a loud, fast roll of drums!

It was over in a moment: the Derby was lost and won!

Instantly the spectators on either side burst the barriers of rope, and the course was obliterated by a rushing, shouting, jostling throng.

'Tom Tit had won!'—'Jim Crow had won!'—'Bubbly Jock had won!' So announced discordant babble of voices.

'Hush! there's the figures!'

Jim Crow was placed first, Tom Tit second, the Favourite —nowhere!

*   *   *

As soon as Clement Lorimer was aware that Snapdragon had lost the Derby, he retired alone into a private room attached to the betting accommodations of the Grand Stand, and locked the door. As he moved towards the table, his eye caught the reflection of his own features in a mirror hanging on the wall; he paused, and gazed upon the glass, then, flinging himself into a chair, muttered,

'The first time I have seen in a mirror the face of a ruined man.'

Then pressing his clenched hands against his forehead, he leant back and mused.

All around him rose the loud murmurs of the crowded race course; the tramp of hurrying feet shook the structure in which he sat. He heard his own name loudly demanded, and from time to time the door was rudely knocked by applicants for admission; but he never stirred or gave token of his presence. A mean spirit might have guessed that the waking dream of the ruined turfite turned on pistols and deadly drugs, but the firm mind of Lorimer gave way to no such morbid fancies. The rudeness of the shock only proved the strength of the sinewy springs of his intellect. It was his first misfortune; for a moment he staggered under it, then he grappled, he wrestled with it, and many minutes had not flown ere the big spirit of the man rose the conqueror from the strife.

A first misfortune is often the turning point of life. If there be nothing in you, down you go—crushed; but if there be the dormant stuff which hereafter will make a good, great, brave man, then be thankful for the shock; and as you rise to the battle, as you feel every mental muscle, every bit of sinew in your mind, swell, and stiffen, and strengthen for the fight, why, thank God for the rough stimulant—jump bravely to your feet; reflect that you must put down your misfortune, or it will put you down; and then, having conquered in your own brain—and if you feel what we have sketched, conquer you will—why climb proudly to the very summit of the opposing woe, trample it down beneath you, and feel that you, a Man—erect upon the ruins of a hostile Circumstance—stand, conquering and to conquer, a God upon a prostrate Titan!

If Clement Lorimer did not speak these words, he felt dimly, yet intensely, the thought which these words convey; and as that thought illumined his soul with a flood of burning, purifying light, he felt, for the first time in his life, the full innate dignity of Mind. An instant more, and he was almost grateful that he had lost the Derby.

'Strange!' he murmured, 'but since last night a presentiment that my life is entering on a stage of storms has taken hold of me. It is not fancy—I am cool, perfectly cool, and can look steadily in upon my soul. It is the warning shadow of coming events which darkens it. Up to this time my hopes have not known a disappointment, my schemes have not known a cross. The tide has turned, and I must pull against it. Aye, and I am glad of it. I have lived long enough in gilded sloth, careless of all but the excitement or the pleasure of the hour. Now for a plunge into the icy current of a struggling life, now to try if its waters will not brace me to dare—to do—aye, and to suffer!'

In a few moments Lorimer had settled his plans. He would go to sea for one week in his yacht, in order to enjoy perfect solitude, and to refresh and re-invigorate his physical powers. Then he proposed to return to town, manfully face his disasters, examine into his affairs, and find, if possible, the clue to the secret of his birth. As soon as he had settled this in his mind, he rose, glanced at the glass, and then proudly murmured to himself,

'No, I have seen many, but I never saw the face of a ruined man so calm before.'

As he continued almost instinctively to gaze upon the glass, he saw that it reproduced another face besides his own. Framed, as it were, in the window opposite to the mirror, was the head and upper part of the figure of a man. The features were distorted with a wild expression of demoniac triumph, and the black eyes glared and sparkled beneath the bushy grey eyebrows.

'A winner by the race,' thought Lorimer. 'Luck seems to have turned his brain.' Then he saw that the man was gazing through the window at the reflection of his (Clement's) own features in the mirror, and it struck him that the mad expression of gratified hate, which glared from the face of the stranger, appeared to fade away as he contemplated the calm features revealed to him by the glass, until at length all indication of strong passion— passion perhaps occasionally uncurbed by the bond of reason—had passed away, leaving the bright eyes illumi- nated only by the light of intellect, and the features noble in their calm placidity. For a moment Lorimer, as though fascinated, continued to gaze upon the two faces reflected in the mirror: his own, pale and young; the stranger's, pale and old. Both pale, and both—ha! what a thought flew through the startled soul of the gazer!—both similar in feature and in expression—the one the young version of the other—as it were the faces of father and son. The vision lasted but for a moment. Lorimer felt again that foreboding of coming events, that undefinable stir within him, as though his soul, forewarned from without, was girding up its loins for great deeds or great suffering. Then, making a desperate effort, he wrenched himself round towards the window—the man was gone. He rushed to the casement, flung it open, and looked out, but hundreds of figures were moving restlessly backwards and forwards. Many faces were there, but the strange old double of his young features was nowhere to be seen; so with flesh, which in spite of himself crept and shuddered, he shut down the window.

As he did so Michael Benosa turned the corner of the Grand Stand, and as he pushed his way amid the crowd muttered to himself.

'So—a calm voice and a strong soul. With the brave the first blow is *not* half the battle. Be it so. I hate to fight —sapling to steel. Now it will be blade to blade, and hilt to hilt. Yet I have the advantage. I have the knowledge! Ha! I have the sun!'

As the old man pronounced these words he flung aloft his arms with a passionate gesture. Immediately a voice sounded in his ears,

'Now, then, old Shandrydan! are you going mad for grief because you've lost a glass of brandy-and-water on the Derby?'

'There's only one specific,' remarked another voice, in a tone of drunken gravity—'there's only one specific against sorrow occasioned by the loss of bets, and that is, to hug yourself in the consciousness that you can't pay them: I'm embraced in that species of hug myself.'

The question and the advice came from the box-seat of a four-in-hand coach, and on that box-seat were stationed Owen Dombler and his friend Mr Spiffler. The former not having lost sufficiently to take away his appetite was eating; the other, being about as much ruined as a gentleman not possessed of either landed or personal property could be, was drinking. The natural consequence was that the clerk was sober and the prophet drunk. As may be supposed, however, the object of their remarks paid little attention to them, and the next moment they were 'chaffing' somebody else.

Meantime Lorimer stood motionless by the window in his solitary room. A rapping at the door caused him to unlock it, and De Witz entered. The captain's face was partly flushed, partly pale, and his hand trembled very much. He sank down into a chair, and looked at Lorimer with a fixed stare. At length he spoke.

'I'm off! By—! is not it a smash? U P, and no mistake!' And the captain uttered a long, loud whistle, which gradually subsided into a species of whine, the which dying away in its turn, the performer finished off with a discordant burst of song, the words keeping some sort of hobbling time to the good old tune of Malbrook, in this wise,

> 'He won it in a canter,
> And so, to end all banter,
> I turned to gay Levanter,
> And walked myself away!

'That's the time of day—eh, Clem? Brussels—Brussels —the sanctuary—the free city of our modern days—I salute thee! Any commands for the *Montagne de la Cour?*'

It was quite easy to see that Captain De Witz had sought for consolation under his misfortune at the same source to which the ingenious Spiffler had applied.

'Here, Lorimer,' he continued, pouring out half a tumbler of wine from a decanter on the table, 'drink, man! Sorrow is as dry as a lime-kiln in the Great Desert.'

Lorimer took up the wine and looked at it.

'How do I know,' he thought, 'but that the devil which is besetting me may not now lurk in that crystal?' Then he threw the glass with its contents into the fire-place, and poured out and drank a tumbler full of clear water. 'There is nothing so cowardly,' he said, 'as Dutch courage.'

At that moment there was heard a clamour of voices in the passage, then a scuffling of feet, and in an instant the door was burst violently open, and from the midst of a shouting, struggling group, Sir Harrowby Trumps dragged Flick forward upon the floor. The coarse, pimply features of the baronet were purple and swollen with passion; the foam he had churned lay in flakes on his thick, worm-like lips; his dress was soiled and disarranged; and his brown, brawny hands, glistening with rings, were twisted in the neckcloth of the poor jockey who, with his white-and-pink jacket almost torn from his back, had evidently been dragged violently along by the maddened turfite.

'Shame! shame! Let go the man! Shame!' shouted the crowd who mustered about the door. 'Shame!—Where's the police? Where's the stewards? Is a man to be throttled for losing a race?'

'Back, ye curs! Back, d— you!' roared Sir Harrowby. 'He's sold the race—he did!'

'For shame, Trumps!' said Lorimer. 'Unloose your grasp!'

The baronet stared at him.

'I tell you he sold the race!' he said between his grinding teeth.

'Hands off, I say, or—'

'Well, then,' thundered Trumps, 'there!' and he pushed poor Flick violently away, and glared at him as he stood pale, and panting, and rolling his eyes wildly about the room.

'Trumps, are you a man—a gentleman? Be cool—be cool, sir! If money has been lost, honour is still at stake.'

'Oh!' roared the excited gambler, still glaring at the jockey. 'Oh, if this country was like Russia, and you were one of my serfs, oh, by the Lord! wouldn't Europe ring with what I'd do to you!'

'Sir Harrowby Trumps,' interposed Lorimer, 'you are in my room. You talk to a person in my service, not in yours. Be silent—or leave us!'

There was a hum of approval from the spectators. Trumps, perceiving that he had no supporters, grumbled out some inarticulate oaths, and flung himself heavily into a chair, wiping the perspiration from his hot, flushed face.

'Well, Flick,' began the calm, rich voice of Lorimer, 'we made ourselves too sure, you see. Snapdragon was a good horse, but not so good as we thought him.'

The jockey made a mighty effort to speak, but there was a

big swelling in his throat; and he moved his lips and gesticulated, but no voice came from his chest.

'I trusted you, Flick,' continued Lorimer. 'I trusted you yesterday, and I trust you today. I know it was not your fault.'

The jockey wrung his hands and shook his head.

'Ah,' said Lorimer, 'not yours! Well, and whose was it?'

Just at this moment the jockey uttered a loud exclamation. Lorimer, we may mention, was standing with his back to the mirror, looking towards the window, and the jockey fronted him. Consequently, when the stranger, whose appearance had already filled Lorimer with such strange emotions, passed again, as he at that moment did before the casement, the owner of Snapdragon saw the reality of that vision in the glass, on which the eyes of the jockey were fixed at the moment he uttered the involuntary cry which proceeded from his lips. Again Lorimer sprang to the window—again he looked vainly for his extraordinary visitant. When he turned into the room, the jockey appeared to have recovered and partially manned himself. He was closely questioned, first, as to the cause of his exclamation, but he gave no satisfactory reply. 'He did not know what had made him behave so—it was involuntary —it was nervousness. Sir Harrowby had used him so roughly. He had seen nothing in particular—nobody in particular. He did not know why they asked him.' As to the race and the horse, Flick's answers, though perfectly respectful, and given with every evidence of deep feeling, appeared to Lorimer unsatisfactory. 'He was disappointed —of course he was: so were many other people. These things did happen sometimes. He could not help it—could not account for it: the race was lost, and there was an end of it. He hoped and trusted for better luck next time.' It was evident nothing more could be made of him, and so for the time he was dismissed.

Lorimer then sat down and wrote a hurried note to Blane with respect to arrangements to be made for settling-day. As he wrote, Trumps and De Witz, who still remained, observed that at almost every second word he cast a keen, quick glance at the window. When he had sealed his despatch, Lorimer stood up and passed his hands across his forehead.

'Like an ancient knight,' he murmured, 'I must go forth to the task alone. Trumps, De Witz, good-bye!'

'Good-bye!' said the baronet: 'and for how long?'

'I know not,' replied Lorimer; 'perhaps for ever!' and passing out he left them staring at each other.

SILVER BLAZE

by Sir Arthur Conan Doyle

Since the creator of Sherlock Holmes went racing occasionally, it should be no surprise to find that he wrote a case for the great detective about crime on the Turf. What is surprising is that Sir Arthur should have got some of his facts wrong and all but made a fool of the usually infallible Holmes! At the heart of the story is the disappearance of Silver Blaze, the favourite for the Wessex Cup, from his stables at King's Pyland—which, incidentally, has been identified as Princetown in Devon. Holmes is brought in to trace the missing animal—which research has shown to have actually existed. For the horse Isonomy, who is said to be his sire, was a remarkable creature who won the Cambridgeshire at Newmarket in 1878, the Manchester Plate and Ascot Gold Cup in 1879 and the Ascot Gold Cup again in 1880, before going to stud the following year.

So far so good. But in the course of the story Sir Arthur describes a race reserved for four and five year-olds, when there is no such thing; an incomplete and incorrect race card; impossible racing odds (fifteen to five) and an injury to the tendons of a horse's ham which is highly unlikely with the instrument specified. Despite these faults, which lay readers would probably not notice, Sir Arthur was proud of the tale and actually bet his wife a small sum that she would not guess the name of the murderer when she came to read the case. And indeed, later detective story writers like Ellery Queen have placed 'Silver Blaze' in the best half-dozen of all the Sherlock Holmes adventures. The reader is now invited to make his own judgment . . .

*   *   *

'I am afraid, Watson, that I shall have to go,' said Holmes, as we sat down together to our breakfast one morning.

'Go! Where to?'

'To Dartmoor—to King's Pyland.'

I was not surprised. Indeed, my only wonder was that he had not already been mixed up in this extraordinary case, which was the one topic of conversation through the length and breadth of England. For a whole day my companion had rambled about the room with his chin upon his chest and his brows knitted, charging and re-charging his pipe with the strongest black tobacco, and absolutely deaf to any of my questions or remarks. Fresh editions of every paper had been sent up by our newsagent only to be glanced over and tossed down into a corner. Yet, silent as he was, I knew perfectly well what it was over which he was brooding. There was but one problem before the public which could challenge his powers of analysis, and that was the singular disappearance of the favourite for the Wessex Cup, and the tragic murder of its trainer. When, therefore, he suddenly announced his intention of setting out for the scene of the drama, it was only what I had both expected and hoped for.

'I should be most happy to go down with you if I should not be in the way,' said I.

'My dear Watson, you would confer a great favour upon me by coming. And I think that your time will not be mis-spent, for there are points about this case which promise to make it an absolutely unique one. We have, I think, just time to catch our train at Paddington, and I will go further into the matter upon our journey. You would oblige me by bringing with you your very excellent field-glass.'

And so it happened that an hour or so later I found myself in the corner of a first-class carriage, flying along, *en route* for Exeter, while Sherlock Holmes, with his sharp, eager face framed in his ear-flapped travelling-cap, dipped rapidly into the bundle of fresh papers which he had procured at Paddington. We had left Reading far behind us before he thrust the last of them under the seat, and offered me his cigar-case.

'We are going well,' said he, looking out of the window,

and glancing at his watch. 'Our rate at present is fifty-three and a half miles an hour.'

'I have not observed the quarter-mile posts,' said I.

'Nor have I. But the telegraph posts upon this line are sixty yards apart, and the calculation is a simple one. I presume that you have already looked into this matter of the murder of John Straker and the disappearance of Silver Blaze?'

'I have seen what the *Telegraph* and the *Chronicle* have to say.'

'It is one of those cases where the art of the reasoner should be used rather for the sifting of details than for the acquiring of fresh evidence. The tragedy has been so uncommon, so complete, and of such personal importance to so many people that we are suffering from a plethora of surmise, conjecture, and hypothesis. The difficulty is to detach the framework of fact—of absolute, undeniable fact—from the embellishments of theorists and reporters. Then, having established ourselves upon this sound basis, it is our duty to see what inferences may be drawn, and which are the special points upon which the whole mystery turns. On Tuesday evening I received telegrams, both from Colonel Ross, the owner of the horse, and from Inspector Gregory, who is looking after the case, inviting my co-operation.'

'Tuesday evening!' I exclaimed. 'And this is Thursday morning. Why did you not go down yesterday?'

'Because I made a blunder, my dear Watson—which is, I am afraid, a more common occurrence than anyone would think who only knew me through your memoirs. The fact is that I could not believe it possible that the most remarkable horse in England could long remain concealed, especially in so sparsely inhabited a place as the north of Dartmoor. From hour to hour yesterday I expected to hear that he had been found, and that his abductor was the murderer of John Straker. When, however, another morning had come and I found that, beyond the arrest of young Fitzroy Simpson, nothing had been done, I felt that it was time for me to take action. Yet in some ways I feel that yesterday has not been wasted.'

'You have formed a theory, then?'

'At least I have a grip of the essential facts of the case. I shall enumerate them to you, for nothing clears up a case so much as stating it to another person, and I can hardly expect your co-operation if I do not show you the position from which we start.'

I lay back against the cushions, puffing at my cigar, while Holmes, leaning forward, with his long thin forefinger checking off the points upon the palm of his left hand, gave me a sketch of the events which had led to our journey.

'Silver Blaze,' said he, 'is from the Isonomy stock, and holds as brilliant a record as his famous ancestor. He is now in his fifth year, and has brought in turn each of the prizes of the turf to Colonel Ross, his fortunate owner. Up to the time of the catastrophe he was first favourite for the Wessex Cup, the betting being three to one on. He has always, however, been a prime favourite with the racing public, and has never yet disappointed them, so that even at short odds enormous sums of money have been laid upon him. It is obvious, therefore, that there were many people who had the strongest interest in preventing Silver Blaze from being there at the fall of the flag next Tuesday.

'This fact was, of course, appreciated at King's Pyland, where the Colonel's training stable is situated. Every pre-caution was taken to guard the favourite. The trainer, John Straker, is a retired jockey, who rode in Colonel Ross's colours before he became too heavy for the weighing-chair. He has served the Colonel for five years as jockey, and for seven as trainer, and has always shown himself to be a zealous and honest servant. Under him were three lads, for the establishment was a small one, containing only four horses in all. One of these lads sat up each night in the stable, while the others slept in the loft. All three bore excellent characters. John Straker, who is a married man, lived in a small villa about two hundred yards from the stables. He has no children, keeps one maid-servant, and is comfortably off. The country round is very lonely, but about half a mile to the north there is a small cluster of villas which have been built by a Tavistock contractor for the use of invalids and others who may wish to enjoy the pure

Dartmoor air. Tavistock itself lies two miles to the west, while across the moor, also about two miles distant, is the larger training establishment of Capleton, which belongs to Lord Backwater, and is managed by Silas Brown. In every other direction the moor is a complete wilderness, inhabited only by a few roaming gipsies. Such was the general situation last Monday night, when the catastrophe occurred.

'On that evening the horses had been exercised and watered as usual, and the stables were locked up at nine o'clock. Two of the lads walked up to the trainer's house, where they had supper in the kitchen, while the third, Ned Hunter, remained on guard. At a few minutes after nine the maid, Edith Baxter, carried down to the stables his supper, which consisted of a dish of curried mutton. She took no liquid, as there was a water-tap in the stables, and it was the rule that the lad on duty should drink nothing else. The maid carried a lantern with her, as it was very dark, and the path ran across the open moor.

'Edith Baxtor was within thirty yards of the stables when a man appeared out of the darkness and called to her to stop. As he stepped into the circle of yellow light thrown by the lantern she saw that he was a person of gentlemanly bearing, dressed in a grey suit of tweed with a cloth cap. He wore gaiters, and carried a heavy stick with a knob to it. She was most impressed, however, by the extreme pallor of his face and by the nervousness of his manner. His age, she thought, would be rather over thirty than under it.

'"Can you tell me where I am?" he asked. "I had almost made up my mind to sleep on the moor when I saw the light of your lantern."

'"You are close to the King's Pyland training stables," she said.

'"Oh, indeed! What a stroke of luck!" he cried. "I understand that a stable boy sleeps there alone every night. Perhaps that is his supper which you are carrying to him. Now I am sure that you would not be too proud to earn the price of a new dress, would you?" He took a piece of white paper folded up out of his waistcoat pocket. "See that the boy has this tonight, and you shall have the prettiest frock that money can buy."

'She was frightened by the earnestness of his manner, and ran past him to the window through which she was accustomed to hand the meals. It was already open, and Hunter was seated at the small table inside. She had begun to tell him of what had happened, when the stranger came up again.

'"Good evening," said he, looking through the window, "I wanted to have a word with you." The girl has sworn that as he spoke she noticed the corner of the little paper packet protruding from his closed hand.

'"What business have you here?" asked the lad.

'"It's business that may put something into your pocket," said the other. "You've two horses in for the Wessex Cup—Silver Blaze and Bayard. Let me have the straight tip, and you won't be a loser. Is it a fact that at the weights Bayard could give the other a hundred yards in five furlongs, and that the stable have put their money on him?"

'"So you're one of those damned touts," cried the lad. "I'll show you how we serve them in King's Pyland." He sprang up and rushed across the stable to loose the dog. The girl fled away to the house, but as she ran she looked back, and saw that the stranger was leaning through the window. A minute later, however, when Hunter rushed out with the hound he was gone, and though the lad ran all round the buildings he failed to find any trace of him.'

'One moment!' I asked. 'Did the stable boy, when he ran out with the dog, leave the door unlocked behind him?'

'Excellent, Watson; excellent!' mumured my companion. 'The importance of the point struck me so forcibly, that I sent a special wire to Dartmoor yesterday to clear the matter up. The boy locked the door before he left it. The window, I may add, was not large enough for a man to get through.

'Hunter waited until his fellow-grooms had returned, when he sent a message up to the trainer and told him what had occurred. Straker was excited at hearing the account, although he does not seem to have quite realized its true significance. It left him, however, vaguely uneasy, and Mrs

Straker, waking at one in the morning, found that he was dressing. In reply to her inquiries, he said that he could not sleep on account of his anxiety about the horses, and that he intended to walk down to the stables to see that all was well. She begged him to remain at home, as she could hear the rain pattering against the windows, but in spite of her entreaties he pulled on his large mackintosh and left the house.

'Mrs Straker awoke at seven in the morning, to find that her husband had not yet returned. She dressed herself hastily, called the maid, and set off for the stables. The door was open; inside, huddled together upon a chair, Hunter was sunk in a state of absolute stupor, the favourite's stall was empty, and there were no signs of his trainer.

'The two lads who slept in the chaff-cutting loft above the harness-room were quickly roused. They had heard nothing during the night, for they are both sound sleepers. Hunter was obviously under the influence of some powerful drug; and, as no sense could be got out of him, he was left to sleep it off while the two lads and the two women ran out in search of the absentees. They still had hopes that the trainer had for some reason taken out the horse for early exercise, but on ascending the knoll near the house, from which all the neighbouring moors were visible, they not only could see no signs of the favourite, but they perceived something which warned them that they were in the presence of a tragedy.

'About a quarter of a mile from the stables, John Straker's overcoat was flapping from a furze bush. Immediately beyond there was a bowl-shaped depression in the moor, and at the bottom of this was found the dead body of the unfortunate trainer. His head had been shattered by a savage blow from some heavy weapon, and he was wounded in the thigh, where there was a long, clean cut, inflicted evidently by some very sharp instrument. It was clear, however, that Straker had defended himself vigorously against his assailants, for in his right hand he held a small knife, which was clotted with blood up to the handle, while in his left he grasped a red and black silk cravat, which was recognized by the maid as having been worn on the preceding evening by the stranger who had visited the stables.

'Hunter, on recovering from his stupor, was also quite positive as to the ownership of the cravat. He was equally certain that the same stranger had, while standing at the window, drugged his curried mutton, and so deprived the stables of their watchman.

'As to the missing horse, there were abundant proofs in the mud which lay at the bottom of the fatal hollow, that he had been there at the time of the struggle. But from that morning he has disappeared; and although a large reward has been offered, and all the gipsies of Dartmoor are on the alert, no news has come of him. Finally an analysis has shown that the remains of his supper, left by the stable lad, contain an appreciable quantity of powdered opium, while the people of the house partook of the same dish on the same night without any ill effect.

'Those are the main facts of the case stripped of all surmise and stated as baldly as possible. I shall now recapitulate what the police have done in the matter.

'Inspector Gregory, to whom the case had been committed, is an extremely competent officer. Were he but gifted with imagination he might rise to great heights in his profession. On his arrival he promptly found and arrested the man upon whom suspicion naturally rested. There was little difficulty in finding him, for he was thoroughly well known in the neighbourhood. His name, it appears, was Fitzroy Simpson. He was a man of excellent birth and education, who had squandered a fortune upon the turf, and who lived now by doing a little quiet and genteel bookmaking in the sporting clubs of London. An examination of his betting-book shows that bets to the amount of five thousand pounds had been registered by him against the favourite.

'On being arrested he volunteered the statement that he had come down to Dartmoor in the hope of getting some information about the King's Pyland horses, and also about Desborough, the second favourite, which was in charge of Silas Brown, at the Capleton stables. He did not attempt to deny that he had acted as described upon the evening before, but declared that he had no sinister designs, and had simply wished to obtain first-hand information. When confronted with the cravat he turned very pale, and was utterly unable to account for its presence in the hand of the murdered man. His wet clothing showed that he had been out in the storm of the night before, and his stick, which was a Penang lawyer, weighted with lead, was just such a weapon as might, by repeated blows, have inflicted the terrible injuries to which the trainer had succumbed.

'On the other hand, there was no wound upon his person, while the state of Straker's knife would show that one, at least, of his assailants must bear his mark upon him. There you have it all in a nutshell, Watson, and if you can give me any light I shall be infinitely obliged to you.'

I had listened with the greatest interest to the statement which Holmes, with characteristic clearness, had laid before me. Though most of the facts were familiar to me, I had not sufficiently appreciated their relative importance, nor their connection with each other.

'Is it not possible,' I suggested, 'that the incised wound upon Straker may have been caused by his own knife in the convulsive struggles which follow any brain injury?'

'It is more than possible; it is probable,' said Holmes. 'In that case, one of the main points in favour of the accused disappears.'

'And yet,' said I, 'even now I fail to understand what the theory of the police can be.'

'I am afraid that whatever theory we state has very grave objections to it,' returned my companion. 'The police imagine, I take it, that this Fitzroy Simpson, having drugged the lad, and having in some way obtained a duplicate key, opened the stable door, and took out the horse, with the intention, apparently, of kidnapping him altogether. His bridle is missing, so that Simpson must have put it on. Then, having left the door open behind him, he was leading the horse away over the moor, when he was either met or overtaken by the trainer. A row naturally ensued, Simpson beat out the trainer's brains with his heavy stick without receiving any injury from the small knife which Straker used in self-defence, and then the thief either led the horse on to some secret hiding-place, or else it may have bolted during the struggle, and be now wandering out on the moors. That is the case as it appears to the police, and improbable as it is, all other explanations are more improbable still. However, I shall very quickly test the matter when I am once upon the spot, and until then I really cannot see how we can get much further than our present position.'

It was evening before we reached the little town of Tavistock, which lies, like the boss of a shield, in the middle of the huge circle of Dartmoor. Two gentlemen were awaiting us at the station; the one a tall fair man with lion-like hair and beard, and curiously penetrating light blue eyes, the other a small alert person, very neat and dapper, in a frock-coat and gaiters, with trim little side-whiskers and an eye-glass. The latter was Colonel Ross, the well-known sportsman, the other Inspector Gregory, a man who was rapidly making his name in the English detective service.

'I am delighted that you have come down, Mr Holmes,' said the Colonel. 'The Inspector here has done all that could possibly be suggested; but I wish to leave no stone unturned in trying to avenge poor Straker, and in recovering my horse.'

'Have there been any fresh developments?' asked Holmes.

'I am sorry to say that we have made very little progress,' said the Inspector. 'We have an open carriage outside, and as you would no doubt like to see the place before the light fails, we might talk it over as we drive.'

A minute later we were all seated in a comfortable landau and were rattling through the quaint old Devonshire town. Inspector Gregory was full of his case, and poured out a stream of remarks, while Holmes threw in an occasional question or interjection. Colonel Ross leaned back with his arms folded and his hat tilted over his eyes, while I listened with interest to the dialogue of the two detectives. Gregory was formulating his theory, which was almost exactly what Holmes had foretold in the train.

'The net is drawn pretty close round Fitzroy Simpson,' he remarked, 'and I believe myself that he is our man. At the

same time, I recognize that the evidence is purely circum-
stantial, and that some new development may upset it.'

'How about Straker's knife?'

'We have quite come to the conclusion that he wounded
himself in his fall.'

'My friend Dr Watson made that suggestion to me as we
came down. If so, it would tell against this man Simpson.'

'Undoubtedly. He has neither a knife nor any sign of a
wound. The evidence against him is certainly very strong.
He had a great interest in the disappearance of the
favourite, he lies under the suspicion of having poisoned
the stable boy, he was undoubtedly out in the storm, he
was armed with a heavy stick, and his cravat was found in
the dead man's hand. I really think we have enough to go
before a jury.'

Holmes shook his head. 'A clever counsel would tear it all
to rags,' said he. 'Why should he take the horse out of the
stable? If he wished to injure it, why could he not do it
there? Has a duplicate key been found in his possession?
What chemist sold him the powdered opium? Above all,
where could he, a stranger to the district, hide a horse, and
such a horse as this? What is his own explanation as to
the paper which he wished the maid to give to the stable
boy?'

'He says that it was a ten-pound note. One was found in
his purse. But your other difficulties are not so formidable
as they seem. He is not a stranger to the district. He has
twice lodged at Tavistock in the summer. The opium was
probably brought from London. The key, having served its
purpose, would be hurled away. The horse may lie at the
bottom of one of the pits or old mines upon the moor.'

'What does he say about the cravat?'

'He acknowledges that it is his, and declares that he had
lost it. But a new element has been introduced into the case
which may account for his leading the horse from the
stable.'

Holmes pricked up his ears.

'We have found traces which show that a party of gipsies
encamped on Monday night within a mile of the spot where
the murder took place. On Tuesday they were gone. Now,

presuming that there was some understanding between Simpson and these gipsies, might he not have been leading the horse to them when he was overtaken, and may they not have him now?'

'It is certainly possible.'

'The moor is being scoured for these gipsies. I have also examined every stable and outhouse in Tavistock, and for a radius of ten miles.'

'There is another training stable quite close, I understand?'

'Yes, and that is a factor which we must certainly not neglect. As Desborough, their horse, was second in the betting, they had an interest in the disappearance of the favourite. Silas Brown, the trainer, is known to have had large bets upon the event, and he was no friend to poor Straker. We have, however, examined the stables, and there is nothing to connect him with the affair.'

'And nothing to connect this man Simpson with the interests of the Capleton stable?'

'Nothing at all.'

Holmes leaned back in the carriage and the conversation ceased. A few minutes later our driver pulled up at a neat little red-brick villa with overhanging eaves, which stood by the road. Some distance off, across a paddock, lay a long grey-tiled outbuilding. In every other direction the low curves of the moor, bronze-coloured from the fading ferns, stretched away to the skyline, broken only by the steeples of Tavistock, and by a cluster of houses away to the westward, which marked the Capleton stables. We all sprang out with the exception of Holmes, who continued to lean back with his eyes fixed upon the sky in front of him, entirely absorbed in his own thoughts. It was only when I touched his arm that he roused himself with a violent start and stepped out of the carriage.

'Excuse me,' said he, turning to Colonel Ross, who had looked at him in some surprise. 'I was day-dreaming.' There was a gleam in his eyes and a suppressed excitement in his manner which convinced me, used as I was to his ways, that his hand was upon a clue, though I could not imagine where he had found it.

'Perhaps you would prefer at once to go on to the scene of the crime, Mr Holmes?' said Gregory.

'I think that I should prefer to stay here a little and go into one or two questions of detail. Straker was brought back here, I presume?'

'Yes, he lies upstairs. The inquest is tomorrow.'

'He has been in your service some years, Colonel Ross?'

'I have always found him an excellent servant.'

'I presume that you made an inventory of what he had in his pockets at the time of his death, Inspector?'

'I have the things themselves in the sitting-room, if you would care to see them.'

'I should be very glad.'

We all filed into the front room, and sat round the central table, while the Inspector unlocked a square tin box and laid a small heap of things before us. There was a box of vestas, two inches of tallow candle, an ADP briar-root pipe, a pouch of sealskin with half an ounce of long-cut cavendish, a silver watch with a gold chain, five sovereigns in gold, an aluminium pencil-case, a few papers, and an ivory-handled knife with a very delicate inflexible blade marked Weiss & Co, London.

'This is a very singular knife,' said Holmes, lifting it up and examining it minutely. 'I presume, as I see blood-stains upon it, that it is the one which was found in the dead man's grasp. Watson, this knife is surely in your line.'

'It is what we call a cataract knife,' said I.

'I thought so. A very delicate blade devised for very delicate work. A strange thing for a man to carry with him upon a rough expedition, especially as it would not shut in his pocket.'

'The tip was guarded by a disc of cork which we found beside his body,' said the Inspector. 'His wife tells us that the knife had lain for some days upon the dressing-table, and that he had picked it up as he left the room. It was a poor weapon, but perhaps the best that he could lay his hand on at the moment.'

'Very possible. How about these papers?'

'Three of them are receipted hay-dealers' accounts. One of them is a letter of instructions from Colonel Ross. This other is a milliner's account for thirty-seven pounds fifteen, made out by Madame Lesurier, of Bond Street, to William Darbyshire. Mrs Straker tells us that Darbyshire was a friend of her husband's, and that occasionally his letters were addressed here.'

'Madame Darbyshire had somewhat expensive tastes,' remarked Holmes, glancing down the account. 'Twenty-two guineas is rather heavy for a single costume. However, there appears to be nothing more to learn, and we may now go down to the scene of the crime.'

As we emerged from the sitting-room a woman who had been waiting in the passage took a step forward and laid her hand upon the Inspector's sleeve. Her face was haggard, and thin, and eager; stamped with the print of a recent horror.

'Have you got them? Have you found them?' she panted.

'No, Mrs Straker; but Mr Holmes, here, has come from London to help us, and we shall do all that is possible.'

'Surely I met you in Plymouth, at a garden-party, some little time ago, Mrs Straker,' said Holmes.

'No, sir; you are mistaken.'

'Dear me; why, I could have sworn to it. You wore a costume of dove-coloured silk with ostrich feather trimming.'

'I never had such a dress, sir,' answered the lady.

'Ah; that quite settles it,' said Holmes; and, with an apology, he followed the Inspector outside. A short walk across the moor took us to the hollow in which the body had been found. At the brink of it was the furze bush upon which the coat had been hung.

'There was no wind that night, I understand,' said Holmes.

'None; but very heavy rain.'

'In that case the overcoat was not blown against the furze bushes, but placed there.'

'Yes, it was laid across the bush.'

'You fill me with interest. I perceive that the ground has been trampled up a good deal. No doubt many feet have been there since Monday night.'

'A piece of matting has been laid here at the side, and we have all stood upon that.'

'Excellent.'

'In this bag I have one of the boots which Straker wore, one of Fitzroy Simpson's shoes, and a cast horseshoe of Silver Blaze.'

'My dear Inspector, you surpass yourself!'

Holmes took the bag, and descending into the hollow he pushed the matting into a more central position. Then stretching himself upon his face and leaning his chin upon his hands he made a careful study of the trampled mud in front of him.

'Halloa!' said he, suddenly, 'what's this?'

It was a wax vesta, half burned, which was so coated with mud that it looked at first like a little chip of wood.

'I cannot think how I came to overlook it,' said the Inspector, with an expression of annoyance.

'It was invisible, buried in the mud. I only saw it because I was looking for it.'

'What! You expected to find it?'

'I thought it not unlikely.' He took the boots from the bag and compared the impressions of each of them with marks upon the ground. Then he clambered up to the rim of the hollow and crawled about among the ferns and bushes.

'I am afraid that there are no more tracks,' said the Inspector. 'I have examined the ground very carefully for a hundred yards in each direction.'

'Indeed!' said Holmes, rising, 'I should not have the impertinence to do it again after what you say. But I should like to take a little walk over the moors before it grows dark, that I may know my ground tomorrow, and I think that I shall put this horseshoe into my pocket for luck.'

Colonel Ross, who had shown some signs of impatience at my companion's quiet and systematic method of work, glanced at his watch.

'I wish you would come back with me, Inspector,' said he. 'There are several points on which I should like your advice, and especially as to whether we do not owe it to the public to remove our horse's name from the entries for the Cup.'

'Certainly not,' cried Holmes, with decision; 'I should let the name stand.'

The Colonel bowed. 'I am very glad to have had your opinion, sir,' said he. 'You will find us at poor Straker's house when you have finished your walk, and we can drive together into Tavistock.'

He turned back with the Inspector, while Holmes and I walked slowly across the moor. The sun was beginning to sink behind the stables of Capleton, and the long sloping plain in front of us was tinged with gold, deepening into rich, ruddy brown where the faded ferns and brambles caught the evening light. But the glories of the landscape were all wasted upon my companion, who was sunk in the deepest thought.

'It's this way, Watson,' he said, at last. 'We may leave the question of who killed John Straker for the instant, and confine ourselves to finding out what has become of the horse. Now, supposing that he broke away during or after the tragedy, where could he have gone to? The horse is a very gregarious creature. If left to himself, his instincts would have been either to return to King's Pyland or go over to Capleton. Why should he run wild upon the moor? He would surely have been seen by now. And why should gipsies kidnap him? These people always clear out when they hear of trouble, for they do not wish to be pestered by the police. They could not hope to sell such a horse. They would run a great risk and gain nothing by taking him. Surely that is clear.'

'Where is he, then?'

'I have already said that he must have gone to King's Pyland or to Capleton. He is not at King's Pyland, therefore he is at Capleton. Let us take that as a working hypothesis, and see what it leads us to. This part of the moor, as the Inspector remarked, is very hard and dry. But it falls away towards Capleton, and you can see from here that there is a long hollow over yonder, which must have been very wet on Monday night. If our supposition is correct, then the horse must have crossed that, and there is the point where we should look for his tracks.'

We had been walking briskly during this conversation,

and a few more minutes brought us to the hollow in question. At Holmes' request I walked down the bank to the right, and he to the left, but I had not taken fifty paces before I heard him give a shout, and saw him waving his hand to me. The track of a horse was plainly outlined in the soft earth in front of him, and the shoe which he took from his pocket exactly fitted the impression.

'See the value of imagination,' said Holmes. 'It is the one quality which Gregory lacks. We imagined what might have happened, acted upon the supposition, and find ourselves justified. Let us proceed.'

We crossed the marshy bottom and passed over a quarter of a mile of dry, hard turf. Again the ground sloped and again we came on the tracks. Then we lost them for half a mile, but only to pick them up once more quite close to Capleton. It was Holmes who saw them first, and he stood pointing with a look of triumph upon his face. A man's track was visible beside the horse's.

'The horse was alone before,' I cried.

'Quite so. It was alone before. Halloa! what is this?'

The double track turned sharp off and took the direction of King's Pyland. Holmes whistled, and we both followed along after it. His eyes were on the trail, but I happened to look a little to one side, and saw to my surprise the same tracks coming back again in the opposite direction.

'One for you, Watson,' said Holmes, when I pointed it out; 'you have saved us a long walk which would have brought us back on our own traces. Let us follow the return track.'

We had not to go far. It ended at the paving of asphalt which led up to the gates of the Capleton stables. As we approached a groom ran out from them.

'We don't want any loiterers about here,' said he.

'I only wished to ask a question,' said Holmes, with his finger and thumb in his waistcoat pocket. 'Should I be too early to see your master, Mr Silas Brown, if I were to call at five o'clock tomorrow morning?'

'Bless you, sir, if anyone is about he will be, for he is always the first stirring. But here he is, sir, to answer your questions for himself. No, sir, no; it's as much as my place is worth to let him see me touch your money. Afterwards, if you like.'

As Sherlock Holmes replaced the half-crown which he had drawn from his pocket, a fierce-looking elderly man strode out from the gate with a hunting-crop swinging in his hand.

'What's this, Dawson?' he cried. 'No gossiping! Go about your business! And you—what the devil do you want here?'

'Ten minutes' talk with you, my good sir,' said Holmes, in the sweetest of voices.

'I've no time to talk to every gadabout. We want no strangers here. Be off, or you may find a dog at your heels.'

Holmes leaned forward and whispered something in the trainer's ear. He started violently and flushed to the temples.

'It's a lie!' he shouted. 'An infernal lie!'

'Very good! Shall we argue about it here in public, or talk it over in your parlour?'

'Oh, come in if you wish to.'

Holmes smiled. 'I shall not keep you more than a few minutes, Watson,' he said. 'Now, Mr Brown, I am quite at your disposal.'

It was quite twenty minutes, and the reds had all faded into greys before Holmes and the trainer reappeared. Never have I seen such a change as had been brought about in Silas Brown in that short time. His face was ashy pale, beads of perspiration shone upon his brow, and his hands shook until the hunting-crop wagged like a branch in the wind. His bullying, overbearing manner was all gone, too, and he cringed along at my companion's side like a dog with its master.

'Your instructions will be done. It shall be done,' said he.

'There must be no mistake,' said Holmes, looking round at him. The other winced as he read the menace in his eyes.

'Oh, no, there shall be no mistake. It shall be there. Should I change it first or not?'

Holmes thought a little and then burst out laughing. 'No, don't,' said he. 'I shall write to you about it. No tricks, now, or—'

'Oh, you can trust me, you can trust me!'

'You must see to it on the day as if it were your own.'

'You can rely upon me.'

'Yes, I think I can. Well, you shall hear from me tomorrow.' He turned upon his heel, disregarding the trembling hand which the other held out to him, and we set off for King's Pyland.

'A more perfect compound of the bully, coward and sneak than Master Silas Brown I have seldom met with,' remarked Holmes, as we trudged along together.

'He has the horse, then?'

'He tried to bluster out of it, but I described to him so exactly what his actions had been upon that morning, that he is convinced that I was watching him. Of course, you observed the peculiarly square toes in the impressions, and that his own boots exactly corresponded to them. Again, of course, no subordinate would have dared to have done such a thing. I described to him how when, according to his custom, he was the first down, he perceived a strange horse wandering over the moor; how he went out to it, and his astonishment at recognizing from the white forehead which has given the favourite its name that chance had put in his power the only horse which could beat the one upon which he had put his money. Then I described how his first impulse had been to lead him back to King's Pyland, and how the devil had shown him how he could hide the horse until the race was over, and how he had led it back and concealed it at Capleton. When I told him every detail he gave it up, and thought only of saving his own skin.'

'But his stables had been searched.'

'Oh, an old horse-faker like him has many a dodge.'

'But are you not afraid to leave the horse in his power now, since he has every interest in injuring it?'

'My dear fellow, he will guard it as the apple of his eye. He knows that his only hope of mercy is to produce it safe.'

'Colonel Ross did not impress me as a man who would be likely to show much mercy in any case.'

'The matter does not rest with Colonel Ross. I follow my own methods, and tell as much or as little as I choose. That is the advantage of being unofficial. I don't know whether you observed it, Watson, but the Colonel's manner has been just a trifle cavalier to me. I am inclined now to have a little amusement at his expense. Say nothing to him about the horse.'

'Certainly not, without your permission.'

'And, of course, this is all quite a minor case compared with the question of who killed John Straker.'

'And you will devote yourself to that?'

'On the contrary, we both go back to London by the night train.'

I was thunderstruck by my friend's words. We had only been a few hours in Devonshire, and that he should give up an investigation which he had begun so brilliantly was quite incomprehensible to me. Not a word more could I draw from him until we were back at the trainer's house. The Colonel and the Inspector were awaiting us in the parlour.

'My friend and I return to town by the midnight express,' said Holmes. 'We have had a charming little breath of your beautiful Dartmoor air.'

The Inspector opened his eyes, and the Colonel's lips curled in a sneer.

'So you despair of arresting the murderer of poor Straker,' said he.

Holmes shrugged his shoulders. 'There are certainly grave difficulties in the way,' said he. 'I have every hope, however, that your horse will start upon Tuesday, and I beg that you will have your jockey in readiness. Might I ask for a photograph of Mr John Straker?'

The Inspector took one from an envelope in his pocket and handed it to him.

'My dear Gregory, you anticipate all my wants. If I might ask you to wait here for an instant, I have a question which I should like to put to the maid.'

'I must say that I am rather disappointed in our London consultant,' said Colonel Ross, bluntly, as my friend left the room. 'I do not see that we are any further than when he came.'

'At least, you have his assurance that your horse will run,' said I.

'Yes, I have his assurance,' said the Colonel, with a shrug of his shoulders. 'I should prefer to have the horse.'

I was about to make some reply in defence of my friend, when he entered the room again.

'Now, gentlemen,' said he, 'I am quite ready for Tavistock.'

As we stepped into the carriage one of the stable lads held the door open for us. A sudden idea seemed to occur to Holmes, for he leaned forward and touched the lad upon the sleeve.

'You have a few sheep in the paddock,' he said. 'Who attends to them?'

'I do, sir.'

'Have you noticed anything amiss with them of late?'

'Well, sir, not of much account; but three of them have gone lame, sir.'

I could see that Holmes was extremely pleased, for he chuckled and rubbed his hands together.

'A long shot, Watson; a very long shot!' said he, pinching my arm. 'Gregory, let me recommend to your attention this singular epidemic among the sheep. Drive on, coachman!'

Colonel Ross still wore an expression which showed the poor opinion which he had formed of my companion's ability, but I saw by the Inspector's face that his attention had been keenly aroused.

'You consider that to be important?' he asked.

'Exceedingly so.'

'Is there any other point to which you would wish to draw my attention?'

'To the curious incident of the dog in the night-time.'

'The dog did nothing in the night-time.'

'That was the curious incident,' remarked Sherlock Holmes.

* * *

Four days later Holmes and I were again in the train bound for Winchester, to see the race for the Wessex Cup. Colonel Ross met us, by appointment, outside the station, and we drove in his drag to the course beyond the town. His face was grave and his manner was cold in the extreme.

'I have seen nothing of my horse,' said he.

'I suppose that you would know him when you saw him?' asked Holmes.

The Colonel was very angry. 'I have been on the turf for twenty years, and never was asked such a question as that before,' said he. 'A child would know Silver Blaze with his white forehead and his mottled off foreleg.'

'How is the betting?'

'Well, that is the curious part of it. You could have got fifteen to one yesterday, but the price has become shorter and shorter, until you can hardly get three to one now.'

'Hum!' said Holmes. 'Somebody knows something, that is clear!'

As the drag drew up in the enclosure near the grand-stand, I glanced at the card to see the entries. It ran:

Wessex Plate. 50 sovs. each, h ft, with 1,000 sovs. added, for four- and five-year olds. Second £300. Third £200. New course (one mile and five furlongs).

1. Mr Heath Newton's The Negro (red cap, cinnamon jacket).
2. Colonel Wardlaw's Pugilist (pink cap, blue and black jacket).
3. Lord Backwater's Desborough (yellow cap and sleeves).
4. Colonel Ross's Silver Blaze (black cap, red jacket).
5. Duke of Balmoral's Iris (yellow and black stripes).
6. Lord Singleford's Rasper (purple cap, black sleeves).

'We scratched our other one and put all hopes on your word,' said the Colonel. 'Why, what is that? Silver Blaze favourite?'

'Five to four against Silver Blaze!' roared the ring. 'Five to four against Silver Blaze! Fifteen to five against Desborough! Five to four on the field!'

'There are the numbers up,' I cried. 'They are all six there.'

'All six there! Then my horse is running,' cried the Colonel, in great agitation. 'But I don't see him. My colours have not passed.'

'Only five have passed. This must be he.'

As I spoke a powerful bay horse swept out from the weighing enclosure and cantered past us, bearing on its back the well-known black and red of the Colonel.

'That's not my horse,' cried the owner. 'That beast has not a white hair upon its body. What is this that you have done, Mr Holmes?'

'Well, well, let us see how he gets on,' said my friend, imperturbably. For a few minutes he gazed through my field-glass. 'Capital! An excellent start!' he cried suddenly. 'There they are, coming round the curve!'

From our drag we had a superb view as they came up the straight. The six horses were so close together that a carpet could have covered them, but half-way up the yellow of the Capleton stable showed to the front. Before they reached us, however, Desborough's bolt was shot, and the Colonel's horse, coming away with a rush, passed the post a good six lengths before its rival, the Duke of Balmoral's Iris making a bad third.

'It's my race anyhow,' gasped the Colonel, passing his hand over his eyes. 'I confess that I can make neither head nor tail of it. Don't you think that you have kept up your mystery long enough, Mr Holmes?'

'Certainly, Colonel. You shall know everything. Let us all go round and have a look at the horse together. Here he is,' he continued, as we made our way into the weighing enclosure where only owners and their friends find admittance. 'You have only to wash his face and his leg in spirits of wine and you will find that he is the same old Silver Blaze as ever.'

'You take my breath away!'

'I found him in the hands of a faker, and took the liberty of running him just as he was sent over.'

'My dear sir, you have done wonders. The horse looks very fit and well. It never went better in its life. I owe you a thousand apologies for having doubted your ability. You have done me a great service by recovering my horse. You would do me a greater still if you could lay your hands on the murderer of John Straker.'

'I have done so,' said Holmes, quietly.

The Colonel and I stared at him in amazement. 'You have got him! Where is he, then?'

'He is here.'

'Here! Where?'

'In my company at the present moment.'

The Colonel flushed angrily. 'I quite recognize that I am under obligations to you, Mr Holmes,' said he, 'but I must regard what you have just said as either a very bad joke or an insult.'

Sherlock Holmes laughed. 'I assure you that I have not associated you with the crime, Colonel,' said he; 'the real murderer is standing immediately behind you!'

He stepped past and laid his hand upon the glossy neck of the thoroughbred.

'The horse!' cried both the Colonel and myself.

'Yes, the horse. And it may lessen his guilt if I say that it was done in self-defence, and that John Straker was a man who was entirely unworthy of your confidence. But there goes the bell; and as I stand to win a little on this next race, I shall defer a more lengthy explanation until a more fitting time.'

*　　*　　*

We had the corner of a Pullman car to ourselves that evening as we whirled back to London, and I fancy that the journey was a short one to Colonel Ross as well as to myself, as we listened to our companion's narrative of the events which had occurred at the Dartmoor training stables upon that Monday night, and the means by which he had unravelled them.

'I confess,' said he, 'that any theories which I had formed from the newspaper reports were entirely erroneous. And yet there were indications there, had they not been overlaid by other details which concealed their true import. I went to Devonshire with the conviction that Fitzroy Simpson was the true culprit, although, of course, I saw that the evidence against him was by no means complete.

'It was while I was in the carriage, just as we reached the trainer's house, that the immense significance of the curried mutton occurred to me. You may remember that I was distrait, and remained sitting after you had all alighted. I was marvelling in my own mind how I could possibly have overlooked so obvious a clue.'

'I confess,' said the Colonel, 'that even now I cannot see how it helps us.'

'It was the first link in my chain of reasoning. Powdered opium is by no means tasteless. The flavour is not disagreeable, but it is perceptible. Were it mixed with any ordinary dish, the eater would undoubtedly detect it, and would probably eat no more. A curry was exactly the medium which would disguise this taste. By no possible supposition could this stranger, Fitzroy Simpson, have caused curry to be served in the trainer's family that night, and it is surely too monstrous a coincidence to suppose that he happened to come along with powdered opium upon the very night when a dish happened to be served which would disguise the flavour. That is unthinkable. Therefore Simpson becomes eliminated from the case, and our attention centres upon Straker and his wife, the only two people who could have chosen curried mutton for supper that night. The opium was added after the dish was set aside for the stable boy, for the others had the same for supper with no ill effects. Which of them, then, had access to that dish without the maid seeing them?

'Before deciding that question I had grasped the significance of the silence of the dog, for one true inference invariably suggests others. The Simpson incident had shown me that a dog was kept in the stables, and yet, though someone had been in and had fetched out a horse, he had not barked enough to arouse the two lads in the loft. Obviously the midnight visitor was someone whom the dog knew well.

'I was already convinced, or almost convinced, that John Straker went down to the stables in the dead of the night and took out Silver Blaze. For what purpose? For a dishonest one, obviously, or why should he drug his own stable boy? And yet I was at a loss to know why. There have been cases before now where trainers have made sure of great sums of money by laying against their own horses, through agents, and then prevented them from winning by fraud. Sometimes it is a pulling jockey. Sometimes it is some surer and subtler means. What was it here? I hoped that the contents of his pockets might help me to form a conclusion.

'And they did so. You cannot have forgotten the singular knife which was found in the dead man's hand, a knife which certainly no sane man would choose for a weapon. It was, as Dr Watson told us, a form of knife which is used for the most delicate operations known in surgery. And it was to be used for a delicate operation that night. You must know, with your wide experience of turf matters, Colonel Ross, that it is possible to make a slight nick upon the tendons of a horse's ham, and to do it subcutaneously so as to leave absolutely no trace. A horse so treated would develop a slight lameness which would be put down to a strain in exercise or a touch of rheumatism, but never to foul play.'

'Villain! Scoundrel!' cried the Colonel.

'We have here the explanation of why John Straker wished to take the horse out on to the moor. So spirited a creature would have certainly roused the soundest of sleepers when it felt the prick of the knife. It was absolutely necessary to do it in the open air.'

'I have been blind!' cried the Colonel. 'Of course, that was why he needed the candle, and struck the match.'

'Undoubtedly. But in examining his belongings, I was fortunate enough to discover, not only the method of the crime, but even its motives. As a man of the world, Colonel, you know that men do not carry other people's bills about in their pockets. We have most of us quite enough to do to settle our own. I at once concluded that Straker was leading a double life, and keeping a second establishment. The nature of the bill showed that there was a lady in the case, and one who had expensive tastes. Liberal as you are with your servants, one hardly expects that they can buy twenty-guinea walking dresses for their women. I questioned Mrs Straker as to the dress without her knowing it, and having satisfied myself that it had never reached her, I made a note of the milliner's address, and felt that by calling there with Straker's photograph, I could easily dispose of the mythical Darbyshire.

'From that time on all was plain. Straker had led out the horse to a hollow where his light would be invisible. Simpson, in his flight, had dropped his cravat, and Straker had picked it up with some idea, perhaps, that he might use it in securing the horse's leg. Once in the hollow he had got behind the horse, and had struck a light, but the creature, frightened at the sudden glare, and with the strange instinct of animals feeling that some mischief was intended, had lashed out, and the steel shoe had struck Straker full on the forehead. He had already, in spite of the rain, taken off his overcoat in order to do his delicate task, and so, as he fell, his knife gashed his thigh. Do I make it clear?'

'Wonderful!' cried the Colonel. 'Wonderful! You might have been there.'

'My final shot was, I confess, a very long one. It struck me that so astute a man as Straker would not undertake this delicate tendon-nicking without a little practice. What could he practise on? My eyes fell upon the sheep, and I asked a question which, rather to my surprise, showed that my surmise was correct.'

'You have made it perfectly clear, Mr Holmes.'

'When I returned to London I called upon the milliner, who at once recognized Straker as an excellent customer, of the name of Darbyshire, who had a very dashing wife with a strong partiality for expensive dresses. I have no doubt that this woman had plunged him over head and ears in debt, and so led him into this miserable plot.'

'You have explained all but one thing,' cried the Colonel. 'Where was the horse?'

'Ah, it bolted and was cared for by one of your neighbours. We must have an amnesty in that direction, I think. This is Clapham Junction, if I am not mistaken, and we shall be in Victoria in less than ten minutes. If you care to smoke a cigar in our rooms, Colonel, I shall be happy to give you any other details which might interest you.'

THE GREAT DERBY SWINDLE

by Guy Boothby

Although Guy Boothby is little remembered today, he created a character who for some years was as familiar to British readers as Sherlock Holmes. This man was Dr Nikola, a sinister and ruthless criminal master-mind who had not a little in common with Professor Moriarty. Dr Nikola appeared in five novels between 1895 and 1901 and helped ensure literary success for the Australian-born writer who had come to England specifically to make his mark.

Boothby was the son of a member of the House of Assembly in Adelaide. He shared his father's love of horse racing, and after he became successful, he spent much of his spare time at the race courses of Southern England. The Turf features in a number of his tales. Simon Carne, the central figure in the following story—one of a series entitled A Prince of Swindlers—has the distinction of being the first gentleman crook in literature (preceding by two years the famous Raffles, created by Sir Arthur Conan Doyle's brother-in-law, E. W. Hornung) and is also a man irresistibly drawn to the world of racing. In 'The Great Derby Swindle' he uses all his ingenuity and cunning to obtain that most cherished ambition of horse owners—a Derby winner.

*　　*　　*

It was seven o'clock on one of the brightest mornings of all that year. The scene was Waterloo Station, where the Earl of Amberley, Lord Orpington, and the Marquis of Laverstock were pacing up and down the main line departure platform, gazing anxiously about them. It was evident from the way they scrutinised every person who approached them, that they were on the look out for someone. This someone ultimately proved to be Simon Carne, who, when he appeared, greeted them with considerable cordiality, at the same time apologizing for his lateness in joining them.

'I think this must be our train,' he said, pointing to the carriages drawn up beside the platform on which they stood. 'At any rate here is my man. By dint of study he has turned himself into a sort of walking Bradshaw, and he will certainly be able to inform us.'

The inimitable Belton deferentially insinuated that his master was right in his conjecture, and then led the way towards a Pullman car which had been attached to the train for the convenience of Carne and his guests. They took their seats, and a few moments later the train moved slowly out of the station. Carne was in the best of spirits, and the fact that he was taking his friends down to the stables of his trainer, William Bent, in order that they might witness a trial of his candidate for the Derby seemed to give him the greatest possible pleasure.

On reaching Merford, the little wayside station nearest the village in which the training stables were situated, they discovered a comfortable four-wheeled conveyance drawn up to receive them. The driver touched his hat, and stated that his master was awaiting them on the Downs; as proved to be the case, for when they left the high road and turned on to the soft turf they saw before them a string of thoroughbreds, and the trainer himself mounted upon his well-known white pony, Columbine.

'Good morning, Bent,' said Carne, as the latter rode up and lifted his hat to the four visitors. 'You see we have kept your promise, and are here to witness the trial you said you had arranged for us.'

'I am glad to see you, sir,' Bent replied. 'And I only hope that what I am about to show you will prove of service to you. The horse is as fit as mortal hands can make him, and if he don't do his best for you next week there will be one person surprised in England, and that one will be myself. As you know, sir, the only horse I dread is

Vulcanite, and the fact cannot be denied that he's a real clinker.'

'Well,' said Carne, 'when we have seen our animal gallop we shall know better how much trust we are to place in him. For my own part I'm not afraid. Vulcanite, as you say, is a good horse, but, if I'm not mistaken, Knight of Malta is a better. Surely this is he coming towards us.'

'That's him,' said the trainer, with a fine disregard for grammar. 'There's no mistaking him, is there? And now, if you'd care to stroll across, we'll see them saddle.'

The party accordingly descended from the carriage, and walked across the turf to the spot where the four thoroughbreds were being divested of their sheets. They made a pretty group; but even the most inexperienced critic could scarcely have failed to pick out Knight of Malta as the best among them. He was a tall, shapely bay, with black points, a trifle light of flesh perhaps, but with clean, flat legs, and low, greyhound-like thighs, sure evidence of the enormous propelling power he was known to possess. His head was perfection itself, though a wee bit too lop-eared if anything. Taken altogether, he looked, what he was, thoroughbred every inch of him. The others of the party were Gasometer, Hydrogen, and Young Romeo, the last named being the particular trial horse of the party. It was a favourite boast of the trainer that the last named was so reliable in his habits, his condition, and his pace, that you would not be far wrong if you were to set your watch by him.

'By the way, Bent,' said Carne, as the boys were lifted into their saddles, 'what weights are the horses carrying?'

'Well, sir, Young Romeo carries 8st. 9lb.; Gasometer, 7st. 8lb.; Hydrogen, 7st. 1lb.; and the Knight, 9st. 11lb. The distance will be the Epsom course, one mile and a half, and the best horse to win. Now, sir, if you're ready we'll get to work.'

He turned to the lad who was to ride Hydrogen.

'Once you are off you will make the running, and bring them along at your best pace to the dip, where Gasometer will, if possible, take it up. After that I leave it to you other boys to make the best race of it you can. You, Blunt,' calling up his head lad, 'go down with them to the post, and get them off to as good a start as possible.'

The horses departed, and Simon Carne and his friends accompanied the trainer to a spot where they would see the finish to the best advantage. Five minutes later an ejaculation from Lord Orpington told them that the horses had started. Each man accordingly clapped his glasses to his eyes, and watched the race before them. Faithful to his instructions, the lad on Hydrogen came straight to the front, and led them a cracker until they descended into the slight dip which marked the end of the first half mile.

Then he retired to the rear, hopelessly done for, and Gasometer took up the running, with Knight of Malta close alongside him, and Young Romeo only half a length away. As they passed the mile post Young Romeo shot to the front, but it soon became evident he had not come to stay. Good horse as he was, there was a better catching him hand over fist. The pace was all that could be desired, and when Knight of Malta swept past the group, winner of the trial by more than his own length, the congratulations Simon Carne received were as cordial as he could possibly desire.

'What did I tell you, sir?' said Bent, with a smile of satisfaction upon his face. 'You see what a good horse he is. There's no mistake about that.'

'Well, let us hope he will do as well a week hence,' Carne replied simply, as he replaced his glasses in their case.

'Amen to that,' remarked Lord Orpington.

'And now, gentlemen,' said the trainer, 'if you will allow me, I will drive you over to my place to breakfast.'

They took their places in the carriage once more, and, Bent having taken the reins, in a few moments they were bowling along the high road towards a neat modern residence standing on a slight eminence on the edge of the Downs. This was the trainer's own place of abode, the stables containing his many precious charges lying a hundred yards or so to the rear.

They were received on the threshold by the trainer's wife, who welcomed them most heartily to Merford. The keen air of the Downs had sharpened their appetites, and when they sat down to table they found they were able to do full justice to the excellent fare provided for them. The meal at an end, they inspected the stables once more, carefully examining the Derby candidate, who seemed none the worse for his morning's exertion, and then Carne left his guests in the big yard to the enjoyment of their cigars, while he accompanied his trainer into the house for a few moments' chat.

'And now sit down, sir,' said Bent, when they reached his own *sanctum*, a cosy apartment, half sitting-room and half office, bearing upon its walls innumerable mementoes of circumstances connected with the owner's lengthy turf experiences. 'I hope you are satisfied with what you saw this morning?'

'Perfectly satisfied,' said Carne, 'but I should like to hear exactly what you think about the race itself.'

'Well, sir, as you may imagine, I have been thinking a good deal about it lately, and this is the conclusion I have come to. If this were an ordinary year, I should say that we possess out and away the best horse in the race; but we must remember that this is not by any means an ordinary year—there's Vulcanite, who they tell me is in the very pink of condition, and who has beaten our horse each time they have met; there's The Mandarin, who won the Two Thousand this week, and who will be certain to come into greater favour as the time shortens, and The Filibuster, who won the Biennial Stakes at the Craven Meeting, a nice enough horse, though I must say I don't fancy him over much myself.'

'I take it, then, that the only horse you really fear is Vulcanite.'

'That's so, sir. If he were not in the list, I should feel as certain of seeing you leading your horse back a winner as any man could well be.'

On looking at his watch Carne discovered that it was time for him to rejoin his friends and be off to the railway station if they desired to catch the train which they had arranged should convey them back to town. So, bidding the trainer and his wife good-bye, they took their places in the carriage once more, and were driven away.

Arriving at Waterloo, they drove to Lord Orpington's club to lunch.

'Do you know you're a very lucky fellow, Carne?' said the Earl of Amberley as they stood on the steps of that institution afterwards, before separating in pursuit of the pleasures of the afternoon. 'You have health, wealth, fame, good looks, one of the finest houses in London, and now one of the prospective winners of the Derby. In fact, you only want one thing to make your existence perfect.'

'And what is that?' asked Carne.

'A wife,' replied Lord Amberley. 'I wonder the girls have let you escape so long.'

'I am not a marrying man,' said Carne; 'how could a fellow like myself, who is here today and gone tomorrow, expect any woman to link her lot with his? Do you remember our first meeting?'

'Perfectly,' replied Lord Amberley. 'When I close my eyes I can see that beautiful marble palace, set in its frame of blue water, as plainly as if it were but yesterday I breakfasted with you there.'

'That was a very fortunate morning for me,' said the other. 'And now here is my cab. I must be off. Good-bye.'

'Good-bye,' cried his friends, as he went down the steps and entered the vehicle. 'Don't forget to let us know if anything further turns up.'

'I will be sure to do so,' said Simon Carne, and then, as he laid himself back on the soft cushions and was driven by way of Waterloo Place to Piccadilly, he added to himself, 'yes, if I can bring off the little scheme I have in my mind, and one or two others which I am preparing, and can manage to get out of England without anyone suspecting that I am the burglar who has outwitted all London, I shall have good cause to say that was a *very* fortunate day for me when I first met his lordship.'

That evening he dined alone. He seemed pre-occupied, and it was evident that he was disappointed about something. Several times on hearing noises in the street outside he questioned his servants as to the cause. At last, however, when Ram Gafur entered the room carrying a telegram upon a salver, his feelings found vent in a sigh of satisfaction. With eager fingers he broke open the envelope, withdrew the contents, and read the message it contained:

'Seven Stars music hall—Whitechapel Road. Ten o'clock.'

There was no signature, but that fact did not seem to trouble him very much. He placed it in his pocket book, and afterwards continued his meal in better spirits. When the servants had left the room he poured himself out a glass of port, and taking a pencil proceeded to make certain calculations upon the back of an envelope. For nearly ten minutes he occupied himself in this way, then he tore the paper into tiny pieces, replaced his pencil in his pocket, and sipped his wine with a satisfaction that was the outcome of perfected arrangements.

'The public excitement,' he said to himself, not without a small touch of pride, 'has scarcely cooled down from the robbery of the famous Wiltshire jewels. Lord Orpington has not as yet discovered the whereabouts of the gold and silver plate which disappeared from his house so mysteriously a week or two ago, while several other people have done their best to catch a gang of burglars who would seem to have set all London at defiance. But if I bring off this new *coup*, they'll forget all their grievances in consideration of this latest and greatest scandal. There'll be scarcely a man in England who won't have something to say upon the subject. By the way, let me see how he stands in the betting tonight.'

He took a paper from the table in the window, and glanced down the sporting column. Vulcanite was evidently the public's choice, Knight of Malta being only second favourite, with The Mandarin a strong third.

'What a hubbub there will be when it becomes known,' said Carne, as he placed the paper on the table again. 'I shall have to take especial care, or some of the storm may blow back on me. I fancy I can hear the newsboys shouting: "Latest news of the turf scandal. The Derby favourite stolen. Vulcanite missing. An attempt made to get at Knight of Malta." Why! It will be twenty years before old England will forget the sensation I am about to give her.'

With a grim chuckle at the idea, he went upstairs to his dressing-room and locked the door. It must have been well after nine o'clock when he emerged again, and, clad in a long ulster, left the house in his private hansom. Passing down Park Lane, he drove along Piccadilly, then by way of the Haymarket, Strand, Ludgate Hill, and Fenchurch Street to the Whitechapel Road. Reaching the corner of Leman Street, he signalled to his man to stop, and jumped out.

His appearance was now entirely changed. Instead of the deformed, scholar-like figure he usually presented, he now resembled a common-place, farmerish individual, with iron-grey hair, a somewhat crafty face, ornamented with bushy eyebrows and a quantity of fluffy whiskers. How he had managed it as he drove along goodness only knows, but that he had effected the change was certain.

Having watched his cab drive away, he strolled along the street until he arrived at a building, the flaring lights of which proclaimed it the Seven Stars Music Hall. He paid his money at the box office, and then walked inside to find a fair-sized building, upon the floor of which were placed possibly a hundred small tables. On the stage at the further end a young lady, boasting a minimum of clothing and a maximum of self-assurance, was explaining, to the dashing accompaniment of the orchestra, the adventures she had experienced 'When Billy and me was courting'.

Acting up to his appearance, Carne called for a 'two of Scotch cold', and, having lit a meerschaum pipe which he took from his waistcoat pocket, prepared to make himself at home. As ten o'clock struck he turned his chair a little, in order that he might have a better view of the door, and waited.

Five minutes must have elapsed before his patience was rewarded. Then two men came in together, and immediately he saw them he turned his face in an opposite direction, and seemed to be taking an absorbing interest in what was happening upon the stage.

One of the men who had entered, and whom he had seemed to recognize—a cadaverous-looking individual in a suit of clothes a size too small for him, a velvet waistcoat at least three sizes too large, a check tie, in which was stuck an enormous horseshoe pin composed of palpably imitation diamonds, boasting no shirt as far as could be seen, and wearing upon his head a top hat of a shape that had been fashionable in the early sixties—stopped, and placed his hand upon his shoulder.

'Mr Blenkins, or I'm a d'isy,' he said. 'Well, who'd ha' thought of seeing you here of all places? Why, it was only this afternoon as me and my friend, Mr Brown here, was a-speaking of you. To think as how you should ha' come up to London just this wery time, and be at the Seven Stars Music 'all, of all other plaices! It's like what the noospapers call a go-insidence, drat me if it ain't. 'Ow are yer, old pal?'

He extended his hand, which Mr Blenkins took, and shook with considerable cordiality. After that, Mr Brown, who from outward appearances was by far the most respectable of the trio, was introduced in the capacity of a gentleman from America, a citizenship that became more apparent when he opened his mouth to speak.

'And what was 'ee speaking of I about?' asked Mr Blenkins, when the trio were comfortably seated at table.

This the diffident Mr Jones, for by that commonplace appellative the seedy gentleman with the magnificent diamonds chose to be called, declined to state. It would appear that he was willing to discuss the news of the day, the price of forage, the prospects of war, the programme proceeding upon the stage, in fact, anything rather than declare the subject of his conversation with Mr Brown that afternoon.

It was not until Mr Brown happened to ask Mr Blenkins what horse he fancied for the Derby that Mr Jones in any degree recovered his self-possession. Then an animated discussion on the forthcoming race was entered upon. How long it would have lasted had not Mr Jones presently declared that the music of the orchestra was too much for him, I cannot say.

Thereupon Mr Brown suggested that they should leave the Hall and proceed to a place of which he knew in a neighbouring street. This they accordingly did, and when they were safely installed in a small room off the bar, Mr Jones, having made certain that there was no one near enough to overhear, unlocked his powers of conversation with whisky and water, and proceeded to speak his mind.

For upwards of an hour they remained closeted in the room together, conversing in an undertone. Then the meeting broke up, Mr Blenkins bidding his friends 'good night' before they left the house.

From the outward appearances of the party, if in these days of seedy millionaires and overdressed bankrupts one may venture to judge by them, he would have been a speculative individual who would have given a five pound note for the worldly wealth of the trio. Yet, had you taken so much trouble, you might have followed Mr Blenkins and have seen him picked up by a smart private hansom at the corner of Leman Street. You might then have gone back to the 'Hen and Feathers', and have followed Mr Brown as far as Osborn Street, and have seen him enter a neat brougham, which was evidently his own private property. Another hansom, also a private one, met Mr Jones in the same thoroughfare, and an hour later two of the number were in Park Lane, while the third was discussing a bottle of Heidseck in a gorgeous private sitting-room on the second floor of the Langham Hotel.

As he entered his dressing-room on his return to Porchester House, Simon Carne glanced at his watch. It was exactly twelve o'clock.

'I hope Belton will not be long,' he said to himself. 'Give him a quarter of an hour to rid himself of the other fellow, and say half-an-hour to get home. In that case he should be here within the next few minutes.'

The thought had scarcely passed through his brain before there was a deferential knock at the door, and next moment Belton, clad in a long great-coat, entered the room.

'You're back sooner than I expected,' said Carne. 'You could not have stayed very long with our friend?'

'I left him soon after you did, sir,' said Belton. 'He was in a hurry to get home, and as there was nothing more to settle I did not attempt to prevent him. I trust you are satisfied, sir, with the result of our adventure.'

'Perfectly satisfied,' said Carne. 'Tomorrow I'll make sure that he's good for the money, and then we'll get to work. In the meantime you had better see about a van and the furniture of which I spoke to you, and also engage a man whom you can rely upon.'

'But what about Merford, sir, and the attempt upon Knight of Malta?'

'I'll see about that on Monday. I have promised Bent to spend the night there.'

'You'll excuse my saying so, sir, I hope,' said Belton, as he poured out his master's hot water and laid his dressing-gown upon the back of a chair, ready for him to put on, 'but it's a terrible risky business. If we don't bring it off, there'll be such a noise in England as has never been heard before. You might murder the Prime Minister, I believe, and it wouldn't count for so much with the people generally as an attempt to steal the Derby favourite.'

'But we shall not fail,' said Carne confidently. 'By this time you ought to know me better than to suppose that. No, no, never fear, Belton; I've got all my plans cut and dried, and even if we fail to get possession of Vulcanite, the odds are a thousand to one against our being suspected of any complicity in the matter. Now you can go to bed. Good night.'

'Good night, sir,' said Belton respectfully, and left the room.

It was one of Simon Carne's peculiarities always to fulfil his engagements in spite of any inconvenience they might cause himself. Accordingly the four o'clock train from Waterloo, on the Monday following the meeting at the Music Hall just narrated, carried him to Merford in pursuance of the promise he had given his trainer.

Reaching the little wayside station on the edge of the Downs, he alighted, to find himself welcomed by his trainer, who lifted his hat respectfully, and wished him good afternoon.

During the drive, Carne spoke of the impending race, and among other things of a letter he had that morning received, warning him of an attempt that would probably be made to obtain possession of his horse. The trainer laughed good humouredly.

'Bless you, sir,' he said, 'that's nothing. You should just

see some of the letters I've got pasted into my scrap book. Most of 'em comes a week or fortnight before a big race. Some of 'em warns me that if I don't prevent the horse from starting, I'm as good as a dead man; others ask me what price I will take to let him finish outside the first three; while more still tell me that if I don't put 'im out of the way altogether, I'll find my house and my wife and family flying up to the clouds under a full charge of dynamite within three days of the race being run. Don't you pay any attention to the letters you receive. I'll look after the horse, and you may be very sure I'll take good care that nothing happens to him.'

'I know that, of course,' said Carne, 'but I thought I'd tell you. You see, I'm only a novice at racing, and perhaps I place more importance just now upon a threat of that kind than I shall do a couple of years hence.'

'Of course,' replied the trainer. 'I understand exactly how you feel, sir. It's quite natural. And now here we are, with the missis standing on the steps to help me give you a hearty welcome.'

They drove up to the door, and when Carne had alighted he was received by the trainer's wife as her lord and master had predicted. His bedroom he discovered, on being conducted to it to prepare for dinner, was at the back of the house, overlooking the stableyard, and possessed a lovely view, extending across the gardens and village towards where the Downs ended and the woods of Herberford began.

'A pretty room,' he said to Belton, as the latter laid out his things upon the bed, 'and very convenient for our purpose. Have you discovered where you are located?'

'Next door, sir.'

'I am glad of that; and what room is beneath us?'

'The kitchen and pantry, sir. With the exception of one at the top of the house, there are no other bedrooms on this side.'

'That is excellent news. Now get me ready as soon as you can.'

During dinner that evening Simon Carne made himself as pleasant as possible to his host and hostess. So affable, indeed, was he that when they retired to rest they confessed to each other that they had never entertained a more charming guest. It was arranged that he should be called at five o'clock on the morning following, in order that he might accompany the trainer to the Downs to see his horse at his exercise.

It was close upon eleven o'clock when he dismissed his valet and threw himself upon his bed with a novel. For upwards of two hours he amused himself with his book; then he rose and dressed himself in the rough suit which his man had put out for him. Having done so, he took a strong rope ladder from his bag, blew out his light, and opened his window. To attach the hooks at the end of the ropes to the inside of the window sill, and to throw the rest outside was the work of a moment. Then, having ascertained that his door was securely locked, he crawled out and descended to the ground. Once there, he waited until he saw Belton's light disappear, and heard his window softly open. Next moment a small black bag was lowered, and following it, by means of another ladder, came the servant himself.

'There is no time to be lost,' said Carne as soon as they were together. 'You must set to work on the big gates, while I do the other business. The men are all asleep; nevertheless, be careful that you make no noise.'

Having given his instructions, he left his servant and made his way across the yard towards the box where Knight of Malta was confined. When he reached it he unfastened the bag he had brought with him, and took from it a brace and a peculiar shaped bit, resembling a large pair of compasses. Uniting these, he oiled the points and applied them to the door, a little above the lock. What he desired to do did not occupy him for more than a minute.

Then he went quietly along the yard to the further boundary, where he had that afternoon noticed a short ladder. By means of this he mounted to the top of the wall, then lifted it up after him and lowered it on the other side, still without making any noise. Instead of dismounting by it, however, he seated himself for a moment astride of it, while he drew on a pair of clumsy boots he had brought with him, suspended round his neck. Then, having chosen his place, he jumped. His weight caused him to leave a good mark on the soft ground on the other side.

He then walked heavily for perhaps fifty yards until he reached the high road. Here he divested himself of the boots, put on his list slippers once more, and returned as speedily as possible to the ladder, which he mounted and drew up after him. Having descended on the other side, he left it standing against the wall, and hastened across the yard towards the gates, where he found Belton just finishing the work he had set him to do.

With the aid of a brace and bit similar to that used by Carne upon the stable door, the lock had been entirely removed and the gate stood open. Belton was evidently satisfied with his work; Carne, however, was not so pleased. He picked up the circle of wood and showed it to his servant. Then, taking the bit, he inserted the screw on the reverse side and gave it two or three turns.

'You might have ruined everything,' he whispered, 'by omitting that. The first carpenter who looked at it would be able to tell that the work was done from the inside. But, thank goodness, I know a trick that will set that right. Now then, give me the pads, and I'll drop them by the door. Then we can return to our rooms.'

Four large blanket pads were handed to him, and he went quietly across and dropped them by the stable door. After that he rejoined Belton, and they made their way, with the assistance of the ladders, back to their own rooms once more.

Half-an-hour later Carne was wrapped in a sweet slumber, from which he did not wake until he was aroused by a tapping at his chamber door. It was the trainer.

'Mr Carne,' cried Bent, in what were plainly agitated tones, 'if you could make it convenient I should be glad to speak to you as soon as possible.'

In something under twenty minutes he was dressed and downstairs. He found the trainer awaiting him in the hall, wearing a very serious face.

'If you will stroll with me as far as the yard, I should like to show you something,' he said.

Carne accordingly took up his hat and followed him out of the house.

'You look unusually serious,' said the latter, as they crossed the garden.

'An attempt has been made to get possession of your horse.'

Carne stopped short in his walk and faced the other.

'What did I tell you yesterday?' he remarked. 'I was certain that that letter was more than an idle warning. But how do you know that an attempt *has* been made?'

'Come, sir, and see for yourself,' said Bent. 'I am sorry to say there is no gainsaying the fact.'

A moment later they had reached the entrance to the stableyard.

'See, sir,' said Bent, pointing to a circular hole which now existed where previously the lock had been. 'The rascals cut out the lock, and thus gained an entry to the yard.'

He picked up the round piece of wood with the lock still attached to it, and showed it to his employer.

'One thing is very certain, the man who cut this hole is a master of his trade, and is also the possessor of fine implements.'

'So it would appear,' said Carne grimly. 'Now, what else is there for me to hear? Is the horse much hurt?'

'Not a bit the worse, sir,' answered Bent. 'They didn't get in at him, you see. Something must have frightened them before they could complete their task. Step this way, sir, if you please, and examine the door of the box for yourself. I have given strict orders that nothing shall be touched until you have seen it.'

They crossed the yard together, and approached the box in question. On the woodwork the commencement of a circle similar to that which had been completed on the yard gates could be plainly distinguished, while on the ground below lay four curious shaped pads, one of which Carne picked up.

'What on earth are these things?' he asked innocently enough.

'Their use is easily explained, sir,' answered the trainer. 'They are intended for tying over the horse's feet, so that when he is led out of his box his plates may make no noise upon the stones. I'd like to have been behind 'em with a whip when they got him out, that's all. The double-dyed rascals to try such a trick upon a horse in my charge.'

'I can understand your indignation,' said Carne. 'It seems to me we have had a narrow escape.'

'Narrow escape, or no narrow escape, I'd have had 'em safely locked up in Merford Police Station by this time,' replied Bent vindictively. 'And now, sir, let me show you how they got out. As far as I can see they must have imagined they heard somebody coming from the house, otherwise they would have left by the gates instead of by this ladder.'

He pointed to the ladder which was still standing where Carne had placed it, and then led him by a side door round to the other side of the wall. Here he pointed to some heavy footmarks upon the turf. Carne examined them closely.

'If the size of his foot is any criterion of his build,' he said, 'he must have been a precious big fellow. Let me see how mine compares with it.'

He placed his neat shoe in one of the imprints before him, and smiled as he noticed how the other overlapped it.

They then made their way to the box, where they found the animal at his breakfast. He lifted his head and glanced round at them, bit at the iron of the manger, and then gave a little playful kick with one of his hind legs.

'He doesn't seem any the worse for his adventure,' said Carne, as the trainer went up to him and ran his hand over his legs.

'Not a bit,' answered the other. 'He's a wonderfully even-tempered horse, and it takes a lot to put him out. If his nerves had been at all upset he wouldn't have licked up his food as clean as he has done.'

Having given another look at him, they left him in charge of his lad, and returned to the house.

The gallop after breakfast confirmed their conclusion that there was nothing the matter, and Simon Carne returned to town ostensibly comforted by Bent's solemn assurance to that effect. That afternoon Lord Calingforth, the owner of

Vulcanite, called upon him. They had met repeatedly, and consequently were on the most intimate terms.

'Good afternoon, Carne,' he said as he entered the room. 'I have come to condole with you upon your misfortune, and to offer you my warmest sympathy.'

'Why, what on earth has happened?' asked Carne as he offered his visitor a cigar.

'God bless my soul, my dear fellow! Haven't you seen the afternoon's paper? Why, it reports the startling news that your stables were broken into last night, and that my rival, Knight of Malta, was missing this morning.'

Carne laughed.

'I wonder what they'll say next,' he said quietly. 'But don't let me appear to deceive you. It is perfectly true that the stables were broken into last night, but the thieves were disturbed, and decamped just as they were forcing the lock of The Knight's box.'

'In that case I congratulate you. What rascally inventions some of these sporting papers do get hold of to be sure. I'm indeed glad to hear that it is not true. The race would have lost half its interest if your horse were out of it. By the way, I suppose you are still as confident as ever?'

'Would you like to test it?'

'Very much, if you feel inclined for a bet.'

'Then I'll have a level thousand pounds with you that my horse beats yours. Both to start or the wager is off. Do you agree?'

'With pleasure. I'll make a note of it.'

The noble Earl jotted the bet down in his book, and then changed the subject by inquiring whether Carne had ever had any transactions with his next door neighbour, Klimo.

'Only on one occasion,' the other replied. 'I consulted him on behalf of the Duke of Wiltshire at the time his wife's diamonds were stolen. To tell the truth, I was half thinking of calling him in to see if he could find the fellow who broke into the stables last night, but on second thoughts I determined not to do so. I did not want to make any more fuss about it than I could help. But what makes you ask about Klimo?'

'Well, to put the matter in a nutshell, there has been a

good deal of small pilfering down at my trainer's place lately, and I want to get it stopped.'

'If I were you I should wait till after the race, and then have him down. If one excites public curiosity just now, one never knows what will happen.'

'I think you are right. Anyhow, I'll act on your advice. Now, what do you say to coming along to the Rooms with me to see how our horses stand in the market? Your presence there would do more than any number of paper denials towards showing the fallacy of this stupid report. Will you come?'

'With pleasure,' said Carne, and in less than five minutes he was sitting beside the noble Earl in his mail phaeton, driving towards the rooms in question.

When he got there, he found Lord Calingforth had stated the case very correctly. The report that Knight of Malta had been stolen, had been widely circulated, and Carne discovered that the animal was, for the moment, almost a dead letter in the market. The presence of his owner, however, was sufficient to stay the panic, and when he had snapped up two or three long bets, which a few moments before had been going begging, the horse began steadily to rise towards his old position.

That night, when Belton waited upon his master at bedtime, he found him, if possible more silent than usual. It was not until his work was well-nigh completed that the other spoke.

'It's a strange thing, Belton,' he said, 'and you may hardly believe it, but if there were not certain reasons to prevent me from being so magnanimous, I would give this matter up and let the race be run on its merits. I don't know that I ever took a scheme in hand with a worse grace. However, as it can't be helped, I suppose I must go through with it. Is the van prepared?'

'It is quite ready, sir.'

'All the furniture arranged as I directed?'

'It is exactly as you wished, sir. I have attended to it myself.'

'And what about the man?'

'I have engaged the young fellow, sir, who assisted me

before. I know he's quick, and I can stake my life that he's trustworthy.'

'I am glad to hear it. He will have need to be. Now for my arrangements. I shall make the attempt on Friday morning next, that is to say, two days from now. You and the man you have just mentioned will take the van and horses to Market Stopford, travelling by the goods train which, I have discovered, reaches the town between four and five in the morning. As soon as you are out of the station, you will start straight away along the high road towards Exbridge, reaching the village between five and six. I shall meet you in the wood alongside the third milestone on the other side, made up for the part I am to play. Do you understand?'

'Perfectly, sir.'

'That will do then. I shall go down to the village tomorrow evening, and you will not hear from me again until you meet me at the place I have named. Good night.'

'Good night, sir.'

Now, it is a well-known fact that if you wish to excite the anger of the inhabitants of Exbridge village, and more particularly of any member of the Pitman Training Establishment, you have but to ask for information concerning a certain blind beggar who put in an appearance there towards sunset on the Thursday preceding the Derby of 18—, and you will do so. When that mysterious individual first came in sight he was creeping along the dusty high road that winds across the Downs from Market Stopford to Beaton Junction, dolorously quavering a ballad that was intended to be, though few would have recognized it, 'The Wearing of the Green'.

On reaching the stables he tapped along the wall with his stick, until he came to the gate. Then, when he was asked his business by the head lad, who had been called up by one of the stable boys, he stated that he was starving, and, with peculiar arts of his own, induced him to provide him with a meal. For upwards of an hour he remained talking with the lads, and then wended his way down the hill towards the village, where he further managed to induce the rector to permit him to occupy one of his outhouses for the night.

After tea he went out and sat on the green, but towards

eight o'clock he crossed the stream at the ford, and made his way up to a little copse, which ornamented a slight eminence, on the opposite side of the village to that upon which the training stables were situated.

How he found his way, considering his infirmity, it is difficult to say, but that he did find it was proved by his presence there. It might also have been noticed that when he was once under cover of the bushes, he gave up tapping the earth with his stick, and walked straight enough, and without apparent hesitation, to the stump of a tree upon which he seated himself.

For some time he enjoyed the beauty of the evening undisturbed by the presence of any other human being. Then he heard a step behind him, and next moment a smart-looking stable lad parted the bushes and came into view.

'Hullo,' said the new-comer. 'So you managed to get here first?'

'So I have,' said the old rascal, 'and it's wonderful when you come to think of it, considering my age, and what a poor old blind chap I be. But I'm glad to find ye've managed to get away, my lad. Now what have ye got to say for yourself?'

'I don't know that I've got anything to say,' replied the boy. 'But this much is certain, what you want can't be done.'

'And a fine young cockerel you are to be sure, to crow so loud that it can't be done,' said the old fellow, with an evil chuckle. 'How do you know it can't?'

'Because I don't see my way,' replied the other. 'It's too dangerous by a long sight. Why, if the guv'nor was to get wind of what you want me to do, England itself wouldn't be big enough to hold us both. You don't know 'im as well as I do.'

'I know him well enough for all practical purposes,' replied the beggar. 'Now, if you've got any more objections to raise, be quick about it. If you haven't, then I'll talk to you. You haven't? Very good then. Now, just hold your jaw, open your ears, and listen to what I've got to say. What time do you go to exercise tomorrow morning?'

'Nine o'clock.'

'Very good, then. You go down on to the Downs, and the Boss sends you off with Vulcanite for a canter. What do you do? Why, you go steadily enough as long as he can see you, but directly you're round on the other side of the hill you stick in your heels and nip into the wood that runs along on your right hand, just as if your horse was bolting with you. Once in there, you go through for half a mile until you come to the stream, ford that, and then cut into the next wood, riding as if the devil himself were after you, until you reach the path above Hangman's Hollow. Do you know the place?'

'I reckon I ought to.'

'Well, then, you just make tracks for it. When you get there you'll find me waiting for you. After that I'll take over command, and get both you and the horse out of England in such a way that nobody will ever suspect. Then there'll be five hundred pounds for your trouble, a safe passage with the horse to South America, and another five hundred the day the nag is set ashore. There's not as much risk as you could take between your finger and thumb, and a lad with a spirit like yours could make a fortune with a thousand pounds on the other side. What have you to say now?'

'It's all very well,' replied the lad, 'but how am I to know that you'll play straight with me?'

'What do you take me for?' said the beggar indignantly, at the same time putting his hand in his coat pocket and producing what looked like a crumpled piece of paper. 'If you doubt me, there's something that may help to convince you. But don't go showing it around tonight, or you'll be giving yourself away, and that'll mean the Stone Jug for you, and "Amen" to all your hopes of a fortune. You'll do as I wish now, I suppose?'

'I'll do it,' said the lad sullenly, as he crumpled the bank note up and put it in his pocket. 'But now I must be off. Since there's been this fuss about Knight of Malta, the Guv'nor has us all in before eight o'clock, and keeps the horse under lock and key, with the head lad sleeping in the box with him.'

'Well, good night to you, and don't you forget about tomorrow morning; niggle the horse about a bit just to make him impatient like, and drop a hint that he's a bit fresh. That will make his bolting look more feasible. Don't leave the track while there's anyone near you, but, as soon as you do, ride like thunder to the place I told you of. I'll see that they're put off the scent as to the way you've gone.'

'All right,' said the lad. 'I don't like it, but I suppose I'm in too deep now to draw back. Good night.'

'Good night, and good luck to you.'

Once he had got rid of the youth, Carne (for it was he) returned by another route to the rector's out-building, where he laid himself down on the straw, and was soon fast asleep. His slumbers lasted till nearly daybreak, when he rose and made his way across country to the small copse above Hangman's Hollow, on the road from Exbridge to Beaton Junction. Here he discovered a large van drawn up, apparently laden with furniture both inside and out. The horses were feeding beneath a tree, and a couple of men were eating their breakfast beside them. On seeing Carne, the taller of the pair—a respectable looking workman, with a big brown beard—rose and touched his hat. The other looked with astonishment at the disreputable beggar standing before them.

'So you arrived here safely,' said Carne. 'If anything you're a little before your time. Boil me a cup of tea, and give me something to eat as quickly as possible, for I am nearly famished. When you have done that, get out the clothes I told you to bring with you, and let me change into them. It wouldn't do for any of the people from the village back yonder to be able to say afterwards that they saw me talking with you in this rig.'

As soon as his hunger was appeased he disappeared into the wood, and dressed himself in his new attire. Another suit of clothes, and an apron such as might be worn by a furniture remover's foreman, a grey wig, a short grey beard and moustache, and a bowler hat, changed his identity completely; indeed, when his rags had been hidden in the hollow of a tree, it would have been a difficult matter to have traced any resemblance between the respectable looking workman eating his breakfast and the disreputable beggar of half-an-hour before.

It was close upon nine o'clock by this time, and as soon as he realized this Carne gave the order to put the horses to. This done, they turned their attention to the back of the van, and then a strange thing became apparent. Though to all appearances, viewed from the open doors at the end, the inside of this giant receptacle was filled to its utmost holding capacity with chests of drawers, chairs, bedsteads, carpets, and other articles of household furniture, yet by pulling a pair of handles it was possible for two men easily to withdraw what looked like half the contents of the van.

The poorest observer would then have noticed that in almost every particular these articles were dummies, affixed to a screen, capable of being removed at a moment's notice. The remainder of the van was fitted after the fashion of a stable, with a manger at the end and a pair of slings dependent from the roof.

The nervous tension produced by the waiting soon became almost more than the men could bear. Minute after minute went slowly by, and still the eagerly expected horse did not put in an appearance. Then Belton, whom Carne had placed on the look-out, came flying towards them with the report that he could hear a sound of galloping hoofs in the wood. A few seconds later the noise could be plainly heard at the van, and almost before they had time to comment upon it, a magnificent thoroughbred, ridden by the stable boy who had talked to the blind beggar on the previous evening, dashed into view, and pulled up beside the van.

'Jump off,' cried Carne, catching at the horse's head, 'and remove the saddle. Now be quick with those cloths, we must rub him down or he'll catch cold.'

When the horse was comparatively dry he was led into the van, which was to be his stable for the next few hours, and, in spite of his protests, slung in such a fashion that his feet did not touch the floor. This business completed, Carne bade the frightened boy get in with him, and take care that he did not, on any account, neigh.

After that the mask of furniture was replaced, and the

doors closed and locked. The men mounted to their places on the box and roof, and the van continued its journey along the high road towards the Junction. But satisfactory as their attempt had so far proved, the danger was by no means over. Scarcely had they proceeded three miles on their way before Carne distinguished the sound of hoofs upon the road behind him. A moment later a young man, mounted on a well-bred horse, came into view, rode up alongside, and signalled to the driver to stop.

'What's the matter?' inquired the latter, as he brought his horses to a standstill. 'Have we dropped anything?'

'Have you seen anything of a boy on a horse?' asked the man, who was so much out of breath that he could scarcely get his words out.

'What sort of a boy, and what sort of a horse?' asked the man on the van.

'A youngish boy,' was the reply, 'seven stone weight, with sandy hair, on a thoroughbred.'

'No: we ain't seen no boy with sandy 'air, ridin' of a thoroughbred 'orse seven stone weight,' said Carne. 'What's 'e been an' done?'

'The horse has bolted with him off the Downs, back yonder,' answered the man. 'The Guv'nor has sent us out in all directions to look for him.'

'Sorry we can't oblige you,' said the driver as he prepared to start his team again. 'Good day to you.'

'Much obliged,' said the horseman, and, when he had turned off into a side road, the van continued its journey till it reached the railway station. A quarter of an hour later it caught the eleven o'clock goods train and set off for the small seaside town of Barworth, on the south coast, where it was shipped on board a steamer which had arrived that morning from London.

Once it was safely transferred from the railway truck to the deck, Carne was accosted by a tall, swarthy individual who, from his importance, seemed to be both the owner and the skipper of the vessel. They went down into the saloon together, and a few moments later an observer, had one been there, might have seen a cheque for a considerable sum of money change hands.

An hour later the *Jessie Branker* was steaming out to sea, and a military-looking individual, not at all to be compared with the industrious mechanic who had shipped the furniture van on board the vessel bound for Spain, stood on the platform of the station waiting for the express train to London. On reaching the metropolis he discovered it surging beneath the weight of a great excitement. The streets re-echoed with the raucous cries of the newsvendors:

'The Derby favourite stolen—Vulcanite missing from his stable!'

Next morning an advertisement appeared in every paper of consequence, offering 'A reward of Five Hundred Pounds for any information which might lead to the conviction of the person or persons who on the morning of May 28th had stolen or caused to be stolen from the Pitman Training Stables, the Derby favourite, Vulcanite, the property of the Right Honourable the Earl of Calingforth.'

The week following, Knight of Malta, owned by Simon Carne, Esq., of Porchester House, Park Lane, won the Derby by a neck, in a scene of intense excitement. The Mandarin being second, and The Filibuster third. It is a strange fact that to this day not a member of the racing world has been able to solve the mystery surrounding the disappearance of one of the greatest horses that ever set foot on an English racecourse.

Today, if Simon Carne thinks of that momentous occasion, when, amid the shouting crowd of Epsom he led his horse back a winner, he smiles softly to himself, and murmurs beneath his breath:

'Valued at twenty thousand pounds, and beaten in the Derby by a furniture van.'

A MYSTERIOUS STABLE

by Nat Gould

Nat Gould was the Dick Francis of his time. From 1890 until his death in 1919, he produced 150 novels which sold in excess of 30 million copies. Every one featured racing in some form or another —although not all were thrillers—and Gould was widely referred to as the 'Prince of Sporting Novelists'. The Times called him 'the most successful writer of best-sellers' and said that any newspaper serialising one of his stories 'could promise itself an increased circulation of 100,000 copies a day'.

By a curious twist of fate, Gould took the opposite route to success from his contemporary, Guy Boothby, publishing his first book, A Double Event, *in Australia in 1890. He had begun his career as a reporter on a small English newspaper, but after six unspectacular years sailed for Australia, where he joined the* Brisbane Daily Telegraph *and became a racing journalist. The excitement and intrigue of horse racing at once caught his imagination, and the raw material which he collected from the Australian courses became the basis for one best-seller after another. Before the end of the century, however, he returned home to England and, switching to tales of the English Turf, continued to enjoy a huge success right up to his death and for some years thereafter, thanks to the twenty-odd unpublished manuscripts that he left among his papers. He earned a fortune from his books, but left little more than £7,000 in his will.*

Although Nat Gould's name is still familiar today, his books are now more collected than read. Curiously, he wrote very few short stories and finding one for this collection has been no easy task. In the end I have plumped for one of the series he wrote for the Daily Graphic *around the turn of the century, about Valentine Martyn, the Race-Course Detective. Martyn is noteworthy as being the very first Turf sleuth in literature.*

*   *   *

Val Martyn was consulted by many people on all matters connected with the seamy side of racing. Many knotty problems and strange doings had he successfully solved.

The Myrtle stables and its trainer, patrons, and jockey now occupied his attention. For the past two or three seasons the running of the Myrtle horses had been so 'in and out' that public attention was fixed on them. Horses that appeared certain of winning had mysteriously lost time and again. So far the authorities had failed to bring the responsible parties to book; there was not sufficient evidence to act upon although there was plenty of suspicion. At last, after a particularly flagrant bit of work, Val Martyn was called in.

It was soon after this that he was sitting, one afternoon, in his usual chair in his house in Chelsea. His bulldog Jack was on the mat at his feet, and his daughter Lillie faced and watched him as he smoked a cigar.

Into the room came Harry Marker; he was engaged to Lillie, and they were to be married during the summer.

Marker owned many good horses. He and Val Martyn had always been friends. The detective would not have trusted the happiness of his only child to any other man.

Val Martyn did not look up as Harry Marker entered the room but appeared to be profoundly studying some problem. Lillie smiled at Harry and motioned him to take a seat.

The detective continued to smoke for some time. He found cigars an aid to concentration. Presently he looked round and saw Harry Marker.

'You came in quietly,' he said with a smile.

'I never care to disturb you when you have your thinking cap on,' was the reply.

'I've got something to think about. They've asked me to tackle the Myrtle stables—the fellows who run them, I mean,' explained Martyn.

'It's about time!' said Harry. 'I wonder they haven't done so before.'

'They fancied the beggars would go too far and commit themselves, and there would have been no need to call me in,' pursued Martyn. 'The Myrtle lot are deuced clever. It's strange how rogues prosper sometimes when honest men cannot come into their own. I'm going to pay a visit to Myrtle stables.'

'Why are you going to Myrtle?' Harry asked.

'To see my old acquaintance, Moses Pinkton,' replied Martyn.

'You don't mean to say the scoundrel is in with the Myrtle crowd!' exclaimed Harry.

'Hand-and-glove; he's one of the rogues who have prospered financially at the expense of honest men,' answered Martyn.

*   *   *

It was Jubilee Meeting at Kempton Park. As usual the famous course was crowded; all the notabilities in the racing world, or nearly so, were present. In the paddock there was the usual crowd to see the Jubilee Stakes runners.

Val Martyn was there, looking spick-and-span, and smoking an unusually big cigar, which was a sure sign of the detective's mental activity.

'Wherever have you been for the past week?' asked Harry Marker.

Martyn smiled.

'I told you I was going to the Myrtle stables,' he replied. 'I went and had an exciting, if not a pleasant time. I'll tell you all about it later on—tonight probably, after you've won the Jubilee with Grey Mist.'

Harry laughed as he replied:

'I'm not so confident about Grey Mist winning today —not half so sanguine as when he landed the Lincoln Handicap last year. Pinkton's Firebrand seems to be regarded as little short of a certainty today.'

Richard Brunt came up.

'Well, my friend, what do you think of things?' he asked the detective.

'You mean, what do I think will win the Jubilee?'

'Yes, has my horse a chance?'

'The Secret? I should say so but he's got to beat Grey Mist.'

'And Firebrand; don't leave him out,' broke in Marker.

'So you fancy Firebrand?' asked Brunt.

'He's been to Myrtle stables gathering information,' said Harry, laughing.

Brunt looked surprised.

'Putting your head in the lion's mouth is a dangerous game,' said he.

Val Martyn laughed.

'I'm used to danger,' he said.

Moses Pinkton walked past and scowled at them. Luke Darton followed him.

'Two of the biggest scoundrels ever seen,' observed Brunt. 'I tried to buy Firebrand. But though I offered a stiff price Pinkton wouldn't sell. He said that he wanted the satisfaction of beating The Secret and Grey Mist.'

'He's not forgotten how we fooled him at Lincoln,' laughed Harry. 'Come and have a look at Grey Mist.'

The sensational favourite of the never-to-be-forgotten Lincoln Handicap was being saddled by Mat Davis, the trainer. In the next stall stood The Secret, a big upstanding chestnut with four white legs and a blaze face.

Both horses were fit and well; they were popular fancies and had been so far some weeks. The public fully expected one of them to win.

Val Martyn walked across the paddock, leaving Harry Marker and Brunt watching their horses. He saw Moses Pinkton attending to Firebrand, with the assistance of the trainer of Myrtle stables; needless to say he was another of the 'doubtful sort'.

Moses Pinkton glared at Martyn.

'Bossing about as usual!' he growled. 'You thought you'd find out something at Myrtle, I suppose, but you failed, as your pals will fail today.'

Val Martyn laughed.

'A nice comfortable place, Myrtle,' he observed. 'You'll be sorry to leave it.'

'Leave it? I'm not going to leave it, not much,' said Moses.

'You're mistaken. You'll be out of it soon. Didn't you know?'

'Know what?' asked Moses.

'That I'm looking out for a more secure place for you —and one or two more,' replied Martyn.

'Well, Foxton, what do you think of your mount?' he asked, as the jockey came up.

Foxton was a small, wizened man. He had been riding for years with various success. He was a very fair horseman but unreliable.

'I think he'll just about win,' answered the jockey.

'You're riding for a mysterious stable,' said Val.

The jockey looked glum.

'I've found 'em all right,' he replied.

Martyn smiled as he walked away.

'I'll do for that devil some day,' said Moses as he looked after him.

'I suppose there's no doubt about Firebrand being able to win?' asked Foxton.

'He'll win by the length of a street if you ride properly,' declared Moses.

'I'm good enough if the horse is good enough,' answered the jockey gruffly. He had no liking for Moses, but he could not pick and choose. Mounts were none too plentiful.

Luke Darton took Moses on one side.

'Grey Mist is well backed. So's The Secret. You're sure Firebrand can beat 'em! There's no mistake?' he said.

'None, he's sure to win,' replied Moses.

'I shall be in a hole if Firebrand loses,' confided Darton; 'it'll ruin me.'

'It won't be the first time you've been broke,' answered Moses.

'I'll expect you to help me out if we lose,' said Darton.

'Of course I'll help you out, with my toe,' replied Moses.

*　　*　　*

A quarter of an hour before the great race the crowd in Tattersall's increased. The roar of the ring was heard all over the course.

The Handicap for the Stakes was considered excellent, and every runner—there were fifteen of them—had some sort of chance. The prices ranged from Firebrand at four to one, down to Sunflower at fifty to one. Grey Mist was second favourite. Then came The Secret, Duckling, Pinmoney, and Caravan.

Firebrand was not a popular favourite. His running had been in and out, and on form he had no pretensions to win a race like the Jubilee. He was backed by a 'clever' division, many of whom always followed a mysterious stable. Myrtle was about the most mysterious of all.

The fifteen horses came on to the course and paraded in front of the stands. They were all well trained and an exceptionally fit lot.

As the horses paraded Caravan suddenly bolted out of the circle; his jockey could not hold him. The horse galloped to the back of the course before being pulled up.

As the horses cantered to the Jubilee starting-post the favourites were cheered. There were plenty of Firebrand's followers to shout for the mysterious stable's candidate.

Foxton carried the pink, yellow sleeves and cap of Pinkton. The horse moved well and had never looked so fit. Brunt said that it would take the best of them all their time to beat him.

Grey Mist and The Secret went freely. Harry Marker's colours—black, green sleeves and cap, were cheered to the echo.

The horses ranged in line at the top of the rise, and at the Jubilee starting-post they formed a bright band of colour across the track. The starter soon had them lined up level and sent them away.

The bugle sounded the start and there was a great shout 'They're off!' The race for the Jubilee Stakes had commenced.

Caravan made the running. As is often the case, the fractious horse at the post got away well at the start. He set a fast pace and carried three or four off their legs so that they fell back; the others were in a cluster.

Firebrand, Grey Mist, The Secret, Pinmoney, Duckling and Sunflower were together. Foxton on Firebrand was determined to have a good place round the turn.

Fred Lyme kept Grey Mist on the rails. Firebrand against him was on the outside; then came The Secret and Sunflower half a length way. The order was maintained until they neared the home turn. Here Sunflower made a spurt, headed the field, and looked like a winner.

It was a bright, clear day, and the colours were easily distinguishable.

As they came to the turn Foxton moved up on Firebrand and the pink jacket and yellow sleeves were conspicuous. The horse was going well. Behind him came Grey Mist still on the rails; then The Secret, and Caravan who had fallen back.

Val Martyn watched the race closely; nothing escaped his keen eyes. He was a good judge of running and knew that Firebrand, the horse from the mysterious stable, was going in great form. He saw Grey Mist moving well on the rails, with The Secret handy. A smile crossed his face; he thought it would be all right. Once in the straight Grey Mist would settle the pretensions of the leaders.

Moses Pinkton and Luke Darton were certain of Firebrand, and no horse could have done better up to now. It meant a fortune to Pinkton if his horse won, and much to Luke Darton.

Grey Mist rounded the bend into the straight without any interference; there was no jostling or crowding but several horses ran wide, losing ground, and giving those better placed a good run.

The stands were packed. All eyes were turned on the horses. No sooner did Sunflower and Firebrand show clearly in front, in the run for home, than a tumult arose which gathered strength as they came along.

Harry Marker felt sanguine; the black-and-green jacket was in a fine position. Brunt was satisfied with the running of The Secret. He hardly expected to beat Grey Mist or Firebrand.

Lillie Martyn, and her friend, Mrs Breaton, grew excited. Grey Mist was their horse. If he won they would land nice sums, and there appeared to be every hope of success.

Sunflower, the hope of the bookmakers, continued to hold the lead; he had a light weight and 'the apprentice' made the most of it.

But Foxton on Firebrand had the measure of the leader; he was satisfied. A clear course was between him and the judge's box, and he felt certain of winning.

He urged his mount forward. As he anticipated, Firebrand easily took the measure of Sunflower, headed him, and led the field by a couple of lengths.

Fred Lyme had a good deal of ground to make up but under no circumstances did he ever lose heart.

Val Martyn, though, was disappointed.

'Firebrand's better than I thought,' he muttered. 'His running must have been all wrong. There's sure to be an inquiry if he wins. I shouldn't wonder if the whole lot are wiped out—serve 'em right, too.'

A tremendous shout from the crowd proclaimed that a change was coming over the aspect of the race.

Grey Mist had gained ground. The Secret was close after him, and Pinmoney pressing him hard.

'Grey Mist! Grey Mist!'

There was no doubt about the enthusiasm as the black-and-green jacket drew nearer to the pink-and-yellow! Harry Marker's horse drew level with Sunflower, passed him, and raced after Firebrand.

There were only two in it now—Firebrand and Grey Mist. The finish would be great, no doubt about it.

Even Val Martyn was thrilled. He was probably more interested in this race than anybody on the course, for he had a 'little scheme' of his own mapped out if Firebrand lost. If the horse won it was another matter, as probably others would deal with the 'mystery lost'.

Moses Pinkton was well nigh beside himself with delight. It looked certain that Firebrand would win. He cared little what happened if the horse won; the stewards might do their worst. The winnings would be safe, what else mattered?

Luke Darton's chance of a lifetime was coming off. He intended to clear out of the country and start his depredations elsewhere, on new ground.

Foxton was so confident that he did not attempt to keep Firebrand on the rails when his mount seemed to prefer the centre of the course.

Fred Lyme shot Grey Mist along, and as the horse had been on the rails all the way he could now finish there. No going round the leader was necessary.

Stride by stride Grey Mist gained on Firebrand. Thousands of people held their breath as they watched the struggle.

On came Grey Mist close to the rails, Fred Lyme driving him hard. Every stride told and brought him nearer to the favourite.

Foxton seemed lost in blissful contemplation of victory. He suffered a rude shock when he caught sight of Grey Mist's head close alongside him; and then he saw the black-and-green jacket and Fred Lyme's determined face.

Up went Foxton's whip, which was about the worst thing he could have done. Firebrand resented it. He put back his ears. It was a bad sign and indicated that he had had enough of it.

Grey Mist drew level; for a moment the horses measured stride for stride. Then Firebrand faltered and the black-and-green was carried forward. In a whirlwind finish Harry Marker's horse got to the front and passed the judge's box half a length in front of Firebrand. Grey Mist had won! The Secret was third.

Deafening cheers greeted the victory. Harry Marker's colours were popular. Lillie's face glowed with delight as she heard the applause.

Moses Pinkton was wild with rage and disappointment; he raved like a madman. Unfortunately he met Luke Darton.

'Out of my way,' roared Moses. 'You always bring bad luck. I never wish to see you again.'

He hurried on to take charge of Firebrand. Darton's face went white.

'Never want to see me again,' he muttered. 'You'll see me

tonight at Myrtle stables. We've a good many things to settle up.'

Pinkton was leading Firebrand away when Brunt stopped him.

'Sell him now, Moses?' he asked, nodding towards the horse.

Moses scowled; he stopped, then said:

'I'm beaten but I'm not done for; I'll sell him at a price.'

'How much?'

'Five thousand.'

'Right!' agreed Brunt, who seldom haggled. 'I believe he's worth it. Hand over the reins. I'll write you a cheque.'

Moses did so, but said:

'Can't you give it me in cash—notes?'

'I'll see,' replied Brunt as he handed over Firebrand to his trainer.

Later on he paid the five thousand pounds in notes and gold. There is seldom a shortage of ready money on the race course.

* * *

Val Martyn disappeared quickly.

'Where's Martyn?' asked Harry Marker.

'Gone!' replied Brunt. 'He told me he was in a hurry; he's probably going to put the finishing touches to Moses and Co.'

Val Martyn arrived in the vicinity of Myrtle stables about ten at night. He was alone but in his pocket was his trusty revolver.

The detective was prepared for 'squalls'; he revelled in them. There was nothing he liked better than a dangerous encounter, provided he got out of it whole and raked in a scoundrel or two.

He had overheard Pinkton and Darton quarrelling at Kempton. That something would happen that night at Myrtle he was certain.

Luke Darton was not a man to stick at anything. Moreover, he knew Pinkton had money on him; and, Martyn conjectured, there was probably a large sum in the house.

Val Martyn watched at Myrtle. He was an adept at hiding in an advantageous position where he could see and remain unseen.

He saw Moses Pinkton arrive and enter the house alone.

It was not until nearly midnight that, by the light of the moon, he spotted Luke Darton creeping cautiously towards the house. With him was the jockey, Foxton.

In a few minutes the two came round to the front door.

'They've made up their minds to knock and get in decently,' thought Martyn.

Darton thumped at the door. There was no reply from within.

Martyn smiled.

'Moses prefers to keep visitors out tonight,' he thought.

Darton, finding no response to his summons, desisted. He had no desire to rouse the stable lads.

The pair disappeared.

Val Martyn stole after them silently, keeping under cover of the house. He heard a slight grating sound. It was Darton opening a window. He recognized this, and looking round the corner saw Foxton disappearing inside. Darton had gone ahead.

Val Martyn went to the window and listened. All was still. He had no wish to run into unnecessary danger. If Darton and Foxton attacked Moses, he (Martyn) would come to the rescue and Moses, in his own defence, would assist him. The situation rather tickled his fancy. Moses assisting him to capture Darton was amusing.

Listening, he fancied he heard a groan.

He waited patiently. Had he heard a struggle he would have gone inside at once, no matter what the risk. He did not think Luke Darton would go quite so far as to commit murder.

He heard steps, then the creak of a bolt, and the back door was opened. Darton came out—and—and looked cautiously round.

He seemed half inclined to go into the house again. He hesitated, went half-way, then stopped.

'He's frightened to go in,' thought Martyn. 'I wonder what happened?'

Darton faced about and commenced to walk away. Val Martyn, with a swift run, was on him.

Darton turned quickly, but the revolver covered his head. The scoundrel shouted with rage. He was trapped.

Quick as a panther Luke Darton sprang at Martyn. The 'bark' of the revolver showed the detective was ready but he missed his aim. This was not surprising for Darton's impetuous rush knocked up his arm.

Luke Darton clung to the detective. Martyn dropped the revolver, it was safer. He was a powerful man and dissipated Darton was no match for him. In a few minutes the detective had him pinned on the ground.

'Give in?' asked Martyn. 'Had enough? What's gone on inside? Where's Foxton?'

'Go and find out,' shouted Darton.

'And leave you here, not likely. I've had a lot of trouble with you, Luke, but I've got you now.'

The stable boys heard the shot and came trooping out.

'Hold him! You'd better rope him,' said Martyn.

'Who're you?' asked Seth, the head lad.

'Val Martyn, the detective.'

Seth started; he had heard of Martyn's many exploits.

'What has happened?' asked Seth.

'I'm going inside to find out. Tie him up,' ordered Martyn.

Seth sent for ropes. Darton was quickly trussed.

Val Martyn went into the house. He found Foxton, the jockey, insensible at the foot up the stairs. Leaving him there he went upstairs.

In a bedroom he found Moses Pinkton dead on the bed, strangled, his eyes bulging. It was a fearful sight.

'There's one rogue the less,' said Martyn as he went to the window and called for Seth.

The head lad came, stumbled over Foxton. Martyn heard him.

'Come upstairs, leave him there!' he shouted.

Seth came into the room. He was horrified when he saw Moses dead.

They searched the room. There was no money in it, but

on examining Luke Darton's clothes Val Martyn found over six thousand pounds on him.

Luke Darton was tried for the murder of Moses Pinkton and sentenced to death. Foxton was acquitted. He satisfied the jury that he had not gone to Myrtle with Darton for the purpose of robbery, still less murder.

THE IRON PRUNE

by Barclay Northcote

Barclay Northcote was America's Nat Gould, a prolific writer of racing stories, many of which appeared as serials in the popular pulp magazine All-Story Weekly *during the early decades of this century. Those of Northcote's novels which were published in book form, like* Death at the Wire *and* The Jockey Slayer, *appeared in paperback and consequently have now become extremely difficult to find.*

Northcote was the son of a Los Angeles bookmaker, Thomas Northcote, and grew up amidst the sights and scenes of racing on the West Coast of America. For a time he even nurtured hopes of becoming a jockey, but grew too big and heavy for this to be feasible. Instead he turned to writing about the thing he had come to know best, the colourful and crafty world of race course gamblers.

This knowledge had been built up in company with his father as he travelled around the race courses of California. The older man had acquired a wide circle of acquaintances among the 'rail-birds', as a section of regular American race goers are called, and it was from these men that Barclay heard the stories that were to provide the raw material for his writing. Four of them were also the inspiration for a quartet of gamblers who feature in many of the tales: John McCarthy alias 'Kid Mothball' and his sidekicks, Saffron, Provo and Felt-Hat Frieslander. They all appear in the story 'The Iron Prune' which Northcote wrote for All-Story Weekly *of March 17, 1917. Apart from being typical of their exploits, it also provides the reader with an authentic picture of horse racing in America at this time.*

*   *   *

Asbestos was the overnight favourite in the sixth race. He was a big, white-stockinged, chestnut gelding, five years old, with an inflammable temperament—the very opposite of his name—which he developed the first moment he faced the barrier as a two-year-old.

On that well-remembered occasion Asbestos had not only 'burned up the track' and galloped home a winner under 'wraps', but he had insisted on maintaining his speed until the next quarter-mile pole.

When his struggling jockey finally turned him and ambled back for the weigh-in, Asbestos hesitated not at all for the needful ceremony just under the judges' stand. With fine but fiendish enthusiasm the handsome horse seized on the idea of going up the stairs leading to the steward's eyrie. Brushing off his demoralized pilot with the same nonchalance that some men forget alimony, he proceeded on reaching the top to bestow an equine kiss on one of the outraged officials by way of thanking them for watching his maiden performance.

Then, striking a *pose plastique*, Asbestos cocked his head owlishly to one side and studied the crowd in the grandstand with the mien of one seeking and deserving public approbation. Thus engaged, he made a movement as though to descend, but, missing his footing, slid the entire flight of steps backwards; near the bottom he turned a complete and unique somersault; fully, freely, and gladly continuing on through the wire fence like a reaper direct from Deering, Illinois, entering a virgin field of timothy.

As though to console the losers who had been unappreciative of his fleetness and to add to the ecstasy of the few who had 'played him on the nose' without the incentive of a form-chart upon which to base an 'alibi' in case he lost, Asbestos now rose with a foolish smile; and, as if seeking to cleanse himself of all guilty stains acquired by his backsliding from the upper storey of the judgment seat, as well as cool his eccentric disposition to a thermal intensity where he would not engender a general conflagration in the stables, he next dove into the 'liverpool', as if he were a candidate for immersion and felt the need of whatever grace would be thus acquired after his rather hectic behaviour.

The liverpool, being a hazard designed to serve the purpose of most hazards and induce a 'flunk' among horses entered in steeplechase events, was adequately provided with steep and slippery sides. Asbestos wallowed around in it for a few minutes, being finally hoisted back to solid earth through the united efforts of numerous stable boys emulating the justly celebrated Mr Hercules.

Having thus gratified his secret craving for name and fame on his 'first out', Asbestos was detained by the aid of several young but lusty hawsers until blanket and blinkers could be brought; then he was towed back to the scales; whereupon it was discovered that some of the lead pads in the saddle had been dislocated by his riotous conduct; after which, his jockey being found seven pounds under weight, Asbestos was disqualified and Lilly Belle's number was run up.

Business of weeping, wailing, and gnashing of teeth on the part of Asbestos' former admirers; more business of incoherent shouts of joy on the part of those who had 'rung in' on Lilly Belle.

Among the former were grouped four shrewd-looking rail-birds—one slim, hatchet-faced youth named John McCarthy, but known far and wide as 'Kid Mothball', because of his weakness for preserving clothing with camphorated ammunition; one Saffron, whose features looked as if they had been recently plunged into a dye-vat intended to receive the imperial robes of a Chinese emperor; next Felt-Hat Frieslander, who abjured sennits and Panamas with equal fervour; and lastly Provo, who hailed from a town of that name in Utah.

'Well, friends,' quoth Kid Mothball, 'we don't start no bungs today in the non-liquidating bank-rolls of them two.' He jerked his thumb towards 'Goldfinger' Ike Bernard and 'Ivory-Eye' Joe Hobbs as the two latter bookmakers commenced to pay off on Lilly Belle's beneficiaries.

'Jigger,' whispered Provo hoarsely. 'Here comes his owner.'

The four partially forgot their disappointment in

commiseration of David Buckley. He was pacing a section of the brick-paved betting-ring in a state of mind that called for a mackintosh rather than material impervious to fire.

For weeks Asbestos had been cherished in the Buckley stables with a view of making a clean-up of staggering dimensions that would send Goldfinger and Ivory-Eye back to their former pastimes of purveying 'iron prunes' in a two-cent restaurant that once adorned Sixth Avenue and Fiftieth Street, New York, and throttling poultry in Washington Market, respectively.

With characteristic secrecy, Kid Mothball had ferreted out the fact that Buckley would back his horse to the limit, and had risen with the joyous lark to verify the rumour by 'clocking it'.

Asbestos worked so well that all four of this little group of earnest seekers for a 'soft spot' had gone after that worthy but overambitious quadruped like a farm-hand after his first bowl of chop-suey.

Hence, slight symptoms of financial unrest after the thoroughbred's turpitude. Hence, also, a miniature snow-fall effect in their vicinity as the quartet shredded the moribund tickets and 'post-mortemed' the circumstances that had harpooned their fond hopes.

'I wisht I'd bet on a saw-horse with brass lungs and Bessemer steel legs,' bleated Felt-Hat.

'We might better 'a' put our dough in a tin stable-bucket and then beat on the door and lissen to that dog romp around in his stall,' echoed Saffron, his ochre complexion acquiring a unique green tinge at thought of his loss.

'Meanin' you could pull it out agin?' queried Mothball, with a smile whose optimism matched the opulent, broad checks in his English walking coat. 'Well, friends,' he continued, after a pause to flick an imaginary bit of dust from his plainly immaculate spats, 'if this was the last race in the world, believe me, I'd be leadin' youse all past the paddock fer the Metropolitan Bellyache Handicap. As it is, havin' throwed out a life-line on Lilly Belle to show fer seven long-lost seeds I run acrost today in the watch-pocket of these here pants, I bites Mooshure Goldfinger's alfalfa stack fer twenty-one iron men. That's eats fer us all, and tomorrow we see if we can't sting 'em more bitter.'

*   *   *

That had been three years before.

It is not often in the course of human events on the Metropolitan Circuit that four devotees of 'the sport of kings' again congregate to discuss the chances of a horse whose eccentricities at the outset of his career have charmed the joy out of life and the 'velvet' out of their pockets into those of the bookmakers.

However, on the beautiful summer afternoon when Morris Park was overflowing with the mad, rollicking crowd, and the frenzy of uncertainty lured on losers and winners alike, this quartet of stalwarts drew together under the joint influence of memory's hypnosis, and the burning desire to revenge themselves on Goldfinger Ike particularly, whose seductive slate was the first to be held aloft when the scratches had been settled.

'I mind the day well when this furnace-linin' fool of a horse pulled all them circus tricks of his'n out at Ogden,' reflected Provo.

'I never played him sence,' hissed Felt-Hat.

'I'm goin' right over now and use him to blow a hole in a puffeckly good tencase note,' avowed Kid Mothball serenely. 'Goldfinger's had that there deposit of our'n all this time and we hain't never seen a cent of intrust.'

Amid a volley of groans from the other three he did that little thing. The odds against Asbestos were three to one.

Mothball came back with his ticket. Suddenly the gong in the betting-ring droned an unwonted signal—and a late scratch was announced. It was Asbestos.

'There you go—chasin' a ghost that'll never walk,' bitterly mourned Saffron. The others were silent.

Asbestos had developed into one of the most willing and consistent horses on the track; and although always a nervous actor at the barrier, had miraculously preserved the same occasional astounding burst of speed in mile events which had been the wonder of the circuit on his 'first out'.

Had it been habitual instead of occasional, his owner would have been able to retire and Asbestos would have always been an odds-on play.

As it was, David Buckley had been accorded only a little better than an even break on the sum total of his thorough-bred's earnings. Just why he should have campaigned the gelding, year in and year out, was problematical. Buckley's judgment, however, was not to be despised.

He had other horses whose average winnings were far higher—for a time. One by one they went the way of all relatively short-lived racing steeds, until, among the original string of twelve, there were not more than two or three who had stabled with this near-phenom the day of his début.

With the regularity of Father Time himself, nevertheless, Asbestos came out, ran well or poorly, in conformance with his mood, and always his owner backed him to win.

Kid Mothball walked back and exchanged his ticket for his original investment. He did not immediately rejoin his friends. Instead he wandered in and out among the crowd, thinking hard; presently he met a pock-marked, wizen-faced little fellow, whose puckered eyes and bald head gave him the air of a gnome—and a mighty wise little gnome, as well.

The gnome took off his hat to wipe his perspiring fore-head. Then was disclosed a most studied attempt to conceal a shortage of hair; what was left of it was plastered in neat but sparse lines down from the centre to his low brow in a greasy series of waves.

'Hello, Pug!' greeted McCarthy.

'Hello, Mothball,' responded Tommy Monahan, who had been a famous jockey in his day, but was now fallen almost as low from his former high estate as Young Griffo, the one-time idol of the prize-ring. Barring the 'cauliflower ear', there was little to choose between them in habits, appearance, or poverty, save that Monahan was too proud to beg, and hence worked at times.

'Say, what do you think of this here scratchin' of Asbestos? How many owners could git away with that after the books had laid a lota bets—hey? The stewards must think Buckley's goin' on the blink—wot? Or, mebbe, they need that quarter-century entry-money—yes?'

Mothball McCarthy regarded his companion with a sententious smile.

'I think that hair of your'n is just like an eoleum harp,' he replied. Suiting the action to the sentiment, he reached out and began to twang each separate lock, meanwhile *pinking* and *panking* like the end-man of a minstrel show.

'Nix on that glee-club stuff,' snorted the other, hastily readjusting his musical locks as carefully as if they were the doors to a bank-vault and thrusting on his hat with a smug satisfaction only to be equalled by a cashier who knows the time-locks are now operating.

'Mebbe you'd like to hear a hundred-bill warble to youse,' ingratiatingly smiled the other.

'Listen, Mothball! If I ever fingered the frills on anything but Mexican money, I'd be out there in the club-house with the owners my own self—inside a week.'

'Info', eh?' taunted Kid Mothball grandiloquently. 'Well, Pug, nothin' short of a knockout would git a rise outa me. Whisper your sorrows, 'nd if it lissens good—youse fer a cut, when th' good thing comes under th' wire.'

'Fer a hundred I'd sell the rest of the hair offen the top of me head!' came back Pug Monahan.

'Aw, yer cheap!' jeered his *vis-à-vis*, as they strolled down toward the paddock. 'I kin buy slightly soiled souls fer fifty each!'

There was something so cryptic about the knowing leer, however, which Monahan bent on him that the rail-bird kept on. Pug might be down and out, but he was as wise as they make 'em, despite his poverty. Wisdom, for that matter, always runs second to luck at the track. And it is proverbial 'the wiser they are, the harder they fall', on the Metropolitan Circuit or off it.

Mothball was no 'Solymun', nor did he pretend to be. He was a bloodhound, however, for those gleanings of real track conditions known as information.

The boob public patronizing the races generally plays superstitions under the name of hunches, and Mothball, on rare occasions, indulged himself in this form of luxury.

The regulars grow grey of hair and dim of eye studying form-charts and the forecasts of handicappers; or now and again take a flier in alleged good things supplied by clever touts who make a speciality of fishing for suckers while owners are running their horses.

But your true rail-bird is out for the 'inside info' ', and it is even more necessary than his daily bread, because it is the source through which that sustenance is derived.

For this reason Kid Mothball allowed himself to amble away from the neighbourhood of the betting-ring. He was assured the premier ex-jockey was really possessed of something that might be worth listening to; whether it was worth risking a bet on he would decide after he heard it.

Although they walked along in ostensible camaraderie, inwardly both were warily making those first advances which characterize opponents.

Pug had something. Mothball wanted it. But that something was of such problematical value—until it had proven its worth—that the rail-bird would not shake himself loose from one solitary centavo until he had 'lamped' Pug's mitt. Pug divined this, and was almost as equally determined not to 'crack open' until he had his price.

There was one thing in Kid Mothball's favour, however: that was his reputation as a square guy.

During five years of 'playing 'em from the ground', he had never been known to break his word. Such an asset is not so uncommon as one would imagine among veterans of the crowd that follow the ponies from one track to another over the metropolitan and other circuits.

The cheap, catch-penny trickster does not last. He may put over one or two double-crosses; he may boast of his superior shrewdness in 'milking' some stable-boy or apprentice jockey, and, owing to the very nature of the conditions governing the transaction, a squeal is unusual on the part of the victim, because to 'let out a roar' is tantamount to discharge from his employment.

But the freemasonry of the racing fraternity is as rigid in matters of fair dealing as if it had temples and lodgerooms scattered all over the world; and the individual who profanes a confidence soon finds himself 'guessing the dogs' in company with the other outsiders.

That was the secret of Kid Mothball's long and fairly prosperous career—his untarnished reputation for 'coming across with the cut'—and never had he, even inferentially, violated a confidence that was reposed in him.

Although frequently broke, as all enthusiasts of the most uncertain game on earth often find themselves—be they owners or otherwise—he rarely borrowed money; and when he did he always paid it back promptly.

Pug Monahan knew all of this, as he appraised the nattily dressed youth who had been a toddler around the stables in the former star rider's halcyon days; where McCarthy, senior, demised these many years, had been a famous trainer.

Pug had seen Mothball grow up on a diet consisting chiefly of the atmosphere of the saddle-room—at times; he had watched him 'wise up' a horse with his dead father's keen, shrewd eyes; he had observed him perched on the rail in the kindergarten days of his equine education; and when Pug's own star had set Kid Mothball's was still steadily rising.

The star was practically at its zenith now, to judge from the shimmer of the faultlessly tailored 'bottle-green' suit which draped his slight but sinewy figure; and the rail-bird might have been easily mistaken at a distance for an enormous stable-fly had he been equipped with a pair of wings to correspond.

Pug sighed.

Kid Mothball smiled.

'Well, old scout, what's on your mind?' he queried.

Monahan impulsively leaned forward and whispered a few words in the other's ear.

'Git out!' jeered McCarthy.

'I guarantee that to be the pure quill dope,' retorted Pug with the dignity of a United States Senator rising to a point of order.

A reminiscent gleam floated into the rail-bird's eyes; his hand stole towards his trouser-pocket.

It emerged clasping a fat roll, several portraits of Thomas Jefferson adorning its exterior, followed by others of the Great Emancipator; Thomas Benton's face next peered out, then that of Silas Wright; hard behind came Washington, Garfield, and even the Goddess of Liberty—in the interior of all the others—who appeared to be acting as her body-guard.

In fact, Kid Mothball seemed to have taken to the habit of carrying a portrait gallery of some of the most illustrious statesmen of his native land, secured from the most enviable of all art-galleries—the Bureau of Engraving and Printing at Washington.

Pug didn't know much history, save that preserved in the archives of formsheets; but he did know 'mazuma', whether by its Hebraic name or otherwise.

He stood breathless, staring at the thousand-dollar, five-hundred-dollar, and smaller bills.

Kid Mothball deftly flicked a portrait of Grover Cleveland, preceding a large, fat X, and tendered it to his informant.

'If this is right,' purred the rail-bird, 'youse kin play this good Dimmycrat on that dog's left eye. If it stays right, youse kin take nine more tickets like this from me on the same dog, when I bet him blind—which I'm goin' to do, after I do a little grand and lofty clockin' around the Dishpan Circuit. You hear me, Pug?'

Pug Monahan gave several evidences to show that at least one of his auditory organs was in such a state of well-being that it would erupt or drop off, or swell up like Kid Griffo's, if he heard much more just then.

*　　*　　*

Just what reasons were behind the withdrawal of Asbestos from the sixth race were not disclosed until the turf-gossip of the newspapers appeared the following morning. These all declared that the horse was not in condition to justify the hopes of his owner, who was prepared, as usual, to back him heavily.

Kid Mothball had no use for newspapers, in turf matters.

'More'n one poor blob has went gallopin' inta the discard a follerin' of them punk tips,' he confided to Saffron, Felt-Hat, and Provo, when the three discussed the curious and most unusual incident of the day before, when the hope of the young rail-bird's 'daily flier' was withdrawn from the sixth.

'Yep, it's mysterious, seein's they had to make it twenty minutes fer a new book and ev'body got home to a cold supper,' opined Provo. 'The stewards is a lot o' stews. Why, it made an awful jam when they did break out and headed for a sound night's sleep.'

'Ya-h-h-h!' echoed Kid Mothball, with a prodigious yawn and an accompanying stretch which threatened to spring the seams under the armpits of his resplendent sack suit of a dark blue. 'Well, friends, seein's how he's out agin today, and with a lot better price hung on him more'n likely, whadda ya say if we cold-chisel Mr Ivory Eye and chew off Ike's gold finger? Are any of youse game?'

'Game to ride a goat that'll lose?' gassupped Felt-Hat Frieslander. 'Why, you hain't got them sticks outen yer eyes yet, Mothball.'

'I've known several goats to lose before,' amiably agreed the leader of the four musketeers, rubbing the optics referred to. 'Lots of times I been a thinkin' as how we oughta quit tryin' to pick winners, 'nd pick losers. If we could pick *all* the losers,' he continued, in reply to the blank look ensuing in the slight pause his curious statement had created, 'then we could lay off them, 'nd play the ones that was left—straight acrost the board.'

'Lissen to him!' sneered Saffron, with a tragic air that would have been most becoming to Edwin Booth in his palmiest days. 'He'll be another Eddie Foy if he stays out tonight agin. Where was you, Mothball?'

'I wasn't feedin' a lota stuss sharks,' pointedly returned the one derided. 'Friends, stuss is no game fer gents that live west of Madison Avenue—take it from me. I'd much ruther eat iron prunes, like I was a doin' last night. They

cost two cents a dish down at Sixth Avenue and Fifty-Third
Street, and Pug Monahan can ride a pan of 'em down to
your plate like he useta pilot a winner at Sheepshead Bay.
Remember Pug?'

'He's a has-been!' shot back Provo, whose impatience to
get down a bet was not well restrained.

'We'll all be—some day,' said Mothball. 'Well, what
does the majority vote about burnin' up our bank-roll on
Asbestos today?'

'I'm away out there watchin' the boys bed down some
horse that won't face the barrier today on that Asbestos
stuff,' said Saffron, extracting a pink evening paper from
his pocket. 'Lissen, Mothball—'nd mebbe you'll save some
money.' He read aloud the following paragraph:

David Buckley, owner of the sometimes consistent,
but more often eccentric, chestnut gelding Asbestos,
was allowed by the stewards to withdraw his entry
from the Yorktown Handicap yesterday owing to his
assurance that the horse was not up to form. Buckley's
reputation is such that this unusual courtesy was
accorded him without hesitation. His confidence in
Asbestos has cost him a pretty penny in past years.
From the start, the thoroughbred has played in weird
luck. And, regardless of what he has done on his last
out, Dave never failed to bet at least five hundred on
him, and many times twice or thrice that amount. His
belief in the horse's good qualities is, at times, one of
the most pathetic things in turf history. However,
some day Dave will ring the bell. He thinks Asbestos is
due to clean up. So he puts him into the big-stake event
today, the Piping Rock Handicap, and at top weight.

'Win or lose,' said Dave last night, 'Asbestos carries
my money. I hope the handicappers have got cold feet.
I haven't, and if I know a horse, Asbestos would race
an aeroplane if he was right—and beat it. That's why I
gave him a day longer and put him into the Piping
Rock.

Kid Mothball nodded.

'Well, yuh gotta hand it to him fer nerve,' he grinned. 'If

youse will stop to think a minit, youse'll remember, friends, that every cloud has a silver-plated linin', even if goldfish don't outlive whales.'

'But this goat hain't got gold hoofs—they're whiter 'n tinfoil,' chimed in Provo. 'How's Asbestos goin' to git home in front, wit' Baby Ruth, Fernrock, Short Grass, and The Wizard ag'in' him? Why, The Wizard could give one flirt of his tail and walk away from him!'

'I never argues,' yawned their mentor as they hung, pop-eyed with excitement, on his reply. 'If you ast me why a man eats iron prunes at two cents a throw I couldn't tell you that, neither. It can't be just because he likes 'em. I didn't. But I ate nine plates of 'em down there at Fifty-Third and Sixth Avenue, and lost a puffeckly good night's sleep. I got enuf pits left to stick all four of us at every quarter-mile post in this yere Pipin' Rock Handicap, and we might throw 'em at Asbestos in relays to speed him along, if youse want to foller my lead.'

'Merciful Hevings!' howled Saffron. 'Do you mean that youse fall fer this stuff?' He waved the pink sheet accusingly.

'You saw it and had to read it to me,' Mothball assured him. 'But wot of it?'

'Wot of it?' echoed Saffron in a sepulchral tone. 'Why, Mothball, this is the reg'lar come-on stuff. Ev'body 'll be out to sting Goldfinger and Ivory-Eye—to say nothin' of the cloutin' they'll try to give the rest of the books. Wot of it? Your new system of pickin' losers is workin' out mighty fine. But you wasn't aimin' to play 'em—didn't you say you'd lay off 'em?'

'Is there a horse by the name of Iron Prune in the overnight list?' asked their tormentor. 'If there is, I'll play him 'stead of Asbestos.'

'Th' best way to play one of them iron prunes,' growled Felt-Hat, 'is to slip it inta a sock 'nd bang Ivory-Eye acrost th' back of th' neck with it. Looky—he's stackin' up more money than is in the Carson City mint.'

There was some slight reason for Felt-Hat's obvious umbrage.

Ivory-Eye evidently anticipated a losing day, judging

from the reams of bills and silver he was handing to his cashier. Goldfinger Ike was not yet in sight. He was always last to arrive, but first to post odds.

Ivory-Eye always ran close up to the other well-known bookie. While Ike kept his auriferous forefinger busy holding up his slate or altering prices, Joe Hobbs utilized his solitary good 'lamp' in following the precedent thus created.

Kid Mothball, however, gave them only a fleeting glance; so did Saffron. The former was scanning the crowd rapidly gathering along the rail inside the main field to watch the exercise boys taking the day's entries out for 'warming up'. The latter was studying the handicapper's forecast in the same pink sheet.

Suddenly his jaundiced face assumed a positively citron-like tinge, and he quacked like a startled duck. Then the countenance which gave him his track-name faded into a mildly luteous, almost cream-coloured tint.

'Git this!' he gasped to Mothball, pointing to the handicapper's chart for the Piping Rock race. '"Asbestos. This is an uncertain horse, likely to break up any race ever started. May float home in front, if he don't start a tango-tea in the clubhouse by mistake. Odds should be twenty to one, instead of three—as yesterday." Don't that lissen like the wrappin' around the little old gold brick?' he demanded.

''Scuse me, friends,' muttered Kid Mothball, 'but if that's old Deacon Monahan over there near Goldfinger's pulpit, I gotta see what the opening hymn's going to be. Wait here fer me.'

'Seems like his belfry shingles gets leakier every day,' he observed. 'Well, youse biscuit-shooters can loaf around. I'm goin' to play Behave Yourself.'

'On the dollar book?' sneered Felt-Hat.

'On the two-dollar book?' roared Provo indignantly. 'And on her pretty nose, too. I suppose you like Blue Thistle so well you'd marry her if somebody'd saw off two of her legs.'

'Coquet's my choice,' sighed Saffron, 'that is, to show. A three-way bet, though, wouldn't be so bad. Since Provo's took to drinkin' root beer his nerves is twicet as strong as

they've been since Saratogy. Coquet, at about a hundred to
one to win, fifty fer place, and twenty to show.'

'I'll scoop up the coin on Little Dipper in the curtain-
raiser,' announced Felt-Hat. 'Not that I think much of her
chances, but I kin be's obstinate as Mothball. Looky him a
readin' a newspaper agin—and wit' Pug Monahan steerin'
him. Pug'll wear that suit of Johnny McCarthy's home
tonight—if he ever gets them ice-tongs mitts of his'n into
that roll, wunst, or I'm a Siberian carpet-sweeper!'

Disgusted, the trio trailed over to the far end of the ring to
play their respective choices.

Mothball was waiting for them at the rail as they
emerged.

'Youse showed good judgment,' said he quietly, as they
exhibited their tickets as the horses paraded past the stand.

'Still lookin' fer Iron Prune?' queried Saffron.

'Oh, no! But let's can this chatter and see how these dogs
bunch up. Watch the apprentice-allowance kids. It's gettin'
to be so bad that they bounce a horse before they bounce the
stewards fer a regular licence.'

'Did Pug have anything down on this race?' demanded
Felt-Hat suspiciously.

'Nothin' but a bad breath,' cheerily returned Kid
Mothball.

'Did youse?' persisted the intrepid head-gear artist.

'Nothin' but high hopes youse is all correck,' grinned the
leader. 'Lissen, friends—I wouldn't part company wit' one
camphor marble on anything today until the Pipin' Rock
bugle. Then, if Iron Prune is an added starter, me, fer him.
If not, I plays Asbestos down to the last fire-brick in little old
N'Yawk. Get me!'

'They're off!' roared the crowd, and the five furlong
maiden race suspended further discussion.

In exactly one minute one and two-fifths seconds Provo
was doing a Moqui fox-trot as Behave Yourself came first
under the wire; Little Dipper was scooping up great wads of
joy for Felt-Hat in second place; and Coquette temporarily
bleached Saffron's liverish face to a coffee-white by beating
out Blue Thistle to show.

'Talk about pickin' em!' jubilated the gentleman last

named. 'Kin you beat that—three in one race? We won't need you long, Mothball! You never pulled anything like that—not even the day you picked Holinden, then Oleander, and touted us onto Zero, after you'd switched to Silver Stockings, out at Emeryville!'

'Nope!' agreed Felt-Hat. 'He did hit three of 'em—but never three in one race.'

'Yep,' churlishly chimed Provo, 'but if you'd parlay —one, two, three—instead of scratchin' your own backs so hard, on three straight races, you'd be wearin' clothes like him. Say, where is he, anyway?'

*　　*　　*

They found him at last when the bookies were waiting the gong to 'open up' for the Piping Rock Handicap. He was with Pug Monahan.

'Still readin' papers?' asked Saffron, casually displaying a stack of bills whose total in numbers—if not in values —would bear comparison with Mothball's own roll.

'Why, friends, I can't read papers very well,' said the sartorial plunger with a slight flush. 'Besides, youse all look after me thataway. I been puttin' in all my time lookin' for that horse, Iron Prune.'

'Aw! Lay off that Iron Prune stuff!' snarled Provo. 'There ain't any horse by that name ever run on the Metropolitan Circuit. How could he git in a stake event like this Whistlin' Pebble purse?'

'Well, I ain't puttin' him in, am I?' replied Mothball with an injured air. 'And I don't want to lay *off* him; I want to lay my whole roll *on* him—to win!'

'Lissen!' exploded Saffron, whose vexation at this mystery was rising even slightly higher than that of the other two, who were like bears in a bee-hive in their eagerness to ascertain Mothball's real intentions. 'You lay that roll of your'n over on the turnstile, and us three'll take turns whirlin' it round while the race is bein' run off. Then, you kin have half of it back agin—that's fair, hain't it? Because you're out to drop it just like the kernels of them iron prunes has been droppin' out of your ears all day.'

'I'd ruther lay it on Asbestos, wrap myself up in his name, and stand in the middle of a bonfire youse guys might build, instid of that,' replied Mothball cheerfully. 'Well, friends, I'm too busy to do anything now but bet.'

He darted away as the gong clanged.

Goldfinger Ike had no sooner hoisted his slate than Kid Mothball shot a thousand-dollar bill before his startled eyes.

'Rub out that 20 to 1 and make it 2!' commanded the faultlessly garbed rail-bird.

'Twenty thousand to one thousand on Asbestos!' droned the book-maker, flicking the portrait of Thomas Jefferson towards the 'take-in' cashier. 'Got any more loose change, dude?'

'Enuf to send youse back to the prune foundry!' retorted Mothball, flipping two portraits of Abraham Lincoln, each adorning a five-hundred-dollar bill, tantalizingly in the air.

'Your shirt looks worth a couple 'o bucks!' Goldfinger suggested as the second ticket came out.

'Your'n won't bring two bits after this race!' elegantly returned Mothball, unhesitatingly following the reply with Thomas Benton, Silas Wright, and several other austere-faced gentlemen whose features in life would have been limned with horror at this treatment.

Goldfinger took each one as unhesitatingly.

Across the alley Ivory-Eye Hobbs was recording a plethora of ten and five dollar bets on the same horse by men who were fighting their way to his book.

Suddenly Goldfinger drew a white chalk-mark through Asbestos's name.

'Aw! You quit, do you?' derided Mothball. 'Well, so-long!'

Felt-Hat, Provo, and Saffron pursued as he made his way hurriedly towards the paddock.

Pug Monahan was there, too.

Likewise, Asbestos was just being led out for inspection.

'Dugan's up!' gloated the former jockey. 'It's all right —Mothball. Got my tickets?'

The nervy little rail-bird displayed the few he had.

All were from Goldfinger Ike's stand.

The other nodded his approval.

'A hundred goes fer youse at twenty to one—if he comes in as you said he would!' confirmed Mothball.

The trainer peered at the girths as the inspection concluded. It was an unusually rigid one, for there had been rumours of late that 'a boat race' was being contemplated.

And, as all well-informed turf patrons know, boat races are taboo on the track, being designed especially for callow college youths with a fondness for aquatic effort. Hence the extra caution of the stewards of the Jockey Club, who desired no taint of scandal to mar the big Piping Rock classic.

'That girth looks a little loose,' said the trainer, turning to the paddock judge.

'Tighten it if you wish,' said that gentleman tersely.

The trainer complied. Also, his big hand tested the stirrup straps; after which Asbestos passed on into the file of horses waiting at the paddock gate, and The Wizard took the eccentric chestnut gelding's place.

Dugan grinned knowingly at Pug Monahan, whose withered features ironed themselves out into a seraphic smile.

Mothball, and his entourage, trailed out and seized on vantage-points near the finish-wire along the rail.

The Piping Rock was six furlongs.

The string of seven starters breasted the barrier promptly, like one docile animal, and got away to a faultless start. Thereafter, for just one minute and fifteen seconds, all of eternity seemed to hover around the heads of Mothball's three chums.

Not for themselves, however, be it said. But for him.

His gameness was as unquestioned as his optimism was unbounded; and his inside info' was generally coequally reliable. Yet the mad manner he had spiked his roll on the most unreliable horse ever known in all of their experience depressed them.

Kid Mothball, however, seemed as serene as the side of a well-cut grindstone. There was not the smallest semblance of anxiety on his lean face. Not even when, in the first two jumps, Asbestos shot out ahead of the field and, under the skilful piloting of Dugan, took the rail with strides that made even The Wizard seem to be standing still, and the balance of the field appear momentarily to be running backward.

Asbestos was five lengths to the good at the first two-furlong pole. Dugan eased him a little as they came around into the stretch; then, leaning forward, gave him his head for a short space; finally, as they flashed past the paddock with The Wizard closing up, Dugan rose in his saddle and—

They were only two jumps from the wire when it happened.

The right stirrup strap parted company, Dugan lurched sidewise involuntarily, pulling wildly at the off-bridle rein to save himself from the fall otherwise certain to occur. And Asbestos, being on his good behaviour, obeyed the bit, turned and started across the track just inside the wire—instead of keeping on and under it, to an easy win.

'I knowed it!' moaned Felt-Hat amid the babel of sound as The Wizard's number went up.

'Knowed what?' asked Mothball.

'That we'd have to phone Bellevue to send fer youse if we had so much as a lead slug or a cigar-coupon left after playin' your choice,' cut in Provo.

'Looky *me!*' shrieked Saffron. 'I'm a bloomin' pauper, just like this here lady-killer that thinks he can pick 'em.'

'Friends,' sighed Mothball, 'you all know my first choice was a goat by the name of Iron Prune—'

He dodged and dove into the crowd as they tried to fall on him as one man.

They paused, exchanging glances of incredulous bewilderment.

'Wot's he laughin' at?' demanded Provo, glaring wildly around.

'At your hat,' snorted Felt-Hat Frieslander, taking his own celebrated head-gear and hurling it over towards the small white ring where The Wizard's jockey was being weighed in.

'But he lost every dime he had to his name—didn't we

see him play Asbestos on the nose?' vociferated Provo. 'My Gawd, his hull head must be full of camphor ice!'

'Naw—grasshoppers, catterpillers, and all them insecks he's afraid will gnaw a hole in his raiment!' gloomed Saffron. 'Well, somebody lend me a bottle of carbolic! That I should survive everything to see this turrible day!' he chanted.

*　　*　　*

They were still futilely seeking for some shadow of reason for Johnny McCarthy's sudden attack of insanity; and they were as far from knowing why he had done what he did and taken his loss in the eccentric way he had, even while the next event was being run off.

'The only thing I kin figger,' said the hatless Felt-Hat at last, 'is that he must 'a' been eaten' in the same oat-bin wit' that Dave Buckley jinx, an'—'

He stopped, his jaw drooping with sheer amazement.

Kid Mothball was floating over their way. Behind him came Pug Monahan—and trailing them were many others.

'Friends,' hissed the rail-bird, whose pockets and arms bulged with bills carrying portraits of all statesmen—living or dead—'form a holler square, quick, 'nd then beat it fer a limousine. We've busted Goldfinger Ike at last, and youse is all in on the percentage, seein's how you follered my play on Ivory-Eye's book.'

They did as bidden.

Speeding down upper Broadway, with the sleeves of several coats doing duty as twine around Pug Monahan's outer garment which had been temporarily transformed into a container for upward of eighty thousand dollars, Mothball imparted the secret.

'I played the Iron Prune. Which is to say, just this: Pug, here, works down in Goldfinger's hash-house—that joint where he got his start, at Fifty-Third and Sixth Avenue. Bein' what he is, Goldfinger couldn't let go that two-cent subtreasury of his'n. I always had a hunch that Dave Buckley'd gone broke on that first out of Asbestos at Reno. 'Cause I knowed he'd bet his life on that chestnut horse. But

I couldn't make out why he stuck to him all these three years. I found out why last night.

'Goldfinger took over Asbestos, under a bill of sale, away back there. And he's been runnin' him under the Buckley colours ever since. Get that? That's why he'd run good one race 'nd bad th' next. Goldfinger growed diamond toes on his crooked book thataway!

'Pug swiped the bill of sale 'nd give it to me. Last night I heard Goldfinger down in that prune emporium of his, tippin' off his friends to lay off Asbestos today. I had to eat all them iron prunes 'nd wear a lousy pair of overalls to git that inside info', too. So I played my last cent on him.

'And Goldfinger cashed my tickets—for if he didn't, he'd never make book agin on the Metropolitan or any other circuit, from Butte to Havana, or from Juarez to Windsor. Nothin' to it a-tall, wunst the stewards ever lamped that bill of sale.'

'We thought you was balmy,' confessed Provo.

'I was just workin' out that new idee of mine,' beamed Mothball, 'of playin' a loser. Only, I put a little more juice on it than I fust figgered I'd have to. Don't forget, friends, termorrow we go after Ivory-Eye—he owes us an honest livin', too.'

'Will Goldfinger Ike quit?' asked Saffron, whose face was now blue with delight.

'Will a cheese smell?' queried the personification of men's clothing styles. 'Or will an iron prune wander from its own fireside? I s'pose, after today, youse 'll all join the longshoremen's union early tomorrow—wot? Just like Pug, here, 'ull ride cockroaches the rest of his hull life, around that two-cent national bank that Goldfinger's got left. But wait till he does come back!'

'He pulled it well—that finish!' averred the hatless one, already dreaming of a fifty-dollar beaver to replace his old top-piece.

'Yes, he'll be back, friends,' went on Mothball dreamily, 'but he'll have to cut in with a new trick or two—somepin' a hull lot newer than that old gag of gettin' a crooked trainer at the last minit to saw a stirrup-strap half in two, so's to fool an honest jockey inta bustin' it clean off when he starts to whip a mount down the stretch.

'My daddy taught me that hide-the-razor-in-yer-fist stunt the same day I got my first long pants. Gee! They was fine pants—until a chigger as big as a Boston bull terrier got in the habit of usin' 'em for a free lunch.

'I wouldn't 'a' dared to play Iron Prune so strong if I hadn't 'a' bet myself I'd buy a new outfit. These here thirty-six suits is gettin' shabby—don't you think so?' he added, turning to Pug Monahan.

Pug leaned forward with a breath so strong it might have propelled the limousine had it been decorously conducted to the carburettor and properly introduced to the spark-plug.

'You sure look like a bum, Mothball!' he averred. 'I'm 'shamed to be seen in public wid youse!'

THE DOWNFALL OF MULLIGAN'S

by Banjo Paterson

Like British and American readers, Australian readers also had a favourite horse racing writer in the early years of this century. He was Andrew 'Banjo' Paterson, whose knowledge of the Turf in his native country was unrivalled and whose commentaries on the sport in print and on the radio were unsurpassed for more than 30 years. Like his American contemporary, Paterson created a group of horse racing enthusiasts—'the sporting men of Mulligan's'—who featured in a number of his tales.

Banjo Paterson had developed his enthusiasm for horses in his childhood and chose sporting journalism as his career. He was for many years a racing journalist on the magazine Truth, and later editor of the Sydney Sportsman. He possessed a marvellous ear for catching the conversations of the people who made up the world of Australian racing, and his weekly broadcasts on ABC radio were notable for the wit and good humour he extracted from this eavesdropping.

Apart from his journalistic work, Paterson published general collections of short stories, poems and a highly-authoritative work, Racehorses and Racing in Australia. Of his stories about the 'sporting men of Mulligan's', the following tale of a 'sting' that goes wrong is among the very best and has been called a classic of Australian short story writing.

* * *

The sporting men of Mulligan's were an exceedingly know-ing lot; in fact, they had obtained the name amongst their neighbours of being a little bit too knowing. They had 'taken down' the adjoining town in a variety of ways. They were always winning maiden plates with horses which were shrewdly suspected to be old and well-tried performers in disguise.

When the sports of Paddy's Flat unearthed a phenomenal runner in the shape of a blackfellow called Frying-pan Joe, the Mulligan contingent immediately took the trouble to discover a blackfellow of their own, and they made a match and won all the Paddy's Flat money with ridiculous ease; then their blackfellow turned out to be a well-known Sydney performer. They had a man who could fight, a man who could be backed to jump five-feet-ten, a man who could kill eight pigeons out of nine at thirty yards, a man who could make a break of fifty or so at billiards if he tried; they could all drink, and they all had that indefinite look of infinite wisdom and conscious superiority which belongs only to those who know something about horseflesh.

They knew a great many things never learnt at Sunday-school. They were experts at cards and dice. They would go to immense trouble to work off any small swindle in the sporting line. In short the general consensus of opinion was that they were a very 'fly' crowd at Mulligan's, and if you went there you wanted to 'keep your eyes skinned' or they'd 'have' you over a threepenny-bit.

There were races at Sydney one Christmas, and a select band of the Mulligan sportsmen were going down to them. They were in high feather, having just won a lot of money from a young Englishman at pigeon-shooting, by the simple method of slipping blank cartridges into his gun when he wasn't looking, and then backing the bird.

They intended to make a fortune out of the Sydney people, and admirers who came to see them off only asked them as a favour to leave money enough in Sydney to make it worth while for another detachment to go down later on. Just as the train was departing a priest came running on to the platform, and was bundled into the carriage where our Mulligan friends were; the door was slammed to, and away they went. His Reverence was hot and perspiring, and for a few minutes mopped himself with a handkerchief, while the silence was unbroken except by the rattle of the train.

After a while one of the Mulligan fraternity got out a pack of cards and proposed a game to while away the time. There was a young squatter in the carriage who looked as if he might be induced to lose a few pounds, and the sportsmen thought they would be neglecting their opportunities if they did not try to 'get a bit to go on with' from him. He agreed to play, and, just as a matter of courtesy, they asked the priest whether he would take a hand.

'What game d'ye play?' he asked, in a melodious brogue.

They explained that any game was equally acceptable to them, but they thought it right to add that they generally played for money.

'Sure an' it don't matter for wanst in a way,' said he —'Oi'll take a hand bedad—Oi'm only going about fifty miles, so Oi can't lose a fortune.'

They lifted a light portmanteau on to their knees to make a table, and five of them—three of the Mulligan crowd and the two strangers—started to have a little game of poker. Things looked rosy for the Mulligan boys, who chuckled as they thought how soon they were making a beginning, and what a magnificent yarn they would have to tell about how they rooked a priest on the way down.

Nothing sensational resulted from the first few deals, and the priest began to ask questions.

'Be ye going to the races?'

They said they were.

'Ah! and Oi suppose ye'll be betting wid thim book-makers—betting on the horses, will yez? They do be terrible knowing men, thim bookmakers, they tell me. I wouldn't bet much if Oi was ye,' he said, with an affable smile. 'If ye go bettin' ye will be took in wid them book-makers.'

The boys listened with a bored air and reckoned that by the time they parted the priest would have learnt that they were well able to look after themselves. They went steadily on with the game, and the priest and the young squatter won slightly; this was part of the plan to lead them on to plunge. They neared the station where the priest was to get out. He had won rather more than they liked, so the signal was passed round to 'put the cross on'. Poker is a game at which a man need not risk much unless he feels inclined, and on this deal the priest stood out. Consequently, when they drew up at his station he was still a few pounds in.

'Bedad,' he said, 'Oi don't loike goin' away wid yer money. Oi'll go on to the next station so as ye can have revinge.' Then he sat down again, and play went on in earnest.

The man of religion seemed to have the Devil's own luck. When he was dealt a good hand he invariably backed it well, and if he had a bad one he would not risk anything. The sports grew painfully anxious as they saw him getting further and further ahead of them, prattling away all the time like a big schoolboy. The squatter was the biggest loser so far, but the priest was the only winner. All the others were out of pocket. His Reverence played with great dash, and seemed to know a lot about the game, so that on arrival at the second station he was a good round sum in pocket.

He rose to leave them with many expressions of regret, and laughingly promised full revenge next time. Just as he was opening the carriage door, one of the Mulligan fraternity said in a stage-whisper, 'He's a blanky sink-pocket. If he can come this far, let him come on to Sydney and play for double the stakes.' Like a shot the priest turned on him.

'Bedad, an' if *that's* yer talk, Oi'll play ye fer double stakes from here to the other side of glory. Do yez think men are mice because they eat cheese? It isn't one of the Ryans would be fearing to give any man is revinge!'

He snorted his defiance at them, grabbed his cards and waded in. The others felt that a crisis was at hand and settled down to play in a dead silence. But the priest kept on winning steadily, and the 'old man' of the Mulligan push saw that something decisive must be done, and decided on a big plunge to get all the money back on one hand. By a dexterous manipulation of the cards he dealt himself four kings, almost the best hand at poker. Then he began with assumed hesitation to bet on his hand, raising the stake little by little.

'Sure ye're trying to bluff, so ye are!' said the priest, and immediately raised it.

The others had dropped out of the game and watched

with painful interest the stake grow and grow. The Mulligan fraternity felt a cheerful certainty that the 'old man' had made things safe, and regarded themselves as mercifully delivered from an unpleasant situation. The priest went on doggedly raising the stake in response to his antagonist's challenges until it had attained huge dimensions.

'Sure that's high enough,' said he, putting into the pool sufficient to entitle him to see his opponent's hand.

The 'old man' with great gravity laid down his four kings, whereat the Mulligan boys let a big sigh of relief escape them.

Then the priest laid down four aces and scooped the pool.

*   *   ·   *

The sportsmen of Mulligan's never quite knew how they got out to Randwick. They borrowed a bit of money in Sydney, and found themselves in the saddling-paddock in a half-dazed condition, trying to realize what had happened to them. During the afternoon they were up at the end of the lawn near the Leger stand and could hear the babel of tongues, small bookmakers, thimble riggers, confidence men, and so on, plying their trades outside. In the tumult of voices they heard one that sounded familiar. Soon suspicion grew into certainty, and they knew that it was the voice of 'Father' Ryan. They walked to the fence and looked over. This is what he was saying:

'Pop it down, gents! Pop it down! If you don't put down a brick you can't pick up a castle! I'll bet no one here can pick the knave of hearts out of these three cards. I'll bet half-a-sovereign no one here can find the knave!'

Then the crowd parted a little, and through the opening they could see him distinctly, doing a great business and showing wonderful dexterity with the pasteboard.

There is still enough money in Sydney to make it worth while for another detachment to come down from Mulligan's; but the next lot will hesitate about playing poker with priests in the train.

THE BROKEN LINK HANDICAP

by Rudyard Kipling

During the era of the British Raj in India, horse racing was one of the most popular sports in the sub-continent. Since those days, race meetings have continued to be held throughout the country although on a smaller scale. That great storyteller, Rudyard Kipling, whose writing is so closely associated with India, not only followed the sport as a young man during the days of the Raj, but also wrote an unforgettable short story about it.

The creator of the immortal Mowgli and Gunga Din was born in Bombay, although he was educated in England, and then returned to India to become a journalist and sub-editor in Lahore. It is believed that he wrote reports on a number of race meetings, and was evidently fascinated by the Indian peoples' delight in gambling. I have been told that there is a strong element of fact in his story, 'The Broken Link Handicap', which he wrote in 1907, but whether or not this is true, it is an outstanding mystery tale, replete with the heat, dust and intrigue of that remarkable country.

*   *   *

There are more ways of running a horse to suit your book than pulling his head off in the straight. Some men forget this. Understand clearly that all racing is rotten—as everything connected with losing money must be. In India, in addition to its inherent rottenness, it has the merit of being two-thirds sham; looking pretty on paper only. Everyone knows everyone else far too well for business purposes. How on earth can you rack and harry and post a man for his losings, when you are fond of his wife, and live in the same

Station with him? He says, 'On the Monday following,' 'I can't settle just yet.' You say, 'All right, old man,' and think yourself lucky if you pull off nine hundred out of a two-thousand-rupee debt. Any way you look at it, Indian racing is immoral, and expensively immoral; which is much worse. If a man wants your money he ought to ask for it, or send round a subscription-list, instead of juggling about the country with an Australian larrikin; a 'brumby', with as much breed as the boy; a brace of *chumars* in goldlaced caps; three or four *ekka*-ponies with hogged manes, and a switch-tailed demirep of a mare called Arab because she has a kink in her flag. Racing leads to the *shroff* quicker than anything else. But if you have no conscience and no sentiments, and good hands, and some knowledge of pace, and ten years' experience of horses, and several thousand rupees a month, I believe that you can occasionally contrive to pay your shoeing-bills.

Did you ever know Shackles—b. w. g., 15.1⅜—coarse, loose, mule-like ears—barrel as long as a gate-post—tough as a telegraph-wire—and the queerest brute that ever looked through a bridle? He was of no brand, being one of an ear-nicked mob taken into the *Bucephalus* at £4:10s. a head to make up freight, and sold raw and out of condition at Calcutta for Rs.275. People who lost money on him called him a 'brumby'; but if ever any horse had Harpoon's shoulders and The Gin's temper, Shackles was that horse. Two miles was his own particular distance. He trained himself, ran himself, and rode himself; and, if his jockey insulted him by giving him hints, he shut up at once and bucked the boy off. He objected to dictation. Two or three of his owners did not understand this, and lost money in consequence. At last he was bought by a man who discovered that, if a race was to be won, Shackles, and Shackles only, would win it in his own way, so long as his jockey sat still. This man had a riding-boy called Brunt—a lad from Perth, West Australia—and he taught Brunt, with a trainer's whip, the hardest thing a jock can learn—to sit still, to sit still, and to keep on sitting still. When Brunt fairly grasped this truth, Shackles devastated the country. No weight could stop him at his own distance; and the fame of

Shackles spread from Ajmir in the South, to Chedputter in the North. There was no horse like Shackles, so long as he was allowed to do his work in his own way. But he was beaten in the end; and the story of his fall is enough to make angels weep.

At the lower end of the Chedputter race course, just before the turn into the straight, the track passes close to a couple of old brick-mounds enclosing a funnel-shaped hollow. The big end of the funnel is not six feet from the railings on the off-side. The astounding peculiarity of the course is that, if you stand at one particular place, about half a mile away, inside the course, and speak at ordinary pitch, your voice just hits the funnel of the brick-mounds and makes a curious whining echo there. A man discovered this one morning by accident while out training with a friend. He marked the place to stand and speak from with a couple of bricks, and he kept his knowledge to himself. *Every* peculiarity of a course is worth remembering in a country where rats play the mischief with the elephant-litter, and Stewards build jumps to suit their own stables. This man ran a very fairish country-bred, a long, racking high mare with the temper of a fiend, and the paces of an airy wandering seraph—a drifty, glidy stretch. The mare was, as a delicate tribute to Mrs Reiver, called 'The Lady Regula Baddun'—or for short, Regula Baddun.

Shackles' jockey, Brunt, was a quite well-behaved boy, but his nerve had been shaken. He began his career by riding jump-races in Melbourne, where a few Stewards want lynching, and was one of the jockeys who came through the awful butchery—perhaps you will recollect it—of the Maribyrnong Plate. The walls were colonial ramparts—logs of *jarrah* spiked into masonry—with wings as strong as Church buttresses. Once in his stride, a horse had to jump or fall. He couldn't run out. In the Maribyrnong Plate twelve horses were jammed at the second wall. Red Hat, leading, fell this side, and threw out The Gled, and the ruck came up behind and the space between wing and wing was one struggling, screaming, kicking shambles. Four jockeys were taken out dead; three were very badly hurt, and Brunt was among the three. He told the story of the Maribyrnong Plate sometimes; and when he described how Whalley on Red Hat, said, as the mare fell under him—'God ha' marcy, I'm done for!' and how, next instant, Sithee There and White Otter had crushed the life out of poor Whalley, and the dust hid a small hell of men and horses, no one marvelled that Brunt had dropped jump-races and Australia together. Regula Baddun's owner knew that story by heart. Brunt never varied it in the telling. He had no education.

Shackles came to the Chedputter Autumn races one year, and his owner walked about insulting the sportsmen of Chedputter generally, till they went to the Honorary Secretary in a body and said, 'Appoint handicappers, and arrange a race which shall break Shackles and humble the pride of his owner.' The Districts rose against Shackles and sent up of their best; Ousel, who was supposed to be able to do his mile in 1–53; Petard, the stud-bred, trained by a cavalry regiment who knew how to train; Gringalet, the ewe-lamb of the 75th; Bobolink, the pride of Peshawar; and many others.

They called that race The Broken-Link Handicap, because it was to smash Shackles; and the Handicappers piled on the weights, and the Fund gave eight hundred rupees, and the distance was 'round the course for all horses'. Shackles' owner said, 'You can arrange the race with regard to Shackles only. So long as you don't bury him under weight-cloths, I don't mind.' Regula Baddun's owner said, 'I throw in my mare to fret Ousel. Six furlongs is Regula's distance, and she will then lie down and die. So also will Ousel, for his jockey doesn't understand a waiting race.' Now, this was a lie, for Regula had been in work for two months at Dehra, and her chances were good, always supposing that Shackles broke a blood-vessel—or Brunt moved on him.

The plunging in the lotteries was fine. They filled eight thousand-rupee lotteries on the Broken-Link Handicap, and the account in the *Pioneer* said that 'favouritism was divided'. In plain English, the various contingents were wild on their respective horses; for the Handicappers had done their work well. The Honorary Secretary shouted himself hoarse through the din; and the smoke of the cheroots was like the smoke, and the rattling of the dice-boxes like the rattle of small-arm fire.

Ten horses started—very level—and Regula Baddun's owner cantered out on his hack to a place inside the circle of the course, where two bricks had been thrown. He faced towards the brick-mounds at the lower end of the course and waited.

The story of the running is in the *Pioneer*. At the end of the first mile, Shackles crept out of the ruck, well on the outside, ready to get round the turn, lay hold of the bit and spin up the straight before the others knew he had got away. Brunt was sitting still, perfectly happy, listening to the 'drum-drum-drum' of the hoofs behind, and knowing that, in about twenty strides, Shackles would draw one deep breath and go up the last half-mile like the 'Flying Dutchman'. As Shackles went short to take the turn and came abreast of the brick-mound, Brunt heard, above the noise of the wind in his ears, a whining, wailing voice on the offside, saying—'God ha' mercy, I'm done for!' In one stride, Brunt saw the whole seething smash of the Maribyrnong Plate before him, started in his saddle, and gave a yell of terror. The start brought the heels into Shackles' side, and the scream hurt Shackles' feelings. He couldn't stop dead; but he put out his feet and slid along for fifty yards, and then, very gravely and judicially, bucked off Brunt—a shaking, terror-stricken lump, while Regula Baddun made a neck-and-neck race with Bobolink up the straight, and won by a short head—Petard a bad third. Shackles' owner, in the Stand, tried to think that his field-glasses had gone wrong. Regula Baddun's owner, waiting by the two bricks, gave one deep sigh of relief, and cantered back to the Stand. He had won, on lotteries and bets, about fifteen thousand.

It was a Broken-Link Handicap with a vengeance. It broke nearly all the men concerned, and nearly broke the heart of Shackles' owner. He went down to interview Brunt. The boy lay, livid and gasping with fright, where he had tumbled off. The sin of losing the race never seemed to strike him. All he knew was that Whalley had 'called' him, that the 'call' was a warning; and, were he cut in two for it, he would never get up again. His nerve had gone altogether, and he only asked his master to give him a good thrashing, and let him go. He was fit for nothing, he said. He got his dismissal, and crept up to the paddock, white as chalk, with blue lips, his knees giving way under him. People said nasty things in the paddock; but Brunt never heeded. He changed into tweeds, took his stick and went down the road, still shaking with fright, and muttering over and over again—'God ha' mercy, I'm done for!' To the best of my knowledge and belief he spoke the truth.

So now you know how the Broken-Link Handicap was run and won. Of course you don't believe it. You would credit anything about Russia's designs on India, or the recommendations of the Currency Commission; but a little bit of sober fact is more than you can stand.

A HORSE OF THE SAME COLOUR

by Edgar Wallace

Few writers of modern fiction are more closely associated with the world of horse racing than Edgar Wallace. In his long series of stories about 'Educated Evans', he created a personality who remains to this day among the best-known characters in racing fiction.

Horse racing was an obsession with Wallace; although he wrote approximately 170 books, 17 plays and countless newspaper articles, essays and short stories, he still somehow found time to attend two and sometimes three race meetings a week. It is said of him that he would cheerfully lose £1,000 in five minutes on a race course, and then recoup the money by dashing off a novel during the weekend.

The critic James Cameron once wrote of Edgar Wallace's interest in the Turf, 'For him, the racecourse was much more than a pastime, much more than a habit, more even than an obsession—it was an addiction. He liked the feel of the place, he liked the sort of people who went there. He enjoyed the company of bookies and jockeys, touts and trainers, con-men and punters. He said that Fleet Street and the races were the only places where he really felt at home. And, of course, there was the betting. Edgar Wallace was not only a mad gambler on the horses, he was, you might say, the cause of mad gambling in others. He was the racing reporter on the Evening Times and edited its racing supplement. He even started two racing sheets of his own. His secretary said of him it must be very difficult for a racing man to study the form of 54 consecutive races, make a selection, and come up with 54 consecutive losers. But Edgar Wallace did—not a bit abashed. "Can't win them all," he would say. Edgar Wallace's trouble was that he hardly ever won any of them!'

Horse racing featured in many of Wallace's stories; apart from the 'Educated Evans' tales, there is the novel, The Twister, *the play,* The Calendar, *and dozens of short stories featuring many of his other famous characters, such as* The Four Just Men, Smithy, P. C. Lee *and Mr J. G. Reeder. The stories of Evans, 'The World's Champion Turf Prophet', as he calls himself, are, for my money, the best of Wallace's horse racing thrillers. Not just because of their style and ingenuity, nor because many people have fond memories of the comedian Max Miller playing Evans on the screen—but perhaps most of all because there is something of the author himself in every one.*

*   *   *

The two-year-old Hesperus was a grey. And the two-year-old Milikins was also a grey. And both their owner and their trainer were hoary-headed men who had grown grey with artfulness.

Mr Tooks (*the* Randolph Tooks) had two stables, one at Lambourn and one in Wiltshire, and to the Wiltshire stable he sent Milikins and to the Lambourn establishment he sent Hesperus, just as soon as he had bought these horses privately from their breeder. Only he changed their names and when the stable boys at Lambourn were talking about the amazing speed of Milikins they were in reality talking of Hesperus.

Only the astute Mr Groom, the trainer, and the astuter Mr Tooks knew this.

Hesperus (wrote the head lad of the Wiltshire stable) isn't worth tuppence: you can leave him out every time he runs.

He was writing to one of his punters, for naughty head lads sometimes have a few correspondents who will give them the odds to a fiver in return for information.

Milikins is a smasher (wrote a literary stable boy who supplied a plutocratic tipster with information). 'We tried him yesterday at level weights with Hard Egg and Dontbelate and he smothered them.'

'Be open and frank about these horses,' said Mr Tooks,

the wily owner. 'If any of these newspaper touts come nosing round your gallops, don't hurt 'em—give 'em a drink. We'll enter Hesperus and Milikins at one meeting, I'll send my own boys to bring the horses on to the course, and we'll skin the ring.'

It is not an offence at law or by the rules of racing to call a horse by any name you wish, so long as he runs by the name he is entered. There is many a high-sounding Derby winner who is called 'Bill' in the stable, and if the stable name for Hesperus was Milikins, nobody was hurt but the stable hands who, contrary to Rule 176, sub-section v, conveyed illicit information.

Educated Evans, the World's Champion Prophet and Turf Adviser, did not ordinarily interest himself in the thoroughbred race-horse, as a horse. To him, a horse was a name in the daily newspapers anchored to the column by a weight, the names of his owner (to which 'Mr' was affixed) and his trainer, who was just Jones or Smith without any mistering nonsense whatever.

But Mr Evans had smelt the early dawn of the gallops and seen the vast uplands of country places, and had, moreover, felt the soul-stir which comes only to those who have sat on the back of a thoroughbred hack. In other words, he had once been the overnight guest of a real trainer, and the exhilaration of the experience had got into his blood and even found its way to his legs. From Isaacs in High Street he acquired a pair of riding breeches and gaiters. He began to take an interest in the horses stabled in the mews, and would often imitate, unconsciously perhaps, the hissing noise that grooms make when they run a dandy brush over a horse's back.

But the most remarkable change that this experience of his had brought about was his passion for observation. He had been twice to Epsom and had shivered on the top of Six Mile Hill whilst innumerable horses that looked very much like one another came at an alarming pace towards him. He had been as far afield as Newmarket—and he had made one most profitable visit to a spot which was somewhere between East Ilsley and Wantage. It may be explained that none of these journeys cost money, a friend and client of his, who did odd cartage-jobs with a motor-van that he had picked up for a song, giving him a lift whenever he was going near to a training centre.

These serious preoccupations of Educated Evans had not escaped the keen eyes of Camden Town. Mr Evans was again in favour. Even the carters at the Midland Goods Station, who had once (so it is said) bribed the driver of a shunting engine to run him over, took him to their arms. His detested rival, Old Sam, had been unlucky. Possibly he was using the wrong kind of pin to find winners, but certain it is that, when the ancient man walked abroad, his beard of many colours floating in the wind, disappointed punters said bitter things to him. The riding breeches and gaiters of Educated Evans were the final blow to Old Sam. He came to Mr Evans' house one night, breathing hops and vengeance, but the Educated Man had gone down into Berkshire overnight.

Early the following morning Mr Groom, the eminent trainer, rode out on to the downs, his string of horses having gone ahead of him. Cantering towards the end of the trial ground, he became aware of a figure on his misty horizon and a big motor lorry drawn up by the side of the road.

'Good-morning, sir,' said Mr Groom politely.

'Good-morning, sir,' said Evans, ready to bolt.

'Are you one of those newspaper gentlemen?' said the amazingly polite trainer.

Evans, who could not tell a lie, admitted that he was.

'Ah! then you'll see an interesting gallop,' said Mr Groom. 'I never object to newspaper gentlemen seeing my trials. What paper do you represent?'

Educated Evans mentioned a journal which would have reeled from Printing House Square to Fleet Street had it but heard.

'It's a good paper but the price is high,' remarked the trainer.

'We're thinkin' of rejuicin' it,' said Evans carelessly. 'I was only sayin' to Lord What's-his-name yesterday, "people won't *pay* fourpence unless you give away a pattern or somethin'—"'

'Here they come!' Groom interrupted as four dots came over the skyline and grew larger every second.

Evans knew enough about horses to see at a glance that the leader was a grey. It flashed past him four lengths ahead of the rest.

'Yes . . . very good,' agreed Groom.

'No, I can't tell you its name—but it is the only grey I have in the stable. Good-morning, Mr—er—'

'Evans,' said the educated man airily. 'You may have heard of me—the celebrated Educated Evans? Braxted . . . don't that recall nothing?'

'Were you named after him?' asked Mr Groom.

The Master of Paddy Lodge, Bayham Mews, shrugged his shoulders.

'I'll write it down for you,' he said, oblivious to Mr Groom's obvious indifference.

Drawing a fat fountain-pen from his pocket (purchased only a few days before from the shilling bargain basement of Pelfridge's) he inscribed his name on a bit of paper he found in his pocket.

'Look out!'

Evans heard the warning shout and stared round. The horses had been pulled up and were returning to where he and the trainer stood. The grey, still fighting for its head, was within a yard of him, and as he looked, the animal spun round like a teetotum.

Pen and paper fell from Evans' hand as he stumbled back. He saw a hoof smash on the pen and a spurting fountain of green ink leap up.

'Keep away from him!' called the trainer sharply, and Evans retreated to the road. He did not even call attention to the loss of his pen.

'That horse didn't seem to like you,' said the trolley driver, as his passenger climbed up.

Evans shrugged again.

'I'm cruel to horses—I admit it,' he confessed. 'He ain't forgot the hidin' I gave him last week.'

Three minutes later he was being rattled towards Newbury, his mind seething with excitement. At the first newspaper shop he stopped and bought a copy of *Horses in*

Training, and turned eagerly to that page which bore the name of Mr Groom's charges.

'Milikins, gr. colt by Grey Fairy—Mill Girl.'

Milikins! Here was a tip, not from the boy that did him, but from his very own eyes!

The Miller, who had been out of town for four days, having gone to Paris to take over the body of Harry Elbert, the well-known fishmonger who, being in a precarious financial position, had packed up a parcel of his employers' money (The Deep Sea Fisheries Limited—The Shops with the Blue Tiles) and gone abroad with the young lady from Higgins the Poulterers.

He came back and, having safely hutched Harry, went in search of Educated Evans.

That learned man he found at his home, Paddy Lodge, and Mr Evans was engaged in the comparatively innocent occupation of frying a sausage.

'Ever heard of Ptolemy, Evans?'

The World's Champion Turf Adviser shook his head.

'Tolly Me?' he frowned. 'That's one of Bennett's hair-trunks, ain't it?'

The Miller spelt the word and the face of his host lit up.

'Oh, you mean Pet-olmy—heard about him? He belongs to the celebrated Adjer Kan an' he can catch pigeons. He's runnin' in the Jubilee—'

'He belongs to quite another gentleman, he's running in the Derby, and they tell me in Paris he can't lose.'

Mr Evans sniffed and turned the sausage with his one-pronged fork.

'There's a horse in the Derby,' he said, with great deliberation, 'that can fall down, eat a good meal, get up an' *then* win it! This horse was tried twenty-one pound better than Sansovino, belongin' to the highly popular Sir Stanley Derby, of Derby House, Newmarket—a personal friend of mine. I've written letters to him.'

'That seems a pretty slight foundation for friendship,' said The Miller dryly. 'Do you call all the people your friends just because you write to 'em?'

'I do,' said Evans significantly. 'If they act honourable.

Everybody don't act honourable. Twenty-one pun' eight shillin's, a basket of greens and a gramophone that don't work—that's all I got out of three hundred clients.'

'It seems a lot,' said The Miller, and Mr Evans sighed in resignation.

'I gave 'em Paddy, 20/1—what a beauty—did I or did I not?'

'You did,' said the officer of the law. 'You sent it out for the Liverpool Cup, but the woman to whom you gave the letters refrained from posting them till Tuesday. In consequence of which you've got a reputation you don't deserve.'

Mr Evans shrugged.

'Maybe I'll get another next week,' he said mysteriously. 'Maybe, when a certain horse comes home alone, I'll get a reputation that won't be deserved, too! Oh, no! Oh, dear no!'

'I hate you when you're sarcastic,' said The Miller. 'Come on! What is this come-home-aloner?'

But Mr Evans was adamantine.

'I'm sorry not to oblige you, Mr Challoner, but I've got competition in my business. There's a certain party— no names no pack-drill—who's fairly doggin' me to get information: him an' his pretty daughter.'

Educated Evans used 'pretty' in the offensive sense to describe Mrs Lube, of whom most people have heard.

It was regrettable that Mr Evans was not of the temperament which makes secrecy possible. All Camden Town knew that the master of Paddy Lodge had a rod in pickle: its actual name he did not tell. He contented himself with 'hints'.

Certainly he hinted to such effect that he had aroused a considerable amount of curiosity, and at the same time had provoked mean-spirited men to discover for themselves the identity of this wonderful horse that he was giving on Thursday, and which, in two incautious moments, he had stated to one person, would win the Birbeck Two-Year-Old Plate at Gatwick, and to another, that it was a grey. When you know the race and the colour of a horse, and there are but two grey horses running, and one of those loudly advertised by every newspaper dealing with the noble sport of horse-racing, it is not difficult to arrive at a conclusion.

'That's it!' said young Harry Gribbs, examining the programme. 'It's Milikins! It'll start at four to one on—that's a nice five pound special, I don't think!'

In other quarters the identity of the animal had been discovered. The Miller called round to see his friend.

'Evans, you're going to lose your connection, my lad,' he said.

Mr Evans was in an irritable, indeed a nervous, state of mind, because he had recognized his indiscretion. In the first place, his secret information was everybody's news. It would be difficult to find a weekly paper that had not put a star against Milikins, except those that had put two.

'And obviously that is the horse you have been gassing about all this week.'

'That's where you're wrong,' snapped Evans, and The Miller stared at him.

'But you said it was a grey; you said it was running in this two-year-old race.'

'Never mind what I said,' Educated Evans looked almost truculent. 'Ain't I entitled to be diplomatical, the same as the well-known Gallypot, the French astrologer, who, when he was asked if the world turned round, replied to the haughty dogs of Venice: "It do and it don't." Ain't I entitled—good lord-'mighty!—to use discretion and artfulness and cleverness? Am I supposed to carry me heart up me sleeve?'

'Calm yourself, Horatius,' said the Miller. 'I meant no harm. Only everybody in Camden Town thinks you're tipping Milikins, and even Old Sam thinks you're losing your dash.'

'So-and-so and so-and-so Old Sam!' said the exasperated Evans.

'Be calm, Elijah!' said The Miller gently. 'And what is that horrible green stuff on your fingers?'

'It's ink that I got for me fountain pen—it won't come orf.'

'Nor will Hesperus,' said Sergeant Challoner, and Evans ground his teeth.

He went back to Paddy House, Bayham Mews, slammed and locked the door and sat for a quarter of an hour glaring at the notice he had run off on his duplicator.

Better than Paddy!
Better than Paddy!
Better than Paddy!

I am sending you one today which can catch pigeons. I am sending you one of the grandest horses that ever looked through a bridal! This one I have touted with my own eyes and seen all its work day by day at great expense! This one is better than Paddy ever knew how to be. He will start at 33/1 and win in a canter.

MILIKINS—FEAR NOTHING.

And don't forget your old and true and tried friend,

EDUCATED EVANS,
Paddy Lodge,
Bayham Mews.

P.S.—Beware of imitations. The police have orders to take into custody any person, old or young, who plaguerises my tips.

Evans had brought into the flat with him a bundle of weekly newspapers, purchased at the local newsagent's, and now he examined the sporting prophecies with interest and despair, as sheet after sheet revealed the implicit faith of the anonymous sporting writers in the superiority of Milikins.

We have seen Milikins do several gallops, and we know that this trainer has a high opinion of him (wrote 'Bow-Wow' in the *Racing Watch Dog*) and there is no doubt that he is a certainty for his race on Saturday, and we have every confidence in giving

MILIKINS.

Evans groaned with every fresh discovery. He realized, in some indefinable way, that his very reputation was at stake. Camden Town was waiting to sneer at him, and he took a sudden and dramatic resolve. Very painfully, he wrote out a new duplicator sheet, substituting for 'Milikins' the word 'Hesperus'. That at least was a grey and was in the same race—for he was committed to a grey.

What did the sporting newspapers say of Hesperus? Even the *Saturday Sports Herald*, whose training correspondents tip every horse in the race, had little to remark in his favour. 'Ours is not good,' said the local correspondent.

Others were equally offensive. Evans groaned again. There was no help for it. Better to send a wild outsider, without a possible chance of winning, than sacrifice his fame for sagacity. Setting his teeth, he finished writing on the wax paper, and the bell of St Pancras' Church was chiming three before he climbed into bed, so weary that he forgot to take off his braces—a precaution he had never neglected before.

Was Camden Town agog at the news it had received? It was.

'Hesperus?' said The Miller, wrinkling his brows, and went in search of the tipster.

But Mr Evans had left by an early rattler for the scene of the contest.

Mr Groom, the eminent trainer, was running both horses, he was glad to see, for a non-runner was almost as damaging to the prestige of a turf prophet as an odds-on favourite.

In what miraculous fashion Mr Evans contrived to get into the most exclusive enclosures at a race meeting, nobody has ever discovered. He is one of the few sportsmen in the world who has had the distinction of being thrown over the rails of the Royal Enclosure at Ascot. Amongst his other battle honours is the experience of being kicked out of Newmarket private stand twice in one day. It is certain he was in the Gatwick paddock, without the title which payment usually confers upon the patrons of racing.

Miller had a day off; his motor-cycle had whizzed him into Surrey, and his profession procured him the same advantage in the matter of admission as Evans had obtained through another cause.

'What's this Hesperus you've sent out?'

'A horse,' said Evans laconically.

'Does it run?'

Mr Evans closed his eyes.

'It will run and will win by the length of the Holloway Road,' he said. 'I've had this horse give to me by the boy that does him, and I've brought down twenty pounds to back him.'

The Miller shook his head.

'Give the money to me: I'll mind it,' he said gently. 'You're ill, Evans. The truth is, you intended giving Milikins, and when you found everybody else was giving it, you switched over.'

Mr Evans raised his shoulders in patient protest.

'Them that laughs last laughs least,' he said cryptically.

It was true he had as much as £25 in his pocket. It was quite untrue that he intended risking so much as a penny upon Hesperus. What he did design was a plunge upon Milikins, that would bring some solace for the losses he would sustain over his idiotic tipping.

Just before the 4.15, he was leaning on the rail, watching the horses parade. There were two greys, but which was Hesperus and which was Milikins, he did not know. Educated Evans never recognized a horse until the jockey got up.

Just as the numbers were going into the frame, The Miller came hurrying to Evans and led him to a quiet corner of the paddock.

'Evans,' he said, 'there's some talk about these horses being mixed up: that Milikins is really Hesperus, and Hesperus Milikins. You told me you saw a trial?'

Evans nodded importantly.

'Then you can tell one horse from the other. Which of those two greys won the trial?'

Evans glanced back at the saddling ring, where the horses were slowly walking. Beyond the fact that they were two greys, he was quite unable to distinguish the trial winner, for two horses, as I have remarked, looked as much alike to Evans as two pairs of boots of similar make and size.

And then there flashed across his mind a recollection of

the alarming incident which had marked the end of the trial.

'Here, hold hard, Miller,' he said agitatedly. 'I can tell you in a twink!'

He hurried back to the ring, followed by Mr Challoner, and presently the greys came along, one following the other. Evans glared down at their feet, and then, with a gurgle of joy, he pointed.

'That's Milikins,' he said. 'See them green spots on his legs? . . . My fountain-pen . . .'

Incoherently he told the story of his loss, which was now to prove his gain.

'That's Milikins,' he said. 'He'll win by the length of Tattersall's . . . that horse is money for nothing,' he went on, forgetting his role of prophet, forgetful of three hundred unfortunate people whom he had begged and implored to back Hesperus. '. . . that horse could stand on his head and win.'

'You daylight robber!' said The Miller softly. 'Then you were bluffing?'

Evans threw out his hands in protest.

'A man of my position has got to fyness,' he said simply, and The Miller was in too much of a hurry to ask for an explanation.

Evans went back to the ring again. There were the green spots on the grey's fetlock. He smiled triumphantly, and, clutching his £20 in a hot hand, he hustled his way into Tattersall's and, taking £35 to £20, climbed up the stand to see his money come home.

'I've got to get it some way or the other, Mr Challoner,' he said to The Miller, who joined him. 'Self-preservation's the first law of betting, and—'

'They're off!'

The start was a straggling one, but Hesperus—even Evans recognized Hesperus now—jumped off in front, was a certain winner at two furlongs, an assured winner at four furlongs, and actually did win by ten lengths.

'Hesperus?' said the dazed Evans. 'The—the thieves and robbers! They've been and run them horses on me!'

And then it slowly dawned upon him that, however

much his pocket might have suffered at Gatwick, his reputation in Camden Town was considerably enhanced.

'Well, well,' he said tolerantly, 'it's a case of information *v.* guesswork. If I'd stayed at home I'd have made a lot of money. I knew they'd rung this horse, and if you hadn't put me off it—'

The Miller gave him one glance, which would have withered an ordinary man. But Evans was no ordinary man.

Said Mr Groom, the trainer, to Mr Tooks, the owner:

'Did you see that ugly little devil looking at the horse's legs? He's a tout or something and came up to my gallops. What did he do? Why, he dropped some green ink on Hesperus. I guessed he'd been sent to find out which was which, so I cleaned Hesperus—and a devil of a job it was—and put a few green spots on Milikins. Artful, eh? I tell you these newspaper chaps want a bit of beating!'

THE SNATCHING OF BOOKIE BOB

by Damon Runyon

There could be no collection of horse racing stories without a contribution from Damon Runyon. The Turf was one of his abiding interests and was transferred to many of his characters —Harry the Horse, Rusty Charlie, Sorrowful Jones, Crooked Dollar Moishe, Cheesecake Ike, The Gimp, Milk Ear Willy, Sleep-out Louie and all the rest.

In an article about Runyon's stories—and in particular the anonymous character who tells them—E. C. Bentley wrote in very Runyonesque fashion, 'Another taste which X (the narrator) has strongly developed is horse race betting: a taste which he shares with practically every guy mentioned in the stories. In fact the only guys I can think of at the moment who do not back horses are two guys who happen to be bookmakers. Some of X's friends, like Hot Horse Herbie, are such guys as never think of anything else in this world but betting on horses; but those who are mainly interested in crime, and so cannot be considered as serious horse-players, mostly devote a good deal of the proceeds to this form of amusement. Playing the horses is a necessary part of X's life.'

Several of Damon Runyon's stories which feature horse racing, such as 'Princess O'Hara' and 'Old Em's Kentucky Home', might well have been included here, but 'The Snatching of Bookie Bob', with its mixture of crime and farce, has long been one of my favourites.

* * *

Now it comes on the spring of 1931, after a long hard winter, and times are very tough indeed, what with the stock market going all to pieces, and banks busting right and left, and the law getting very nasty about this and that, and one thing and another, and many citizens of this town are compelled to do the best they can.

There is very little scratch anywhere and along Broadway many citizens are wearing their last year's clothes and have practically nothing to bet on the races or anything else, and it is a condition that will touch anybody's heart.

So I am not surprised to hear rumours that the snatching of certain parties is going on in spots, because while snatching is by no means a high-class business, and is even considered somewhat illegal, it is something to tide over the hard times.

Furthermore, I am not surprised to hear that this snatching is being done by a character by the name of Harry the Horse, who comes from Brooklyn, and who is a character who does not care much what sort of business he is in, and who is mobbed up with other characters from Brooklyn such as Spanish John and Little Isadore, who do not care what sort of business they are in, either.

In fact, Harry the Horse and Spanish John and Little Isadore are very hard characters in every respect, and there is considerable indignation expressed around and about when they move over from Brooklyn into Manhattan and start snatching, because the citizens of Manhattan feel that if there is any snatching done in their territory, they are entitled to do it themselves.

But Harry the Horse and Spanish John and Little Isadore pay no attention whatever to local sentiment and go on the snatch on a pretty fair scale, and by and by I am hearing rumours of some very nice scores. These scores are not extra large scores, to be sure, but they are enough to keep the wolf from the door, and in fact from three different doors, and before long Harry the Horse and Spanish John and Little Isadore are around the race-tracks betting on the horses, because if there is one thing they are all very fond of, it is betting on the horses.

Now many citizens have the wrong idea entirely of the snatching business. Many citizens think that all there is to snatching is to round up the party who is to be snatched and then just snatch him, putting him away somewhere until his family or friends dig up enough scratch to pay whatever price the snatchers are asking. Very few citizens understand that the snatching business must be well organized and very systematic.

In the first place, if you are going to do any snatching, you cannot snatch just anybody. You must know who you are snatching, because naturally it is no good snatching somebody who does not have any scratch to settle with. And you cannot tell by the way a party looks or how he lives in this town if he has any scratch, because many a party who is around in automobiles, and wearing good clothes, and chucking quite a swell is nothing but the phonus bolonus and does not have any real scratch whatever.

So of course such a party is no good for snatching, and of course guys who are on the snatch cannot go around inquiring into bank accounts, or asking how much this and that party has in a safe-deposit vault, because such questions are apt to make citizens wonder why, and it is very dangerous to get citizens to wondering why about anything. So the only way guys who are on the snatch can find out about parties worth snatching is to make a connection with some guy who can put the finger on the right party.

The finger guy must know the party he fingers has plenty of ready scratch to begin with, and he must also know that this party is such as is not apt to make too much disturbance about being snatched, such as telling the gendarmes. The party may be a legitimate party, such as a business guy, but he will have reasons why he does not wish it to get out that he is snatched, and the finger must know these reasons. Maybe the party is not leading the right sort of life, such as running around with blondes when he has an ever-loving wife and seven children in Mamaroneck, but does not care to have his habits known, as is apt to happen if he is snatched, especially if he is snatched when he is with a blonde.

And sometimes the party is such a party as does not care to have matches run up and down the bottom of his feet, which often happens to parties who are snatched and who do not seem to wish to settle their bill promptly, because many parties are very ticklish on the bottom of the feet, especially if the matches are lit. On the other hand, maybe the party is not a legitimate guy, such as a party who is running a crap game or a swell speakeasy, or who has some other dodge he does not care to have come out, and who also does not care about having his feet tickled.

Such a party is very good indeed for the snatching business, because he is pretty apt to settle without any argument. And after a party settles one snatching, it will be considered very unethical for anybody else to snatch him again very soon, so he is not likely to make any fuss about the matter. The finger guy gets a commission of twenty-five per cent of the settlement, and one and all are satisfied and much fresh scratch comes into circulation, which is very good for the merchants. And while the party who is snatched may know who snatches him, one thing he never knows is who puts the finger on him, this being considered a trade secret.

I am talking to Waldo Winchester, the newspaper scribe, one night and something about the snatching business comes up, and Waldo Winchester is trying to tell me that it is one of the oldest dodges in the world, only Waldo calls it kidnapping, which is a title that will be very repulsive to guys who are on the snatch nowadays. Waldo Winchester claims that hundreds of years ago guys are around snatching parties, male and female, and holding them for ransom, and furthermore Waldo Winchester says they even snatch very little children and Waldo states that it is all a very, very wicked proposition.

Well, I can see where Waldo is right about it being wicked to snatch dolls and little children, but of course no guys who are on the snatch nowadays will ever think of such a thing, because who is going to settle for a doll in these times when you can scarcely even give them away? As for little children, they are apt to be a great nuisance, because their mammas are sure to go running around hollering bloody murder about them, and furthermore little children are very dangerous indeed, what with being apt to break out with measles and mumps and one thing and another any minute and give it to everybody in the neighbourhood.

Well, anyway, knowing that Harry the Horse and Spanish John and Little Isadore are now on the snatch, I am by no means pleased to see them come along one Tuesday evening when I am standing at the corner of Fiftieth and Broadway, although of course I give them a very jolly hello, and say I hope and trust they are feeling nicely.

They stand there talking to me a few minutes, and I am very glad indeed that Johnny Brannigan, the strong-arm cop, does not happen along and see us, because it will give Johnny a very bad impression of me to see me in such company, even though I am not responsible for the company. But naturally I cannot haul off and walk away from this company at once, because Harry the Horse and Spanish John and Little Isadore may get the idea that I am playing the chill for them, and will feel hurt.

'Well,' I say to Harry the Horse, 'how are things going, Harry?'

'They are going no good,' Harry says. 'We do not beat a race in four days. In fact,' he says, 'we go overboard today. We are washed out. We owe every bookmaker at the track that will trust us, and now we are out trying to raise some scratch to pay off. A guy must pay his bookmaker no matter what.'

Well, of course this is very true, indeed, because if a guy does not pay his bookmaker it will lower his business standing quite some, as the bookmaker is sure to go around putting the blast on him, so I am pleased to hear Harry the Horse mention such honourable principles.

'By the way,' Harry says, 'do you know a guy by the name of Bookie Bob?'

Now I do not know Bookie Bob personally, but of course I know who Bookie Bob is, and so does everybody else in this town that ever goes to a race track, because Bookie Bob is the biggest bookmaker around and about, and has plenty of scratch. Furthermore, it is the opinion of one and all that Bookie Bob will die with this scratch, because he is considered a very close guy with his scratch. In fact, Bookie Bob is considered closer than a dead heat.

He is a short fat guy with a bald head, and his head is always shaking a little from side to side, which some say is a

186

touch of palsy, but which most citizens believe comes of Bookie Bob shaking his head 'No' to guys asking for credit in betting on the races. He has an ever-loving wife, who is a very quiet little old doll with grey hair and a very sad look in her eyes, but nobody can blame her for this when they figure that she lives with Bookie Bob for many years.

I often see Bookie Bob and his ever-loving wife eating in different joints along in the Forties, because they seem to have no home except an hotel, and many a time I hear Bookie Bob giving her a going-over about something or other, and generally it is about the price of something she orders to eat, so I judge Bookie Bob is as tough with his ever-loving wife about scratch as he is with everybody else. In fact, I hear him bawling her out one night because she has on a new hat which she says costs her six bucks, and Bookie Bob wishes to know if she is trying to ruin him with her extravagances.

But of course I am not criticizing Bookie Bob for squawking about the hat, because for all I know six bucks may be too much for a doll to pay for a hat, at that. And furthermore, maybe Bookie Bob has the right idea about keeping down his ever-loving wife's appetite, because I know many a guy in this town who is practically ruined by dolls eating too much on him.

'Well,' I say to Harry the Horse, 'if Bookie Bob is one of the bookmakers you owe, I am greatly surprised to see that you seem to have both eyes in your head, because I never before hear of Bookie Bob letting anybody owe him without giving him at least one of their eyes for security. In fact,' I say, 'Bookie Bob is such a guy as will not give you the right time if he has two watches.'

'No,' Harry the Horse says, 'we do not owe Bookie Bob. But,' he says, 'he will be owing us before long. We are going to put the snatch on Bookie Bob.'

Well, this is most disquieting news to me, not because I care if they snatch Bookie Bob or not, but because somebody may see me talking to them who will remember about it when Bookie Bob is snatched. But of course it will not be good policy for me to show Harry the Horse and Spanish

John and Little Isadore that I am nervous, so I only speak as follows:

'Harry,' I say, 'every man knows his own business best, and I judge you know what you are doing. But,' I say, 'you are snatching a hard guy when you snatch Bookie Bob. A very hard guy, indeed. In fact,' I say, 'I hear the softest thing about him is his front teeth, so it may be very difficult for you to get him to settle after you snatch him.'

'No,' Harry the Horse says, 'we will have no trouble about it. Our finger gives us Bookie Bob's hole card, and it is a most surprising thing, indeed. But,' Harry the Horse says, 'you come upon many surprising things in human nature when you are on the snatch. Bookie Bob's hole card is his ever-loving wife's opinion of him.

'You see,' Harry the Horse says, 'Bookie Bob has been putting himself away with his ever-loving wife for years, as a very important guy in this town, with much power and influence, although of course Bookie Bob knows very well he stands about as good as a broken leg. In fact,' Harry the Horse says, 'Bookie Bob figures that his ever-loving wife is the only one in the world who looks on him as a big guy, and he will sacrifice even his scratch, or anyway some of it, rather than let her know that guys have such little respect for him as to put the snatch on him. It is what you call psychology,' Harry the Horse says.

Well, this does not make good sense to me, and I am thinking to myself that the psychology that Harry the Horse really figures to work out nice on Bookie Bob is tickling his feet with matches, but I am not anxious to stand there arguing about it, and pretty soon I bid them all good evening, very polite, and take the wind, and I do not see Harry the Horse or Spanish John or Little Isadore again for a month.

In the meantime, I hear gossip here and there that Bookie Bob is missing for several days, and when he finally shows up again he gives it out that he is very sick during his absence, but I can put two and two together as well as anybody in this town and I figure that Bookie Bob is snatched by Harry the Horse and Spanish John and Little Isadore, and the chances are it costs him plenty.

So I am looking for Harry the Horse and Spanish John and Little Isadore to be around the race track with plenty of scratch and betting them higher than a cat's back, but they never show up, and what is more I hear they leave Manhattan and are back in Brooklyn working every day handling beer. Naturally this is very surprising to me, because the way things are running beer is a tough dodge just now, and there is very little profit in same, and I figure that with the scratch they must make off Bookie Bob, Harry the Horse and Spanish John and Little Isadore have a right to be taking things easy.

Now one night I am in Good Time Charley Bernstein's little speak in Forty-eighth Street, talking of this and that with Charley, when in comes Harry the Horse, looking very weary and by no means prosperous. Naturally I gave him a large hello, and by and by we get to gabbing together and I ask him whatever becomes of the Bookie Bob matter, and Harry the Horse tells me as follows:

Yes [Harry the Horse says], we snatch Bookie Bob all right. In fact, we snatch him the very next night after we are talking to you, or on a Wednesday night. Our finger tells us Bookie Bob is going to a wake over in his old neighbourhood on Tenth Avenue, near Thirty-eighth Street, and this is where we pick him up.

He is leaving the place in his car along about midnight, and of course Bookie Bob is alone as he seldom lets anybody ride with him because of the wear and tear on his car cushions, and Little Isadore swings our flivver in front of him and makes him stop. Naturally Bookie Bob is greatly surprised when I poke my head into his car and tell him I wish the pleasure of his company for a short time, and at first he is inclined to argue the matter, saying I must make a mistake, but I put the old convincer on him by letting him peek down the snozzle of my John Roscoe.

We lock his car and throw the keys away, and then we take Bookie Bob in our car and go to a certain spot on Eighth Avenue where we have a nice little apartment all ready. When we get there I tell Bookie Bob that he can call up anybody he wishes and state that the snatch is on him and that it will require twenty-five G's, cash money, to take it off, but of course I also tell Bookie Bob that he is not to mention where he is or something may happen to him.

Well, I will say one thing for Bookie Bob, although everybody is always weighing in the sacks on him and saying he is no good—he takes it like a gentleman, and very calm and businesslike.

Furthermore, he does not seem alarmed, as many citizens are when they find themselves in such a situation. He recognizes the justice of our claim at once, saying as follows:

'I will telephone my partner, Sam Salt,' he says. 'He is the only one I can think of who is apt to have have such a sum as twenty-five G's cash money. But,' he says, 'if you gentlemen will pardon the question, because this is a new experience to me, how do I know everything will be okay for me after you get the scratch?'

'Why,' I say to Bookie Bob, somewhat indignant, 'it is well known to one and all in this town that my word is my bond. There are two things I am bound to do,' I say, 'and one is to keep my word in such a situation as this, and the other is to pay anything I owe a bookmaker, no matter what, for these are obligations of honour with me.'

'Well,' Bookie Bob says, 'of course I do not know you gentlemen, and, in fact, I do not remember ever seeing any of you, although your face is somewhat familiar, but if you pay your bookmaker you are an honest guy, and one in a million. In fact,' Bookie Bob says, 'if I have all the scratch that is owing to me around this town, I will not be telephoning anybody for such a sum as twenty-five G's. I will have such a sum in my pants pocket for change.'

Now Bookie Bob calls a certain number and talks to somebody there but he does not get Sam Salt, and he seems much disappointed when he hangs up the receiver again.

'This is a very tough break for me,' he says. 'Sam Salt goes to Atlantic City an hour ago on very important business and will not be back until tomorrow evening, and they do not know where he is to stay in Atlantic City. 'And,' Bookie Bob says, 'I cannot think of anybody else to call up to get this scratch, especially anybody I will care to have know I am in this situation.'

'Why not call your ever-loving wife?' I say. 'Maybe she can dig up this kind of scratch.'

'Say,' Bookie Bob says, 'you do not suppose I am chump enough to give my ever-loving wife twenty-five G's, or even let her know where she can get her dukes on twenty-five G's belonging to me, do you? I give my ever-loving wife ten bucks per week for spending money,' Bookie Bob says, 'and this is enough scratch for any doll, especially when you figure I pay for her meals.'

Well, there seems to be nothing we can do except wait until Sam Salt gets back, but we let Bookie Bob call his ever-loving wife, as Bookie Bob says he does not wish to have her worrying about his absence, and tells her a big lie about having to go to Jersey City to sit up with a sick Brother Elk.

Well, it is now nearly four o'clock in the morning, so we put Bookie Bob in a room with Little Isadore to sleep, although, personally, I consider making a guy sleep with Little Isadore very cruel treatment, and Spanish John and I take turns keeping awake and watching out that Bookie Bob does not take the air on us before paying us off. To tell the truth, Little Isadore and Spanish John are somewhat disappointed that Bookie Bob agrees to settle so promptly, because they are looking forward to tickling his feet with great relish.

Now Bookie Bob turns out to be very good company when he wakes up the next morning, because he knows a lot of racetrack stories and plenty of scandal, and he keeps us much interested at breakfast. He talks along with us as if he knows us all his life, and he seems very nonchalant indeed, but the chances are he will not be so nonchalant if I tell him about Spanish John's thought.

Well, about noon Spanish John goes out of the apartment and comes back with a racing sheet, because he knows Little Isadore and I will be wishing to know what is running in different spots although we do not have anything to bet on these races, or any way of betting on them, because we are overboard with every bookmaker we know.

Now Bookie Bob is also much interested in the matter of what is running, especially at Belmont, and he is bending over the table with me and Spanish John and Little Isadore, looking at the sheet, when Spanish John speaks as follows:

'My goodness,' Spanish John says, 'a spot such as this fifth race with Questionnaire at four to five is like finding money in the street. I only wish I have a few bobs to bet on him at such a price,' Spanish John says.

'Why,' Bookie Bob says, very polite, 'if you gentlemen wish to bet on these races I will gladly book to you. It is a good way to pass away the time while we are waiting for Sam Salt, unless you will rather play pinochle?'

'But,' I say, 'we have no scratch to play the races, at least not much.'

'Well,' Bookie Bob says, 'I will take your markers, because I hear what you say about always paying your bookmaker, and you put yourself away with me as an honest guy, and these other gentlemen also impress me as honest guys.'

Now what happens but we begin betting Bookie Bob on the different races, not only at Belmont, but at all the other tracks in the country, for Little Isadore and Spanish John and I are guys who like plenty of action when we start betting on the horses. We write out markers for whatever we wish to bet and hand them to Bookie Bob, and Bookie Bob sticks these markers in an inside pocket, and along in the late afternoon it looks as if he has a tumour on his chest.

We get the race results by 'phone off a poolroom downtown as fast as they come off, and also the prices, and it is a lot of fun, and Little Isadore and Spanish John and Bookie Bob and I are all little pals together until all the races are over and Bookie Bob takes out the markers and starts counting himself up.

It comes out then that I owe Bookie Bob ten G's, and Spanish John owes him six G's, and Little Isadore owes him four G's, as Little Isadore beats him a couple of races out west.

Well, about this time, Bookie Bob manages to get Sam Salt on the 'phone, and explains to Sam that he is to go to a certain safe-deposit box and get out twenty-five G's, and then wait until midnight and hire himself a taxicab and start riding around the block between Fifty-first and Fifty-second, from Eighth to Ninth avenues, and to keep riding until somebody flags the cab and takes the scratch off him.

Naturally Sam Salt understands right away that the snatch is on Bookie Bob, and he agrees to do as he is told, but he says he cannot do it until the following night because he knows there is not twenty-five G's in the box and he will have to get the difference at the track the next day. So there we are with another day in the apartment and Spanish John and Little Isadore and I are just as well pleased because Bookie Bob has us hooked and we naturally wish to wiggle off.

But the next day is worse than ever. In all the years I am playing the horses I never have such a tough day, and Spanish John and Little Isadore are just as bad. In fact, we are all going so bad that Bookie Bob seems to feel sorry for us and often lays us a couple of points above the track prices, but it does no good. At the end of the day, I am in a total of twenty G's, while Spanish John owes fifteen, and Little Isadore fifteen, a total of fifty G's among the three of us. But we are never any hands to hold post-mortems on bad days, so Little Isadore goes out to a delicatessen store and lugs in a lot of nice things to eat, and we have a fine dinner, and then we sit around with Bookie Bob telling stories, and even singing a few songs together until time to meet Sam Salt.

When it comes on midnight Spanish John goes out and lays for Sam, and gets a little valise off of Sam Salt. Then Spanish John comes back to the apartment and we open the valise and the twenty-five G's are there okay, and we cut this scratch three ways.

Then I tell Bookie Bob he is free to go on about his business, and good luck to him, at that, but Bookie Bob looks at me as if he is very much surprised, and hurt, and says to me like this:

'Well, gentlemen, thank you for your courtesy, but what about the scratch you owe me? What about these markers? Surely, gentlemen, you will pay your bookmaker?'

Well, of course we owe Bookie Bob these markers, all right, and of course a man must pay his bookmaker, no matter what, so I hand over my bit and Bookie Bob puts down something in a little note-book that he takes out of his kick.

Then Spanish John and Little Isadore hand over their dough, too, and Bookie Bob puts down something more in the little note-book.

'Now,' Bookie Bob says, 'I credit each of your accounts with these payments, but you gentlemen still owe me a matter of twenty-five G's over and above the twenty-five I credit you with, and I hope and trust you will make arrangements to settle this at once because,' he says, 'I do not care to extend such accommodations over any considerable period.'

'But,' I say, 'we do not have any more scratch after paying you the twenty-five G's on account.'

'Listen,' Bookie Bob says, dropping his voice down to a whisper, 'what about putting the snatch on my partner, Sam Salt, and I will wait over a couple of days with you and keep booking to you, and maybe you can pull yourselves out. But of course,' Bookie Bob whispers, 'I will be entitled to twenty-five per cent of the snatch for putting the finger on Sam for you.'

But Spanish John and Little Isadore are sick and tired of Bookie Bob and will not listen to staying in the apartment any longer, because they say he is a jinx to them and they cannot beat him in any manner, shape or form. Furthermore, I am personally anxious to get away because something Bookie Bob says reminds me of something.

It reminds me that besides the scratch we owe him, we forget to take out six G's two-fifty for the party who puts the finger on Bookie Bob for us, and this is a very serious matter indeed, because anybody will tell you that failing to pay a finger is considered a very dirty trick. Furthermore, if it gets around that you fail to pay a finger, nobody else will ever finger for you.

So [Harry the Horse says] we quit the snatching business because there is no use continuing while this obligation is outstanding against us, and we go back to Brooklyn to earn enough scratch to pay our just debts.

We are paying off Bookie Bob's IOU a little at a time, because we do not wish to ever have anybody say we welsh on a bookmaker, and furthermore we are paying off the six G's two-fifty commission we owe our finger.

And while it is tough going, I am glad to say our honest effort is doing somebody a little good, because I see Bookie Bob's ever-loving wife the other night all dressed up in new clothes and looking very happy, indeed.

And while a guy is telling me she is looking so happy because she gets a large legacy from an uncle who dies in Switzerland, and is now independent of Bookie Bob, I only hope and trust [Harry the Horse says] that it never gets out that our finger in this case is nobody but Bookie Bob's ever-loving wife.

THE RACE-GANG RACKET

by Frank Johnston

Although Frank Johnston would never have claimed to be a Damon Runyon, his knowledge of the seamy side of British racing gave his stories and books a flavour of authenticity few other writers of his time on this side of the Atlantic could match. Indeed, his novels like Highway Robber's Derby and Turf Racketeers were best-sellers in the Nineteen Thirties.

Johnston was for years a race meeting reporter and tipster and boasted a range of friends from stable boys to top jockeys and from lowly punters to influential horse-owning members of the nobility. He was a man in the know where racing matters were concerned, and the information he gathered which he was unable to publish in the press was instead utilized in his novels and stories such as the series featuring Marcus Thaine, 'The Turf Crook', published in 1937. Johnston said of Thaine, 'He is a crook—there can be no hedging from that fact. But there is the saving grace that he does not knowingly swindle anyone who cannot afford to lose—or does not deserve to do so.' And of the series as a whole, he commented, 'Although many of the episodes concerning "The Turf Crook" have been based on incidents which have actually occurred in racing, it must be made clear that all the characters in the stories are entirely fictitious and any similarity is purely coincidental.'

I thought that it might reassure the reader to know that, before reading the extraordinary story of 'The Race-Gang Racket'.

* * *

Educated by the cinema and the Yellow Press that the United States of America is overridden with racketeers, the public have come to accept this as a definite fact. If you talk to people who have visited America, they will tell you of the most diabolical schemes to obtain money without giving anything in return.

If, however, you were to reply that the game has been played in this country—in one way or another—since the Romans arrived, and that it is still being done in the most open and flagrant manner, they would probably laugh at you.

I, Marcus Thaine, will relate to you a story in which I was personally concerned and which you may hardly credit; nevertheless, I can vouch for the truth of the statements. Afterwards you may change your mind and will understand that, while we do not make a song of the rackets that are played right under our noses every day, their existence is undeniable.

In the States, for instance, there might spring up overnight in a certain city a 'Taxi Owners' and Drivers' Protection Association'. Drivers of cabs would be approached and asked to join the Association, the subscription to which might be five dollars a week. Some would pay, but others would refuse. Then the racket is brought into operation. The 'big shot' just tips off his toughs, and the unfortunate driver who has refused to become a member finds that his tyres have been slit, his windscreen smashed, and his recording clock damaged beyond repair.

Then he is approached again. 'If you were a member of the Association we could have protected you against that,' he is told.

What can the man do? He knows what has happened, yet could not prove anything. To go to the police would be so much waste of time.

That is only one instance. They have 'Protection Associations' for so many things in America. Milkmen, grocers, bakers, candlestick-makers—each and every trade and profession is subject to the grand 'racket' game that has swept the Western Continent. And they think it is new? That it is an entirely post-war evolution of a progressive people? Forgive me if I smile.

This 'racket' business was worked to the bone before

poor old Henry VIII was married for the last time. On and off it has been revived in mild forms, and still exists in many directions today. But it is not advertised, neither has it reached such proportions as to be a menace to the public here.

Having said quite enough about the subject, I will get down to brass tacks and confess that I was once concerned in a very slick racket that equalled in ingenuity anything the Americans have ever conceived. Naturally one associates such a thing with something that has ready money—and quick money at that—attached to the end of it. And because you know I have been in the racing world most of my life you will expect my story to be associated with the Turf. I shall not disappoint you.

It is going back a few years—exactly how many I prefer not to say—but let it suffice that it was after the war and was round about the time when the race-gang feud was running, and that the subject received—every now and then—a good deal of notice from the newspapers.

Regular race goers knew that the situation had been exaggerated by the Press, but a gullible public, who did not understand the Turf, really believed that race courses swarmed with men armed to the teeth, and who brandished razors and bludgeons at the slightest provocation. What utter nonsense it was! But I suppose the reporters enjoyed themselves 'writing up' these lurid details.

Incidentally, I'd like to bet that all they ever knew about racing was to have a couple of bob on a horse with a bookie up an alley. I may be wrong, of course, but whenever I read a racing item on a news page, and it has not been written by the accredited sporting representative of the paper, I nearly always smile. These 'stories' bristle with inaccuracies and incorrect technical details. Even when the 'news-men' have only a couple of lines to write under a picture they flop —and how!

Here is an example that some of you may recall. It is only a year or so ago that a leading daily paper printed a photograph of horses passing the stands at Sandown Park. The words under the picture went something like this:

> Jumping the *fence* in front of the stands in the Kingston *Hurdle* Race at Sandown Park yesterday.

The italics are mine.

It does not need an expert knowledge of racing to see what is wrong, for the veriest tyro must know that the horses do not jump *fences* in a hurdle race. I mention this just to show you that newspapers do not always give you the right stuff—except when their racing men do the story.

To get back on the rails. At the time of this race-gang feud—if we must call it a feud—there was a certain amount of truth in the reports,but the fights occurred only when one gang thought that another was poaching upon its preserves.

We'll cut that part out. The point is that at this time I and a few others conceived a really brilliant scheme whereby we could 'collect' some easy money. I should like to say at this stage that the newspapers had helped us to a great extent —at least, in so far that even a number of racing people had it at the back of their minds that one of the 'gangs' might start something really tough if they were thwarted.

I do not mind admitting that the original idea was mine. It occurred to me one day after a series of hopeless outsiders had triumphed. I watched disconsolate punters wending their weary way off the course, while the bookies were grinning and literally counting the small fortunes they had won that day.

The satisfaction on the faces of the layers of odds was galling—and the thought occurred to me: 'Wouldn't it be a grand thing to go along the line and touch them all— they've got plenty, and it would serve them right for betting under the odds and skinning the public.'

I had, that day, seen one man lay 6 to 1 to a little backer about a horse that was returned at 16 to 1, and which— on the book and according to the money that had been invested on it—ought to have been 160 to 1 or more. To the general surprise, this horse skated home alone, and probably staggered its trainer as well as the rest of us.

This was before the days of the Totalisator, and before the bookies were charged enormous sums to bet at a meeting. I hold different views now about skinning them, because I know how hard it is for bookies to carry on. The race course companies take toll in a most unfair manner, and the layers have put over a million pounds more into racing than they would have done under the old scale, which cannot be called equitable, particularly as little of the money has gone into the game—merely into the pockets of the executives. However, in the old days bookies paid only admission fees to the course, or to the ring in which they operated.

There were minor 'rackets', of course. The men who shouted the runners got a rake-off; those who sold the boards with the names of the runners printed on them touched for more than the value of the goods they provided; and, lastly, the men who provided the 'marked cards' tickled to a pretty tune.

This marked-card business is, by the way, something of which the public know very little. An hour before racing you will see groups of bookies, or their clerks or runners, gathered in little circles. They will be noting on their race cards the remarks made by the man who has collected the information that will affect betting throughout the afternoon. He will—in ways best known to himself—collate information regarding arrivals, and of any commissions that have been placed early, and in the most uncanny way will get to know which horses will be backed for good money. He can naturally couple with these items his own judgment of form, hence when the books open up on a race they nearly always agree as to which horse is favourite, which is second favourite, and the various 'dangers', their cards having been marked with a dot, 'C', or 'X', as the case may be.

None of these people I have mentioned really earn the money the bookies pay them, but they are all part and parcel of the make-up of racing, and there you are.

My intention was something very different. I scouted round and approached Jeff Murdoch on the subject. He was tickled to death about it. 'You're a marvel, Thaine,' he said. 'Why, it'll be like shelling peas.'

'Maybe,' I replied, 'but if you'll come in it will help. There ought to be three or four of us, perhaps five. What we ought to do is to find a couple of old bruisers who are not known generally and who look really tough. Do you know anyone who will fill the bill?'

Jeff was a marvel. He knew everyone who had been near The Ring for thirty years, as well as all the boys of Stepney and Bow, while the Bethnal Greenites were like cousins to him. On his suggestion we roped in Spike Taylor and 'Erb Bootle. They were a couple of tough-looking guys, and no mistake, and were willing to do anything for half a bar (10s.) a day. I gave them instructions when Jeff brought them along to a pub in the Blackfriars Road.

'We're going down to Kempton today,' I commenced, 'and your job won't take half an hour. All you have to do is to walk along behind Jeff and me and look as though you're out for trouble. We want bodyguards who'll give us a hand if we don't meet friends. Get that?'

They 'got it' all right, and we set off from Waterloo keenly excited at the prospect. Incidentally, for all our 'big talk', Jeff and I had barely enough to pay the fares down, and it was just as well that we intended working only 'outside' on the course, and not entering the rings, as admission to the park was only a few bob all told.

We waited until the second race was over, then I gave the signal that the 'racket' was about to commence. Incidentally, I had spent the time looking round to see if any of the gangs were about in force. They were not, so everything was set fair.

In the park at Kempton the bookies stand in one long line about thirty yards from the rails in the straight, with a dozen or so extending at a right angle opposite the winning post where the course bends round. Nowadays there are not half so many of them, but there was more money about ten years or so ago, and consequently more men 'standing up' at the meetings. On the particular day I remember there were about forty bookies working on the course, apart from those in the Silver Ring and Tattersall's.

We began at the end of the line opposite the winning post. The first bookie I approached was only a small operator, but he had enjoyed a 'skinner' on the second race, and was drinking beer out of a bottle when I went up to him. Jeff

Murdoch was at my side, and our toughs only a few paces away, standing about as though they would almost like to fight each other just for the sake of not getting bored.

I led off this way: 'Give us a dollar.'

'What for?' he demanded.

'Never mind what for; give us a dollar, or . . .'

He glanced round and spotted Spike Taylor and 'Erb Bootle. I could see he was wavering, suspecting—just as I hoped he would—that some of the boys were busy. Then I clinched the matter. 'Better drop to us, or the Birmingham lot'll be along. You'll need help then.'

Goodness knows what he thought, but he dipped into the bag and parted with some silver.

We went steadily down the line, and the bookies had apparently noted that the others we had 'tapped' had paid up. In one case we had a point-blank refusal, however, and that was where we played the trump card. 'Don't blame me if you get into trouble,' I told him; 'you've had your chance.'

Altogether we did pretty well, touching some of the bigger men for currency notes, and at the end of an hour had collected over £20 for our 'trouble'. It was not bad, but not as good as I had hoped, although I intended it to be a regular practice at southern meetings, and to work the dodge two or three times a week, according to the fixtures.

Well, after the fourth race I called the others to one side. 'You remember Newman, who didn't drop?' I said, and they nodded. 'Well, he's in for trouble. Follow me and back me up. He's not going to bet any more today unless he pays.'

We hastened along to where the man was betting. He was shouting the odds, and a number of backers were standing round. As I reached the pitch I picked up a betting ticket with his name on it. It had, of course, been paid out, and was torn, but that didn't matter to me.

The other three were close on my heels when I pushed through and handed the ticket to Newman. 'Four pounds,' I demanded.

'Four pounds—eighty-one,' he repeated, but the clerk

told him the claim was wrong, and that the bet had been paid. 'I've paid this once!' he shouted. 'Why, the ticket's torn! Don't come that stuff with me.'

I repeated my demand for the money and swore that I had not been paid. Murdoch supported me grandly. He joined in and shouted back that he had been with me all the time and knew I had not received the money. Spike Taylor and 'Erb Bootle then did their stuff in a manner that might have been expected. Their language was a treat, and would have made a Billingsgate porter turn green with envy. As the man steadfastly refused to pay out on the supposed bet, they threatened. 'We'll smash yer up if yer don't pay our pal!' they roared.

'Serve 'im right, too,' shouted Murdoch. 'Come on, boys—if he won't pay out, treat him like a welsher. That's what he is—a welsher. Hey, listen, all you mugs,' he went on, addressing the crowd, 'he won't pay up. Chuck him over.'

I drew close up to Newman. 'Now then, what's it going to be,' I hissed, 'will you pay up, or take what's coming to you?'

His reply was to hit me a smashing blow on the mouth. That was enough. I staggered back, but Spike and 'Erb did their stuff in grand style. They lashed out right and left, and Jeff joined in with them. As soon as I regained my feet I went after Newman like a tiger. No man could hit me like that and get away with it.

All in a flash a free fight had started, but we were four to their three, and had the added advantage that two of us, at least, had experience of the ring. The bookie's clerk was knocked out, and the runner took to his heels and ran for dear life. Meanwhile Spike and I gave Newman a very rough time. Blows literally rained on him, until Murdoch gave a shout, 'Cops!', and we ran off and mingled with the crowd.

It was easy enough to get away, and we left the course knowing that Newman would not be able to bet on any more races that day. He had been the victim of his courage, but we knew that the example would do us a lot of good and make our path easier in future. Everyone would know that we meant business, and I was convinced that news of the affray would soon get round.

We next worked the game at Hurst Park, and to many of the bookies I passed on the 'information' that: 'We've got our orders, and it'll be worse for you than it was for Newman if you don't drop. The others'll all be down here tomorrow.'

That did the trick. There were a few who argued, but we just made it clear that we could give them 'protection' from being molested in the course of their business, and they contributed varying amounts to our 'fund'.

During that week there happened to be a gang fight between the Birmingham crowd and a number of Londoners. The Midlanders were defeated, and four of them were taken to hospital, while the others escaped, and this did us a power of good. For a week or so we reaped a richer harvest than ever, and I began to think that the game would go on indefinitely. Our 'takings' were averaging over £100 a week, and it was as simple as kiss your hand.

The public were quite ignorant of what was going on. How could they suspect that the four men going 'along the line' were working a racket at the expense of the bookmakers? True, there were a few suspicious glances, but in the 'outside' crowd there is seldom anyone to interfere.

Naturally we took a few precautions, and did not attempt any 'business' when an Inspector of Police was about, but the ordinary uniformed men were practically ignored. Too many of their brethren worked the 'racket' of making street bookies drop—and still do to this day, for that matter—for us to worry about them.

Now and again, of course, we had to let some of the bookies off. The public were not always the mugs they are believed to be, and with a series of well-backed horses winning, our chances of collecting were considerably reduced. Some of the bookies would have to dip deeply into their bags to pay out genuine 'winnings', and in such cases I took the view that it would be better to let a man off rather than rouse him to desperation. To bleed them dry every time would not enable us to keep it up, and I was a bit 'windy' that some of the layers would unite and defy our threats to put them out of business.

Then the end came—at least, for us—but I believe that others have since played the same game at various times. How it happened I do not quite know, but I have very good reason to believe that it was our first 'victim', Newman, who spiked our guns.

We were on the way to another fixture at Kempton Park, and as there was a big race on I suggested to Jeff that we went out for an extra sum from each of the bookies. 'There may be some new men,' I pointed out, 'and we'll make 'em drop heavy if an outsider wins the big'un.'

By this time Spike and 'Erb had demanded a considerably bigger share of the takings, and I had been forced to agree. They also managed to pick up easy money in other ways on and off the course, and were—for them—doing very well.

In due course we reached the entrance gates at the Sunbury course, and I went up to the turnstile with a handful of silver to pay the admission fees for the four of us. To my surprise I felt a tap on the shoulder. 'Not you,' said a sharp voice. 'You don't want to go racing, neither do your pals. Get out of it.'

'What's the idea?' I demanded. 'I'm paying to go in, aren't I? What's the matter with me?'

The square-shouldered man who confronted me had 'police' written all over him, and behind him were some more plain-clothes men, while there were a number of constables within easy call.

'Just that we don't like your face,' he told me. 'You'd better beat it before we take you inside. Keep out of racing, and you'll save yourself getting into trouble. That's all; now hop it.'

Opposition would have been useless. I knew that, because I've seen others treated the same way. There was an incident at Folkestone that has long remained in my memory. A well-known pickpocket thought he would have a day's work on the course, but they stopped him at the gate and kept him out.

There was nothing else to do but to get back to town, and while Spike and 'Erb uttered terrible threats, they were 'wide' enough not to attempt any of the desperate deeds they planned, for they knew that it was a waste of time getting up against the police, which would only mean trouble for all of us.

But, as I say, it was a grand racket while it lasted, and just shows what you can get away with on mere bluff—plus an occasional demonstration; and I'd like to bet that the Yanks have never tried the same dodge on their race tracks—yet.

THE ASCOT TRAGEDY

by H. C. Bailey

*The aristocratic Reggie Fortune was on the other side of the fence
from Marcus Thaine, yet he enjoyed similar public acclaim; he was
'perhaps the most popular sleuth in England between the world
wars', according to Chris Steinbrunner and Otto Penzler in their*
Encyclopedia of Mystery and Detection.
*Like Frank Johnston, Heny Christopher Bailey was a London
newspaperman, although he specialized in the drama of the theatre
rather than that of the race course. He was, however, a keen
follower of racing (although he had an intense dislike of gambling),
and his detective, Reggie Fortune, tackled several cases with a Turf
background. Fortune is an unusual detective in that he is a
practising physician and surgeon who acts as a special adviser to
Scotland Yard on medical matters. He is plump, younger-looking
than his years and a dedicated gourmet. In all, H. C. Bailey
published over a dozen books of Reggie Fortune's adventures
between 1920 and 1943.*

*In 'The Ascot Tragedy', Reggie is at his most perceptive and
painstaking in tracking down a killer who has struck dramatically
during one of the great meetings of the racing calendar.*

*   *   *

'The Ascot Tragedy'—that is what it would have been
called in the evening papers if they had known all about it.
They did not. They made the most of the mystery, you
remember; it was not good for them or you to know that the
sequel was a sequel. But there is no reason why the flats
should not be joined now.

So let us begin at Ascot on the morning of that Cup Day. One of our fine summers, the course rather yellow, the lawns rather brown, a haze of heat over the distant woodland, and sunshine flaming about the flounces and silk hats. There were already many of both in the Royal Enclosure (it was a year of flounces), and among them, dapper, debonair, everybody's friend, the youngest middle-aged man in Europe. He, of course, is the Hon Sidney Lomas, the Chief of the Criminal Investigation Department, though mistaken by some outsiders for a comic actor of fame. Tripping back from a joke with the stewards, he discovered, sprawling solitary on the end of one of the seats, Mr Fortune, the adviser of him and all other official and important people when surgery, medicine or kindred sciences can elucidate what is or is not crime. No one looks more prosperous than Reginald Fortune. He is plump and pinkly healthy, he and his tailor treat each other with respect, his countenance has the amiability of a nice boy.

But on this occasion Lomas found fault with him. 'Why, Fortune, you're very pensive. Have you lost the lady of your present affections? Or backed a wrong 'un?'

'Go away. No fellow has a right to be as cool as you look. Go quite away. I feel like the three fellows in the Bible who sang in the furnace. How can you jest, Lomas? I have no affections. I cannot love, to bet I am ashamed. I always win. Half-crowns. Why is the world thus, Lomas?'

'My dear fellow, you're not yourself. You look quite professional.'

Reggie fortune groaned. 'I am. This place worries me. I am anatomical, ethnological, anthropological.'

'Good Gad,' said Lomas.

'Yes. A distressing place, look at it;' he waved a stick.

The people in the Royal Enclosure were as pleasant to behold as usual. Comely girls and women who had been comely passed in frocks of which many were pretty and few garish; their men were of a blameless, inconspicuous uniformity.

'What is he?' said Reggie Fortune. 'I ask you. Look at his feet.'

What Lomas saw was a man dressed like all the rest of

them and as well set up, but of a darker complexion. He did not see anything remarkable. 'The big fellow?' he said. 'He is a little weak at the knee. But what's the matter with him?'

'Who is he?' said Reggie Fortune.

Lomas shrugged. 'Not English, of course. Rather a half-caste colour, isn't he? From one of the smaller legations, I suppose, Balkan or South American.' He waved a hand to some elegant aliens who were at that moment kissing ladies' hands with florid grace. 'They all come here, you know.'

'I don't know,' said Reggie Fortune peevishly. 'Half-caste? Half what caste? Look at his feet.' Now the man's feet, well displayed beneath white spats, were large and flat but distinguished by their heels, which stuck out behind extravagantly. 'That is the negro heel.'

'My dear Fortune! The fellow is no more a negro than I am,' Lomas protested: and indeed the man's hair was straight and sleek and he had a good enough nose, and he was far from black.

'The negro or Hamitic heel,' Reggie Fortune drowsily persisted. 'I suspect the Hamitic or negro leg. And otherwise up above. And it's all very distressing, Lomas.'

'An Egyptian or perhaps an Arab: probably a Foreign Office pet,' Lomas consoled him. 'That would get him into the Royal Enclosure.'

Lomas was then removed by a duchess and Reggie Fortune tilted his hat still farther over his eyes and pondered whether it would be wise to drink before lunch and was dreamily aware of other people on his seat, an old man darkly tanned and soldierly in the custody of a little woman brilliantly dressed and terribly vivacious. She chattered without a pause, she made eyes, she made affectionate movements and little caresses. The old man though helpless seemed to be thinking of something else. And Reggie Fortune sketched lower and still lower estimates of human nature.

They went away at last when everybody went away to gather in a crowd at the gates and along the railings for the coming of the King. You will please to observe that the time must have been about one o'clock.

Reggie Fortune, one of the few, remained on his seat. He heard the cheering down the course and had sufficient presence of mind to stand up and take off his hat as the distant band began to play. Over the heads of the crowd he saw the red coats of the postilions and a gleam of the grey of the team as the King's carriage swept round into the enclosure. The rest of the procession passed and the crowd melted away. But one man remained by the railings alone. He was tall and thin and he leaned limply against the railings, one arm hanging over them. After a little while he turned on his heel and fell in a heap.

Two of the green-coated wardens of the gate ran up to him. 'Oh, Lord,' Reggie Fortune groaned, 'why did I be a doctor?' But before he could get through the flurry of people the man was being carried away.

The gift of Lomas for arriving where he wants to be displayed itself. Lomas slid through the crowd and took his arm, 'Stout fellow! Come along. It's Sir Arthur Dean. Touch of sun, what?'

'Arthur Deàn? That's the Persia man, the pundit on the Middle East?'

'That's the fellow. Getting old, you know. One of the best.'

Into the room where the old man lay came the shouting over the first race. By the door Lomas and an inspector of police talked in low tones, glancing now and then at Reggie, who was busy.

'Merry Man! Merry Man! Merry Man!' the crowd roared outside.

Reggie straightened his bent back and stood looking down at his patient. Lomas came forward. 'Anything we can get you, Fortune? Would you like some assistance?'

'You can't assist him,' said Reggie. 'He's dead.'

'Merry Man!' the crowd triumphed. 'Merry Man!'

'Good Gad!' said Lomas. 'Poor fellow. One of the best. Well, well, what is it? Heart failure?'

'The heart generally fails when you die,' Reggie mumbled: he still stared down at the body and the wonted benignity of his face was lost in expressionless reserve. 'Do you know if he has any people down here?'

'It's possible. There is a married son. I'll have him looked for.' Lomas sent his inspector off.

'I saw the old man with a woman just before he died,' Reggie murmured, and Lomas put up his eyeglass.

'Did you though? Very sudden, wasn't it? And he was all alone when he died.'

'When he fell,' Reggie mumbled the correction. 'Yes, highly sudden.'

'What was the cause of death, Fortune?'

'I wonder,' Reggie muttered. He went down on his knees by the body, he looked long and closely into the eyes, he opened the clothes . . . and to the eyes he came back again. Then there was a tap at the door and Lomas having conferred there came back and said, 'The son and his wife. I'll tell them. I suppose they can see the body?'

'They'd better see the body,' said Reggie, and as Lomas went out he began to cover and arrange it. He was laying the right arm by the side when he checked and held it up to the light. On the back of the hand was a tiny drop of blood and a red smear. He looked close and found such a hole as a pin might make.

From the room outside came a woman's cry, then a deep man's voice in some agitation, and Lomas opened the door. 'This is Mr Fortune, the surgeon who was with your father at once. Major Dean and Mrs Dean, Fortune.'

Reggie bowed and studied them. The man was a soldierly fellow, with his father's keen, wary face. But it was the woman Reggie watched, the woman who was saying, 'I was with him only half an hour ago,' and twisting her hands nervously.

'Most of that half-hour he has been dead. Where did you leave him, madam?' Reggie said.

Husband and wife stared at him. 'Why, in the Royal Enclosure, of course. In the crowd when the King came. I—I lost him. Somebody spoke to me. Yes, it was Sybil. And I never saw him again.'

Reggie stepped aside from the body. She shuddered and hid her face in her hands. 'His eyes—his eyes,' she murmured.

Major Dean blew his nose. 'This rather knocks one over,' he said. 'What's the cause of death, sir?'

'Can you help me?' said Reggie.

'I? What do you mean?'

'Nothing wrong with his heart, was there?'

'Never heard of it. He didn't use doctors. Never was ill.'

Reggie stroked his chin. 'I suppose he hadn't been to an oculist lately?'

'Not he. His eyes were as good as mine. Wonderful good. He used to brag of it. He was rising seventy and no glasses. Good Lord, what's that got to do with it? I want to know why he died.'

'So do I. And I can't tell you,' said Reggie.

'What? I say—what? You mean a post-mortem. That's horrible.'

'My dear Major, it is most distressing,' Lomas purred. 'I assure you anything in our power—sympathize with your feelings, quite, quite. But the Coroner would insist, you know; we have no choice.'

'As you were saying,' Reggie chimed in, 'we want to know why he died.'

Major Dean drew a long breath. 'That's all right, that's all right,' he said. 'The old dad!' and he came to his father's side and knelt down, and his wife stood by him, her hand on his shoulder. He looked a moment into the dead face, and closed the eyes and looked long.

From this scene Reggie and Lomas drew back. In the silence they heard the man and woman breathing unsteadily. Lomas sighed his sympathy. Mrs Dean whispered, 'His mouth! Oh, Claude, his mouth!' and with a sudden darting movement wiped away some froth from the pale lips. Then she too knelt and she kissed the brow. Her husband lifted the dead right hand to hold it for a while. And then he reached across to the key chain, took off the keys, slipped them into his pocket and helped his wife to her feet.

Reggie turned a still expressionless face on Lomas. Lomas still exhibited grave official sorrow.

'Well—er—thanks very much for all you've done,' Major Dean addressed them both. 'You've been very kind. We feel that. And if you will let me know as soon as you know anything—rather a relief.'

'Quite, quite.' Lomas held out his hand; Major Dean took it. 'Yes, I'm so sorry, but you see we must take charge of everything for the present.' He let the Major's hand go and still held out his own.

Dean flushed. 'What, his keys?'

'Thank you,' said Lomas, and at last received them. 'I was thinking about his papers, you know.'

'I can promise you they'll be safe.'

'Oh, well, that settles it!' Dean laughed. 'You know where to find me,' and he took his wife, who was plainly eager to speak to him, away.

Lomas dandled the keys in his hand. 'I wonder what's in their minds? And what's in yours, Fortune?'

'Man was murdered,' said Reggie.

Lomas groaned, 'I was afraid you had that for me. But surely it's not possible?'

'It ought not to be,' Reggie admitted. 'At a quarter to one he was quite alive, rather bored perhaps, but as fit as me. At a quarter past he was dead. What happened in between?'

'Why, he was in sight the whole time—'

'All among the most respectable people in England. Yet he dies suddenly of asphyxia and heart failure. Why?'

'Well, some obscure heart trouble—' Lomas protested.

'He was in the pink. He never used doctors. You heard them say so. He hadn't even been to an oculist.'

'A fellow doesn't always know,' Lomas urged. 'There are all sorts of heart weakness.'

'Not this sort.' Reggie shook his head. 'And the eyes. Did you see how those two were afraid of his eyes? Your eyes won't look like that when you die of heart failure. They might if an oculist had put Belladonna in 'em to examine you. But there was no oculist. Dilated pupils, foam at the mouth, cold flesh. He was poisoned. It might have been aconitine. But aconitine don't kill so quick or quite so quiet.'

'What is aconitine?'

'Oh, wolf-bane. Blue-rocket. You can get it from other plants. Only this is too quick. It slew him like prussic acid and much more peacefully. Some alkaloid poison of the aconite family, possibly unclassified. Probably it was put into him by that fresh puncture in his hand while he was packed in the crowd, just a scratch, just a jab with a hollow needle. An easy murder if you could trust your stuff. And when we do the post-mortem we'll find that everything points to death by a poison we can't trace.'

'Thanks, so much,' said Lomas. 'It is for this we employ experts.'

'Well, the police also must earn their bread. Who is he?'

'He was the great authority on the Middle East. Old Indian civilian long retired. Lately political adviser to the Government of Media. You know all that.'

'Yes. Who wanted him dead?' said Reggie.

'Oh, my dear fellow!' Lomas spread out his hands. 'The world is wide.'

'Yes. The world also is very evil. The time also is waxing late. Same like the hymn says. What about those papers son and co were so keen on?'

Lomas laughed. 'If you could believe I have a little intelligence, it would so soothe me. Our people have been warned to take charge of his flat.'

'Active fellow. Let's go and see what they found.'

It was not much more than an hour before a policeman was letting them into Sir Arthur Dean's flat in Westminster. An inspector of police led the way to the study. 'Anything of interest, Morton?' Lomas said.

'Well, sir, nothing you could call out of the way. When we came, the servants had heard of the death and they were upset. Sir Arthur's man, he opened the door to me fairly crying. Been with him thirty years, fine old-fashioned fellow, would be talking about his master.'

Lomas and Reggie looked at each other, but the inspector swept on.

'Then in this room, sir, there was Sir Arthur's executor, Colonel Osbert, getting out papers. I had to tell him that wouldn't do. Rather stiff he was. He is a military man. Well, sir, I put it to him, orders are orders, and he took it very well. But he let me see pretty plain he didn't like it. He was quite the gentleman, but he put it to me we had no business in Sir Arthur's affairs unless we thought there was foul play. Well, of course, I couldn't answer that. He talked a good deal, fishing, you might say. All he got out of me was that I couldn't allow anything to be touched. So he said he would take it up with the Commissioner and went off. That's all, sir.'

'Who is he?' said Reggie.

'His card, sir. Colonel Osbert, late Indian Army.'

'Do you know if he was who he said he was?' Lomas asked.

The inspector was startled. 'Well, sir, the servants knew him. Sir Arthur's man, he let him in, says he's Sir Arthur's oldest friend. I had no reason to detain him.'

'That's all right, Morton,' said Lomas. 'Well, what time did you get here?'

'Your message came two o'clock, sir. I should say we were here by a quarter past.'

Lomas nodded and dismissed him. 'Quick work,' he said with a cock of his eye at Reggie. 'We can time it all by the King. He drove up the course at ten past one. Till the procession came Sir Arthur was alive. We didn't pick him up till five minutes after, at the least. No one knew he was dead till you had examined him. No one knew then but me and my men. And yet Colonel Osbert in London knows of the death in time to get round here and get to work on the dead man's papers before two-fifteen. He knew the man was dead as soon as we did who were looking at the body. Damme, he has very early information.'

'Yes. One to you, Lomas. And a nasty one for Colonel Osbert. Our active and intelligent police force. If you hadn't been up and doing and sent your bright boys round, Colonel Osbert might have got away with what he wanted. And he wouldn't have had to explain how he knew too much.'

'When was the poison given? Say between five to one and ten past. At that time the murderer was in the Royal Enclosure. If he had his car waiting handy, could he get here before two-fifteen?'

'Well—if his car was a flier, and there were no flies on his chauffeur and he had luck all the way, I suppose it's possible. But I don't believe in it. I should say Osbert didn't do the job.'

Lomas sprang up and called the inspector. He wanted to know what Colonel Osbert was wearing. Colonel Osbert was in a lounge suit of grey flannel. Lomas sat down again and lit a cigarette. 'I'm afraid that will do for an alibi, Fortune,' he sighed. 'Your hypothetical murderer was in the Royal Enclosure. Therefore—'

'He was in topper and tails, same like us. The uniform of respectability. Of course, he could have done a change in his car. But I don't think it. No. Osbert won't do. But what was he after?'

Lomas stood up and looked round the room. It had the ordinary furniture of an old-fashioned study and in addition several modern steel chests of drawers for filing documents. 'Well, he set some value on his papers,' Lomas said.

'Lots of honest toil before you, Lomas, old thing.' Reggie smiled, and while Lomas fell to work with the keys he wandered about picking up a bowl here, a brass tray there. 'He kept to his own line,' he remarked. 'Everything is Asiatic.'

'You may well say so,' Lomas groaned, frowning over a mass of papers.

But Reggie's attention was diverted. Somebody had rung the bell and there was talk in the hall. He made out a woman's voice. 'I fancy this is our young friend the daughter-in-law,' he murmured.

Lomas looked up at him. 'I had a notion you didn't take to her, Fortune. Do you want to see her?'

'God forbid,' said Reggie. 'She's thin, Lomas, she's too thin.'

In a moment or two a discreet tap introduced Inspector Morton. 'Mrs Dean, deceased's daughter-in-law, sir,' he reported. 'Asked to see the man-servant. I saw no objection, me being present. They were both much distressed, sir. She asked him if Colonel Osbert had been here. Seemed upset when she heard he was here before us. Asked if he had taken anything away. The servant told her we weren't letting anything be touched. That didn't seem to satisfy her.

She said something nasty about the police being always too late. Meant for me, I suppose.'

'I rather fancy it was meant for me,' said Reggie. 'It's a bad business.'

'I don't think the Colonel got away with anything, sir. He was sitting down to the diary on the table there when we came in.'

'All right.' Lomas waved him away. 'Damn, it is a bad business. What am I to do with this, Fortune?' He held up papers in a strange script, papers of all sorts and sizes, some torn and discoloured, some fresh.

Reggie went to look. 'Arabic,' he said. 'And this is Persian.' He studied them for a while. 'A sort of dossier, a lot of evidence about some case or person. Lomas, old thing, you'll have to call in the Foreign Office.'

'Lord, we can translate them ourselves. It's the mass of it!'

'Yes, lot of light reading. I think I should have a talk to the Foreign Office. Well, that's your show. Me for the body.'

Lomas lay back in his chair. 'What's in your head?'

'I won't let anything into my head. There is no evidence. But I'm wondering if we'll ever get any. It's a beautiful crime—as a crime. A wicked world, Lomas, old thing.'

On the day after, Reggie Fortune came into Lomas's room at Scotland Yard and shook his head and lit one of Lomas's largest cigars and fell into a chair. 'Unsatisfactory, highly unsatisfactory,' he announced. 'I took Harvey down with me. You couldn't have a better opinion except mine, and he agrees with me.'

'And what do you say?'

'I say, nothing doing. He had no medical history. There was nothing the matter with the man, yet he died of heart failure and suffocation. That means poisoning by aconitine or a similar alkaloid. But there is no poison in the price list which would in a quarter of an hour kill quietly and without fuss a man in perfect health. I have no doubt a poison was injected into him by that puncture on the hand, but I don't know what it was. We'll have some analysis done, of course, but I expect nothing of that. There'll be no trace.'

'Unique case.'

'I wouldn't say that. You remember I thought General Blaker was poisoned. He was mixed up with Asiatics, too. There were queer circumstances about the death of that Greek millionaire in Rome two years ago. The world's old and men have been poisoning each other for five thousand years and science only began to look into it yesterday. There's a lot of drugs in the world that you can't buy at the chemist's.'

'Good Gad,' Lomas protested, 'we're in Scotland Yard, not the "Arabian Nights". What you mean is you can't do anything?'

'Even so. Can you? Who wanted him dead?'

'Nobody but a lunatic. He had no money to leave. He was on the best terms with his son. He was a popular old boy, never had an enemy. He had no secrets—most respectable —lived all his life in public.'

'And yet his son snatched at his keys before he was cold. And his dear old friend Osbert knew of his death before he was dead and made a bee-line for his papers. By the way, what was in his papers?'

Lomas shrugged. 'Our fellows are working at 'em.'

'And who is Osbert?'

'Well, you know, he's coming to see me. He put in his protest to the Commissioner, and they were going to turn him down, of course. But I thought I'd like to listen to Colonel Osbert.'

'Me, too,' said Reggie.

'By all means, my dear fellow. But he seems quite genuine. He is the executor. He is an old friend, about the oldest living. Not a spot on his record. Long Indian service.'

'Only son and daughter don't seem to trust him. Only he also is a bit Asiatic.'

'Oh, my dear Fortune—' Lomas was protesting when Colonel Osbert came.

You will find a hundred men like him on any day in the service clubs. He was small and brown and neat, even dapper, but a trifle stiff in the joints. His manner of speech was a drawl concluding with a bark.

Reggie lay back in his chair and admired the bland

fluency with which Lomas said nothing in reply to the
parade-ground demands of Colonel Osbert. Colonel
Osbert wanted to know (if we may reduce many sentences
to one) what Lomas meant by refusing him possession of
Sir Arthur Dean's papers. And Lomas continued to reply
that he meant nothing in particular.

'Sudden death at Ascot—in the Royal Enclosure, too,' he
explained. 'That's very startling and conspicuous. The poor
fellow hadn't been ill, as far as we can learn. Naturally we
have to seek for any explanation.'

So at last Osbert came out with: 'What, sir, you don't
mean to say, sir—suspect foul play?'

'Oh, my dear Colonel, you wouldn't suggest that?'

'I, sir? Never entered my head. Poor dear Arthur! A
shock, sir. A blow! Getting old, of course, like the rest of
us.'

'Ah, had he been failing?' said Reggie sympathetically.

'Well, well, well. We none of us grow younger, sir.'
Colonel Osbert shook his head. 'But upon my soul, Mr
Lomas, I don't understand the action of your department.'

'I'm so sorry you should say that,' Lomas sighed. 'Now I
wonder if you have particular reason for wanting Sir
Arthur's papers at once?'

'My good sir, I am his executor. It's my duty to take
charge of his papers.'

'Quite, quite. Well, they're all safe, you know. His death
must have been a great shock to you, Colonel.'

'Shock, sir? A blow, a blow. Poor dear Arthur!'

'Yes, too bad,' Lomas mourned: and voice and face were
all kindly innocence as he babbled on: 'I suppose you heard
about it from his son?'

Colonel Osbert paused to clear his throat. Colonel Osbert
stopped that one. 'Major Dean? No, sir. No. Point of fact, I
don't know who the fellow was. Some fellow called me up
on the 'phone and told me poor dear Arthur had fallen
down dead on the course. Upon my soul, I was knocked
over, absolutely knocked over. When I came to myself I
rushed round to secure his papers.'

'Why, did you think somebody would be after
them?'

'My dear sir!' Colonel Osbert protested. 'Really, now really. It was my duty. Arthur was always very strict with his papers. I thought of his wishes.'

'Quite, quite,' Lomas purred, and artless as ever he went on: 'Mrs Dean was round at the flat, too.'

'God bless my soul!' said Colonel Osbert.

'I wonder if you could tell me: is there anyone who would have an interest in getting hold of his papers?'

Colonel Osbert again cleared his throat. 'I can tell you this, sir. I don't understand the position of Mrs Dean and her husband. And I shall be glad, I don't mind owning, I shall be very glad to have poor dear Arthur's papers in my hands.'

'Ah, thank you so much,' said Lomas, and with bland adroitness got Colonel Osbert outside the door.

'He's not such a fool as he looks,' Reggie murmured. 'But there's better brains in it than his, Lomas, old thing. A bad business, quite a bad business.'

And then a clerk came in. Lomas read the letter he brought and said: 'Good Gad! You're an offensive person, Fortune. Why did you tell me to go to the Foreign Office? Here is the Foreign Office. Now we shall be in the affair for life. The Foreign Office wants me to see His Excellency Mustapha Firouz.'

'Accompanied by Sindbad the Sailor and Chu Chin Chow?' said Reggie. 'Who is he?'

'Oh, he's quite real. He's the Median Minister. He—Why what is it now?' The question was to the clerk, who had come back with a card.

'Says he's anxious to see you immediately, sir. It's very urgent, and he won't keep you long.'

'Major Dean,' Lomas read, and lifted an eyebrow.

'Oh, rather. Let 'em all come,' said Reggie.

It was Major Dean, and Major Dean ill at ease. He had a difficulty in beginning. He discovered Reggie. 'Hallo! I say, can you tell me anything?' he blurted out.

'I can't,' said Reggie sharply. 'I don't know why your father died,' and Major Dean winced.

'I thought you had something to tell us, Major,' Lomas said.

'Do you believe he was murdered? I've a right to ask that.'

'But it's a very grave suggestion,' Lomas purred. 'Do you know of anyone who had a motive for killing your father?'

'It's this filthy mystery,' the Major cried. 'If he was murdered, I suppose he was poisoned. But how?'

'Or why?' said Reggie.

The Major fidgeted. 'I dare say he knew too much,' he said. 'You know he was the adviser to the Median Government. He had some pretty serious stuff through his hands. I don't know what. He was always great on official secrecy. But I know he thought it was pretty damning for someone.'

'Ah, thanks very much,' Lomas said.

But the Major seemed unable to go.

'I mean to say, make sure you have all his papers and stick to 'em.'

Lomas and Reggie studied him. 'I wonder why you say that?' Lomas asked. 'The papers would naturally pass to Colonel Osbert.'

'I know. Osbert was the guv'nor's best pal, worse luck. I wouldn't trust him round the corner. That's what I mean. Now I've done it, I suppose;' he gave a grim chuckle. 'It is done, anyway;' and he was in a hurry to go.

Reggie stood up and stretched himself. 'This is pretty thick,' said he, 'and we've got His Excellency the Pasha of Nine Tales on the doorstep.'

Into the room was brought a man who made them feel short, a towering man draped in folds of white. Above that flowing raiment rose a majestic head, a head finely proportioned, framed in hair and beard of black strewn with grey. The face was aquiline and bold, but of a singular calm, and the dark eyes were veiled in thought. He bowed to each man twice, sat down and composed his robe about him, and it was long before he spoke. 'I thank you for your great courtesy;' each word came alone as if it was hard to him. 'I have this to say. He who is gone he was the friend of my people. To him we turned always and he did not fail. In him we had our trust. Now, sir, I must tell you we have our enemies, who are also, as it seems to us, your enemies. Those whom you call the Turks, they would do evil to us which would be evil to you. Of this we had writings in their hands and the hands of those they use. These I gave to him who is gone that he should tell us what we should do. For your ways are not our ways nor your law our law. Now he is gone, and I am troubled lest those papers fall again into the hands of the Turks.'

'Who is it that Your Excellency fears? Can you tell me of any man?' Lomas said.

'I know of none here. For the Turks are not here in the open and this is a great land of many people. Yet in all lands all things can be bought at a price. Even life and death. This only I say. If our papers go to your King and the Ministers of your King it is well and very well. If they are rendered to me that also may be well. But if they go I know not where, I say this is not just.'

'I can promise Your Excellency they will go before the Foreign Office.'

The Median stood up and bowed. 'In England I never seek justice in vain,' he said.

And when he was gone, 'Good Gad, how little he knows,' said Lomas. 'Well, Fortune?' but Reggie only lit a cigar and curled himself up on the sofa. 'What I like about you is that you never say I told you so. But you did. It is a Foreign Office touch,' and still Reggie silently smoked. 'Why, the thing's clear enough, isn't it?'

'Clear?' said Reggie. 'Oh, Peter! Clear?'

'Well, Sir Arthur had in his hands papers damaging to these blood-and-thunder Young Turks. It occurred to them that if he could die suddenly they might arrange to get the papers into their hands. So Sir Arthur is murdered, and either Osbert the executor or Major Dean the son is bribed to hand over the papers.'

'In the words of the late Tennyson,' said Reggie,

'And if it is so, so it is, you know;
And if it be so, so be it.

But it's not interesting, Lomas, old thing.'

'It would be interesting to hear you find a flaw in it,' said Lomas.

Reggie shook his head. 'Nary flaw.'

'For my part,' said Lomas with some heat, 'I prefer to understand why a crime was committed. I find it useful. But I am only a policeman.'

'And so say all of us.' Reggie sat up. 'Then why talk like a politician? Who did it and how are we going to do him in? That's our little job.'

'Whoever it was, we've bilked him,' said Lomas. 'He has got nothing for his pains. The papers will go before the Foreign Office and then back to the Median Legation. A futile crime. I find a good deal of satisfaction in that.'

'You're easy pleased then.' Reggie's amiability was passing away. 'A futile crime: thanks to the active and intelligent police force. But damn it, the man was murdered.'

'My dear Fortune, can I help it? It's not the first and it won't be the last murder in which there is no evidence. You're pleased to be bitter about it. But you can't even tell me how the man was murdered. A poison unknown to the twentieth-century expert. No doubt that annoys you. But you needn't turn and rend me. There is also one more murder unknown to the twentieth-century policeman. But I can't make evidence any more than you. We suspect either Osbert or Major Dean had a hand in it. But we don't know which and we don't know that either was the murderer. If we could prove that they were mixed up with the Young Turks, if we knew the man they dealt with we should have no case against them. Why, if we could find some Young Turk hireling was in the Royal Enclosure we should have no proof he was the murderer. We couldn't have,' Lomas shrugged. 'Humanly speaking, it's a case in which there can be no conviction.'

'My only aunt, don't I know that?' Reggie cried. 'And do you remember what the old Caliph said, "In England I never seek justice in vain"? Well, that stings, Lomas – humanly speaking.'

'Great heavens, what am I to do? What do you want to do?'

Reggie Fortune looked at him. The benign face of Reggie Fortune was set in hard lines. 'There's something about the voice of a brother's blood crying from the ground,' he said slowly.

'My dear fellow! Oh, my dear fellow, if you are going to preach,' Lomas protested.

'I'm not. I'm going to tea,' said Reggie Fortune. 'Elise has got the trick of some new cakes. They're somewhat genial.'

They did not meet again till the inquest.

It was horribly hot in court. The newspaper reporters of themselves would have filled, if given adequate space, a larger room. They sat in each other's pockets and thus yielded places to the general public, represented by a motley collection of those whom the coroner's officer permitted himself to call Nosey Parkers: frocks which might have come out of a revue chorus beside frocks which would well become a charwoman. And the Hon Sidney Lomas murmured in the ear of his henchman Superintendent Bell, 'I see several people who ought to be hanged, Bell, but no one who will give us the chance.'

Mr Reginald Fortune, that eminent surgeon, pathologist and what not, called to the witness-box, was languid and visibly bored with the whole affair. He surveyed the court in one weary, dreamy glance and gazed at the coroner as if seeking, but without hope, some reason for his unpleasant existence. Yes, he had seen Sir Arthur immediately after death. He had formed the opinion that Sir Arthur died of asphyxia and heart failure. Yes, heart failure and asphyxia. He was, however, surprised.

From the reporters' table there was a general look of hungry interest. But one young gentleman who had grown fat in the service of crime breathed heavily in his neighbour's ear: 'Nothing doing: I know old Fortune. This is a wash-out.'

Mr Fortune had lost interest in his own evidence. He was looking sleepily round the court. The coroner had to recall his wandering mind. 'You were surprised, Mr Fortune?'

'Oh, ah. Well, I couldn't explain the suddenness of the attack, the symptoms and so forth. So with the assistance of Dr Harvey I made a further examination. We went into the matter with care and used every known test. There is no evidence to be found that any other factor was present than the natural causes of death.'

'But that does not explain the sudden failure of the heart.'

'I don't explain it,' said Reggie. 'I can't.'

'Medicine,' said the coroner sagely, 'still has its myster-
ies. We must remember, gentlemen, that Sir Arthur had
already completed our allotted span, the Psalmist's three
score years and ten. I am much obliged to you, Mr Fortune.'

And after that, as the fat young gentleman complained,
there was nothing in it. The jury found that Sir Arthur's
death was from natural causes and that they sympathized
with the family. So much for the Ascot mystery. There
remains the sequel.

When the court broke up and sought, panting, the open
air, 'He is neat, sir, isn't he?' said Lomas's henchman,
Superintendent Bell. 'Very adroit, is Mr Fortune. That
couldn't have been much better done.' And Lomas smiled.
It was in each man's simple heart that the Criminal Investigation Department was well rid of a bad business. They
sought Reggie to give him lunch.

But Reggie was already outside; Reggie was strolling, as
one for whom time has no meaning, towards the station.
He was caught up by the plump young reporter, who
would like you to call him a crime specialist. 'Well, Mr
Fortune,' he said in his ingratiating way, 'good morning.
How are you, sir? I say, you have put it across us in the
Dean case.'

The crime specialist then had opportunities for psycho-
logical study as Mr Fortune's expression performed a series
of quick changes. But it settled down into bland and ami-
able surprise. 'My dear fellow,' said Mr Fortune, 'how are
you? But what's the trouble? There's nothing in the Dean
case, never was.'

'No, that's just it. And we were all out for a first-class
crime story. After all the talk there's been, natural causes is
pretty paltry.'

Reggie laughed. 'Sorry, sorry. We can't make crimes for
you. But why did you talk? There was nothing to talk
about.'

'I say, you know, that's a bit thick,' the crime specialist
protested.

'My dear chap,' said Reggie modestly, 'if the doctor on

the spot hadn't happened to be me, you would never have thought of the case. Nothing else in it.'

'Oh, well, come now, Mr Fortune! I mean to say – what about the CID holding up all the old man's papers and turning down his executor?'

Reggie was not surprised, he was bewildered. 'Say it again slowly and distinctly,' he entreated, and when that was done he was as one who tries not to laugh. 'And very nice, too. My dear fellow, what more do you want? There's a story for you.'

'Well, it's never been officially denied,' said the young man.

'Fancy that!' Reggie chuckled.

'But between ourselves, Mr Fortune—'

'It's a great story,' Reggie chuckled. 'But really – Well, I ask you!' and he slid away.

In the hotel lounge he found Bell and Lomas and cocktails. 'Pleasure before business, as ever,' he reproached them, and ordered one for himself.

'And what have you been doing, then?' Lomas asked.

'I have been consoling the Fourth Estate. That great institution the Press, Mr Lomas, sir. Through one of Gilligan's young lions. Out of the mouths of babes and sucklings—'

'I wish you wouldn't talk to reporters,' Lomas complained.

'You're so haughty. By the way, what was Ludlow Blenkinhorn doing here?' He referred to a solicitor of more ability than standing. 'Osbert was here and his solicitor, the young Deans and their solicitor. Who was old Blenkinhorn representing?'

Bell and Lomas looked at each other. 'Didn't see the fellow,' said Lomas.

'Mr Fortune's quite right, sir. Blenkinhorn was standing with the public. And that's odd, too.'

'Highly odd. Lomas, my dear old thing, I wish you'd watch Blenkinhorn's office and Osbert's flat for any chaps who look a bit exotic, a bit foreign—and follow him up if you find one.'

Lomas groaned. 'Surely we've done with the case.'

'Ye-es. But there's some fellow who hasn't. And he has a pretty taste in poisons. And he's still wanting papers.'

'We've nothing to act on, you know,' Lomas protested.

'Oh, not a thing, not a thing. But he might have.'

Lomas nodded and Superintendent Bell went to the telephone.

When Mr Fortune read *The Daily Post* in the morning he smiled upon his devilled kidneys. Its report of the inquest was begun with a little pompous descriptive work. 'The mystery of the Ascot Tragedy was solved yesterday. In the cold sanity of the coroner's court the excitement of the last few days received its quietus. Two minutes of scientific evidence from Mr Fortune—' and so on until young omniscience worked up to its private little scoop. 'The melodramatic rumours of sensational developments in the case have thus only availed to expose the fatuity of their inventors.' (This was meant for some rival papers.) 'It may now be stated bluntly that nothing in the case ever gave rise to speculation among well-informed people, and that the stories of impounding documents and so forth have no foundation in fact.'

But about lunch time Mr Fortune received a curt summons from the Hon Sidney Lomas and instantly obeyed it. 'Well, you know, I thought I should be hearing from you,' he smiled. 'I felt, as it were, you couldn't live without me long.'

'Did you, by Jove!' said Lomas bitterly. 'I've been wishing all the morning you had been dead some time. Look at that!' He tossed across the table a marked copy of *The Daily Post*.

'Yes, I was enjoying that at breakfast. A noble institution, the British Press, Lomas. A great power. If you know how to use it.'

'I wish to God you wouldn't spoof reporters. It's a low taste. And it's a damned nuisance. I can't contradict the rag and—'

'No, you can't contradict it. I banked on that,' Reggie chuckled.

'Did you indeed? And pray what the devil are you at? I have had Osbert here raving mad—'

'Yes, I thought it would stir up Osbert. What's his line?'

'Wants the papers, of course. And as you very well know, confound you, they're all at the Foreign Office, the cream of them, and likely to be. He says we've no right to keep them after this. Nonsense, of course, but devilish inconvenient to answer. And at last the old man was quite pathetic, says it isn't fair to him to give out we haven't touched the papers. No more it is. He was begging me to contradict it officially. I could hardly get rid of him.'

'Busy times for Lomas.'

'Damn it, I have been at it all the morning. Old Ludlow Blenkinhorn turned up, too.'

'I have clicked, haven't I?' Reggie chuckled.

'Confound you. He says he has a client with claims on the estate and is informed by the executor that all papers have been taken by us. Now he has read your damned article and he wants to know if the executor is lying.'

'That is a conundrum, isn't it? And who is Mr Ludlow Blenkinhorn's client?'

'He didn't say, of course.'

'What a surprise. And your fellows watching his office, do they say?'

Lomas took up a scrap of paper. 'They have sent us something. A man of foreign or mulatto appearance called on him first thing this morning. Was followed to a Bayswater lodging-house. Is known there as Sherif. Mr A. Sherif. Thought to be an Egyptian.'

'The negro or Hamitic heel!' Reggie murmured. 'Do you remember, Lomas, old thing?'

'Good Gad!' Lomas dropped his eye-glass. 'But what the devil can we do?'

'Watch and pray,' said Reggie. 'Your fellows watch Sherif and Blenkinhorn and Osbert and you pray. Do you pray much, Lomas?'

They went in fact to lunch. They were not long back when a detective speaking over the telephone reported that a man of mulatto appearance had called on Colonel Osbert. Reggie sprang up. 'Come on, Lomas. We'll have them in the act and bluff the whole thing out of them.'

'What act?'

'Collusion. This Egyptian-Syrian-negroid-Young Turk and the respectable executor. Come on, man.'

In five minutes they were mounting to Colonel Osbert's flat. His servant could not say whether Colonel Osbert was at home. Lomas produced his card. 'Colonel Osbert will see me,' he announced, and fixed the man with a glassy stare.

'Well, sir, I beg pardon, sir. There's a gentleman with him.'

'At once,' said Lomas and walked into the hall.

The man still hesitated. From one of the rooms could be heard voices in some excitement. Lomas and Reggie made for that door. But as they approached there was a cry, a horrible shrill cry, and the sound of a scuffle. Reggie sprang forward. Someone rushed out of the room and Reggie, the smaller man, went down before him. Lomas clutched at him and was kicked in the stomach. The fellow was off. Reggie picked himself out of the hatstand and ran after him. Lomas, in a heap, gasping and hiccoughing, fumbled in his pocket. 'B-b-blow,' he stammered to the stupefied servant, and held out a whistle. 'Like hell. Blow!'

A long peal sounded through the block of flats.

Down below a solid man strolled out of the porter's lodge just as a gentleman of dark complexion and large feet was hurrying through the door. The solid man put out a leg. Another solid man outside received the gentleman on his bosom. They had then some strenuous moments. By the time Reggie reached them three hats were on the ground, but a pair of handcuffs clasped the coffee-coloured wrists.

'His pockets,' Reggie panted, 'his waistcoat pockets.'

The captive said something which no one understood, and struggled. One of the detectives held out a small white-metal case. Reggie took from it a hypodermic syringe. 'I didn't think you were so up-to-date,' said Reggie. 'What did you put in it? Well, well, I suppose you won't tell me. Take him away.'

He went back to find Lomas and the servant looking at Colonel Osbert. Colonel Osbert lay on the floor. There was froth at his lips and on his wrist a spot of blood. Reggie knelt down beside him . . .

'Too late?' Lomas said hoarsely.

Reggie rose. 'Well, you can put it that way,' he said. 'It's the end.'

In Lomas's room Reggie spread himself on a sofa and watched Lomas drink whisky and soda. 'A ghastly business,' Lomas said: he was still pale and unsteady. 'That creature is a wild beast.'

'He'll go where he belongs,' said Reggie, who was eating bread and butter. 'All according to plan.'

'Plan? My God, the man runs amok!'

'Oh, no, no, no. He wanted those papers for his employers. He contracted with Osbert to hand them over when Dean was dead. He murdered Dean and Osbert couldn't deliver the goods. So I told him through the papers that Osbert had them. He thought Osbert was bilking him and went to have it out with him. Osbert didn't satisfy him, he was sure he had been done and he made Osbert pay for it. All according to plan.'

Lomas set down his glass. 'Fortune,' he said nervously, 'Fortune—do you mean—when you put that in the paper —you meant the thing to end like this?'

'Well, what are we here for?' said Reggie. 'But you know you're forgetting the real interest of the case.'

'Am I?' said Lomas weakly.

'Yes. What is his poison?'

'Oh, good Gad,' said Lomas.

HORSE OF DEATH

by Ralph Straus

If there is one theme that has fascinated writers about the Turf more than any other it is that of being able to prophesy winners. Not by luck, or even by fixing the race, but simply by being able to foresee which horse is going to win. Among all such stories that I have read, 'Horse of Death' is quite outstanding, both in terms of the plot and the remarkable denouement.

The author, Ralph Straus, was a popular novelist and biographer whose abiding interest was in the Sport of Kings, for he listed his hobbies in Who's Who *quite simply as 'Horse Racing and Real Tennis'. His interest developed while he was a student at Cambridge, and race meetings are a feature of some of his most popular books, including* The Unseemly Adventure *and* A Whip for the Woman. *Straus also ran his own private printing press, and from this issued a number of tracts about racing which are now much sought-after by collectors of racing memorabilia. There is, however, no better story with which to represent him in this collection than the narrative of the mysterious events surrounding the 'Horse of Death'.*

*   *   *

John Chester and I were sitting in the smoking-room of the House of Commons—I had been listening to the Indian debate—when the conversation turned on the matter of coincidence.

'Has it ever occurred to you,' he asked, 'that the most extraordinary thing about coincidence is its rarity? What I mean is this: if a husband dies in Switzerland or California or Cape Town, and his loving wife sees him weeding his garden at Clapham at the identical moment, the papers make use of the lady to the extent, sometimes, of a column. Similar cases are quoted, and if it happens to be September at the time, a regular correspondence ensues. You know the kind of thing. But surely the really singular part of the business is the number of husbands who die in Switzerland or California or Cape Town *without* showing themselves in their garden at Clapham.'

I could not help laughing.

'But isn't it so?'

'I dare say.'

'Of course it is, but everybody is naturally more interested in the one case in which, according to the loving wife, the man does show himself, and, forgetting the nine hundred and ninety-nine other cases in which he doesn't, assumes that here is clear proof of supernatural phenomena.'

'On the other hand,' I ventured, 'some well-authenticated cases are so very extraordinary—'

'But why shouldn't they be extraordinary? Everything is extraordinary. Why, I could give you an instance . . .'

'Please do,' said I, and smiled. John Chester was nicely trapped for a story, and knew it, for he shrugged his shoulders and emptied his glass, and passed me a cigar and lit one himself, and smoked for a few moments in silence.

* * *

'A few years ago,' he began, 'I was knocked up with work and went down to the little fishing village of Claniston, in Kent. I had motored through it once or twice before, and had been given excellent luncheons at the inn there, and the landlady had told me then that I might have a bed on reasonable terms whenever I chose. Claniston is miles away from a railway station, and it seemed just the place for a really tired man. So down I went and proposed to do nothing for a week but eat and sleep and look at the sea.

'I arrived, I remember, in the afternoon, and as I was being driven to the inn I noticed in a field just off the road preparations for one of those fairs which move round the country, staying no more than a night or two at each village. And Mrs Larkins, my landlady, remarked on the coincidence of my arrival and the fair's.

'"We shall all of us be there tonight," she informed me, "me and my son and Eliza." She spoke in tones which implied that I was expected to accompany them, and go I did, with Mrs Larkins, and her great hulking villainous son, and Eliza, who was the maid-of-all-work. We became separated before long, I am glad to say, but by that time I had ridden on the roundabout, and seen the fattest lady on earth—she was nearly as stout as old Lady Raynescourt —and had felt sad for the human skeleton, and had watched those detestable swinging-boats, and thrown wooden balls at coconuts, and had witnessed what was called for some curious reason a prize-fight, and in general done what was expected of me. I had even been squirted by some village maiden keen to show me that she was as good as myself. A fair, you know, is a splendid thing to make you young again.

'I suppose I had been there half an hour, and was well inured to the screeching strains of the automatic orchestra and the shouting and the hundreds of other noises, and was about to walk home, when I saw a small crowd gather outside one of the tents on the outskirts of the fair. I walked across and listened to a man dressed as Mephistopheles, who was howling at the top of his raucous voice.

'For the small sum of fourpence, I learned, you could witness, inside his tent, the wonderful exhibition of Professor Torino, whose clairvoyant exploits had charmed and mystified every crowned head and learned scientist in Europe. The crowd seemed uncertain what to do, but I, as you know, have a liking for such things, and I boldly made my way up to Mephistopheles, paid my fourpence like a man, and was shown into the tent.

'Here there were two or three rows of chairs facing a rude stage hidden from view by a red curtain with yellow flowers painted on it. For nearly a minute I was the sole audience, but my patronage had evidently decided the crowd, for it streamed in, and in a very short while the tent was full.

Mephistopheles appeared, walked up to the curtain, and drew it aside to disclose an antique sofa, behind which an acetylene lamp was burning with peculiar brilliance.

'I was rather pleased with that acetylene lamp. It hinted at mystery, and the audience was obviously impressed. Little things like that, you know, mean much to an entertainment such as Mephistopheles was about to give us. I prepared to enjoy myself.

'Well, Mephistopheles climbed on to the stage, which stood a foot off the ground, and made another speech. That was his great point. I think that man could have made speeches on any subject under the sun. He informed us that at enormous cost he had secured the services of the two geniuses who had mystified and charmed all the kings and queens they had ever met during a career which had extended . . . and so on. That took about ten minutes, and we were just beginning to be a little impatient when he gave a half-turn and beckoned to somebody behind.

'Then a man with grey hair and a black moustache came on and bowed awkwardly. He was followed by a thin woman dressed in a dirty white garment that gave out a faint rustle. Her sunken eyes and tired face suggested—oh, everything that was horrible and degrading and ugly. Then her husband, in a feeble voice, gave an epitome of what he proposed to do. He muttered some unintelligible information about the various universities which had presumably honoured him, showing us at the same time a silver medal at his breast. Then he made some passes over his wife. The thin woman shivered and fell back—with some skill—on to the sofa where she lay motionless.

'Then we were invited to put any question we chose to "the lady in the trance". I watched the audience carefully. They did not quite know what to make of the thing, and nobody spoke. So, in order to set the ball rolling, I asked a question about a certain colleague of mine, and the reply was—what shall I say?—well, it was skilful. It was so skilful that it aroused my admiration, and feeling that I was expected to say something, I murmured "Quite right", and clapped my hands. The audience, duly impressed, followed suit.

'"Any further questions you would care to put?" asked Torino.

'"The winner of the Bridbury Stakes?" asked somebody behind me. I turned round and saw the dirty-faced son of my landlady.

'"Alas! we cannot answer any such question." Torino's tones were apologetic. "The law of the land . . . the police . . ." He trailed off into some explanation.

For a moment I feared trouble—Claniston is a sporting village—but a rustic who had not heard young Larkins' question bawled out an inquiry about some matter of local interest. His friends backed him up, and the Bridbury Stakes were forgotten. Torino turned to his wife, who gave an answer that appeared popular, for there was loud applause. And the entertainment continued until Mephistopheles decided that we had been given our full fourpennyworth, and passed round a bag for donations. Then we slipped out, and I started to walk back to the inn.'

*   *   *

John Chester paused to attend to his cigar.

'Now I don't pretend,' he continued, 'to give you reasons for thinking that Mme Torino was never in a trance at all. That is beside the point—and for all I care she may have been in that state which the newspapers and popular entertainers like to call clairvoyant. The real point is this: it was a very dark night, and, contrary to my expectation, I was not in the least tired. That is the infernal irony of things. The first opportunity I had had in which to laze I felt extremely wide-awake and energetic. Sleep was imposs-ible. The night was warm, and I decided to take a walk over the cliffs. Mrs Larkins had given me a latch-key.

'Well, I must have walked over the downs for nearly an hour before I came once again into Claniston. I had passed not a soul, and the night was so dark that at times I could hardly see my way at all. Claniston is sufficiently primitive to have no lamps at all in its single street. The private entrance to my inn was at the end of a narrow passage. I had come, as I thought, to this passage, but must have walked up another path which led to the door of a large barn, standing next to the inn and used for storing hay and straw. I was about to go back when I heard a curious sound like a moan, and stood still. Then a harsh voice swore, and a thin ray of light came through a chink in the door.

'Wondering what was happening, I put my eye to that chink, and witnessed as delightful a little melodrama as ever the old Lyceum audiences can have enjoyed. For there on the carpet of straw was the estimable Larkins pointing a revolver, whether loaded or not I cannot tell you, at the unfortunate Torino and his wife. I have never seen two people so terrified. There was a single candle set on an old box, and it was casting almost as curious a light as the acetylene lamp of the rather more legitimate entertainment I had been witnessing an hour ago.

'Well, I watched and listened. I ought, I suppose, to have fetched the village constable, and so helped him to well-earned promotion, but I did not. I just watched, fascinated. And then I understood the meaning of it all, for Torino was making the usual passes over his wife, who fell back on to the straw and lay still.

'"What do you wish to know?" asked the poor man, retaining even in these trying conditions a professional air.

'"Oi want yew to answer me just this one 'ere question. Wot's the 'orse as 'll win the Bridbury Stakes next Thursday? Now, none o' your rotting nonsense. I know as 'ow yew can tell these things, and in this 'ere case, yew've got to."

'So that was it, you see: a polite little piece of—well, blackmail, carried out quite securely in this old barn, with an unfortunate and trespassing witness in the shape of an inquisitive member of Parliament.

'Torino, I could see, was smiling pathetically. I wondered what he would do. Here was surely a test of his genuineness. On the other hand it might merely be a test of his artistry. Which it was I'll leave for you to decide.'

'What did he say?' I asked, unable to refrain longer from the interruptions which long experience has taught me are exceedingly distasteful (except at certain well-marked moments) to John Chester.

'He said a thing which gave him my sympathy. He looked at that hulking bully of a Larkins and said: "Then you believe in my wife's powers of clairvoyance?"

'The man's lower lip stuck out as he played with his revolver. "None o' that," he said, and I could see that he was suspicious of trickery. "None of yer long words as a feller can't make 'ead or tail of. Oi wants a plain answer to a plain question. Then we can say good night. Now, wot's the 'orse as'll win the Bridbury Stakes? Oi thinks Oi knows, but Oi wants to 'ear yewer old woman say the same thing." He smiled grimly.

'"You wish to know the winner of the Bridbury Stakes, run next Thursday? I will ask my wife. But you promise to go if we give you an answer?"

'"We settled all that afore," said my landlady's son, showing irritation. "Yew keep to yewer part of the business, an' Oi'll keep to mine."

'Which seemed fair. I waited, not daring to move. Torino had turned to his wife, muttering words which I could not hear. Larkins looked on with interest. The second entertainment that evening had every chance of being more satisfactory to him than the first, in addition to which it had cost him fourpence less. I could almost bring myself to admire his determination. Quite a lot of skill must have been expended on staging this scene in the barn, and I wondered how he had managed to do it.

'And then the woman spoke. She spoke in perfectly clear tones. I heard every word.

'"There is a park," she said, "with crowds of people. They're all shouting. Something is exciting them. I don't quite understand what they're doing. Ah, there is a horse, and another galloping past them. It is a race course. They are cheering a horse coming out of the paddock." She paused for a moment, and her audience's mouth opened wide with astonishment. He forgot to point the revolver at the professor. "Yes, a lot of horses," she went on in her dull, even tones, "are coming from the paddock. I can see them distinctly . . . but something is happening. I can't quite understand. A big brown horse with a white star on its forehead . . ."

'"Yes, yes, that's White Star," cried Larkins excitedly. "Go on, Missus, that's my fancy."

'"This brown horse—why, it has no rider! It must have broken away. The jockey has been thrown at the paddock gates. Oh, it has kicked a man near the railings. Poor man, he has been kicked badly. Yes, I can see distinctly. It is dashing down the course. The jockey is following. Now they have captured the horse. It is restive, but I think it will win. Yes, I am sure it will win . . ."

'"Gawd! White Star!" shouted the audience. "She means White Star right enough. Go on. Will it win? My fancy. Oi'll get twelve as sure as . . . Go on, Missus. If it wins, Oi'll . . ."

'The revolver was forgotten.

'The woman went on speaking. "Yes, the jockey is on the horse again. The man who was kicked is dying. He'll die in a moment. Can't you see him dying with the crowd round him?"

'"'Ere, that's nuth'n t' do with the race. Come on an' tell us if White Star wins."

'"He's dead," said the woman in reply. "Now the horses are at the post. They've started. They're running round the bend. I know the winner. It's the horse that escaped from the paddock. It is third now. The jockey has red and white colours on his coat. I can see them. Can't you see them? Look, the people are cheering. There! My horse has won—the big horse with the white star . . ." She stopped, and Torino turned to his audience.

'"That's all," said he.

'"White Star?" asked Larkins.

'"Yes, White Star will win the Bridbury Stakes."

'"My fancy," repeated the man pompously, "an' a damn good price it'll be, too. Back it." Torino shook his head sadly. The other put the revolver into his pocket. "Thanks. 'Ere, give us yewer 'and. Yew've behaved like a gen'elman. Shake."

'I waited to see Torino put out a trembling hand, and silently walked down that dark passage and away over the downs again. I could not go in just then, and it must have been one o'clock before I finally turned in.

'I was wondering, you see, what I should do.'

'You went, of course, to see the race run?'

John Chester smiled. 'My dear fellow,' said he, 'don't you see that the Torinos were clever people. They knew that the man would go as soon as they answered his question, and go I've no doubt he did. How the question was answered could hardly matter, could it? Besides, if the Torinos were able to prophesy the winners of races, you don't suppose they would have been performing in booths for a bare pittance?'

'No, I don't,' said I.

'Very well, then,' said John Chester for the second time that evening.

'I arranged to go to Bridbury on the day of the race, and a very remarkable race it proved to be.'

'But I suppose White Star won the race?' I persisted.

'It was a remarkable race,' was all the reply I received, and was conscious that my interruption had been out of place.

*   *   *

'Yes,' he repeated after a pause that was considerably longer than usual, 'it was a remarkable race. I shall not easily forget it. And I am not a superstitious person. I am not even a person who cares particularly about risking his money on horses. But that day at Bridbury I put two pounds each way on a large horse with a white star on its forehead. I remember being told at the time by Sir John Lade that the horse had no chance whatever against his own animal, but pointed out that I was there for a holiday, and reserved to myself the luxury of backing my, or rather Madame Torino's fancy.

'Well, the great race came on, and the ring was shouting itself hoarse. I discovered that Sir John Lade's horse, Otway the Second, was favourite. Denizen came next, White Star a mere outsider at twelves. One or two horses had come out of the paddock, and were cantering up the course. I myself was standing in one of the enclosures.

'Suddenly I was aware of a slight stir near the paddock gates, and a moment later a riderless horse dashed out and began a mad gallop after the others. It swerved towards the railings just opposite to where I was standing. The crowd, of course, was pressing. One man, I could see, was leaning forward with a knee on the ground. He seemed to irritate the animal, which in another second had struck out at him, kicking his head . . .

'Oh, yes, it sounds curious, but it undoubtedly happened much as Mme Torino had foretold, and I began to see a chance of winning some money. It was all done so quickly that few realized what was happening until all was over. The man who had been kicked fell back with a groan, and they took him away. Then the jockey who had been thrown by the gates came running out. They secured the runaway further down the course, and in a few moments all was quiet.

'The race was run.'

'With White Star the winner?'

'If you studied your Racing Calender, you would know that he won by what is called a short head from Otway the Second. I remember chaffing Sir John Lade about the horse afterwards. I won nearly thirty pounds, and blessed the Torinos.'

'It was an extraordinary coincidence,' said I.

'Wasn't it?' smiled John Chester. 'But that, as you have guessed, was not all.'

'Not all?'

'The man who was kicked died a few minutes later.'

'Just as the woman had predicted!'

'Precisely!'

There came another pause, but shorter this time, while John Chester puffed at his cigar. 'I walked across the course,' he went on, 'and found a small crowd standing round the man who'd been kicked. Two men with a stretcher arrived at the same moment. I saw them lift up the bleeding figure. Not a pleasant sight. No. I recognised him, too.'

'You . . .'

'Oh, of course, the man who'd been kicked was young Larkins.'

The division bell was ringing.

HORSESHOES FOR LUCK

by Anthony Gilbert

For a good many years òne of the best kept secrets in crime and mystery story circles was that the popular author 'Anthony Gilbert' was in actual fact a woman, Lucy Beatrice Malleson. Perhaps because her mother wanted her to be a teacher rather than the writer she herself set out to become, Miss Malleson built an aura of mystery around her identity as difficult to penetrate as those she created in her many successful novels. It must surely have amused her—and also given her satisfaction—before the secret came out, to read reviews such as this one in the News Chronicle: *'I know of no author of this type of tale who is more skilled at making a good story seem brilliant by sheer force of writing and clear perception of* his *own characters.'*

Miss Malleson was also a follower of racing, and several meetings provide the background to important moments in her stories. In the following short story, 'Horseshoes for Luck', her knowledge of the Turf is clearly evident in a mystery which her police sleuth, Inspector Field, sets out to solve . . .

* * *

'Luck?' said the stranger on my left. 'Tell that to the Marines. There's no such thing. It's nothing but superstition, and any sensible man will tell you the same. Look at these people that won't see the new moon through glass, throw salt over their left shoulder, won't walk under a ladder or sit down thirteen at table—are they any luckier than anyone else? You bet they aren't. I had a pal once, full of ideas about one thing being lucky and something else being fatal. He bought a pub, a free house it was, and he called it the "Three Horseshoes". Full of what he was going to do with it, make it into a regular hotel, with a garage and a bowling green. Bound to be lucky with a name like that, he thought. But the first week some loafer smashed up the bar, and the second week his wife skipped off with a commercial traveller, who hadn't even paid his account, and the week after that the barmaid helped herself to the till.'

'He should ha' nailed three horseshoes over the door,' said someone else.

'That wouldn't ha' made a scrap of difference,' said my companion scornfully. 'There's no such thing as luck. What do you say?' and he turned expectantly to Inspector Field.

'Anyone can have horseshoes for me,' Field said promptly. 'They're like that other superstition, that a man that's a gambler must be a good sportsman. It doesn't follow. Ever heard of Cheesehampton?'

Two or three men nodded. 'They've got some very fine stables there.'

'It's because of those very stables I went down there. It was a hotbed of racing folk. The time I was there was just before Goodwood, and I was there because one racing man wasn't quite the sportsman you might expect.

'The day before I started we'd heard from the local police that the people at Cheesehampton were being bothered with anonymous letters. You keep getting outbreaks in various parts of the country and sometimes they're dangerous and sometimes not. Mostly they're the work of lunatics. All sorts of quite ridiculous people were getting them, people who had no more reason to fear the police than an archangel. It wasn't so much that the letters constituted blackmail—mostly they were too silly for that—but some folk were getting upset and it was felt generally that the thing should be stopped. Whoever was responsible didn't ask for money: he'd put his meaning something like this:

> You think no one knows what happened at Brighton on the 4th June last. But I do. Beware.

It was like a story in a kids' magazine, but there must have been some truth in some of the suggestions, because people were jumpy. Even people who hadn't had letters were getting that way. Guilty conscience, I suppose.

'Well, this had been going on for some time when the writer overstepped his mark. There was a big man there called Bayliss, a rabid race goer with his own stables. Apart from horses he really hadn't any life at all. He wasn't married, never opened a book, never heard a note of music. It was horses with him all the time. I'd been at Cheese-hampton only a few hours when he came in waving one of these silly sheets.

'"Look here," he shouted, "I'll tell you who this fellow is. Read this."

'So I read it. It was the usual thing, written on the same kind of paper in the same obviously faked hand. It said:

If you do not withdraw Bluebeard from the race for the Cup, the whole world shall hear the truth about A.

'"Who's A.?" I said, and he told me Alcock, his jockey, who was going to ride Bluebeard for the Cup.

'"What's this chap talking about?" I went on, and Bayliss looked murder and said: "About a year ago I had a couple of horses running in a big race, and biggish odds on both. I backed one heavily myself, and wouldn't say anything definite about the other. She was a mare and very tempera-mental, particularly in wet weather, as mares often are. That was a drenching summer, and though she could make a very good pace if conditions suited her, she was no use unless she was pleased. Alcock was up that day, and if anyone could have coaxed a spurt out of her he was the man, but she was sulky, and even he could do nothing. A neighbour of mine, another racing man called Grey, whose property marches with mine, had a lot of money on her; he'd seen Alcock exercising her and knew she could make a fine pace. Of course, I didn't tell him not to put money on her—what man would? Anyway, I'm superstitious enough to believe that if you start warning people against your horse it'll get the inevitable reaction. The result was that Grey backed her heavily and lost a packet; afterwards he came round breathing death and swore that Alcock had pulled the beast. It was so vilely untrue that I was tempted to take action. I told him, anyhow, he could go to the stewards, but naturally he wasn't going to chance being run in for libel, and the damages would have been pretty heavy. I'm well-known round here and so is Alcock, and Grey hadn't a leg to stand on, and knew it. Still, he did what he could by dropping hints here and there, nothing definite enough to take up, but deucedly unpleasant for me, and galling as hell for Alcock. Fortunately, from my point of view, he's not a very popular chap, and no one paid much attention. But what I am afraid of is that if the yarn goes round often enough, he may shake Alcock's confidence. The boy's got nothing to fear, actually, but if he gets the notion that anyone believes this ridiculous yarn, it'll shake him to pieces, and he'll be no use to me or anyone else. And Grey knows that. Naturally, I'm inclined to back my own stable, but I'm not the only man hereabouts that knows that Bluebeard, with Alcock up, will sweep the field next week."

'I hung around picking up scraps of local talk, and I was told that Bayliss hadn't overstated the case. One man said: "If Alcock were on a rocking-horse he'd get somewhere," which might be intended as a compliment, but made the story Grey was spreading sound a bit more likely.

'Bayliss told me he hadn't any intention of taking any notice of the threats, but all the same he wanted some assurance that no harm should befall his jockey. I asked him what proof he had that Grey had actually written the letters, and he had to admit that there was none.

'"Still," he urged, "no one else has a motive, while Grey's reeks to Heaven. He's running a horse of his own, and he backed him some time ago at very heavy odds. He's not a bad horse, either, but he won't stand a chance with Bluebeard, and both of us know it. Grey's in desperately low water, and everything depends on his beast winning the race."

'It appeared that Grey's horse was second favourite, but there didn't seem much doubt in the minds of those best qualified to know that Bluebeard would beat him, though it might be a close thing. I found out, too, that Bayliss's story of Grey being very deeply dipped was no more than the truth.

'"He'd get me warned off, if he could, but since he can't, he'll stop at nothing to put Bluebeard or Alcock or both where they can't threaten him."

'You can see for yourselves it wasn't a very easy position. I couldn't accuse Grey of being the author of the anonymous letters, but it didn't seem to me any harm going round to see him. After all, he might have had one himself. Grey was a laconic sort of fellow; no, he said, he hadn't been pestered; people with nothing to hide generally weren't, which shows you how much he knew about human nature, or life, for that matter. I must say I didn't take to him—a big swaggering sort of chap, too well-dressed for me. I like tailor's dummies in a window, but nowhere else. Besides, his manner irritated me. You could see him putting a policeman in his place every time he opened his mouth. I came away feeling a good deal of sympathy for Bayliss.

'Coming through the village I ran against Bayliss again.

'"Look here, Inspector," he said, "I've had another of these blasted things; and this time it's deadly serious."

'The new letter read:

You had better withdraw your horse while you have the chance. Alcock will never ride him.

'"That's tantamount to a threat of murder," said Bayliss excitedly.

'"Threat of bodily harm perhaps," I agreed, "or it might just mean there's some monkey trick on foot to keep him out of the way till after the race. You'd better keep an eye on him."

'I wasn't able to get any definite evidence against Grey, but I thought I'd feel a lot more comfortable when the race had been run. Going back, I thought it all sounded a bit silly; this is England, and you don't kidnap men in broad daylight. But it didn't sound so silly twenty-four hours later when a man as white as paper came to find me and said: "If you please, sir, there's been an accident. It's Alcock.

They've just found him in a clump of bushes over by Milton Heath."

'"What's wrong with him?" I asked sharply, and though I think by this time I expected the answer I got, I felt a bit sick when the fellow said: "He's dead all right. Been dead for some hours. Mr Bayliss is half crazy."

'"Thrown?" I asked, and the chap looked sick in his turn and told me: "Must have been. And Bluebeard lost his head—he was always an excitable brute; no one but Alcock could ride him—and trampled on him."

'I went along. They hadn't moved the body, because Bayliss, as soon as he heard, swore it was foul play, though it was as clear a case of a man being kicked by a horse as ever I'd seen. Alcock must have gone clean over the beast's head, we decided. Bluebeard had pitched him alongside a bracken clump, and the horse, either frightened by the accident or hurt itself, had done the rest.

'"It looks as though he saw Bluebeard meant trouble," said Bayliss, who, I believe, was upset about the boy for his own sake, quite apart from losing the race. "Look at the grass here; he must have tried to drag himself out of the horse's way. It's all crushed and trampled."

'"Did he know this part of the country?" I asked, and was told that he brought the horse here every day.

'"Of course, I never supposed he'd come to grief, riding, and you can say what you like, Inspector, this isn't a natural death. Someone scared the horse crazy. He wouldn't have lashed out at his jockey otherwise."

'I suggested the usual things—a sudden shot, though who'd be shooting there I couldn't suggest—a piece of paper blowing under Bluebeard's nose, though there was no sign of any—but Bayliss wasn't satisfied.

'All the same, it was difficult to see what else could have happened. The doctor said there could be no doubt about cause of death. Evidence showed that the upper part of the head had been crushed by a horse's hoof.

'"Are there any marks of ill-usage on the horse?" I asked, and Bayliss said he was all right except for a pair of cut knees, but naturally he wouldn't be able to run in the race forty-eight hours hence. That was when I began to think that, after all, there might be something fishy about the whole affair. A fall on turf and bracken doesn't result in cut knees. Grazing and scraping—yes—but cuts—no. When I saw the horse I got more suspicious still; I'm handier with a motor cycle, I confess, when it comes to getting about, but even I know a bad cut when I see one. The place where the accident had happened was just over a slope where a few trees grew, and as I thought about it a new idea came to me. I walked up to the trees and began to examine them, and I found, as I'd half begun to expect, marks on the trunks of two of them, where the bark had been rasped very recently.

'"What's the matter?" Bayliss demanded.

'"Just what I want to know," I told him, and I began to hunt on the ground. I was remembering Bayliss's comment that the grass round the place where Alcock lay had been badly trampled. Well, I found the same condition here. Half a dozen men might have been stamping on it. Alcock hadn't threshed about much—the doctor was of opinion that he must have been killed outright by the blow—because there were no bloodstains anywhere, and in any case he had pitched several yards away from the trees. That looked as though it might have been trodden on purpose, and the purpose was to conceal footprints. You couldn't get the smallest trace from that mess. Presently, after about forty minutes, during which I thought Bayliss was going to break a blood-vessel—I found what I was looking for—two or three little chips of wire.'

'You mean, someone had stretched wire across the path to make the lad take a toss?'

'Exactly. And it must have been someone who knew that Alcock would be coming hell-for-leather down that stretch. Well, that accounted for the cuts on the horse's legs, and whoever was responsible must have slipped out afterwards and cut the wire with a pair of clippers. That got us on a way and proved that Bayliss was right when he spoke of foul play; but it didn't mean that Grey was the man responsible.

'Bayliss nearly drove me off my head following me round and saying: "It's murder, I tell you, murder! Bluebeard wouldn't trample his own jockey if he hadn't been frantic."

'Someone suggested that the horse might have had his

back to the jockey and so didn't know what he was doing, but that wouldn't work either. The position in which the lad was lying showed that. The queer thing was that, if Bluebeard had been in a state of frenzy, he shouldn't have smashed in the whole head. It looked as though there had been just one blow and that he'd cantered back to his stable.

'Well, I thought of this and that, tested a theory and turned it down, and then I asked to see the horse. He'd come back all right on his own account, so it didn't look as though there had been a plot to kill him. I wasn't even convinced yet that whoever was responsible had intended to kill the jockey. After all, there was no need to do that, and murder's an ugly game, with ugly consequences for the murderer.

'At the stables the grooms were looking a bit askance at Bluebeard. Nobody likes a horse that kills its jockey; besides, he was known to have a queer temper at the best of times. I said I wanted to see his feet. For a minute no one moved, then Bayliss came shoving past me and lifted the great feet, one after the other, for me to examine. As he stood back, saying: "Well?" I felt myself sweating.

'"You're right, sir," I told him. "There's more than a toss to this. It's murder."

'You see, there wasn't a trace of blood on any of those four hooves. And yet Alcock had been killed by a blow from a horse, and the wound was too deep, too frightful, for no trace to be left on the shoe.

'Bayliss was still shouting that Grey was behind this, and I went off to inquire into Grey's movements, though I had to handle the affair pretty carefully. I hadn't an iota of evidence against the fellow. I asked him whether he'd been in the neighbourhood of Milton Heath that morning, and if so, if he'd seen anyone hanging about, but he told me he'd spent his time at the golf club, going round on his own.

'Well, several people remembered seeing Grey at the club, and one man admitted he had lunched with him. I asked if he'd employed a caddie, but it appeared he hadn't. He felt he might foozle half his shots, he explained, and he'd feel less of a fool if he were by himself. Well, that was reasonable enough. Few men are heroes to their caddies. I inquired about Grey's stable, but it appeared none of his horses had been out that morning, and he hadn't hired a hack. Besides, he'd been on the golf course, and a man can't be in two places at the same time. The only thing I did discover that might conceivably help was that the golf course ran quite close to the place where Alcock had been found.

'I thought and I thought. Suppose he'd timed himself to be at this particular spot at the time when Alcock would probably be passing? Even so, how could he have been responsible for the jockey's death? He'd been carrying golf clubs, certainly, but Alcock had been killed by a blow from a horse's hoof.

'And then, suddenly, I knew what had happened. Don't ask me how. If it wasn't for these gleams of inspiration the life of a policeman would be harder than it is, and it's hard enough, heaven knows, what with criminals being so unsporting and detective writers giving them so many hints. I went down to see the village blacksmith.

' "Shod any horses for Mr Grey lately?" I asked him.

' "One," he told me. "A mare. About a week ago."

' "Going a bit lame, wasn't she?"

' "Well, no, not that I could see. Don't know what he wanted her shod for, come to that."

'But I knew. Grey had come down himself, which was a bit unusual, for he was one of these high and mighty chaps, who think themselves a cut above the rest of the world. After that I went up to Mr Grey's house, choosing a time when he wasn't there, and told the servant that I was expected and I'd wait. They put me in the library and I routed among his books and found what I'd expected. Mind you, in a way I don't know that I wanted to find it, because even a policeman doesn't like to think of what humanity is capable of. But I was right. I even got the weapon in due course, as ugly an object as ever I've seen.' He took a pencil out of his pocket and began to draw something on the back of an envelope. 'Know what this is?' he asked us.

Well, there wasn't much question as to that. It was a stick like a club, with a horseshoe on one end. When we began to understand, we knew what he meant when he said he'd half-hoped he wouldn't find it. There was a famous Continental criminal called The Spider, who'd liked making use of it. Paris was his happy hunting-ground, till they ran him down at last. His method was to get a couple of horseshoes and fasten them on to a wooden club, and you had as murderous an implement as any criminal could desire. Grey had read his story, and seen in it a fine chance to put Alcock out and secure his own future. He must have waited till the boy came past, took a toss over the wire, and then murdered him.

'But was that necessary?' we asked. 'Wouldn't it have been enough if he'd incapacitated Bluebeard?'

'He couldn't afford not to put the jockey out of the way,' Field told us, with a shade of contempt for our slower intellects. 'Alcock would know the horse hadn't come down by himself. And Grey had got to clear the wire before anyone discovered his share in the plot. He literally didn't dare let Alcock live. And I suppose he thought he was safe enough. Any doctor would have sworn death was caused by the kick of a horse. There'd been a horse on the spot, a queer-tempered horse at that. Grey thought Bluebeard would get the blame, and he'd save his own skin. He was steeped in debt and worse; if he couldn't put up a considerable sum of money he'd have got five years, and I suppose he thought it was worth risking his life. He planned it all pretty carefully; the anonymous letters began arriving long before any hint of danger threatened Bayliss and his jockey. A more feeble criminal would have sent one to himself, but he didn't make that mistake. But it's a fact that no criminal ever remembers everything, and what Grey forgot was that there would be no blood on Bluebeard's hoofs. Or perhaps he thought no one else would think of that. And so,' he wound up, passing his tankard to be refilled for the third time, 'when I hear about horseshoes being lucky, I remember two men who were killed by them, as you might say, and it's not the kind of luck I'd appreciate.'

LONG SHOT

by Ellery Queen

Like Anthony Gilbert, Ellery Queen is a pseudonym, but of two writers instead of one—American-born cousins, Frederic Dannay and Manfred B. Lee—who perfected the difficult art of writing mystery fiction in partnership. Ellery also enjoys the distinction of being the detective hero of his own stories, a ploy deliberately used by his creators in the hope that the author's name would be more easily remembered if it appeared throughout the book; and the works have been published with great success around the world, as well as being made into films and radio and television series. The monthly publication, The Ellery Queen Mystery Magazine, *which Dannay and Lee started in 1941, became famous for the talented writers it developed, and the US mystery critic Anthony Boucher once observed that the magazine had 'published every important crime writer who ever wrote a short story'.*

The two men who were Ellery Queen were actually very different in character: Dannay was quiet and scholarly, while Lee was a lively extrovert with a great interest in sport. It was he who provided the background knowledge for Ellery Queen collections such as Sporting Blood *and the group of sports stories that make up* The New Adventures of Ellery Queen. *It is from the latter book that 'Long Shot' is extracted, as ingenious a mystery of the Turf as you could wish to find.*

* * *

'One moment, dear. My favourite fly's just walked into the parlour,' cried Paula Paris into her ashes-of-roses telephone. 'Oh, Ellery, do sit down! . . . No, dear, you're fishing. This one's a grim hombre with silv'ry eyes, and I have an option on him. Call me tomorrow about the Garbo excitement. And I'll expect your flash the moment Crawford springs her new *coiffure* on palpitating Miss America.'

And, the serious business of her Hollywood gossip column concluded, Miss Paris hung up and turned her lips pursily towards Mr Queen. Mr Queen had cured Miss Paris of homophobia, or morbid fear of crowds, by the brilliant counter-psychology of making love to her. Alas for the best-laid plans! The patient had promptly succumbed to the cure and, what was worse, in succumbing had infected the physician, too.

'I do believe,' murmured the lovely patient, 'that I need an extended treatment, Doctor Queen.'

So the poor fellow absently gave Miss Paris an extended treatment, after which he rubbed the lipstick from his mouth.

'No oomph,' said Miss Paris critically, holding him off and surveying his gloomy countenance. 'Ellery Queen, you're in a mess again.'

'Hollywood,' mumbled Mr Queen. 'The land God forgot. No logic. Disorderly creation. The abiding place of chaos. Paula, your Hollywood is driving me c-double-o-ditto!'

'You poor imposed-upon Wimpie,' crooned Miss Paris, drawing him onto her spacious maple settee. 'Tell Paula all about the nasty old place.'

So, with Miss Paris's soft arms about him, Mr Queen unburdened himself. It seemed that Magna Studios ('The Movies Magnificent'), to whom his soul was chartered, had ordered him as one of its staff writers to concoct a horse-racing plot with a fresh patina. A mystery, of course, since Mr Queen was supposed to know something about crime.

'With fifty writers on the lot who spend all their time —and money—following the ponies,' complained Mr Queen bitterly, 'of course they have to pick on the one serf in their thrall who doesn't know a fetlock from a wither. Paula, I'm a sunk scrivener.'

'You don't know *anything* about racing?'

'I'm not interested in racing. I've never even *seen* a race,' said Mr Queen doggedly.

'Imagine that!' said Paula, awed. And she was silent. After a while Mr Queen twisted in her embrace and said in accusing despair: 'Paula, you're thinking of something.'

She kissed him and sprang from the settee. 'The wrong tense, darling. I've *thought* of something!'

* * *

Paula told him all about old John Scott as they drove out into the green and yellow ranch country.

Scott was a vast, shapeless Caledonian with a face as craggy as his native heaths and a disposition not less dour. His inner landscape was bleak except where horses breathed and browsed; and this vulnerable spot had proved his undoing, for he had made two fortunes breeding thoroughbreds and had lost both by racing and betting on them.

'Old John's never stood for any of the crooked dodges of the racing game,' said Paula. 'He fired Weed Williams, the best jockey he ever had, and had him blackballed by every decent track in the country, so that Williams became a saddle-maker or something, just because of a peccadillo another owner would have winked at. And yet—the inconsistent old coot!—a few years later he gave Williams's son a job, and Whitey's going to ride Danger, John's best horse, in the Handicap next Saturday.'

'You mean the $100,000 Santa Anita Handicap everybody's in a dither about out here?'

'Yes. Anyway, old John's got a scrunchy little ranch, Danger, his daughter Kathryn, and practically nothing else except a stable of also-rans and breeding disappointments.'

'So far,' remarked Mr Queen, 'it sounds like the beginning of a Class B movie.'

'Except,' sighed Paula, 'that it's not entertaining. John's really on a spot. If Whitey doesn't ride Danger to a win in the Handicap, it's the end of the road for John Scott . . . Speaking about roads, here we are.'

They turned into a dirt road and ploughed dustily towards a ramshackle ranch-house. The road was pitted, the fences dilapidated, the grassland patchy with neglect.

'With all his troubles,' grinned Ellery, 'I fancy he won't take kindly to this quest for Racing in Five Easy Lessons.'

'Meeting a full-grown man who knows nothing about racing may give the old gentleman a laugh. Lord knows he needs one.'

A Mexican cook directed them to Scott's private track, and they found him leaning his weight upon a sagging rail, his small buried eyes puckered on a cloud of dust eddying along the track at the far turn. His thick fingers clutched a stop-watch.

A man in high-heeled boots sat on the rail two yards away, a shotgun in his lap pointing carelessly at the head of a too well-dressed gentleman with a foreign air who was talking to the back of Scott's shaggy head. The well-dressed man sat in a glistening roadster beside a hard-faced chauffeur.

'You got my proposition, John?' said the well-dressed man, with a toothy smile. 'You got it?'

'Get the hell off my ranch, Santelli,' said John Scott, without turning his head.

'Sure,' said Santelli, still smiling. 'You think my proposition over, hey, or maybe somethin' happen to your nag, hey?'

They saw the old man quiver, but he did not turn; and Santelli nodded curtly to his driver. The big roadster roared away.

The dust-cloud on the track rolled towards them and they saw a small, taut figure in sweater and cap perched atop a gigantic stallion, black-coated and lustrous with sweat. The horse was bounding along like a huge cat, his neck arched. He thundered magnificently by.

'2.02⅘,' they heard Scott mutter to his stop-watch. 'Rosemont's ten-furlong time for the Handicap in '37. Not bad . . . Whitey!' he bellowed to the jockey, who had pulled the black stallion up. 'Rub him down good!'

The jockey grinned and pranced Danger towards the adjacent stables.

The man with the shotgun drawled: 'You got more company, John.'

The old man whirled, frowning deeply; his craggy face broke into a thousand wrinkles and he engulfed Paula's slim hand in his two paws. 'Paula! It's fine to see ye. Who's this?' he demanded, fastening his cold keen eyes on Ellery.

'Mr Ellery Queen. But how is Katie? And Danger?'

'You saw him.' Scott gazed after the dancing horse. 'Fit as a fiddle. He'll carry the handicap weight of a hundred and twenty pounds Saturday an' never feel it. Did it just now with the leads on him. Paula, did ye see that murderin' scallywag?'

'The fashion-plate who just drove away?'

'That was Santelli, and ye heard what he said might happen to Danger.' The old man stared bitterly down the road.

'Santelli!' Paula's serene face was shocked.

'Bill, go look after the stallion.' The man with the shotgun slipped off the rail and waddled towards the stable. 'Just made me an offer for my stable. Hell, the dirty thievin' bookie owns the biggest stable west o' the Rockies—what's he want with my picayune outfit?'

'He owns Broomstick, the Handicap favourite, doesn't he?' asked Paula quietly. 'And Danger is figured strongly in the running, isn't he?'

'Quoted five to one now, but track odds'll shorten his price. Broomstick's two to five,' growled Scott.

'It's very simple, then. By buying your horse, Santelli can control the race, owning the two best horses.'

'Lassie, lassie,' sighed Scott. 'I'm an old mon, an' I know these thieves. Handicap purse is $100,000. And Santelli just offered me $100,000 for my stable!' Paula whistled. 'It don't wash. My whole shebang ain't worth it. Danger's no cinch to win. Is Santelli buyin' up all the other horses in the race, too?—the big outfits? I tell ye it's somethin' else, and it's rotten.' Then he shook his heavy shoulders straight. 'But here I am gabbin' about my troubles. What brings ye out here, lassie?'

'Mr Queen here, who's a—well, a friend of mine,' said Paula, colouring, 'has to think up a horse-racing plot for a movie, and I thought you could help him. He doesn't know a thing about racing.'

Scott stared at Mr Queen, who coughed apologetically. 'Well, sir, I don't know but that ye're not a lucky mon. Ye're welcome to the run o' the place. Go over an' talk to Whitey; he knows the racket backwards. I'll be with ye in a few minutes.'

The old man lumbered off, and Paula and Ellery sauntered towards the stables.

'Who is this ogre Santelli?' asked Ellery with a frown.

'A gambler and bookmaker with a national hook-up.' Paula shivered a little. 'Poor John. I don't like it, Ellery.'

They turned a corner of the big stable and almost bumped into a young man and a young woman in the lee of the wall, clutching each other desperately and kissing as if they were about to be torn apart for eternity.

'Pardon *us*,' said Paula, pulling Ellery back.

The young lady, her eyes crystal with tears, blinked at her. 'Is—is that Paula Paris?' she sniffled.

'The same, Kathryn,' smiled Paula. 'Mr Queen, Miss Scott. What on earth's the matter?'

'Everything,' cried Miss Scott tragically. 'Oh, Paula, we're in the most awful trouble!'

Her amorous companion backed bashfully off. He was a slender young man clad in grimy, odoriferous overalls. He wore spectacles floury with the chaff of oats, and there was a grease smudge on one emotional nostril.

'Miss Paris—Mr Queen. This is Hank Halliday, my—my boy-friend,' sobbed Kathryn.

'I see the whole plot,' said Paula sympathetically. 'Papa doesn't approve of Katie's taking up with a stablehand, the snob! and it's tragedy all around.'

'Hank *isn't* a stablehand,' cried Kathryn, dashing the tears from her cheeks, which were rosy with indignation. 'He's a college graduate who—'

'Kate,' said the odoriferous young man with dignity, 'let me explain, please. Miss Paris, I have a character deficiency. I am a physical coward.'

'Heavens, so am I!' said Paula.

'But a man, you see . . . I am particularly afraid of

animals. Horses, specifically.' Mr Halliday shuddered. 'I took this—this filthy job to conquer my unreasonable fear.' Mr Halliday's sensitive chin hardened. 'I have not yet conquered it, but when I do I shall find myself a real job. And then,' he said firmly, embracing Miss Scott's trembling shoulders, 'I shall marry Kathryn, papa or no papa.'

'Oh, I hate him for being so mean!' sobbed Katie.

'And I—' began Mr Halliday sombrely.

'Hankus-Pankus!' yelled a voice from the stable. 'What the hell you paid for, anyway? Come clean up this mess before I slough you one!'

'Yes, Mr Williams,' said Hankus-Pankus hastily, and he hurried away with an apologetic half-bow. His lady-love ran sobbing off towards the ranch-house.

Mr Queen and Miss Paris regarded each other. Then Mr Queen said: 'I'm getting a plot, b'gosh, but it's the wrong one.'

'Poor kids,' sighed Paula. 'Well, talk to Whitey Williams and see if the divine spark ignites.'

*   *   *

During the next several days Mr Queen ambled about the Scott ranch, talking to Jockey Williams, to the bespectacled Mr Halliday—who, he discovered, knew as little about racing as he and cared even less—to a continuously tearful Kathryn, to the guard named Bill—who slept in the stable near Danger with one hand on his shotgun—and to old John himself. He learned much about jockeys, touts, racing procedure, gear, handicaps, purses, forfeits, stewards, the ways of bookmakers, famous races and horses and owners and tracks; but the divine spark perversely refused to ignite.

So, on Friday at dusk, when he found himself unaccountably ignored at the Scott ranch, he glumly drove up into the Hollywood hills for a laving in the waters of Gilead.

He found Paula in her garden soothing two anguished young people. Katie Scott was still weeping and Mr Halliday, the self-confessed craven, for once dressed in an odourless garment, was awkwardly pawing her golden hair.

'More tragedy?' said Mr Queen. 'I should have known. I've just come from your father's ranch, and there's a pall over it.'

'Well, there should be!' cried Kathryn. 'I told my father where *he* gets off. Treating Hank that way! I'll never speak to him as long as I live! He's—he's *unnatural*!'

'Now, Katie,' said Mr Halliday reprovingly, 'that's no way to speak of your own father.'

'Hank Halliday, if you had one spark of manhood—!'

Mr Halliday stiffened as if his beloved had jabbed him with the end of a live wire.

'I didn't mean that, Hankus,' sobbed Kathryn, throwing herself into his arms. 'I know you can't help being a coward. But when he knocked you down and you didn't even—'

Mr Halliday worked the left side of his jaw thoughtfully. 'You know, Mr Queen, something happened to me when Mr Scott struck me. For an instant I felt a strange—er—lust. I really believe if I'd had a revolver—and if I knew how to handle one—I might easily have committed murder then. I saw—I believe that's the phrase—red.'

'Hank!' cried Katie in horror.

Hank sighed, the homicidal light dying out of his faded blue eyes.

'Old John,' explained Paula, winking at Ellery, 'found these two cuddling again in the stable, and I suppose he thought it was setting a bad example for Danger, whose mind should be on the race tomorrow; so he fired Hank, and Katie blew up and told John off, and she's left his home for ever.'

'To discharge me is his privilege,' said Mr Halliday coldly, 'but now I owe him no loyalty whatever. I shall *not* bet on Danger to win the Handicap!'

'I hope the big brute loses,' sobbed Katie.

'Now, Kate,' said Paula firmly, 'I've heard enough of this nonsense. I'm going to speak to you like a Dutch aunt.'

Katie sobbed on.

'Mr Halliday,' said Mr Queen formally, 'I believe this is our cue to seek a slight libation.'

'Kathryn!'

'Hank!'
Mr Queen and Miss Paris tore the lovers apart.

* * *

It was a little after ten o'clock when Miss Scott, no longer weeping but facially still tear-ravaged, crept out of Miss Paris's white frame house and got into her dusty little car.

As she turned her key in the ignition lock and stepped on the starter, a harsh bass voice from the shadows of the back seat said: 'Don't yell. Don't make a sound. Turn your car around and keep going till I tell you to stop.'

'Eek!' screeched Miss Scott.

A big leathery hand clamped over her trembling mouth.

After a few moments the car moved away.

* * *

Mr Queen called for Miss Paris the next day and they settled down to a snail's pace, heading for Arcadia eastward, near which lay the beautiful Santa Anita race course.

'What happened to Lachrymose Katie last night?' demanded Mr Queen.

'Oh, I got her to go back to the ranch. She left me a little after ten, a very miserable little girl. What did you do with Hankus-Pankus?'

'I oiled him thoroughly and then took him home. He'd hired a room in a Hollywood boarding-house. He cried on my shoulder all the way. It seems old John also kicked him in the seat of his pants, and he's been brooding murderously over it.'

'Poor Hankus. The only honest male I've ever met.'

'I'm afraid of horses, too,' said Mr Queen hurriedly.

'Oh, you! You're detestable. You haven't kissed me once today.'

Only the cooling balm of Miss Paris's lips, applied at various points along US Route 66, kept Mr Queen's temper from boiling over. The roads were sluggish with traffic. At the track it was even worse. It seemed as though every last soul in Southern California had converged upon Santa Anita at once, in every manner of conveyance, from the dusty Model T's of dirt farmers to the shiny metal monsters of the movie stars. The magnificent stands seethed with noisy thousands, a wriggling mosaic of colour and movement. The sky was blue, the sun warm, zephyrs blew, and the track was fast. A race was being run, and the sleek animals were small and fleet and sharply focused in the clear light.

'What a marvellous day for the Handicap!' cried Paula, dragging Ellery along. 'Oh, there's Bing, and Al Jolson, and Bob Burns! . . . Hello! . . . And Joan and Clark and Carole . . .'

Despite Miss Paris's over-enthusiastic trail-breaking, Mr Queen arrived at the track stalls in one piece. They found old John Scott watching with the intentness of a Red Indian as a stablehand kneaded Danger's velvety forelegs. There was a stony set to Scott's gnarled face that made Paula cry: 'John! Is anything wrong with Danger?'

'Danger's all right,' said the old man curtly. 'It's Kate. We had a blow-up over that Halliday boy an' she ran out on me.'

'Nonsense, John. I sent her back home last night myself.'

'She was at your place? She didn't come home.'

'She didn't?' Paula's little nose wrinkled.

'I guess,' growled Scott, 'she's run off with that Halliday coward. He's not a mon, the lily-livered—'

'We can't all be heroes, John. He's a good boy, and he loves Katie.'

The old man stared stubbornly at his stallion, and after a moment they left and made their way towards their box.

'Funny,' said Paula in a scared voice. 'She couldn't have run off with Hank; he was with you. And I'd swear she meant to go back to the ranch last night.'

'Now, Paula,' said Mr Queen gently. 'She's all right.' But his eyes were thoughtful and a little perturbed.

*　　*　　*

Their box was not far from the paddock. During the preliminary races, Paula kept searching the sea of faces with her binoculars.

'Well, well,' said Mr Queen suddenly, and Paula became

conscious of a rolling thunder from the stands about them.

'What's the matter? What's happened?'

'Broomstick, the favourite, has been scratched,' said Mr Queen dryly.

'Broomstick? Santelli's horse?' Paula stared at him, paling. 'But why? Ellery, there's something in this—'

'It seems he's pulled a tendon and can't run.'

'Do you think,' whispered Paula, 'that Santelli had anything to do with Katie's . . . not getting . . . home?'

'Possible,' muttered Ellery. 'But I can't seem to fit the blinking thing—'

'Here they come!'

The shout shook the stands. A line of regal animals began to emerge from the paddock. Paula and Ellery rose with the other restless thousands, and craned. The Handicap contestants were parading to the post!

There was High Tor, who had gone lame in the stretch at the Derby two years before and had not run a race since. This was to be his come-back; the insiders held him in a contempt which the public apparently shared, for he was quoted at fifty to one. There was little Fighting Billy. There was Equator, prancing sedately along with Buzz Hickey up. There was Danger! Glossy black, gigantic, imperial, Danger was nervous. Whitey Williams was having a difficult time controlling him and a stablehand was struggling at his bit.

Old John Scott, his big shapeless body unmistakable even at this distance, lumbered from the paddock towards his dancing stallion, apparently to soothe him.

Paula gasped. Ellery said quickly: 'What is it?'

'There's Hank Halliday in the crowd. Up there! Right above the spot where Danger's passing. About fifty feet from John Scott. And Kathryn's not with him!'

Ellery took the glasses from her and located Halliday.

Paula sank into her chair. 'Ellery, I've the queerest feeling. There's something wrong. See how pale he is . . .'

The powerful glasses brought Halliday to within a few inches of Ellery's eyes. The boy's glasses were steamed over; he was shaking, as if he had a chill; and yet Ellery could see the globules of perspiration on his cheeks.

And then Mr Queen stiffened very abruptly.

John Scott had just reached the head of Danger; his thick arm was coming up to pull the stallion's head down. And in that instant Mr Hankus-Pankus Halliday fumbled in his clothes; and in the next his hand appeared clasping a snubnosed automatic. Mr Queen very nearly cried out. For, the short barrel wavering, the automatic in Mr Halliday's trembling hands pointed in the general direction of John Scott, there was an explosion, and a puff of smoke blew out of the muzzle.

Miss Paris leaped to her feet, and Miss Paris did cry out.

'Why, the crazy young fool!' said Mr Queen dazedly.

Frightened by the shot, which had gone wild, Danger reared. The other horses began to kick and dance. In a moment the place below boiled with panic-stricken thoroughbreds. Scott, clinging to Danger's head, half-turned in an immense astonishment and looked inquiringly upwards. Whitey struggled desperately to control the frantic stallion.

And then Mr Halliday shot again. And again. And a fourth time. And at some instant, in the spaces between those shots, the rearing horse got between John Scott and the automatic in Mr Halliday's shaking hand.

Danger's four feet left the turf. Then, whinnying in agony, flanks heaving, he toppled over on his side.

'Oh, gosh; oh, *gosh*,' said Paula, biting her handkerchief.

'Let's go!' shouted Mr Queen, and he plunged for the spot.

*   *   *

By the time they reached the place where Mr Halliday had fearfully discharged his automatic, the bespectacled youth had disappeared. The people who had stood about him were still too stunned to move. Elsewhere, the stands were in pandemonium.

In the confusion, Ellery and Paula managed to slip through the inadequate track-police cordon hastily thrown about the fallen Danger and his milling rivals. They found old John on his knees beside the black stallion, his big hands steadily stroking the glossy, veined neck. Whitey, pale and bewildered-looking, had stripped off the tiny saddle, and the track veterinary was examining a bullet-wound in Danger's side, near the shoulder. A group of track officials conferred excitedly near by.

'He saved my life,' said old John in a low voice to no one in particular. 'He saved my life.'

The veterinary looked up. 'Sorry, Mr Scott,' he said grimly. 'Danger won't run this race.'

'No. I suppose not.' Scott licked his leathery lips. 'Is it—mon, is it serious?'

'Can't tell till I dig out the bullet. We'll have to get him out of here and into the hospital right away.'

An official said: 'Tough luck, Scott. You may be sure we'll do our best to find the scoundrel who shot your horse.'

The old man's lips twisted. He climbed to his feet and looked down at the heaving flanks of his fallen thorough-bred. Whitey Williams trudged away with Danger's gear, head hanging.

A moment later the loud-speaker system proclaimed that Danger, Number 5, had been scratched, and that the Handicap would be run immediately the other contestants could be quieted and lined up at the stall-barrier.

'All right, folks, clear out,' said a track policeman, as a hospital van rushed up, followed by a hoisting truck.

'What are you doing about the man who shot this horse?' demanded Mr Queen, not moving.

'Ellery,' whispered Paula nervously, tugging at his arm.

'We'll get him; got a good description. Move on, please.'

'Well,' said Mr Queen slowly, 'I know who he is, do you see?'

'Ellery!'

'I saw him and recognized him.'

They were ushered into the Steward's office just as the announcement was made that High Tor, at fifty to one, had won the Santa Anita Handicap, purse $100,000, by two and a half lengths . . . almost as long a shot, in one sense, as the shot which had laid poor Danger low, commented Mr Queen to Miss Paris, *sotto voce*.

'Halliday?' said John Scott, with heavy contempt. 'That yellow-livered pup try to shoot me?'

'I couldn't possibly be mistaken, Mr Scott,' said Ellery.

'I saw him, too, John,' sighed Paula.

'Who is this Halliday?' demanded the chief of the track police.

Scott told him in monosyllables, relating their quarrel of the day before. 'I knocked him down an' kicked him. I guess the only way he could get back at me was with a gun. An' Danger took the rap, poor beastie.' For the first time his voice shook.

'Well, we'll get him; he can't have left the park,' said the police chief grimly. 'I've got it sealed tighter than a drum.'

'Did you know,' murmured Mr Queen, 'that Mr Scott's daughter Kathryn has been missing since last night?'

Old John flushed slowly. 'You think—my Kate had somethin' to do—'

'Don't be silly, John!' said Paula.

'At any rate,' said Mr Queen dryly, 'her disappearance and the attack here today can't be a coincidence. I'd advise you to start a search for Miss Scott immediately. And, by the way, send for Danger's gear. I'd like to examine it.'

'Say, who the devil are you?' growled the chief.

Mr Queen told him negligently. The chief looked properly awed. He telephoned to various police headquarters, and he sent for Danger's gear.

Whitey Williams, still in his silks, carried the high small racing saddle in and dumped it on the floor.

'John, I'm awful sorry about what happened,' he said in a low voice.

'It ain't your fault, Whitey.' The big shoulders drooped.

'Ah, Williams, thank you,' said Mr Queen briskly. 'This *is* the saddle Danger was wearing a few minutes ago?'

'Yes, sir.'

'Exactly as it was when you stripped it off him after the shots?'

'Yes, sir.'

'Has anyone had an opportunity to tamper with it?'

'No, sir. I been with it ever since, and no one's come near it but me.'

Mr Queen nodded and knelt to examine the empty-pocketed saddle. Observing the scorched hole in the flap, his brow puckered in perplexity.

'By the way, Whitey,' he asked, 'how much do you weigh?'

'Hundred and seven.'

Mr Queen frowned. He rose, dusted his knees delicately and beckoned the chief of police. They conferred in undertones. The policeman looked baffled, shrugged, and hurried out.

When he returned, a certain familiar-appearing gentleman in too-perfect clothes and a foreign air accompanied him. The gentleman looked sad.

'I hear some crackpot took a couple o' shots at you, John,' he said sorrowfully, 'an' got your nag instead. Tough luck.'

There was a somewhat quizzical humour behind this ambiguous statement which brought old John's head up in a flash of belligerence.

'You dirty, thievin'—'

'Mr Santelli,' greeted Mr Queen. 'When did you know that Broomstick would have to be scratched?'

'Broomstick?' Mr Santelli looked mildly surprised at this irrelevant question. 'Why, last week.'

'So that's why you offered to buy Scott's stable—to get control of Danger?'

'Sure,' Mr Santelli smiled genially. 'He was hot. With my nag out, he looked like a cinch.'

'Mr Santelli, you're what is colloquially known as a cock-eyed liar.' Mr Santelli ceased smiling. 'You wanted to buy Danger not to see him win, but to see him lose!'

Mr Santelli looked unhappy. 'Who is this,' he appealed to the police chief, 'Mister Wacky himself?'

'In my embryonic way,' said Mr Queen, 'I have been making a few inquiries in the last several days and my information has it that your bookmaking organization covered a lot of Danger money when Danger was five to one.'

'Say, you got somethin' there,' said Mr Santelli, suddenly deciding to be candid.

'You covered about $200,000, didn't you?'

'Wow,' said Mr Santelli. 'This guy's got ideas, ain't he?'

'So,' smiled Mr Queen, 'if Danger won the Handicap you stood to drop a very frigid million dollars, did you not?'

'But it's my old friend John some guy tried to rub out,'

pointed out Mr Santelli gently. 'Go peddle your papers somewheres else, Mister Wack.'

John Scott looked bewilderedly from the gambler to Mr Queen. His jaw-muscles were bunched and jerky.

At this moment a special officer deposited among them Mr Hankus-Pankus Halliday, his spectacles awry on his nose and his collar ripped away from his prominent Adam's-apple.

* * *

John Scott sprang towards him, but Ellery caught his flailing arms in time to prevent a slaughter.

'Murderer! Scallywag! Horse-killer!' roared old John. 'What did ye do with my lassie?'

Mr Halliday said gravely: 'Mr Scott, you have my sympathy.'

The old man's mouth flew open. Mr Halliday folded his scrawny arms with dignity, glaring at the policeman who had brought him in. 'There was no necessity to manhandle me. I'm quite ready to face the—er—music. But I shall not answer any questions.'

'No gat on him, Chief,' said the policeman by his side.

'What did you do with the automatic?' demanded the chief. No answer. 'You admit you had it in for Mr Scott and tried to kill him?' No answer. 'Where is Miss Scott?'

'You see,' said Mr Halliday stonily, 'how useless it is.'

'Hankus-Pankus,' murmured Mr Queen, 'you are superb. You don't know where Kathryn is, do you?'

Hankus-Pankus instantly looked alarmed. 'Oh, I say, Mr Queen. Don't make me talk. Please!'

'But you're expectin' her to join you here, aren't you?'

Hankus paled. The policeman said: 'He's a nut. He didn't even try to make a get-away. He didn't even fight back.'

'Hank! Darling! Father!' cried Katie Scott; and, straggle-haired and dusty-faced, she flew into the office and flung herself upon Mr Halliday's thin bosom.

'Katie!' screamed Paula, flying to the girl and embracing her; and in a moment all three, Paula and Kathryn and Hankus, were weeping in concert, while old John's jaw dropped even lower and all but Mr Queen, who was smiling, stood rooted to their bits of Space in timeless stupefaction.

Then Miss Scott ran to her father and clung to him, and old John's shoulders lifted a little, even though the expression of bewilderment persisted; and she burrowed her head into her father's deep, broad chest.

In the midst of this incredible scene the track veterinary bustled in and said: 'Good news, Mr Scott. I've extracted the bullet and, while the wound is deep, I give you my word Danger will be as good as ever when it's healed.' And he bustled out.

And Mr Queen, his smile broadening, said: 'Well, well, a pretty comedy of errors.'

'Comedy!' growled old John over his daughter's golden curls. 'D'ye call a murderous attempt on my life a comedy?' And he glared fiercely at Mr Hank Halliday, who was at the moment borrowing a handkerchief from the policeman with which to wipe his eyes.

'My dear Mr Scott,' replied Mr Queen, 'there has been no attempt on your life. The shots were not fired at you. From the very first Danger, and Danger only, was intended to be the victim of the shooting.'

'What's this?' cried Paula.

'No, no, Whitey,' said Mr Queen, smiling still more broadly. 'The door, I promise you, is well guarded.'

The jockey snarled: 'Yah, he's off his nut. Next thing you'll say I plugged the nag. How could I be on Danger's back and at the same time fifty feet away in the grandstand? A million guys saw this screwball fire those shots!'

'A difficulty,' replied Mr Queen, bowing, 'I shall be delighted to resolve. Danger, ladies and gentlemen, was handicapped officially to carry one hundred and twenty pounds in the Santa Anita Handicap. This means that when his jockey, carrying the gear, stepped upon the scales in the weighing-out ceremony just before the race, the combined weight of jockey and gear had to come to exactly one hundred and twenty pounds; or Mr Whitey Williams would never have been allowed by the track officials to mount his horse.'

'What's that got to do with it?' demanded the chief, eyeing Mr Whitey Williams in a hard, unfeeling way.

'Everything. For Mr Williams told us only a few minutes ago that he weighs only a hundred and seven pounds. Consequently the racing saddle Danger wore when he was shot must have contained various lead weights which, combined with the weight of the saddle, made up the difference between a hundred and seven pounds, Mr Williams's weight, and a hundred and twenty pounds, the handicap weight. Is that correct?'

'Sure. Anybody knows that.'

'Yes, yes, elementary, in Mr Holmes's imperishable phrase. Nevertheless,' continued Mr Queen, walking over and prodding with his toe the saddle Whitey Williams had fetched to the office, 'when I examined this saddle *there were no lead weights in its pockets.* And Mr Williams assured me no one had tampered with the saddle since he had removed it from Danger's back. But this was impossible, since without the lead weights Mr Williams and the saddle would have weighed out at less than a hundred and twenty pounds on the scales.

'And so I knew,' said Mr Queen, 'that Williams had weighed out with a different saddle, that when he was shot Danger was wearing a different saddle, that the saddle Williams lugged away from the wounded horse was a different saddle; that he secreted it somewhere on the premises and fetched here on our request a *second* saddle —this one on the floor—which he had prepared beforehand with a bullet-hole nicely placed in the proper spot. And the reason he did this was that obviously there was something in that first saddle he didn't want anyone to see. And what could that have been but a special pocket containing an automatic, which in the confusion following Mr Halliday's first, signal shot, Mr Williams calmly discharged into Danger's body by simply stooping over as he struggled with the frightened horse, putting his hand into the pocket, and firing while Mr Halliday was discharging his three other futile shots fifty feet away? Mr Halliday, you see, couldn't be trusted to hit Danger from such a distance, because Mr Halliday is a stranger to firearms; he might even hit Mr Williams instead, if he hit anything. That's why I believe Mr Halliday was using blank cartridges and threw the automatic away.'

The jockey's voice was strident, panicky. 'You're crazy! Special saddle. Who ever heard—'

Mr Queen, still smiling, went to the door, opened it, and said: 'Ah, you've found it, I see. Let's have it. In Danger's stall? Clumsy, clumsy.'

He returned with a racing saddle; and Whitey cursed and then grew still. Mr Queen and the police chief and John Scott examined the saddle and, surely enough, there was a special pocket stitched into the flap, above the iron hoop, and in the pocket there was a snub-nosed automatic. And the bullet-hole piercing the special pocket had the scorched speckled appearance of powder-burns.

'But where,' muttered the chief, 'does Halliday figure? I don't get him at all.'

'Very few people would,' said Mr Queen, 'because Mr Halliday is, in his modest way, unique among bipeds.'

'Huh?'

'Why, he was Whitey's accomplice—weren't you, Hankus?'

Hankus gulped and said: 'Yes. I mean no. I mean—'

'But I'm sure Hank wouldn't—' Katie began to cry.

'You see,' said Mr Queen briskly, 'Whitey wanted a set-up whereby he would be the last person in California to be suspected of having shot Danger. The quarrel between John Scott and Hank gave him a ready-made instrument. If he could make Hank seem to do the shooting, with Hank's obvious motive against Mr Scott, then nobody would suspect his own part in the affair.

'But to bend Hank to his will he had to have a hold on Hank. What was Mr Halliday's Achilles heel? Why, his passion for Katie Scott. So last night Whitey's father, Weed Williams, I imagine—wasn't he the jockey you chased from the American turf many years ago, Mr Scott, and who became a saddle-maker?—kidnapped Katie Scott, and then communicated with Hankus-Pankus and told him just what to do today if he ever expected to see his beloved alive again. And Hankus-Pankus took the gun they provided him with, and listened very carefully, and agreed to do everything they told him to do, and promised he would not breathe a word of the truth afterwards, even if he had to go to jail for his crime, because if he did, you see, something terrible would happen to the incomparable Katie.'

Mr Halliday gulped, his Adam's-apple bobbing violently.

'An' all the time this skunk,' growled John Scott, glaring at the cowering jockey, 'an' his weasel of a father, they sat back an' laughed at a brave mon, because they were havin' their piddling revenge on me, ruining me!' Old John shambled like a bear towards Mr Halliday. 'An' I am a shamed mon today, Hank Halliday. For that was the bravest thing I ever did hear of. An' even if I've lost my chance for the Handicap purse, through no fault of yours, and I'm a ruined maggot, here's my hand.'

Mr Halliday took it absently, meanwhile fumbling with his other hand in his pocket. 'By the way,' he said, 'who did win the Handicap, if I may ask? I was so busy, you see—'

'High Tor,' said somebody in the babble.

'Really? Then I must cash this ticket,' said Mr Halliday with a note of faint interest.

'Two thousand dollars!' gasped Paula, goggling at the ticket. 'He bet two thousand dollars on High Tor at fifty to one!'

'Yes, a little nest-egg my mother left me,' said Mr Halliday. He seemed embarrassed. 'I'm sorry, Mr Scott. You made me angry when you—er—kicked me in the pants, so I didn't bet it on Danger. And High Tor was such a beautiful name.'

'Oh, Hank,' sobbed Katie, beginning to strangle him.

'So now, Mr Scott,' said Hankus-Pankus with dignity, 'may I marry Katie and set you up in the racing business again?'

'Happy days!' bellowed old John, seizing his future son-in-law in a rib-cracking embrace.

'Happy days,' muttered Mr Queen, seizing Miss Paris and heading her for the nearest bar.

Heigh, Danger!

JORKENS CONSULTS A PROPHET

by Lord Dunsany

Lord Dunsany, an eccentric Irish nobleman who is chiefly remem-
bered today as a writer of fantasy fiction, was similar to Dick
Francis in that he was a rider who turned his experiences into
fiction. Dunsany would never have claimed to be a jockey in the
same class as Francis, but he was a doughty rider and was said to be
at his best when racing for a bet!

As the 18th Baron Dunsany, he inherited a castle in County
Meath and there earned the reputation of being a 'fashionable
sportsman' by raising cricket teams to play on a special pitch cut
each year out of an area of open pasture land, as well as construct-
ing a steeplechase course around his estate. Dunsany owned a
number of excellent horses, the best of which he raced at local
meetings, usually with professional jockeys in the saddle. How-
ever, stories of his own race meetings, at which he took on friends
and other landowners for wagers of hundreds of pounds, are still
legendary in County Meath.

There is more than a little of Dunsany in his fictional character,
Jorkens, a clubman who delights in telling the most bizarre and
often unlikely stories to a group of friends. A number of these
concern horse racing, and my favourite is 'Jorkens Consults a
Prophet' which I hope the reader will find as memorable as I do.

*   *   *

It was the usual thing at the Billiards Club, a thing that
happens too often: Jorkens was known to be coming up the
stairs, and one or two members, simply with the deliberate
intention of getting the conversation where he was unlikely

to join in, that is to say away from Africa or any of the wilder lands, had chosen philosophy for their discussion. Free will or destiny was the general trend of their argument. I found it merely dull. But the moment Jorkens heard them, his eye brightened up.

'There is a lot to be said for destiny,' said Jorkens, 'but you can't ignore free will.'

'What do you mean?' said one of the philosophers.

And then Terbut joined in.

'Do you know anything about either of them?' he said.

'Yes,' said Jorkens. 'As it happens I do. I thought I knew about one of them, and it turned out I didn't, but I had quite a considerable experience of the other. I'll tell you about it. It was like this. I was a good deal interested in destiny, not so much from the point of view from which you are looking at it, but as a practical proposition. I said to myself, things are bound to happen, and there's no stopping them; and if one could find out someone who knew what those things were, there'd be a great deal of money in it. And, mind you, it was not I that was having wild fancies about it: plenty of people claimed to know the future, and do so still. Well, I investigated the claims of one of them. I went to him and I said, "You foretell the future?"

'"I do," he said.

'"Can you tell what is going to win the Derby?" I asked.

'"I can," he said.

'Well, it wasn't the Derby that I wanted to know about, it was a race meeting a long way from here, but it served my purpose just as well, and I asked him if he could tell me what was going to win that. So he brought out a lot of silks and began unwrapping them, all of them different colours; and when he had taken off about nine of them, there was a crystal, not quite smooth, but lightly carved on the surface with things like leaves; rather like an artichoke. Then he lit a powder in a little agate saucer, which made a smoke with a queer smell and made everything dim all round, but not the crystal. The crystal remained as bright as ever. When he moved it slightly in his hand things moved in the crystal: you could see them quite clearly. And then he told me the name of the horse that would win that race, and the name of the second and the third. He did more than that, he showed me the actual race in the crystal with the three horses leading it past the post and their colours clear and distinct. Now, that was a queer thing to do. The horses were unmistakable: I recognized all three of them afterwards; but, to make sure, I jotted down the colours that the jockeys were wearing. He let me see that race again and again. It was clear and bright, in spite of the smoke all round me; in fact the grass was greener than it ever is naturally, and the colours the jockeys wore were more like enamel than silk. But you simply couldn't mistake them. Of course I paid him; I paid him a good deal; in fact the blackguard demanded £5, and wouldn't take less. But, after all, the information was worth it. Then I got out of the room as fast as I could, away from the scented smoke, to breathe the fresh air, and because I didn't like the fellow at all. I had the name of the winning horse from the conjurer's lips, and I had seen the race with my own eyes. Did I tell you that he let me see the race over and over again, so that I got the colours quite clear? I bought some coloured chalks and jotted down sketches of them. I very soon found what the horses were, and who their owners were and what their colours; and the colours I had seen in the crystal were perfectly right. Well, do you know, I didn't have a penny on that race. I just went and watched it. And there were the horses, every single one of them, just as I had seen them in the crystal. And the man was perfectly right about the name of the winner, and of the second and third. It was an odd and surprising experience to see that race in the crystal repeated before my eyes, all the horses I had seen, all the colours and even the exact distances between each, which I had noticed in the crystal and made rough notes of. I was a good deal surprised, but I didn't waste any time wondering: I saw that I was on a good thing, and I went straight back to that rather sinister fellow that burned the scented smoke. I said, "I want to see another race, and I will give you £10 this time." I did that so as not to have any argument as to whether or not he would show me another, for I knew now that it was an excessively good thing. Well, he burned the smoke again in the agate saucer while he held the crystal in his hand; and the room grew dim once more and the crystal shone brighter and I saw another race. Again he told me the names of the three winners, and again I jotted them down and made little sketches of all the colours with the coloured pencils, which I had in my pocket this time. It was a big race, a very big one, and it was coming on in about three weeks' time. Well, I concentrated on the winner. Of course I could have got fabulous odds, if I had backed all those three horses to come in in the right order, but I didn't want to give too much away: I didn't want people to suspect that I had had dealings with a clairvoyant, and so to find out that my bet was a bet on a certainty. I had a good deal of money in those days, and I concentrated on the winner. I put all the money I had on him, spreading it over various bookies, and I borrowed a good deal more; and the odds were six to one. What with the cash I had borrowed and what with the stuff I owned, I stood to be ten times richer on the afternoon of that race than I had been on the same morning. I am not going to tell you what race it was; because, if what I tell you gets out, I don't want some fellow to get up and say that that's not the way races are run there. They are run in that way of course, only I don't want to say so.

'The day before I made my final arrangements with the bookies I went back to the damned fellow with the crystal and scented smoke, to ask him if he was sure of what he had been talking about, that is to say that Pullover would win that race, with a jockey wearing blue and yellow hoops. He said he knew well what he was talking about, and that that horse would win. And he asked me if the other race had not gone exactly as he had predicted, which of course made me look rather silly and quite unreasonably anxious. But it was then that he touched on a topic that I think you were just talking about. He said that free will was some sort of force that was almost equal, I think he said, to destiny; and that if I were to take a gun and shoot the horse as he came by, or injure it severely before the race, then of course it would not win, but that according to the will and the actions of everybody else in the world, and every horse, that horse would win the race. Only two men, he and I, knew anything of the future, as far as that horse was concerned: he certainly would do nothing whatever, and took an oath accordingly, and, provided that I exerted no free will against what was planned for the horse, it was destined that it must win. He also repeated the names of the second and third, with which I had nothing to do, for the reason that I have told you. The whole thing seemed very reasonable and, indeed, obvious. Of course if I took violent measures against whatever was ordained, the thing could not happen; just as, if you divert a river, it won't go its old way to the sea, but leave it alone, and it will.

'The day of the race I went and saw the horses in the ring. And I had seen every one of them in the crystal. The colours of three of the jockeys I had of course sketched in coloured pencil, and I had the sketch in my pocket. And there the three jockeys were, all walking about. The winner was absolutely unmistakable, even without the blue and yellow hoops: he was a bright chestnut with a clear white star on his forehead.

'I watched the race. And the second horse that I had seen in the crystal, white with red spots, and the third horse, green jacket and cap with white sleeves, were coming along nicely; but the odd thing was that my winner suddenly went a bit short far out in the country, and I saw him through my glasses dropping back. When the man had said "if you shoot the horse, he won't win," I had said to the damned fellow, "Do you think I should be such a fool?" But I had done a more foolish thing really. I had backed the horse too heavily for the bookies. They couldn't afford to let him win. If I said that that jockey with his blue and yellow hoops had received any money from them, he would turn out to be still alive and would sue me for libel. But he had a young family; and a thousand-pound note comes in wonderfully handy in bringing up two or three children. Yes, the second horse was first, and the third horse was second, and then came the field: the race was wonderfully like what I had seen in the crystal, only that my chestnut horse with the white star, ridden by blue and yellow hoops, was right back with a little bunch that came cantering past at the end. Of course it was all my own fault: I'd played free will against destiny. And, as I was never able to make out in what proportions they work, I never had anything to do with that kind of thing any more.'

THE OWNERS' HANDICAP

by Leslie Charteris

Another writer who is also a good horseman is Leslie Charteris, creator of one of the most popular characters in crime literature —Simon Templar, better known as the 'Saint', and widely referred to as 'the modern Robin Hood'. The Saint has been the hero of more than 40 novels and innumerable radio, televisions and film adaptations which have starred many famous actors, from Louis Hayward (the first Saint in 1938) to Roger Moore, the most recent.

Leslie Charteris introduced a lot of himself into the Saint who is nòt only tall, handsome and elegantly dressed, but an expert shot, a skilled pilot and a fine horseman. Despite his love of the good life, the Saint has rarely been involved in the world of horse racing, but when he decides to bring an unscrupulous bookmaker to heel, he displays considerable knowledge of the racing world, as well as his customary expertise in outthinking and outmanoeuvring his enemy. This is an engrossing adventure of the Saint, as intriguing as any that Leslie Charteris has written.

*   *   *

'The art of crime,' said Simon Templar, carefully mayonnaising a section of *truite à la gelée*, 'is to be versatile. Repetition breeds contempt—and promotion for flat-footed oafs from Scotland Yard. I assure you, Pat, I have never felt the slightest urge to be the means of helping any detective on his upward climb. Therefore we soak bucket-shops one week and bootleggers the next, and poor old Chief Inspector Teal never knows where he is.'

Patricia Holm fingered the stem of her wineglass with a

far-away smile. Perhaps the smile was a trifle wistful. Perhaps it wasn't. You never knew. But she had been the Saint's partner in outlawry long enough to know what any such oratorical opening as that portended; and she smiled.

'It dawns upon me,' said the Saint, 'that our talents have not yet been applied to the crooked angles of the Sport of Kings.'

'I don't know,' said Patricia mildly. 'After picking the winner of the Derby with a pin, and the winner of the Oaks with a pack of cards—'

Simon waved away the argument.

'You may think,' he remarked, 'that we came here to celebrate. But we didn't. Not exactly. We came here to feast our eyes on the celebrations of a brace of lads of the village who always tap the champagne here when they've brought off a coup. Let me introduce you. They're sitting at the corner table behind me on your right.'

The girl glanced casually across the restaurant in the direction indicated. She located the two men at once— there were three magnums on the table in front of them, and their appearance was definitely hilarious.

Simon finished his plate and ordered strawberries and cream.

'The fat one with the face like an egg and the diamond tie-pin is Mr Joseph Mackintyre. He wasn't always Mackintyre, but what the hell? He's a very successful bookmaker; and, believe it or not, Pat, I've got an account with him.'

'I suppose he doesn't know who you are?'

'That's where you're wrong. He does know—and the idea simply tickles him to death. It's the funniest thing he has to talk about. He lets me run an account, pays me when I win, and gets a cheque on the nail when I lose. And all the time he's splitting his sides, telling all his friends about it, and watching everything I do with an eagle eye—just waiting to catch me trying to put something across him.'

'Who's the thin one?'

'That's Vincent Lesbon. Origin believed to be Levantine. He owns the horses, and the way those horses run is nobody's business. Lesbon wins with 'em when he feels like it, and Mackintyre fields against 'em so generously that the starting price usually goes out to the hundred-to-eight mark. It's an old racket, but they work it well.'

Patricia nodded. She was still waiting for the sequel that was bound to come—the reckless light in the Saint's eyes presaged it like a red sky at morning. But he annihilated his strawberries with innocent deliberation before he leaned back in his chair and grinned at her.

'Let's go racing tomorrow,' he said. 'I want to buy a horse.'

They went down to Kempton Park, and arrived when the runners for the second race were going up. The race was a selling plate; with the aid of his faithful pin, Simon selected an outsider that finished third; but the favourite won easily by two lengths. They went round to the ring after the numbers were posted, and the Saint had to bid up to four hundred guineas before he became the proud owner of Hill Billy.

As the circle of buyers and bystanders broke up, Simon felt a hand on his arm. He looked round, and saw a small thick-set man in check breeches and a bowler hat who had the unmistakable air of an ex-jockey.

'Excuse me, sir—have you arranged with a trainer to take care of your horse? My name's Mart Farrell. If I could do anything for you—'

Simon gazed thoughtfully at his new acquisition, which was being held by an expectant groom.

'Why, yes,' he murmured. 'I suppose I can't put the thing in my pocket and take it home. Let's go and have a drink.'

They strolled over to the bar. Simon knew Farrell's name as that of one of the straightest trainers on the Turf, and he was glad that one of his problems had been solved so easily.

'Think we'll win some more races?' he murmured, as the drinks were set up.

'Hill Billy's a good horse,' said the trainer judiciously. 'I used to have him in my stable when he was a two-year-old. I think he'll beat most things in his class if the handicaps give him a run. By the way, sir, I don't know your name.'

It occurred to the Saint that his baptismal title was perhaps too notorious for him to be able to hide the nucleus of his racing stud under a bushel, and for once he had no desire to attract undue publicity.

'Hill Billy belongs to the lady,' he said. 'Miss Patricia Holm. I'm just helping her to watch it.'

As far as Simon Templar was concerned, Hill Billy's career had only one object, and that was to run in a race in which one of the Mackintyre-Lesbon stud was also a competitor. The suitability of the fixture was rather more important and more difficult to be sure of, but his luck was in. Early the next week he learned that Hill Billy was favourably handicapped in the Owners' Plate at Gatwick on the following Saturday, and it so happened that his most serious opponent was a horse named Rickaway, owned by Mr Vincent Lesbon.

Simon drove down to Epsom early the next morning and saw Hill Billy at exercise. Afterwards he had a talk with Farrell.

'Hill Billy could win the first race at Windsor next week if the going's good,' said the trainer. 'I'd like to save him for it—it'd be a nice win for you. He's got the beating of most of the other entries.'

'Couldn't he win the Owners' Handicap on Saturday?' asked the Saint; and Farrell pursed his lips.

'It depends on what they decide to do with Rickaway, sir. I don't like betting on a race when Mr Lesbon has a runner—if I may say so between ourselves. Lesbon had a filly in my stable last year, and I had to tell him I couldn't keep it. The jockey went up before the stewards after the way it ran one day at Newmarket, and that sort of thing doesn't do a trainer's reputation any good. Rickaway's been running down the course on his last three outings, but the way I work out the Owners' Handicap is that he could win if he wanted to.'

Simon nodded.

'Miss Holm rather wants to run at Gatwick, though,' he said. 'She's got an aunt or something from the North coming down for the week-end, and naturally she's keen to show off her new toy.'

Farrell shrugged cheerfully.

'Oh, well, sir, I suppose the ladies have got to have their

way. I'll run Hill Billy at Gatwick if Miss Holm tells me to, but I couldn't advise her to have much of a bet. I'm afraid Rickaway might do well if he's a trier.'

Simon went back to London jubilantly.

'It's a match between Hill Billy and Rickaway,' he said. 'In other words, Pat, between Saintliness and sin. Don't you think the angels might do a job for us?'

One angel did a job for them, anyway. It was Mr Vincent Lesbon's first experience of any such exquisite interference with his racing activities; and it may be mentioned that he was a very susceptible man.

This happened on the Gatwick Friday. The Mackintyre-Lesbon combination was putting in no smart work that day, and Mr Lesbon had whiled away the afternoon at a betting club in Long Acre, where he would sometimes beguile the time with innocuous half-crown punting between sessions at the snooker table. He stayed there until after the result of the last race was through on the tape, and then took a taxi to his flat in Maida Vale to dress for an evening's diversion.

Feminine visitors of the synthetic blonde variety were never rare at his apartment; but they usually came by invitation, and when they were not invited the call generally foreboded unpleasant news. The girl who stood on Mr Lesbon's doorstep this evening, with the air of having waited there for a long time, was an exception. Mr Lesbon's sensitive conscience cleared when he saw her face.

'May I—may I speak to you for a minute?'

Mr Lesbon hesitated fractionally. Then he smiled—which did not make him more beautiful.

'Yes, of course. Come in.'

He fitted his key in the lock and led the way through to his sitting-room. Shedding his hat and gloves, he inspected the girl more closely. She was tall and straight as a sapling, with an easy grace of carriage that was not lost on him. Her face was one of the loveliest he had ever seen; and his practised eye told him that the cornfield gold of her hair owed nothing to artifice.

'What is it, my dear?'

'It's . . . Oh, I don't know how to begin! I've got no right to come and see you, Mr Lesbon, but—there wasn't any other way.'

'Won't you sit down?'

One of Mr Lesbon's few illusions was that women loved him for himself. He was a devotee of the more glutinous productions of the cinema, and prided himself on his polished technique.

He offered her a cigarette, and sat on the arm of her chair.

'Tell me what's the trouble, and I'll see what we can do about it.'

'Well—you see—it's my brother . . . I'm afraid he's rather young and—well, silly. He's been backing horses. He's lost a lot of money, ever so much more than he can pay. You must know how easy it is. Putting on more and more to try and make up for his losses, and still losing . . . Well, he works in a bank; and his bookmaker's threatened to write to the manager if he doesn't pay up. Of course, Derek would lose his job at once . . .'

Mr Lesbon sighed.

'Dear me!' he said.

'Oh, I'm not trying to ask for money! Don't think that. I shouldn't be such a fool. But—well, Derek's made a friend of a man who's a trainer. His name's Farrell—I've met him, and I think he's quite straight. He's tried to make Derek give up betting, but it wasn't any good. However, he's got a horse in his stable called Hill Billy—I don't know anything about horses, but apparently Farrell said Hill Billy would be a certainty tomorrow if your horse didn't win. He advised Derek to do something about it—clear his losses and give it up for good.' The girl twisted her handkerchief nervously. 'He said—please don't think I'm being rude, Mr Lesbon, but I'm just trying to be honest—he said you didn't always want to win—and—and—perhaps if I came and saw you—'

She looked up at Rickaway's owner with liquid eyes, her lower lip trembling a little. Mr Lesbon's breath came a shade faster.

'I know Farrell,' he said, as quietly as he could. 'I had a horse in his stable last year, and he asked me to take it away—just because I didn't always want to win with it. He's changed his principles rather suddenly.'

'I—I'm sure he'd never have done it if it wasn't for Derek, Mr Lesbon. He's really fond of the boy. Derek's awfully nice. He's a bit wild, but . . . Well, you see, I'm four years older than he is, and I simply have to look after him. I'd do anything for him.'

Lesbon cleared his throat.

'Yes, yes, my dear. Naturally.' He patted her hand. 'I see your predicament. So you want me to lose the race. Well, if Farrell's so fond of Derek, why doesn't he scratch Hill Billy and let the boy win on Rickaway?'

'Because—oh, I suppose I can't help telling you. He said no one ever knew what your horses were going to do, and perhaps you mightn't be wanting to win with Rickaway tomorrow.'

Lesbon rose and poured himself out a glass of whisky.

'My dear, what a thing it is to have a reputation!' He gestured picturesquely. 'But I suppose we can't all be paragons of virtue . . . But still, that's quite a lot for you to ask me to do. Interfering with horses is a serious offence—a very serious offence. You can be warned off for it. You can be branded, metaphorically. Your whole career'—Mr Lesbon repeated his gesture—'can be ruined!'

The girl bit her lip.

'Did you know that?' demanded Lesbon.

'I—I suppose I must have realised it. But when you're only thinking about someone you love—'

'Yes, I understand.' Lesbon drained his glass. 'You would do anything to save your brother. Isn't that what you said?'

He sat on the arm of the chair again, searching her face. There was no misreading the significance of his gaze.

The girl avoided his eyes.

'How much do you think you could do, my dear?' he whispered.

'No!' Suddenly she looked at him again, her lovely face pale and tragic. 'You couldn't want that—you couldn't be so—'

'Couldn't I?' The man laughed. 'My dear, you're too

innocent!' He went back to the decanter. 'Well, I respect your innocence. I respect it enormously. We won't say any more about—unpleasant things like that. I will be philanthropical. Rickaway will lose. And there are no strings to it. I give way to a charming and courageous lady.'

She sprang up.

'Mr Lesbon! Do you mean that—will you really—'

'My dear, I will,' pronounced Mr Lesbon thickly. 'I will present your courage with the reward that it deserves. Of course,' he added, 'if you feel very grateful—after Rickaway has lost—and if you would like to come to a little supper party—I should be delighted. I should feel honoured. Now, if you weren't doing anything after the races on Saturday—'

The girl looked up into his face.

'I should love to come,' she said huskily. 'I think you're the kindest man I've ever known. I'll be on the course tomorrow, and if you still think you'd like to see me again—'

'My dear, nothing in the world could please me more!' Lesbon put a hand on her shoulder and pressed her towards the door. 'Now you run along home and forget all about it. I'm only too happy to be able to help such a charming lady.'

Patricia Holm walked round the block in which Mr Lesbon's flat was situated, and found Simon Templar waiting patiently at the wheel of his car. She stepped in beside him, and they whirled down into the line of traffic that was crawling towards Marble Arch.

'How d'you like Vincent?' asked the Saint, and Patricia shivered.

'If I'd known what he was like at close quarters, I'd never have gone,' she said. 'He's got hot, slimy hands, and the way he looks at you . . . But I think I did the job well.'

Simon smiled a little, and flicked the car through a gap between two taxis that gave him half an inch to spare on either wing.

'So that for once we can give the pin a rest,' he said.

Saturday morning dawned clear and fine, which was

very nearly a record for the season. What was more, it stayed fine; and Mart Farrell was optimistic.

'The going's just right for Hill Billy,' he said. 'If he's ever going to beat Rickaway he'll have to do it today. Perhaps your aunt might have five shillings on him after all, Miss Holm.'

Patricia's eyebrows lifted vaguely.

'My—er—'

'Miss Holm's aunt got up this morning with a bilious attack,' said the Saint glibly. 'It's all very annoying after we've put on this race for her benefit, but since Hill Billy's here he'd better have the run.'

The Owners' Handicap stood fourth on the card. They lunched on the course, and afterwards the Saint made an excuse to leave Patricia in the Silver Ring and went into Tattersalls' with Farrell. Mr Lesbon favoured the more expensive enclosure, and the Saint was not inclined to give him the chance to acquire any premature doubts.

The runners for the three-thirty were being put in the frame, and Farrell went off to give his blessing to a charge of his that was booked to go to the post. Simon strolled down to the rails and faced the expansive smile of Mr Mackintyre.

'You having anything on this one, Mr Templar?' asked the bookie juicily.

'I don't think so,' said the Saint. 'But there's a fast one coming to you in the next race. Look out!'

As he wandered away, he heard Mr Mackintyre chortling over the unparalleled humour of the situation in the ear of his next-door neighbour.

Simon watched the finish of the three-thirty, and went to find Farrell.

'I've got a first-class jockey to ride Hill Billy,' the trainer told him. 'He came to my place this morning and tried him out, and he thinks we've a good chance. Lesbon is putting Penterham up—he's a funny rider. Does a lot of Lesbon's work, so it doesn't tell us anything.'

'We'll soon see what happens,' said the Saint calmly.

He stayed to see Hill Billy saddled, and then went back to where the opening odds were being shouted. With his hands in his pockets, he sauntered leisurely up and down the line of bawling bookmakers, listening to the fluctuation of the prices. Hill Billy opened favourite at two to one, with Rickaway a close second at threes—in spite of its owner's dubious reputation. Another horse named Tilbury, which had originally been quoted at eight to one, suddenly came in demand at nine to two. Simon overheard snatches of the gossip that was flashing along the line, and smiled to himself. The Mackintyre-Lesbon combination was expert at drawing that particular brand of red herring across the trail, and the Saint could guess at the source of the rumour. Hill Billy weakened to five to two, while Tilbury pressed close behind it from fours to threes. Rickaway faded out to five to one.

'There are always mugs who'll go for a horse just because other people are backing it,' Mr Mackintyre muttered to his clerk; and then he saw the Saint coming up. 'Well, Mr Templar, what's this fast one you promised me?'

'Hill Billy's the name,' said the Saint, 'and I guess it's good for a hundred.'

'Two hundred and fifty pounds to one hundred for Mr Templar,' said Mackintyre lusciously, and watched his clerk entering up the bet.

When he looked up the Saint had gone.

Tilbury dropped back to seven to two, and Hill Billy stayed solid at two and a half. Just before the 'off' Mr Mackintyre shouted 'Six to one, Rickaway,' and had the satisfaction of seeing the odds go down before the recorder closed his notebook.

He mopped his brow, and found Mr Lesbon beside him.

'I wired off five hundred pounds to ten different offices,' said Lesbon. 'A little more of this and I'll be moving into Park Lane. When that girl came to see me I nearly fainted. What does that man Templar take us for?'

'I don't know,' said Mr Mackintyre phlegmatically.

A general bellow from the crowd announced the 'off', and Mr Mackintyre mounted his stool and watched the race through his field glasses.

'Tilbury's jumped off in front; Hill Billy's third, and Rickaway's going well on the outside . . . Rickaway's moving up, and Hill Billy's on a tight rein . . . Hill Billy's gone up to second. The rest of the field's packed behind, but they don't look like springing any surprises . . . Tilbury's finished. He's falling back. Hill Billy leads, Mandrake running second, Rickaway half a length behind with plenty in hand . . . Penterham's using the whip, and Rickaway's picking up. He's level with Mandrake—no, he's got it by a short head. Hill Billy's a length in front, and they're putting everything in for the finish.'

The roar of the crowd grew louder as the field entered the last furlong. Mackintyre raised his voice.

'Mandrake's out of it, and Rickaway's coming up. Hill Billy's flat out with Rickaway's nose at his saddle . . . Hill Billy's making a race of it. It's neck-and-neck now. Penterham left it a bit late. Rickaway's gaining slowly—'

The yelling of the crowd rose to a final crescendo, and suddenly died away. Mr Mackintyre dropped his glasses and stepped down from his perch.

'Well,' he said comfortably, 'that's three thousand pounds.'

The two men shook hands gravely and turned to find Simon Templar drifting towards them with a thin cigar in his mouth.

'Too bad about Hill Billy, Mr Templar,' remarked Mackintyre succulently. 'Rickaway only did it by a neck, though I won't say he mightn't have done better if he'd started his sprint a bit sooner.'

Simon Templar removed the cigar.

'Oh, I don't know,' he said. 'As a matter of fact, I rather changed my mind about Hill Billy's chance just before the "off". I was over at the telegraph office, and I didn't think I'd be able to reach you in time, so I wired another bet to your London office. Only a small one—six hundred pounds, if you want to know. I hope Vincent's winnings will stand it.' He beamed seraphically at Mr Lesbon, whose face had suddenly gone a sickly grey. 'Of course you recognised Miss Holm—she isn't easy to forget, and I saw you noticing her at the Savoy the other night.'

There was an awful silence.

'By the way,' said the Saint, patting Mr Lesbon affably on the shoulder, 'she tells me you've got hot, slimy hands.

Apart from that, your technique makes Clark Gable look like something the cat brought in. Just a friendly tip, old dear.'

He waved to the two stupefied men and wandered away; and they stood gaping dumbly at his retreating back.

It was Mr Lesbon who spoke first, after a long and pregnant interval.

'Of course you won't settle, Joe,' he said half-heartedly.

'Won't I?' snarled Mr Mackintyre. 'And let him have me up before Tattersalls' Committee for welshing? I've *got* to settle, you fool!'

Mr Mackintyre choked.

Then he cleared his throat. He had a great deal more to say, and he wanted to say it distinctly.

THE RACING ROBOT

by Robert Bloch

Robert Bloch's crime thriller, Psycho, *is not only a classic in its own right, but also the inspiration for Alfred Hitchock's most famous film and its recent sequel,* Psycho 2. *Although the dramatic and chilling story ensured Bloch's fame, it has tended to overshadow much of his other work, in both the mystery and horror genres, where his considerable output of books and short stories during the past fifty years has confirmed him as a gifted and compulsively readable storyteller.*

Although many of his stories are concerned with the darker side of life, Bloch has a wickedly sardonic sense of humour; indeed, he confesses that one of his youthful ambitions was to be a comedian. This streak of wit is seen at its best in his popular series character, Lefty Feep, a Runyonesque figure much given to persuing dubious money-making schemes. Lefty is described as 'an indoor sportsman' with an eye for race horses that usually lose. In the following story he becomes involved in an idea that appears to be foolproof: the use of a robot jockey to win races, but as with any tale that bears Robert Bloch's name, the outcome is totally unexpected.

*   *   *

Jack's shack was almost empty the other night, and so was I. I ordered a stack of wheat cakes and began to wade into them with a knife, fork, and lots of gusto.

Somewhere between the fourth and fifth wheat cake I suddenly noticed a human thumb. The thumb wriggled up and down, pressing the fifth wheat cake back on the plate.

A voice assailed my ears.

'Send back the platter—don't eat this batter.'

I raised my head quickly and stared.

Lefty Feep was standing at the side of my table. The tall, angular indoor sportsman was grinning broadly.

'Lefty Feep!' I exclaimed. 'You're a sight for sore eyes!'

And he was. Feep was wearing a creation designed to make anybody's eyes sore. A checked overcoat, striped trousers, and polka-dot spats hung on his frame, reading from top to bottom. He was carrying a huge cigar and, as I looked, he puffed fifty cents worth of smoke into my face.

'Do not make with the cakes,' Feep insisted, pushing my plate aside. He signalled for a waiter.

'Me and my friend here wish a few pounds of caviar,' he ordered.

The waiter's mouth hung open.

'Also tell the chef to go out and catch a couple humming birds by the tongue. Female humming birds—they are more delicate, if you follow me.'

The waiter followed, with a sarcastic grin.

'Caviar and humming birds' tongues, you say? I suppose you want some champagne, too, with a little Chinese lettuce on the side—you mooching bum!'

Lefty Feep disregarded the criticism. 'Champagne is a good idea,' he nodded. 'But forget us with the lettuce. I got plenty of lettuce right here.'

Reaching into his pocket he pulled out a big wad of bills.

The waiter retreated as Feep sat down next to me.

'Quite a roll you've got there,' I remarked.

'Sure,' said Feep. 'It looks good even without butter.'

Curiosity got the better of me. 'Where in the world did you make all this money?' I demanded.

Feep shrugged. 'It's in the bag with a nag.'

'How?'

'My hay starts to pay.'

'What do you mean, in English?'

'I win a horse race,' he explained.

'But I thought you usually lost on the races,' I remarked.

'Usually I do,' admitted Lefty Feep. 'In fact up to recently I figure the only way I can clean up on a horse is to become a street-sweeper.'

'But you were lucky this time?'

'Smart is the word, buddy,' Feep beamed. 'Let me tell you how it all happens. It is amazing and amusing.'

I got up hastily. I could smell another story coming on. 'Some other time, perhaps,' I mumbled. 'Must go now. I've got a blind date.'

'She must be, if she goes out with you,' Feep retorted.

I tried to dodge, but his outstretched foot tripped me back into my seat.

'There. Now you are comfortable,' said Lefty Feep. 'So kindly flap your ears to these remarkable remarks.'

And as I flapped my ears, Lefty Feep flapped his tongue and began to speak.

*   *   *

It all starts out one day last week when I am strolling down the street enjoying the sunshine and fresh air. I might as well enjoy sunshine and fresh air, since my landlady puts me out of my room.

It seems I do not make a dent in my rent lately, but this does not bother me half as much as the strolling. You see, I am strolling on my hands and knees. The idea is I am trying to look like a dog, so my creditors won't know me.

At the moment I happen to be crouching next to a lamp post, cursing the name of Gorilla Gabface.

This is not the first time I take Gorilla Gabface's name in vain, because he plays plenty of unwashed tricks on me before. But this last trick is the worst—it is the reason why I am down and out. Down on my knees and out of my room.

Because Gorilla Gabface lately buys himself a race horse. Naturally he tells me about it and I take a look at the plug. To me the nag has all the earmarks of a phony pony, and I tell Gabface so. He gets sore and suggests I place a slight wager against the horse if I don't like it.

Which I do, playing the favourite in a race the next day. And Gorilla Gabface's horse beats the favourite.

I cannot figure this out, because his horse is such a fugitive from a milk-wagon. So the next day I bet again and Gabface's horse comes in. And the next day.

The result is I am now flat broke. And I am just beginning to figure out why. Gabface is crookeder than a Jap diplomat, and I now realize he must be doping his horse. Also he is using a lightweight jockey and weighing him in with lead in his ears and mouth.

This I realize. But I also realize it is too late for me to do anything about it. Gorilla Gabface is still winning races, and all I can do is run races with my creditors.

So there I am, crouching by the lamp post and wondering if I can find a bone somewhere.

Then I happen to look up and I see the sign.

'HORSECRACKER INSTITUTE.'

And all at once I remember that this is the place where Sylvester Skeetch and Mordecai Meetch have their laboratory. They are a couple of scientific Americans—two professors without a quiz show. They are always cooking up some screwy idea or theory, and I happen to recall that I once collect fifty bucks from them when I assist in an experiment.

The experiment doesn't work, but neither do I—and I get the fifty bucks anyway.

So that gives me an idea. Why not stroll into the HORSECRACKER INSTITUTE and see if they are bouncing any screwballs today?

I get up off my knees faster than I do in a dice-game when somebody looks at my dice. In two minutes I am up the stairs and in the laboratory.

The outer room is empty. So I push in the other door and take a look.

*   *   *

Sylvester Skeetch and Mordecai Meetch are bending over a big white table. They are wearing dark glasses and those scientific nightgowns. A big light shines down on the table, and also shines on the knives and saws in their hands. Skeetch is sewing something up and mumbling to himself.

I tiptoe over and sneak a peek.

Then I give a gulp.

They have a body on the table and they are sewing it up!

Absolutely—there is a guy lying out on the table, and they are cross-stitching his neck for him!

'Hippocrates' oath!' I mutter, or some such profanity.

Skeetch and Meetch wheel around. Their glasses glare. Then they recognize me. Meetch smiles.

'Well, if it isn't Feep!' he says. 'Glad to see you again.'

I can only stare at the body on the table.

'What kind of morgue *smorgasbord* are you cooking up there?' I gasp, which is something to gasp.

'Nothing at all,' Meetch answers. 'How's our patient, Skeetch?'

'Fine.'

'Patient?' I say.

'Well, you might call him that.' Meetch turns around. 'Ready to get up now?'

Sure enough—I see that the guy on the table is smiling. He nods when Meetch talks to him. I stand there waiting for his sewed head to fall off, but it doesn't.

Instead the guy sits up then stands up.

So does my hair.

'Feep,' says Skeetch, 'Shake hands with Robert.'

I look at Robert. He stands stiff-jointed with a very wooden smile on his face. But he holds out his hand and I grab it. We shake very gently.

He stops shaking hands.

I don't.

Then I look down at my hand to see what I am holding. His arm! It comes off at the shoulder!

'Curse it!' yells Meetch. 'You aren't glued tight enough!'

He grabs the arm, grabs Robert, and throws him down on the table again. Skeetch runs over with a big can of glue and another needle.

I can't bear to look. I cover my eyes.

*   *   *

Skeetch taps me on the shoulder after a while.

'Peekaboo,' he says. 'You can come out now. It's all right.'

'All right?' I say. 'Tearing guys arms off is all right? I guess I don't know my own strength.'

Skeetch laughs.

'Take a look,' he suggests.

I look. Robert is back on his feet. The arm is on again.

'Ulp!' I remark.

Meetch chuckles. 'You're fooled, too,' he grins. 'You think Robert is a man, eh?'

'What else?'

'Well, he's not. He's our newest invention, that's all.'

'Invention?'

'Of course. Feep—meet Robert the Robot.'

'A robot—one of those mechanical men?'

Meetch nods.

'But aren't they always some kind of tin or steel? And don't you have to press a lot of buttons to make them work?'

'Not any more,' Skeetch tells me. 'Robert the Robot is made out of nothing but wires, electrical batteries, synthetic brain and nerve tissue, reclaimed rubber, and plastic wood.'

'Plastic wood?'

'Feel his face and hands. Marvellous likeness, isn't it? Very artistic modelling, just like flesh.'

'But he's alive—he can talk and move—'

'Of course. The synthetic brain and nerve tissue takes care of that. Certain embolistic difficulties must be accounted for, and there's a synaptic differential to be eliminated or compensated for, but—'

Meetch interrupts.

'Never mind all that,' he says. 'What Skeetch is trying to tell you is—we are successful. We create a synthetic human being, a robot. Robert the Robot is the latest scientific achievement, the crowning triumph of this Institute!'

Robert the Robot smiles and bows.

I shrug my shoulders. 'Very interesting,' I admit. 'But now what? What are you going to do with this plastic personality?'

Skeetch scratches his noggin.

'There is an important point. I haven't the faintest idea of what to do with Robert the Robot.'

'Neither have I,' Meetch chimes in. 'Of course we must examine his potentialities. See what kind of a brain he has. Why, right now he's as simple as a new-born babe.'

Robert the Robot stands there with a silly grin on his wooden puss.

'But he walks and talks,' I object. 'That is not simple.'

'Part of the process already under control,' Skeetch says. 'He can speak and understand—but he cannot think. Or can he? That is something we must find out about. What can a robot like this do? What is he capable of? What are his limitations?'

'I dunno,' says Robert the Robot, fingering the suit of clothes they put on him.

'There's the answer!' Meetch sighs. 'He dunno! Skeetch, it's going to be a terrific problem studying and educating this creation of ours! A scientific check will require months of observation.'

'Yes,' Skeetch agrees with a groan. 'And here we are, up to our necks on those rocket-ship plans, too! How are we going to sandwich in enough time to train our creation?'

*　　*　　*

Right here is where I get an idea.

'Why not let me show Robert the Robot around?' I suggest.

'You?'

'Why not? I am in the know. I can teach him plenty. I can show him the ropes. For a small fee, of course.'

Meetch looks at Skeetch. Skeetch looks at Meetch. Neither of them are getting any bargain from this exchange of glances. But Skeetch speaks.

'You might do it. But will you take care of Robert for us? Will you check his reactions regularly?'

'Not only his reactions but also his oil,' I promise.

'No need for that. Robert the Robot is self-operating. No gears, no cogs, nothing to wind up, nothing to run down. No food, water, oil, nothing to plug in.'

'Wrap it up,' I order. 'That's for me.'

'All right,' says Meetch. 'Here's fifty dollars. Take Robert the Robot for a week and see if you can teach him anything.'

'From me he'll learn plenty,' I assure him. 'All the angles and lots of curves, too.'

'We expect a full report,' Skeetch warns me.

'You'll get it.'

So they hand me fifty smackeroos and I waltz down the stairs with Robert the Robot at my heels.

When we get out to the doorway, I turn and take a squint at Robert again.

He doesn't look bad. In his blue suit and white shirt he resembles a window-dummy—but a high class window-dummy. The plastic wood face and hands look like the real flesh. He has nice eyes and a cheerful smile. Not exactly a movie star, but he will pass in a crowd. There is a little glue around his neckline, but not enough to attract attention. A very remarkable personality—this Robert the Robot.

But looks are not everything, and I figure I won't take any chances. If he is going to be my pal for a week, I might as well wise him up a little. I do not wish for him to make any bad breaks in society, and it is my job to see that he is Emily Posted.

'Well, Robert,' I tell him. 'Here we go into the big city.'

'What's a city?' he asks, with a straight face.

'What's a city? Why a city is—a lot of buildings with mortgages on them. A place where people live.'

'What are people?'

'People? Why, persons. Human beings. Like me.'

'You're a human being?'

'Don't say it in that nasty tone of voice. Of course I am. And you are going to pretend that you're one, too.'

'What do human beings do?'

'Why, I eat and sleep.'

'What are they?'

'Eating is something you do with food after cooking it.'

'What's cooking?'

*   *   *

Slang he talks! So I explain about food and eating, and then I explain sleeping.

He shakes his head. 'I don't see anything in it,' he tells me. 'I will not eat or sleep. What else do people do?'

'They work.' So I tell him about jobs and working.

'But why do they work?'

'In order to get money so they can eat and sleep.'

Robert the Robot grins. 'People are silly, then,' he decides. 'I don't want to be a people.'

'Person,' I correct him. 'Watch your grammar. People means a whole snag of finks. A person is just one lug.'

'Finks and lugs,' the Robot mumbles.

'Come on, let's walk around for a while,' I suggest.

And off we go on a conducted tour. It is the first time I ever show a Robot the sights of the big city, but he is not a bad guy as dummies go. It really gives me a bang to point out the joints, and Robert gets quite enthusiastic.

What really gives him the old jolt is the machinery. The cars and busses and trains are quite a thrill. Being a robot, naturally he is interested in mechanical stuff. So we watch neon signs and adding machines and I take him over to see a printing press and a couple factories. In fact, it is after dark before I manage to tear him away from a clothes-pin factory.

We stand outside and wait for a car near a drug-store. Robert the Robot happens to notice the weighing machine.

'What is that?' he asks.

So of course I have to explain what a weighing machine is. And just for fun I slip a penny in the slot and let him weigh himself. A card comes out with his weight on it.

Robert the Robot weighs 85 lbs.

That is curious. Here is a robot, looking like a full-grown man, and he only weighs 85 pounds. The plastic wood, of course.

'You're quite a lightweight,' I remark. 'Funny.'

Only on second thought it isn't funny.

It's wonderful!

'Eighty-five pounds!' I yell. 'Come on, Robert—we're going places!'

'Home?' he asks.

'No, not home,' I answer. 'We are going to the amusement park!'

And that is just where we do go.

* * *

I take Robert the Robot out to the carnival. Nobody notices him, of course, or thinks he is any different. They do not realize he is a robot. They also do not realize he is a gold-mine—but I do.

I get him into the carnival and I throw him on the merry-go-round right away. Put him right on the wooden horses.

'This is nice,' he tells me, sliding up and down and hanging onto the brass pole.

'Let go the pole and see if you can ride,' I suggest.

He does. He can ride.

We go around again.

'Why are we doing this?' asks Robert the Robot.

'You'll find out,' I answer.

Because I know what I'm doing. I'm teaching Robert the Robot how to ride.

Here is a robot who looks like a human being. He only weighs 85 pounds. If he can ride—what a jockey he will make!

I can put weights on him when he weighs in that will make him plenty heavy. Then I remove them and he goes back to just 85 pounds on a horse. And Gorilla Gabface, for all his crookedness, can't get a jockey weighing 85 pounds. I will enter a race, bet with Gabface, and let the robot ride a horse I put my money on. It's a cinch.

After I give Robert the Robot a few more riding lessons I hustle him out of the carnival. We walk along the street and I explain my plan to him.

I tell him what a race is, and what live horses are, and how to handle one.

'Tomorrow you will ride like that,' I finish up. 'You will win a lot of money. That means plenty of groceries and a nice place to sleep.'

Robert the Robot shakes his wooden head.

'But I do not like groceries and I never sleep,' he complains. 'Besides, I am not sure that one of these horses, as you call them, is safe for me. My arms might fall off again.'

'You'll like it,' I argue.

'No. I rather look at some more machinery,' says Robert the Robot. 'Beautiful wheels and pistons.'

'Beautiful baloney!' I sneer.

'Yes,' whispers Robert the Robot. 'Beautiful.'

'What?' I turn my head.

'A beautiful baloney, you call her?' breathes Robert the Robot.

He is staring off into space. I squint and follow his gaze.

Robert the Robot is looking into a department store window. He is gawking at a window dummy standing there. A blonde window dummy with long false eyelashes, wearing a negligée.

'A beautiful baloney,' he whispers.

'You are wrong, Robert,' I correct him. 'Women are not baloneys. They are generally referred to in polite circles as tomatoes. Or wenches. Or ginch. Of course, this one is just a window dumm—'

*　　*　　*

Then I catch myself in time. Because another idea hits me.

'Robert,' I whisper.

He does not hear me, he is so busy giving this window dummy the old eye.

'Robert, do you like her?'

'Oh, yes,' he sighs. 'I like her.'

Yes, I am right. He doesn't know any better—he falls for this window dummy. So I go right ahead with my idea.

'Robert, how would you like to have her for a girl-friend?'

'Girl-friend?'

I start to explain what a girl-friend is, but I don't need to. He catches on. He shakes his head so fast the stitches nearly break on his neck. And almost cracks his plastic lips with a smile.

'I will see to it,' I promise. 'If you will run this race tomorrow for me.'

'Well—'

'Think of it, Robert! She will be sitting up in the grand-stand watching you ride. Watching you win! You'll be a hero!'

'Do you think she'll like me?' asks Robert. 'I can't seem to get her to smile at me.'

Then I catch on. *He* thinks the window-dummy is alive, the way he is!

'She's marvellous,' he breathes. 'Wonderful how she manages to stand still all this time without ever moving.'

'Sure,' I agree. 'Most women won't stand still for a minute.'

'Why doesn't she talk?' he asks.

'Listen,' I tell him. 'When you hang around dames as long as I do, you will be grateful to find one who doesn't talk.'

'Maybe so,' says Robert the Robot.

'Well, then, how about it?' I ask, giving him the needle. 'If she comes along, will you ride in a race tomorrow?'

'Yes,' he says.

So I pat him on his wooden back and dash into the department store. It is closed, of course, but I locate the watchman and the head designer. I tell the head designer I wish to buy his window-dummy.

'You want that dummy?' ask the designer jerk.

'Well,' I say, kind of embarrassed, 'I don't really want it. It's for a friend. A present—like a doll.'

'Awfully big for a doll,' says the designer jerk.

'I have an awfully big friend,' I explain.

So to make a long story short, I finally walk off with the dummy for twenty bucks. This is a lot of hay, but I figure I will be making bales of hay when the sun shines on the race-track tomorrow.

In a few minutes I am back on the street, dragging the dummy across my back.

'Robert, meet your new girl-friend,' I say. 'Here she is.'

'What's her name?' he asks, very gullible.

'Oh—her name is Roberta,' I tell him.

He reaches out to shake hands. I wag the dummy's arm.

'Can't she walk?' he inquires.

'Have a heart,' I explain. 'The poor girl stands on her feet all day long. She is tired.'

'I am not tired.'

'You are not a woman,' I snap. 'No, I will carry her home. She must be ready to go to the race tomorrow.'

*　　*　　*

I do carry her home. I give the landlady the back rent and she gives me a little back talk, and then I settle Robert the Robot in one room and lock Roberta the window-dummy in the other room.

'Got to keep it proper,' I tell Robert. 'Now I must go out and make final arrangements.'

Which is just what I do.

I head for the stable.

I am looking for a personality by the name of Horse-Sense Homer, a dear friend of mine who is quite a jack around the track. He owns a horse of his own—a nag if there ever was one—and I fancy he will be currying him in a hurry tonight.

Which he is. I step into the stable and the first person I recognize is Horse-Sense Homer himself. I do not see him in the dark but I can tell he is a stable man, because he has such an air about him.

'Homer,' I yell. 'It's me—Lefty Feep!'

He turns on a lantern and I see he is lying down on the straw, asleep. Next to him is his scrawny horse.

'Who's your friend?' I inquire.

Horse-Sense Homer smiles. 'The best nag I own,' he tells me. 'The name is Glue Factory.'

'You're telling me?'

'A great horse,' he insists. 'Watch her win tomorrow.'

'Got a good jockey?'

'Fair. I'm depending on Glue Factory, though.'

'Well, I've got your troubles all packed up,' I tell him. 'I just pick up a jockey for you.'

'Pick up?'

'With one hand,' I assure him. 'He's that light.'

'No midgets.'

'A full-grown man,' I come back. 'Great rider, too. You can't lose. He only weighs 85 pounds.'

'85 pounds?'

'A wonder. And just to show you how much confidence I have in him, I'm going to bet all your money on winning.'

'All my money, eh? With who?'

'Gorilla Gabface,' I answer. 'He is racing his steed against you, is he not?'

'Right,' says Horse-Sense Homer, frowning. 'You know I am a little afraid. That horse of his, Cut Plug, is a pretty fast filly.'

'Don't be silly with that filly!' I sneer.

'But Gabface's horse always wins.'

'Not now he doesn't. Not with my 85-pound jockey.'

'Well, Lefty, wait a minute now—'

'No time to wait. Got to place the bet.' I grab his wallet and run off. He stares after me, shaking his head.

*　　*　　*

I shake my feet back to town and into Gorilla Gabface's pool parlour where he hangs out, particularly around the chins.

And there sits the fat slob himself, grinning from ear to ear. When I walk in he laughs.

'Well, if it isn't Lefty Feep,' he cracks. 'And pretty sagging, too! What's the matter, Lefty—you lose your racing form?'

I just hand him the onion eye.

'I guess my Cut Plug teaches you a lesson at the track today,' he chuckles. 'Maybe now you will learn to stop horsing around.'

Then I give it to him.

'Listen, Gabface. Is it true that you plan to enter that horse-doctor's delight of yours in tomorrow's race?'

'The fifth race, to be exact,' Gabface answers. 'And what is it to you? Want to make a bet on him winning?'

'No,' I come back. 'But I will make a little wager with you that Cut Plug gets beat by another steed.'

'Such as which?'

'I am betting on Glue Factory,' I tell him.

'Glue Factory?' Gabface laughs again and several windows fall out. 'Why that oat-burner does not win a race since Paul Revere sells her back in 1776.'

'She wins tomorrow,' I state. 'Do you wish to amble into a gamble?'

'I will bet against you Feep,' Gabface sneers. 'What amount do you wish to wager? A dime? Or does somebody hand you a quarter?'

'I will bet $500,' I tell him.

Gabface sits up.

'Where do you get $500 and how do you hide the body?' he scoffs.

'Here is the dough.' I wave the wallet at him.

He smiles. 'All right. It's a bet. I will see you at the track tomorrow with my wheelbarrow. I need it to carry the winnings in.'

He jerks his head all at once.

'Who is the jockey?' he asks. 'Horse-Sense Homer's regular boy?'

'I got a new jockey for this race,' I tell him. 'Fellow by the name of Robert.'

'Never hear of him.'

'You will,' I predict. And walk out.

*　　*　　*

So the deal is fixed. I put up the dough, the bet is on, and all I do now is arrange final details. The next morning I go down and get racing togs for Robert the Robot and have him weighed in. I put a few weights inside his stomach and sew him back up and he tips the scales at 125. While we weigh Gabface comes in with his jockey. He also tips the scales at 125, but he has a mouthful of pennies or something and does not say anything. I figure he really goes for about 118—and with Robert the Robot at 85, he is a cinch to win.

Gabface doesn't think so. He comes over and looks at Robert. Robert is nothing much to look at. His wooden face and painted smile do not show up very well in the daylight, and he moves very stiff and awkward, just as anybody would if they had wooden hips.

'So this is your new jockey?' grins Gabface, looking Robert up and down. He stares hard, and for a minute I am afraid he will realize that Robert, in spite of the plastic wood, is just a mechanical man.

But he only sniffs and says, 'Fine specimen. Must be out on a bender last night from the way his face looks. He shouldn't ride a horse today. A pink elephant is better.'

I do not comment, but take Robert the Robot out of there in a speedy hurry.

How do you feel?' I ask him.

'Feel? What's feel?' he comes back.

'Never mind. Are you ready to race today?'

'Will Roberta watch me?'

'Right in the stands with me,' I promise.

This cheers him up. We go around to the stable and I introduce him to Glue Factory and give him a few pointers on riding. This isn't really important, because the horse will race by itself, and all that bothers it is weight. So it's a cinch.

The only one who worries now is Horse-Sense Homer. He happens to come up and say hello while Robert and I stand there.

'You the marvellous jockey Feep tells me about?' he says, slapping Robert on the back.

'Oooooh!' says Robert the Robot and falls down. One of his legs buckles and comes off at the knee.

'Jumping steeple-chase!' yells Homer. 'I cripple him for life! Get a doctor—get an ambulance—police—'

'Get some glue,' I tell him, very calmly.

'Glue? But his leg—'

'I will glue it on again.'

'Glue a man's leg on?'

'He is only a dummy,' I explain. 'A robot. A mechanical man. There is nothing to worry about.'

Homer takes this all in and his face turns a delicate shade of blue.

'Nothing to worry about?' he gasps. 'You mean you bet my $500 that you will win a race with a dummy for a jockey?'

'But he is very smart for a dummy,' I assure Homer.

'Look,' I say, putting his leg back on, 'he is made out of

plastic wood.' And bend the foot backwards. 'Soft as mud.'

'Don't do that,' Homer shrieks. 'Your name is mud, Feep! You put $500 of mine into the paws of Gorilla Gabface with this crazy stunt.'

'Don't burn your bridges until you come to them,' I cheer him up. 'Just watch Robert the Robot race.'

'I am going to close my eyes and lie down,' Homer sighs.

* * *

Then the bugle blows for the first race and I run off. I get Robert in his racing togs and pull them over his plastic body. I give him his last-minute instructions. But he looks worried.

'What about Roberta?' he says. 'What about her?'

'She is waiting in the stands to see you,' I needle him. 'Here—she sends you this to wear.'

And I pull out a part of the window-dummy's wig I clip off.

'A lock of her hair!' whispers Robert the Robot. 'Gee!'

'Now get in there and win,' I coach. 'The fifth race is coming up.' And I turn him over to Homer.

Then I go back to the stands. Here I sit in a box with Roberta the window-dummy next to me like I promise. I dig her up a nice dress to wear and drag her along to a seat. She has to be carried in, but nobody notices very much— everybody being on their feet and screaming while they watch the races.

Comes the fifth race. Comes the horses. Comes Cut Plug and Glue Factory. Comes the break at the barrier. And they're off!

Robert the Robot sails along in his saddle. Cut Plug's jockey gives him the old boot and spur. But Glue Factory takes the lead. With scarcely no weight to carry, she is really feeling her oats. I see Robert bouncing up and down and the horse gallops around the inside stretch and then heads for home.

The crowd roars. Glue Factory is a long shot. And Cut

Plug, the favourite, is all shot. Because Glue Factory wins in a breeze. Five lengths!

'Yeeeoowee!' yells a loud voice in my ear. It turns out to be my own voice.

'I am robbed!' screams another voice from in back of me.

I turn around and see Gorilla Gabface dancing up and down on one foot in a rage polka.

'Give me the dough,' I call to him, in a very sweet tone of voice.

'Why you—' Gabface begins. But he never goes any further in his description because he suddenly notices Roberta the window-dummy sitting next to me.

'Ladies present,' he mumbles. 'Is this your latest flame, Lefty?'

I keep Roberta's back turned. 'No,' I explain. 'She is the—the girl-friend of my jockey.'

'Oh, that dirty—' Gabface commences. And catches himself once more. He shakes his head. 'I still do not see how you win,' he groans. 'The horse looks like it isn't carrying any weight at all.'

'Pay up,' I say, very patient.

'All right, Feep. You get a break this time. But it doesn't happen again.'

'Oh no?' I see a chance to get really even with this crook. 'What do you plan to do? Give that nag of yours a shot of dynamite in his oats to make him start off with a bang?'

'Do you mean to infer that I pull a fixed race?' Gabface grunts.

'Who cares?' I grin. 'No matter what you do from now on, I win all the races.'

'So? Perhaps you wish to make another bet? I am racing my horse again Saturday,' Gabface snarls.

This is just what I like to hear.

'Certainly I will wager. Shall we say a cool grand this time?' I suggest.

'That is plenty icy.' Gabface is hedging.

'Afraid, eh?'

'Listen you,' says Gabface, sticking his chins out. 'I am not afraid of man nor beast—and one of those categories must cover you. I will bet the thousand. My horse against that plug you and Homer run.'

So it is a bet.

* * *

Gabface leaves and I run down to meet Robert the Robot and Horse-Sense Homer.

Horse-Sense is very excited. He cannot believe the race is won. When I tell him about the new bet he is happier than ever.

Robert the Robot is happy, too. I bring him a whole handful of hair from the window-dummy's wig and say she pulls it out in her excitement.

He is anxious to race again.

'This is more fun than the merry-go-round,' he admits.

So it is settled. Robert the Robot and Roberta the dummy go home with me in a cab. I keep them separated and act as chaperone when we get to my dump.

Starting early the next morning I take Robert down to the stable for a workout. Only two more days to go and I don't wish to take chances. I know Gorilla Gabface is sore, and when he gets sore he gets mean, and when he gets mean he is dangerous, and when he is dangerous there is trouble ahead.

He will do anything to win the race Saturday, I know. So the next two days I train Robert and guard him carefully. I also have Horse-Sense Homer guard his horse, too. Gorilla Gabface will not get a chance to pull any funny business, I figure. And on Friday afternoon everything is all set for the big day tomorrow.

Until we get home.

Then I discover my mistake. I spend all this time guarding Robert the Robot and the horse. Roberta is left home alone.

And when we return to the house she is gone!

Vanished!

'Where is Roberta?' squeaks Robert, hopping around the room in excitement.

'Probably she goes to the beauty parlour to get her hair fixed,' I stall. 'She will pull a lot out tomorrow when you win.'

But I am panicky.

I jump two feet when the doorbell rings.

Then I get to the door, open it, and look out. There is no one there. But standing in the hall is Roberta.

She looks all right. Whoever takes her does no damage.

I drag her in and show her to Robert. He cheers up and stays cheerful all evening.

But I worry.

*   *   *

Saturday morning, the day of the big race, finds me down at the tracks quite early indeed. Horse-Sense Homer takes Glue Factory out for exercise and reports she is very fast today. Robert the Robot goes into the stables to rest. But me—I head for the stall where Gorilla Gabface keeps his oat meal-ticket.

Sure enough, there he is. And when he sees me he cannot keep the nasty grin off his puss.

'So,' I accuse him. 'You are the one who kidnaps my jockey's girl-friend.'

'Who kidnaps who?' he comes back. 'Nobody puts the snatch on her. She is back, isn't she?'

'Yes,' I admit. 'But you grab her in the first place.'

Gabface leers.

'Maybe I do. Maybe I figure on queering the race by making your jockey feel upset about his girl-friend,' he hints. 'But I do not realize then that the girl-friend is a window-dummy.'

'So what? Everybody has a hobby.'

'Window-dummies aren't hobbies,' Gabface goes on. 'You know, Feep, I get to thinking when I find out this. I get to thinking about what kind of a personality might have a window-dummy for a heartburn. Perhaps, I figure, he is a dummy himself.'

'You're slightly but completely screwy,' I suggest.

'Maybe. Maybe not.' Gabface grins in his chins. 'It adds

up, doesn't it? Your horse races like she doesn't carry much weight.'

'But a live dummy is ridiculous,' I stall.

Gabface nods. 'I agree with you, Feep,' he tells me. 'And there will be no such nonsense in today's race.'

'What do you mean?'

'I send some of the boys around to examine your jockey,' he informs me.

'Hey, what do you mean?' I yell.

'Can't put anything over on me,' he comes back. 'See you after the race. I can use that thousand.'

I do not waste any more time. I heat my feet running back to the stable where I leave Robert the Robot.

I rush in. 'Robert!' I screech. 'Where are you?'

No answer. I see no one in the gloom.

But as I rush across the floor I stumble. Stumble on Robert the Robot. Or what's left of Robert the Robot.

*   *   *

Robert the Robot is lying in a heap on the stable floor. He does not look human any more. He resembles a small junk pile.

Gorilla's boys really interview him. In fact they tear him to pieces!

Sure enough, there is nothing on the floor but torn clothes, twisted wires and cords, and a lot of scraps of plastic wood. I bend down and pick up a handful. It kneads between my fingers.

'Poor Robert,' I whisper, thinking of the Robot.

'Poor me!' I also whisper, thinking of the thousand berries.

'All set?' It is Horse-Sense Homer, running in panting. 'I just get a fresh hunch we win,' he announces. 'So I plank one thousand more on the nose to win. Odds are three to one! We will clean up!'

'Clean up this mess,' I suggest.

'What is it?' Homer asks.

'It's our jockey. That's what it is.'

And I explain.

'But we can't race Glue Factory, then. We lose all our dough! And to think I put it all on her nose!'

'Wait a minute!' I stare down and get an inspiration. Crazy, but an idea.

'We need a jockey?' I say.

'Of course we do,' wails Homer.

'You got one. Me.'

'You—Feep?'

'Why not? I weigh about 130.'

'Too much. Gabface's horse will beat us unless we get an edge in weight or something.'

'We will get something,' I promise him. 'Robert the Robot will win for us yet.'

'But he's busted and you're riding.'

'Leave it to me,' I promise him.

The bugle sounds.

'Hurry up—where's the nag?' I yell, picking up what is left of Robert the Robot and dashing for the stable entrance.

Homer shrugs but follows me.

Fifteen minutes later I am wearing racing togs and jogging out to the post on Glue Factory.

Gabface is standing next to his pony and when he sees us coming up to the starting post he nearly falls over.

'You—riding this race?' he gasps.

The hypo he is trying to slip his horse falls out of his hand.

'Winning this race,' I grin. 'By a nose.'

'You're nuts,' he yells.

'You'll see,' I call back. 'You can't stop Robert the Robot. We win by a nose.'

'I will hold my nose,' Gabface says. 'But if I hold it until you limp past the finish line I will suffocate.'

'Is that a promise?'

'Good-bye, Feep. And say good-bye to your money, too,' he calls after me.

I bend down and pat Glue Factory on the neck as we get ready to run. She is in good form, but I am heavy. And I am depending on just one thing to win.

But my worries dissolve in a cloud of dust.

We're off. Way, way off!

I keep watching Gabface's horse—Cut Plug. He comes up strong. I give my nag the old pressure. We are neck and neck. We pull away from the rest. We round the turn. The crowd is busting lungs all over the place.

We head for home. I bend over in the saddle. Cut plug is even with me. I see the finish line ahead. We are neck and neck. And then I give one last boot. Glue Factory jerks her head out. We cross the finish line.

We win—by a nose!

And that, of course, is where I get all my money.

*   *   *

Lefty Feep sat back and relighted his cigar with a dollar bill.

'Some story,' he commented.

'Some hooey,' I said.

'Who's hooey?'

'You,' I answered. 'To begin with, what did those scientists say when you told them their robot was ruined?'

'Nothing. They will build another one anyway. Right now they are all mixed up building a rocket ship and they do not even pay attention when I report to them. No trouble there at all.'

'All right,' I sighed. 'But there is one other thing wrong with this story of yours. How did you manage to win this race? You're heavier than the average jockey. Even if your horse was in good form, I don't see how you could win by a nose, as you say.'

'Well,' Feep admitted, 'I really don't win.'

'Aha, I thought so!'

'Robert the Robot wins the race, like I tell Gabface.'

'But Robert the Robot was torn to pieces.'

'I know. But he still wins by a nose.'

'How?'

'It's this way,' said Lefty Feep. 'My horse is almost as fast as Gabface's this day. In fact, without doping his nag, the two horses will run about even, I figure. So I can ride as jockey and come in neck and neck.'

'But you won by a nose.'

'That is where Robert the Robot really wins,' Feep

grinned. 'You see, when he is busted, I merely take some of the plastic wood from Robert the Robot's body and—'

'And what?'

'And I mould an extra long nose to glue on the horse!'

THE GRAND NATIONAL CASE

by Julian Symons

Julian Symons is one of the most admired and respected figures among modern crime writers, both as a historian of the genre and as a highly accomplished author of mystery novels and short stories. His novel The Colour of Murder *(1957) was voted the best of the year by the British Crime Writers' Association, while his study of the detective story,* Bloody Murder, *published in 1972, won a special award from the Mystery Writers of America. He is also an influential reviewer of crime fiction and has published an important listing of 'The Hundred Best Crime Stories'.*

Apart from his crime novels, which are frequently based on real-life cases, Julian Symons has written a series of short stories about a resourceful private detective, Francis Quarles, which have appeared in Ellery Queen's Mystery Magazine *and in two collections. 'The Grand National Case' is one of the detective's toughest challenges, leading to a particularly dramatic climax.*

* * *

'With my son up he can do it,' Sir Reginald Bartley said emphatically. 'There's no better amateur in the country than Harry. I tell you I'm not sorry Baker can't ride him.'

There was something challenging in his tone. Trainer Norman Johnson, wooden-faced, bow-legged, said non-committally, 'He can ride, your son, I'm not denying it.'

'And Lucky Charm's a fine horse.'

'Ay, there's nothing against the horse,' Johnson said.

'Then what's the matter with you, man? A few days ago you were keen as mustard, telling me I had a chance of leading in my first National winner. Today you're enthusiastic as the cat who started lapping a saucer of cream and found it was sour milk.'

'I wouldn't want to raise false hopes, Sir Reginald, that's all. Here comes Lucky Charm.'

'And here comes Harry.'

Private detective Francis Quarles stood with them in the paddock at Aintree and listened to this conversation with interest. Horse racing was one of the few subjects about which he had no specialized knowledge, and he was here only because he had been tracking down the man who later became known as the Liverpool Forger. Quarles had once cleared up a troublesome series of robberies committed in the chain of department stores owned by Sir Reginald, and when they met again at the Adelphi Hotel the business magnate had invited the private detective to be his guest at Aintree.

In the hotel that morning Quarles had learned that Lucky Charm was a forty to one outsider in this year's Grand National, that its jockey Baker had fallen and put out his shoulder on the previous day, and that Lucky Charm would now be ridden by Sir Reginald's son Harry.

Now he looked at the big-shouldered powerful-looking black horse with the number 8 on his saddle cloth, who was being led round by a stable boy. Then at the young man who walked up to them wearing a jacket of distinctive cerise and gold hoops.

'How is it, Harry? All set?' asked Sir Reginald.

'Why not?' Harry Bartley had the kind of dark, arrogant good looks that Quarles always distrusted.

'We're all ready to lead him in,' Sir Reginald said, with what seemed to Quarles almost fatuous complacency. 'We know we've got the horse and the jockey, too, Harry my boy.'

Johnson said nothing. Harry Bartley pulled a handkerchief out of his breast pocket and blew his nose.

'Got your lucky charm?' the owner persisted.

'Of course.' Harry's voice was slightly blurred, as though he had had a tooth out. From the same pocket he produced a rabbit's paw, kissed it and put it back carefully.

'There's Mountain Pride,' said Sir Reginald a little wistfully. Mountain Pride, Quarles knew, was the favourite, a bay gelding with a white star on his forehead.

'Time to go.' Harry Bartley gave them a casual nod and turned away, walking a little erratically across the paddock to the place where the stable boy stood, holding Lucky Charm. Had he been drinking, Quarles wondered?

'Good luck,' his father called. 'Better be getting along to the stand.' Sir Reginald was a choleric little man, and now his face was purple as he turned to the trainer. 'You may not like the boy, but you could have wished him luck.'

Johnson's wooden expression did not change. 'You know I wish Lucky Charm all the luck there is, Sir Reginald.'

'Trouble with Johnson is, he's sulking,' Sir Reginald said when they were in the stand. 'Insisted Baker should ride the horse when I wanted Harry. I gave way, after all Baker's a professional, fine jockey. Then, when Baker was injured, wanted to have some stable boy and I put my foot down.'

'What has he got against your son?'

Sir Reginald looked at Quarles out of the corner of one slightly bloodshot eye. 'The boy's a bit wild, y'know. Nothing wrong with him, but—a bit wild. There they go.'

The horses had paraded in front of the stand and now they were going down to the starting post. Bright March sunlight illuminated the course and even Francis Quarles, who was not particularly susceptible to such things, found something delightful in the scene. The men and women in the stands and the crowd chattering along the rails, the men with their raglans and mackintoshes and the patches of colour in women's coats and hats, the ballet-like grace of the horses and the vivid yet melting green of the Aintree background . . .

Quarles pulled himself up on the edge of sentiment. His companion said sharply, 'Harry's having trouble.'

The horses were at the starting post. Quarles raised his glasses. After a moment he picked out Lucky Charm. The black horse was refusing to get into line with the rest. Three times Harry Bartley brought him up and he turned away.

Sir Reginald tapped the stick he carried on the ground. 'Come on now, Harry, show him who's master. Never known Lucky Charm like this before.'

'Is he used to your son?'

The question was not well received. 'Harry can ride any horse,' Bartley snapped. Then he drew in his breath and his voice joined with thousands of others in the cry: 'They're off.'

Now in the stand a mass of binoculars was raised to follow the progress of some thirty horses over some of the most testing fences in the world. Now bookmakers looked anxious, punters let cigars go out, women twisted race cards in gloved hands. Everything now depended on the jumping skill and staying power of horses who had been trained for months in preparation for this day, and on the adeptness of the jockeys in nursing their charges and then urging them forward to some moment of supreme endeavour.

The horses came up in a bunch to the first fence, rose to it, cleared it. Thousands of throats exhaled and articulated sighingly the words: 'They're over.'

They were not all over, Quarles saw. A jockey lay on the ground, a jockey wearing red jacket and white cap. A riderless horse ran on.

On to the second jump and the third, a six-foot ditch with a four-foot-nine fence on the other side of it. Now there was a cry: 'O'Grady's down. Double or Quits is down. Bonny Dundee's down.' There were more riderless horses, more jockeys on the ground who stumbled to their feet and ran to the rails when all the runners had passed.

Past Becher's they came and round the Canal Turn and then over Valentine's, the field beginning to string out.

'There's Mountain Pride in front,' Sir Reginald cried. 'And Johnny Come Lately and Lost Horizon. And Lucky Charm's with them.' Almost under his breath he muttered, 'But I don't like the way the boy's handling him.'

The horses came round towards the stand. Quarles watched the cerise and gold jacket take the fourteenth fence, and it seemed to him that Harry Bartley was not so much riding as desperately clinging on to the horse. They

came to the fifteenth fence, the Chair, which is one of the
most awkward at Aintree, a six-foot ditch and then a fence
five-foot-two in height which rises roughly in a chair's
shape.

Mountain Pride soared over, and so did the two horses
that followed. Then came the cerise and gold jacket. Lucky
Charm rose to the fence and went over beautifully, but as
he landed the jockey seemed simply to slip off and lay
prone on the turf. Lucky Charm ran on, the rest of the field
thundered by.

Sir Reginald lowered his glasses slowly. 'That's that. Not
my Grand National, I'm afraid.'

Quarles waited for the figure on the turf to get up, but it
did not move. Ambulance men beside the jump ran on to
the course with a stretcher, bent over the jockey. Still he did
not move as they lifted him on to the stretcher.

They watched in stupefaction as the ambulance men
carried him away. Then Sir Reginald, his usually ruddy face
white as milk, said: 'Come on, man, come on.'

'What about the race?'

'To hell with the race,' Sir Reginald cried. 'I want to know
what's happened to my son.'

*   *   *

The limp body of Harry Bartley was carried round to the
course hospital, in the administrative block. Doctor
Ferguson, the local doctor, had just begun his examination
when the door of the ward was pushed open and a handsome grey-haired man, with a pair of binoculars slung
round his neck, came in.

'Ferguson? My name's Ramsay, I'm Harry's doctor.
We've met before, up here last year. Is the boy badly hurt?'

'As far as I can see he's received no injury at all. There's
something very wrong though, his pulse is feeble and
irregular. Was he subject to any kind of fits, do you know?'

'Harry? Not to my knowledge.' Ferguson made way as
Doctor Ramsay approached the body and bent over it. He
straightened up with a puzzled frown. 'Have you smelt
round the nose and mouth?'

'No, I haven't. I'd only begun to examine him.' Ferguson bent over too and caught the smell of bitter almonds. 'My God, he's taken poison.'

'Taken it—or it's been administered to him.' Ramsay's face was grave. 'The question is what, and how? It's not cyanide, obviously, or he wouldn't be alive now.'

'I must telephone—' Doctor Ferguson broke off as Sir Reginald and Francis Quarles, followed by trainer Norman Johnson, came into the room. Ramsay went over to Sir Reginald and placed a hand on his arm.

'Bartley, I won't mince words. You must be prepared for a shock. Harry has been poisoned in some way, and there's very little we can do for him.'

'He'll be all right?'

'It's touch and go,' Ramsay said evasively. He watched Francis Quarles approach the body. 'Who's that?'

Sir Reginald told him.

Quarles bent over the unconscious figure, looked at its pale face and purple lips and nose, smelt the flavour of bitter almonds. He came over to Ramsay, who had now been joined by Ferguson. Sir Reginald introduced the detective.

'Have you gentlemen made up your minds about this case?' Quarles asked. He spoke in a faintly languid manner which made Ramsay, who was brisk and soldierly, bristle slightly.

'Not yet. In your superior wisdom I suppose you have done so.'

'Have you considered nitro benzene?'

'Nitro benzene,' Doctor Ferguson said thoughtfully. 'Yes, that would explain the prussic acid symptoms, but I don't see why it should have occurred to you.'

'I know little about horse racing, but something about poisoning,' Quarles said. 'And I had the opportunity of seeing Harry Bartley just before the race. His appearance then seemed to me very strange. His speech was blurred and he walked unsteadily. The unworthy thought crossed my mind that he might be drunk, but as you will know such an appearance of drunkenness is a common symptom in nitro benzene poisoning.'

There was silence. Ramsay shifted uncomfortably. Sir Reginald said, 'What are we waiting for? If there's no ambulance let's get him in to Liverpool in my car.'

Ferguson crossed over to Harry Bartley again, felt pulse and heart and then drew a sheet up over the face. Ramsay said to Sir Reginald, 'He's gone. I wanted to break it gently. There was never any chance.'

'But when we came in Ferguson here was telephoning—'

'I was telephoning the police superintendent on the course,' Ferguson said. 'There'll need to be an investigation. This is a bad business.'

Francis Quarles took no part in the flurry of conversation that followed the arrival of the police superintendent and the other officers with him. Instead he went over to the wooden-faced trainer Norman Johnson, and took him outside. They paced up and down in hearing of the excited crowds who were cheering the victory of Mountain Pride, and Quarles asked questions.

'Harry Bartley may have died by accident, but I would bet a hundred pounds that he was murdered. Now there's one obvious question I should like to have answered by a racing expert. Is it likely that he was killed to prevent Lucky Charm winning the National?'

Johnson paused for an appreciable time before he said bluntly: 'No.'

'It's unlikely?'

'You can put it out of your mind. I'm not saying horse racing's pure as snow, Mr Quarles. Far from it. Horses have been nobbled before now, horses have been doped. But favourites, not forty to one outsiders. And horses, not men.'

'You mean—?'

'If anyone wanted to stop Lucky Charm they'd go for the horse, not the man. Kill a horse and get caught, you may go to prison. Kill a man—well, it's murder.'

'Sir Reginald seemed very optimistic about his horse's chances in the National. What did you feel?'

The trainer rubbed his chin, making a sound like a saw cutting wood. 'With Baker up, he was a good outsider, a nice each way bet. Hadn't quite the class for it, but you never can tell. He liked Baker, did Lucky Charm.'

'And he didn't like Harry Bartley?'

'Hated him. Bartley used the whip more than he need. Lucky Charm wasn't a horse you could treat that way. I tried to persuade Sir Reginald to give the ride to another jockey, but it was no good.'

'You shared the horse's dislike of Harry Bartley, I gather.'

The trainer said nothing. His faded blue eyes stared into the distance, the Red Indian impassiveness of his features did not change. 'Was there a special reason for that?'

Slowly and without passion, Norman Johnson said, 'Sir Reginald Bartley is a man I respect and like, none more so. I don't know how he came to have such a son. He couldn't be trusted with a woman, he couldn't be trusted to pay his debts, he was a good rider but he couldn't be trusted to treat a horse decently.'

'But there's something personal in your dislike,' Quarles insisted.

Johnson brought his blue eyes out of the middle distance and focused them on Quarles. 'You'll learn about it soon enough. It might as well be from me. I had a daughter named Mary. She was a good girl until she took up with Harry Bartley. He was always around the stables, every day for weeks, and I was fool enough not to realize what he was after. Until Mary went away with him and left me a note, I understood it then well enough. That was six months ago. He walked out on her after a few weeks. She put her head in a gas oven.'

'I see.'

'When I've worked out my contract with Sir Reginald, I'm asking him to take his horses away.'

Quarles said softly, 'Some people might call that a motive for murder.'

'I don't deny it, Mr Quarles. It happens that I didn't kill him, that's all.' Johnson drove the fist of one hand into the palm of the other, and his voice for the first time vibrated with excitement. 'But if you ever find his murderer you'll find he has a pesonal reason, a reason like mine. For me, I hope you never find him. I say good luck to the man or woman who killed Harry Bartley.'

*　*　*

Back in the course hospital Quarles met young Inspector Makepeace, who had been working with him in running down the Liverpool Forger.

Makepeace looked at the private detective with a wry smile. 'You seem to manage to be where things happen, Mr Quarles. I understand you saw young Bartley before the race.'

Quarles told him the impression he had formed that Bartley might be drunk, and the outcome of his conversation with Johnson. The Inspector listened with interest.

'I should say Johnson's right, and this was almost certainly the working out of a private enmity. As you say, he's got a motive himself, although I'm keeping an open mind about that. In return I don't mind telling you that we've got a pretty good idea of how the poison was administered. Miss Moore here has been very helpful about that. She was engaged to Harry Bartley.'

Miss Jennifer Moore had a round innocent face and dark hair. She had been crying. 'But Inspector, I only said—'

'Bear with me a moment,' Inspector Makepeace asked. Quarles, whose own sense of modesty was conspicuous by its absence, noted mentally that Makepeace had a good conceit of himself. 'I don't know whether you know much about nitro benzene poisoning, Mr Quarles?'

'I know that nitro benzene is comparatively easy to make,' Quarles answered. 'It is generally taken in the form of a liquid although it is equally poisonous as a vapour—I remember the case of a young man who spilt nitro benzene on his clothes, became stupefied and finally collapsed in coma and died. But the most interesting thing about it is that there is an interval between taking the poison and its effects appearing, which can vary from a quarter of an hour to three hours, or longer in the case of vapour. Is that what you were going to tell me?'

The Inspector laughed a little uncomfortably. 'You're a

bit of a walking encyclopaedia, aren't you? That's pretty much what I was going to say, yes. You'll see that if we can trace the course of Bartley's eating and drinking today we should be able to see when he took the poison. Now it so happens that we can do just that. Doctor Ramsay, would you come over here, please?'

The poker-backed doctor came forward.

'I understand Harry Bartley came to see you this morning.'

Ramsay nodded. 'I'm staying with friends a couple of miles outside Liverpool. Harry rang me up this morning before nine o'clock. He was pretty jittery, wanted something to pep him up. He was out at the place I'm staying before half-past nine and I gave him a couple of pills, put two more in a box for him in case he needed to take them before the race.'

'They were in his clothes in the changing-room,' Makepeace said to Quarles with a smile. 'I can see your eyes fixed thoughtfully on Doctor Ramsay, but Ferguson here assures me that any pills taken at half-past nine must have had effect well before the time of the race. Now, follow the course of events, Quarles. Bartley returned to the hotel by ten o'clock, met Miss Moore in the lobby and said that he was going up to his room to write some letters. She arranged to pick him up at about twelve, because they were going to a cocktail party. She picked him up then and they went to the cocktail party, which was given by a friend of theirs. There, Miss Moore can testify, Harry Bartley drank *just one glass of orange juice.*'

'What about lunch?' Quarles asked the girl.

She shook her head. 'Harry was worried about making the weight. He came and watched Bill and me eat lunch and didn't touch anything, not so much as a piece of toast or a glass of water.'

'Bill?'

She coloured slightly. 'Doctor Ramsay and I have known each other for years. He can bear out what I say. We had lunch on the course, and after it Harry went off to the changing-room. Of course he may have drunk something after that.'

'Most unlikely,' Ferguson said. 'Particularly if he was worried about making the weight.'

'So you see we're down to the glass of orange juice.' The Inspector smoothed his fair hair with some complacency.

'Apparently,' Quarles agreed. 'At lunch, did he show any sign of confusion, blurred speech, unsteady walk, anything like that?'

Both Ramsay and Jennifer Moore returned decided negatives.

'Come on now, Mr Quarles,' Makepeace said with a smile. 'The fact is you're reluctant to admit that the police are ever quick off the mark, and this time we've surprised you.'

'It isn't that, my dear Inspector. Something's worrying me, and I don't quite know what it is. Something that I've seen, or that's happened or that's been said. I shall be interested to know the result of the post-mortem.'

'The PM?' The Inspector was startled. 'Surely you don't doubt that—'

'That he died of nitro benzene poisoning? No, I don't, but there's still something that tantalizes me about it. Ah, here are his personal possessions. Interesting.'

The detective paused by a table on which a number of articles lay in two separate piles. One of them contained the things Bartley had been wearing during the race, the other came from his clothes in the changing-room.

In the first pile were Lucky Charm's saddle, the cerise and gold shirt and cap, and the breeches Bartley had been wearing. Here too, isolated and pathetic, was the rabbit's paw charm he had kissed, neatly ticketed: 'Found in pocket.'

The things in the other pile were naturally more numerous, sports jacket, vest, shirt and grey trousers, gold wristwatch, keys on a ring, silver and copper coins, a wallet with notes and other papers, three letters. Inspector Makepeace picked up one of these letters and handed it to Quarles.

It was a letter written in a sprawling hand by a woman who used violet ink, and it was full of bitter reproaches, in painfully familiar phrasing. 'Cast me off like an old shoe . . . given you everything a woman can give . . . shan't let you get away with it . . . sooner see you dead than married to somebody else.' Why is it, Quarles wondered, that at times of strong emotion, almost all of us express ourselves in clichés? The letter began 'Darling Harry' and was signed 'Hilary'.

'You haven't traced the writer of this letter yet?' The undercurrent of sarcasm in Quarles's voice was so faint that Inspector Makepeace missed it.

'Give us a chance, Mr Quarles. Between you and me I'm not inclined to attach too much importance to it, shouldn't be surprised to learn that there were half a dozen women in Master Harry's life. I'm more interested in getting a complete list of guests at that cocktail party. Nothing very informative here, I'm afraid.'

'On the contrary,' Quarles said.

Makepeace stared. 'You mean there's something I've missed—'

'You haven't missed anything, but something's missing that should be here. You should be able to deduce it yourself. Now I'm more anxious than ever to know the result of the post-mortem.'

*　　*　　*

Sir Reginald Bartley paced up and down the drawing-room of his suite. His voice had lost none of its vigour, but his appearance was pitiably different from that of the jaunty little man who had talked about leading in the Grand National winner twenty-four hours earlier. There was an unshaved patch on his chin, his face was pallid and his hand trembled slightly.

'I want this murderer caught,' he said. 'I want to see him in the dock, I want to hear the judge pronounce sentence on him. That police Inspector is smart, but I believe you're smarter, Quarles. I want you to investigate this case, and if you catch the man who poisoned my son you can write your own cheque.'

Quarles looked at him intently. 'Why do you call it a man? There is a general belief that most poisoners are women.'

'Man or woman.' Sir Reginald made an impatient gesture to indicate that this was merely splitting hairs. 'I want them in the dock.'

'Then you'll have to be franker with me than you have been so far. You might begin by telling me what you know about Hilary.'

'Hilary?' Sir Reginald's surprise seemed genuine. 'That's not a name I've ever heard in relation to Harry.'

'She wrote an interesting letter to your son.' Quarles did not pursue the point. 'Norman Johnson said that your son behaved very badly to his daughter.'

Sir Reginald blew his nose emphatically. 'She was a foolish girl, wouldn't leave him alone. I'm not denying that Harry was sometimes wild. But there was never any real harm in him.'

'Johnson's story was that your son lured this girl away from home, lived with her for a short time and then walked out on her. Do you accept that?'

'I've really no idea. Harry was of age. I knew little about that side of his life. I don't see,' he added stiffly, 'that it's our place to sit in moral judgment on him.'

'It's not a question of moral judgment,' Quarles said patiently. 'I'm trying to get at facts. What do you think of Miss Moore?'

'A very nice girl, very nice indeed,' said Sir Reginald emphatically.

'She'd only recently become engaged to your son, I believe?'

'About three weeks ago, yes. She is—was—very much in love with him.'

'Doctor Ramsay had known her for years?'

'Yes. Known Harry for many years too, for the matter of that, pretty well ever since he was a boy. Good chap, Ramsay, pulled me through a bad go of pneumonia a couple of years ago, just after my wife died.'

Quarles stood up. His eyes, hard and black, stared at Sir Reginald, who bore their gaze uneasily. 'I accept the commission. But you will realise, Sir Reginald, that I am no respecter of persons. You are engaging me to discover the truth, regardless of consequences.'

Sir Reginald repeated after him: 'Regardless of consequences.'

In the hotel lobby Quarles heard himself being paged. He stopped the boy, and was told that Miss Moore was in the lounge and would like to speak to him. He found her talking in a deserted corner of the room to a dark-skinned, rather too beautifully-dressed young man, with a fine hooked nose.

'This is Paul Lapetaine, who was Harry's great friend,' she said. 'As a matter of fact it was through Jack that I met Harry, and it was Paul who gave the cocktail party yesterday.'

'Is that so?' Quarles looked at Lapetaine with interest, wondering about his ancestry. Indian perhaps? Or even Red Indian? Turkish? 'Are you a racing man, Mr Lapetaine?'

'I am an art dealer.' Lapetaine smiled, showing pointed yellowish teeth. 'But I am interested in horse racing, yes. I like the excitement. I like to gamble, I was very fond of Harry. So I came up for the National. I am almost ashamed of it, but I had a good win.'

'You backed Mountain Pride?'

'I did. I had just a little saver on Lucky Charm, for sentiment's sake as you might say, but I did not think he had quite—how shall I put it?—the class for the race.'

'You watched it, of course?'

'No, Mr Quarles.' Lapetaine looked down at his elegant suède shoes. 'I was engaged on urgent business.'

Jennifer Moore said impatiently, 'Look here, Mr Quarles, there's something, I want you to tell me. Has Sir Reginald asked you to investigate this case?' Quarles nodded. 'I hope you won't.'

'Why not?'

'It can't possibly do any good. Harry's dead, and nothing can bring him back. And it might—well, might embarrass people who haven't any connection with it.'

Lapetaine listened with a malicious smile. Quarles said quietly, 'I see. Your engagement is very recent, isn't it, Miss Moore?'

'Harry and I met for the first time five weeks ago. It sounds silly, I expect, but we fell in love at first sight. Within a fortnight we were engaged.'

'Should I be right in thinking that Doctor Ramsay feels some affection for you, and that you are afraid my investigations may involve him?'

Still with that slightly objectionable smile, Lapetaine said: 'I can tell you exactly what Jennifer is afraid of. Ramsay has been sweet on her for years. Now, you know that Harry went out to see Ramsay on the morning of the race to get some pep tablets. What was to stop Ramsay from giving him three more, one of them filled with nitro benzene, and saying, "Take one of these at twelve-thirty, my boy, and you'll ride as you've never ridden before." It simply happened that Harry took the poisoned tablet first. The timing would be just about right.'

The girl buried her face in her hands. 'You shouldn't have—'

'My dear, Mr Quarles is an intelligent man. I should be surprised if that idea had not already occurred to him.'

Quarles looked at him. 'You seem to know a good deal about the operation of nitro benzene, Mr Lapetaine.'

Unperturbed, the art dealer showed his teeth. 'I trained for a medical degree in youth before I—what shall I say? —discovered my vocation.'

'There are certain objections to that idea,' Quarles began, when a page boy came running up.

'Mr Quarles, sir. Telephone for you.'

On the telephone Quarles heard Inspector Makepeace's voice, raw with irritation. 'We've got the result of the PM. I don't know how you guessed, but you were perfectly right.'

'There was no question of guessing,' Quarles said indignantly. 'My suggestion was the result of deduction from observed facts.'

'Anyway, It seems to leave us just where we began.'

'Oh no,' Quarles said softly. 'I have told you exactly what happened before and during the race. Surely it leaves only one possible explanation.'

He went back to the lounge, and addressed Jennifer Moore. 'You need not worry any further, Miss Moore, about Doctor Ramsay or anyone else having administered a poisonous pill to Harry Bartley. I have just learned the result of the post-mortem. There was only a trace of nitro benzene in the stomach.'

They looked at him in astonishment, Lapetaine with his mouth slightly open. 'I will spell out the meaning of that for you. Harry Bartley was not poisoned by a pill or by the orange juice he drank at your cocktail party, Mr Lapetaine. He was poisoned by nitro benzene, yes, but in the form of vapour.'

*　　*　　*

Lapetaine had been surprised by Quarles's revelation but, as the detective admitted to himself with some admiration, the art dealer was a cool card. After the initial shock he nodded.

'Will you excuse me? I must remember to make a note of an appointment.' He scribbled something on a sheet of paper torn from a diary and said with a smile, 'I am relieved. You will no longer suspect me of poisoning my guest's orange juice, which would hardly have been playing the game, as you might say.'

Jennifer Moore seemed bewildered. 'I thought it must be the orange juice. If it was vapour, then—well, I simply don't understand. Perhaps it was an accident.'

'It was not an accident,' Francis Quarles said. 'You can see that my investigations may be useful after all, Miss Moore.'

'I suppose so,' she said a little doubtfully. 'Good-bye, Mr Quarles.'

Lapetaine held out his hand to say good-bye, and when Quarles took it he found a piece of paper in his palm. He opened it after they had turned away, and saw that it was the paper torn from Lapetaine's diary. On it he had scribbled: *Can you meet me in ten minutes at Kismet Coffee House, down the street?*

Ten minutes later Quarles pushed open the door of the Kismet Coffee House. In one of the cubicles he found the darkly handsome Lapetaine, drinking black coffee.

'Mr Quarles, you'll think me immensely mysterious, but—'

'Not at all. It was plain enough from your note that you wanted to talk to me when Miss Moore was not present. From that I deduce that you want to talk about a woman connected with Harry Bartley, and that it would upset Miss Moore to hear about her. I admit, however, that I am making no more than an informed guess when I suggest that her name is Hilary.'

Lapetaine looked at Quarles with his mouth open, then laughed unconvincingly. 'My word, Mr Quarles, it's not much use trying to keep secrets from you. I didn't know you'd ever heard of Hilary Hall.'

'I didn't say that I had. But now that you have told me her name, you may as well go on with the story. I take it that she was a friend of Harry Bartley's.'

'She certainly was. Hilary's a night-club singer, the star turn at the Lady Love, which is a newish club just off Piccadilly. She's a red-head with a tremendous temper. When she heard that Harry was engaged to be married, she really hit the roof. Harry had played around with a lot of girls in his time, you know.'

Quarles nodded. 'I do know. But about Miss Hall.'

Lapetaine leaned forward. 'This I'll bet you don't know, Mr Quarles, and neither does anybody else. Hilary Hall came up here the day before the race, and she came to make trouble. She telephoned Harry that evening and he went to see her, tried to quieten her down, but without much effect. She rang Harry again at that cocktail party I gave the morning before the race, but I spoke to her. I spent the afternoon of the race arguing with her.' Lapetaine smiled. 'She finally agreed that a thousand pounds might help to soothe her injured feelings. I think you should talk to her.'

'I think so too. Why didn't you give this information to the police, Mr Lapetaine?'

The art dealer looked down at his shoes. 'I didn't think Hilary could be involved, but after what you tell me about vapour – I don't know. If I'm going to get into any trouble myself, then with me it's strictly number one. Hilary's gone back to London. You'll find her at the Lady Love.'

Francis Quarles talked on the telephone to the owner of the Lady Love night club, and then took a plane from Liverpool to London. He arrived at the night club, caught a glimpse of a cabaret turn ending, and pushed his way backstage among a crowd of blondes and brunettes, wondering as he had often done before why a dozen half-dressed girls should be so much less attractive than one.

He tapped on the door of a room that was labelled 'Miss Hall'. A deep, harsh voice said, 'All right.'

Hilary Hall was sitting in front of a looking-glass and her reflection frowned out at him. Her beauty was like a physical blow after the commonplace prettiness of the dancing girls outside. Yet on a second look it was not really beauty, Quarles saw, but simply the combination of flaming red hair, a milk-white skin and certain unusual physical features—the thick brows that almost met in the middle, the jutting red underlip, the powerful shoulders. This was a woman whom you could easily imagine as a murderess, although such an exercise of the imagination, as Quarles well knew, could easily be misleading.

'I was told you were coming,' she said in that rusty, attractive voice. 'And I've seen your picture in the papers. What do you want?'

'I would like you to answer some questions.'

'I'm on in ten minutes. You've got till then.' She had not turned round.

Quarles said, 'I can put it simply. You were in love with Harry Bartley. You wrote him a threatening letter after his engagement. You went up to Liverpool to cause trouble.'

Her thick brows were drawn together. 'So what? He's dead now. I never went near the course, Mr Dick.'

Quarles said softly, 'He came to see you that night before the race.'

She swung round now and faced him. Her eyes were snapping with temper. She looked magnificent. 'Of course he did, after I'd rung him up. He came to pour out all his troubles and say how sorry he was it had to be good-bye. He didn't want to marry that silly little bit he'd got engaged to. She had money, that was all. Can you imagine any man preferring her to me?'

She paused and Quarles, although not particularly susceptible, felt a kind of shiver run down his back.

'He had other troubles too,' she said. 'A frightful cold that he was afraid might develop into flu and make it difficult for him to ride that damned horse. Said he'd have to do something about it. Altogether, he was pretty low.'

'You were very much in love with him?'

Looking down at her scarlet fingernails she said, 'He was a man.'

With a deprecating cough Quarles said, 'But you were prepared to accept a thousand pounds to soothe your feelings.'

She struck the dressing-table sharply with clenched fist. 'That filthy little dago Paul Lapetaine's been talking to you. He was after me himself, but he never got to first base. I like men, not dressed-up dolls. Yes, I said I'd take the money. I needed it. I knew Harry would never put a ring on my finger. You can think what you like about it.'

'What I think,' Quarles said abruptly, 'is that you're an honest woman.'

Her heavy frown changed into a smile. 'You're all right.'

A head poked through the door, a voice said, 'On in two minutes, Miss Hall.'

'Look here,' she said, 'I'm on now, but why don't you stay here, we'll talk afterwards, have a drink. I want to find Harry's murderer as much as you do.'

'I should be delighted to have a drink, and honoured if you would allow me to take you out to supper,' the detective said. 'But we won't talk about the case. The case is solved.'

*　　*　　*

Francis Quarles's secretary Molly Player was a neatly attractive – but not too attractive – blonde. He had told her something about the people involved in the case, and now as they arrived and she took them all in to Quarles's office overlooking Trafalgar Square, she found some amusement in comparing the detective's remarks with the reality.

Sir Reginald came first, pale and anxious ('self-made man, vulgar and cocky, but really cut to pieces by his son's death,' Quarles had said), and he was closely followed by Doctor Ramsay ('every inch a soldier, so military he seems phoney, but in fact he was an army doctor, and a good one'). Then came Jennifer Moore wearing a becoming amount of black, with elegant Paul Lapetaine. 'She looks and talks like a mouse, but that doesn't mean she *is* a mouse,' Quarles had said thoughtfully of Miss Moore. Lapetaine he had dismissed briskly. 'One of nature's spivs.'

Then, on her own, in a glory of furs and radiating bright sex, Hilary Hall. 'You can't miss *her*, Molly, any more than you can miss the sun coming out,' Quarles said. 'An orange sun,' he added as an afterthought. 'High in the sky, a scorcher.'

Last of all Norman Johnson, the brown-faced bow-legged trainer of Lucky Charm. About him Quarles's comment had been tersest of all. 'Pokerface.'

Molly Player let them all in. Then she sat down and tried to type a report, but found herself making a number of mistakes. She remembered Quarles's last words to her: 'One of these six, Molly, is a murderer.'

Francis Quarles sat back in the big chair behind his desk, and said pleasantly to the six people, 'One of you is a murderer.'

His office was large, but it had only four chairs for visitors, so that Paul Lapetaine stretched his elegant legs from a stool, and Doctor Ramsay sat in a window-seat from which he could look down on the square far below with its pigeons, its children and its lions. Jennifer Moore sat next to Ramsay, as far away as possible from Hilary Hall.

'It may be of interest to you all,' Quarles continued didactically, 'to know how I discovered the murderer, after Sir Reginald had engaged me to investigate.

'I considered first the question of motive, and I found that five of you had motives, of a kind, for killing Harry Bartley. Johnson, trainer of the horse he rode, was angry because Bartley had treated his daughter badly. Miss Hall had been thrown over by Bartley, and had written him a threatening letter.

'Miss Moore might have discovered that Bartley went to see Miss Hall on the night before the race. She looks a quiet young lady, but quiet young ladies have been known to poison through jealousy.

'Paul Lapetaine I should judge to have been jealous also of Bartley's success with women, and especially with Hilary Hall. Doctor Ramsay was obviously fond of Miss Moore, and had been for years. He must have had bitter feelings when he learned that she was going to marry a man like Harry Bartley.'

Ramsay on his window-seat made a motion of protest. Sir Reginald said: 'You have no right to talk about my son like that.'

Quarles's voice was harsh. 'I'm sorry, Sir Reginald. I told you that this inquiry might be disagreeable for you. I don't condone murder, but I must admit that your son strikes me as an unpleasant character.

'Let us move on from motive to opportunity. Bartley was killed by nitro benzene, and it was thought at first that he had drunk the poison in a glass of orange juice, or perhaps taken it in the form of pills. There was a thought in Miss Moore's mind, or perhaps Lapetaine put it there, the idea that Doctor Ramsay might have given Bartley a tablet filled with nitro benzene when Bartley came to see him early on the morning of the race.

'The post-mortem proved conclusively that this idea was mistaken. Dr Ramsay's tablets were perfectly harmless. Hartley had not been killed by nitro benzene introduced into his stomach. He had been poisoned by it in the form of vapour. This was the essential feature of the crime. The last vital clue, however, was provided by Miss Hall. She told me that on the night before the race, when Bartley came to see her, he complained of a bad nose cold that he feared might develop into influenza.'

There was silence in the room. Then Jennifer Moore said

timidly, 'I suppose I knew that, too. I mean, I knew Harry was sniffing a lot and had a bit of a cold, but I still don't understand why it should be important.'

'Quite early in the case I said that I remembered an affair in which a young man spilt nitro benzene on his clothes, became stupefied, collapsed in coma and died. Something like that happened to Harry Bartley.'

'His clothes weren't poisoned.' That was Johnson, speaking for the first time.

'No. He was killed by a handkerchief impregnated with nitro benzene, which he used frequently because he had a cold.'

Hilary Hall objected, in her rusty voice, 'I don't believe that that points to anybody in particular.'

'There are two other things I should tell you. When I met Harry Bartley in the paddock I noticed that he used a handkerchief to wipe his nose. After the race, when his things were laid out on a table, the handkerchief was no longer there.'

'It came out when he fell from the horse,' Ramsay suggested.

'No. Because the rabbit's paw which he had tucked into his pocket at the same time was still there. The handkerchief had been stolen.'

Sir Reginald rubbed his chin. 'I may be slow, but I simply don't see how that can be possible. Nobody came near Harry's body—' He stopped.

'That isn't true,' Quarles said. 'But it is true that only one person fulfils all our murderer's qualifications. He had to be a person who disliked Harry Bartley. He had to possess some knowledge of the properties of nitro benzene. He had to know that Bartley had a cold, and would frequently wipe his nose with a handkerchief. He had to be a person from whom Bartley would have accepted a handkerchief—having been told that it was impregnated with what our murderer might have said was oil of eucalyptus, good for a cold. Finally, he had to be a person who had access to Bartley very soon after he collapsed. He was able to bend over the body—making an examination, shall we say?—and abstract the handkerchief.

'The police are outside, Doctor Ramsay, it's no good trying to use that gun in your hip pocket.'

Doctor Ramsay was on his feet now, and the gun was in his hand. 'I'm not sorry for what I did,' he said. 'Not in the least. Harry was a dirty little devil with girls, had been since he was a boy. I'd always loved you, Jennifer, although I've never said it. In the wrong age group, I know. When I heard he'd got hold of you I just couldn't stand it. Don't come near me, now. I don't want to hurt anybody else.'

'Bill.' Jennifer Moore held out a hand to him. 'Please don't—'

Ramsay flung up the window. 'You don't think I'm going to endure the farce of a trial, do you? It's better this way, for me and for everybody else.' He stepped out on to the ledge, and looked for a moment at the pigeons and the children, the placid lions and Nelson on his pillar. Then he jumped.

A DERBY HORSE

by Michael Innes

Michael Innes has been described by the Times Literary Supplement as 'in a class by himself among writers of detective fiction', and his detective hero, John Appleby, as one of the most erudite sleuths in mystery fiction. Michael Innes' real name is John Innes Mackintosh Stewart. The son of a Scottish professor, he seemed destined from his youth for the life of an academic. Educated at Edinburgh Academy and Oriel College, Oxford, where he won the Matthew Arnold Memorial Prize, he spent five years at the University of Leeds as lecturer in English and ten years as Jury Professor of English at the University of Adelaide, Australia, before becoming a Student of Christ Church, Oxford.

Innes' interest in crime fiction developed as a form of relaxation from his tutorial duties; apart from several novels and collections of short stories under his own name, he has written 29 books about the immaculate Appleby, charting his career through the ranks at Scotland Yard until he is made Commissioner and retires with a knighthood, although even in retirement he finds himself continually being drawn into cases. Not surprisingly, a good number are set against academic backgrounds, but in 'A Derby Horse' we find him revealing more than a little insight into the world of horse racing.

*   *   *

'Such curious names,' Mrs Mutter murmured, and let an eye travel vaguely down her card. 'Gay Time and Postman's Path and Summer Rain. Often *witty*, of course—one sees that when one looks at the names of the dear creatures' fathers and mothers—but inadequately *equine*, if you understand me.'

'Nonsense, m'dear.' Mrs Mutter's husband had tipped back his chair the better to scan through his binoculars the vast carpet of humanity covering the downs. 'You couldn't call a likely colt Dobbin, or a well-bred filly Dapple or Daisy . . . But what a tremendous turn-out there is. Biggest crowd, if you ask me, since 'forty-six—Airborne's race.'

'And the time's creeping on, and the excitement's creeping up.' Lady Appleby had glanced at her watch.

'Anxious about your husband—eh?' Mr Mutter shook his head. 'Exacting, being high up in the police. Hope he hasn't been detained by somebody's pinching the favourite. Or perhaps—'

'Nothing of that sort.' A new voice was heard—that of Sir John Appleby himself as he strolled up to join his party. 'But I did not long ago have to do with a Derby horse that went rather badly missing. Have you ever known, Mutter, a strong colt, closely knit and with the quarters of a sprinter, disappear into thin air? Disconcerting experience.'

'But no doubt instructive.' Mutter dropped his binoculars. 'And you've just got time to tell us about it.'

*   *   *

Appleby sat down. 'It began with a frantic telephone-call from a certain Major Gunton, who trains near Blandford. Pantomime had vanished.'

Mrs Mutter made one of her well-known charming gestures. 'What did I say? Such *curious* names. Who could take seriously a horse called that?'

'Gunton did, and so did the brute's owner. They had entered Pantomime for this very Derby.'

'Hasn't that to be done very young?' Mrs Mutter was eager for knowledge. 'Like Eton boys, and that sort of thing?'

Mutter groaned. 'As yearlings, m'dear. Appleby, go on.'

*   *   *

'Pantomime was being sent from Blandford to Newbury. The journey, which was to be made by road—'

'It would be in one of those horrid little boxes.' Mrs Mutter was expressive. 'Almost like *coffins*, supposing horses to *have* coffins. The poor things can't so much as turn round.'

'It wouldn't be to their advantage to do so.' Appleby took the point seriously. 'Bumpy, you know. But the box was certainly what you describe—a simple, open affair, hitched to the back of an estate-wagon. Gunton had a reliable man called Merry, who saw to getting Pantomime into the thing at about dusk one fine autumn evening. Gunton himself came out and saw that the creature was safely locked in; and then Merry and a stable-lad got into the wagon and drove off. Short of a road accident, Pantomime seemed as safe as houses. And until Salisbury, if Merry could be believed, he *was* safe. After that, it grew dark. And in the dark—again if Merry could be believed—some mysterious violation of the very laws of nature took place. In other words, when the box arrived in Newbury, Pantomime had disappeared.'

Mutter raised his eyebrows. 'Lock tampered with?'

'No. And they hadn't had to pull up during the whole journey.'

'Then Pantomime must have *jumped*.' Mrs Mutter was horrified.

Appleby shook his head. 'Quite impossible. Those boxes give a horse no room for tricks. There seemed only one conceivable explanation: that some Brobdingnagian bird had descended on poor little Pantomime and carried him off in his beak.

*   *   *

'I was working on a case in Oxford when I got the message asking me to take over this queer affair. There wasn't much more information forthcoming than what I've given you, but of course there was a description of the horse: a chestnut with black spots on the hind quarters—like Eclipse and Pantaloon, I was told by a man at the Yard who specialises in the Stud-Book. With this I set out very early on the morning following the disappearance, intending to drive straight to Blandford, and from there retrace Pantomime's last journey if it should be necessary.

'I had got to Newbury, and was wondering whether Andover would be a good place to stop for breakfast, when I ran into fog. It seemed best to press on—and I must confess that probably I pressed on pretty fast. Still, policemen do well always to drive with a bit of extra care; and I was doing nothing that any normal contingency could render dangerous. Nevertheless, I had an accident. At one moment I had been staring into empty air—or fog. The next, there was a solid object plumb in front of my bonnet, and this was followed by a slight but ominous impact before I brought the car to a stop. For a second I wondered whether I'd fallen asleep at the wheel. For what I had *seen* in that moment decidedly suggested a dream. It had been a substantial chestnut mass, diversified with black spots.

*　　*　　*

'I climbed out and ran back. There, sure enough—and with all the appearance of having been hurled violently into a high hedge—I glimpsed the figure of a chestnut colt. But it was only for a moment; the wretched fog was getting worse, with drifting patches as thick as a horse-blanket. Pantomime was obscured for a couple of seconds—and when the place cleared again he had vanished.

'That was all to the good, since it meant he could scarcely have broken any bones. The road was empty, so I concluded he had forced his way through the hedge. I followed suit—it wasn't a comfortable dive—and there he was. But by *there* I mean a quarter of a mile off. He seemed to have done that in about twenty seconds.'

Mutter chuckled. 'A Derby horse, decidedly. Mahmoud's record for the twelve furlongs—'

'Quite so. Well, off I went in pursuit—and presently the dream had turned to nightmare. It's an odd bit of country —open, undulating, and covered with scattered patches of gorse which seem to have been blown into all sorts of fantastic shapes by the wind. What with the fog thrown in, it was easy to feel oneself hunting the hapless Pantomime amid a sort of menagerie of prehistoric monsters. And Pantomime was—well, illusive. For one thing, he had more than flat-racing in him. At one moment I even had a confused notion that he had cleared a hay-stack. And this was the more surprising, since he did now appear to have injured himself. I was getting no more than peeps at him, but his gait was certainly queer. And if horses get concussion—well, Pantomime was badly concussed.

'The end came quickly. Somewhere near by there was a chap out with a shot-gun after rabbits—a silly employment in those conditions—and he was coming near enough to worry me. Suddenly I rounded a clump of gorse and came upon Pantomime apparently cornered and at bay. I had just time to feel that there was something pretty weirdly wrong when the creature rose in air like a tiger and came sailing down at me. At the same instant I heard a patter of shot at my feet—it was the silly ass with the gun blazing away at goodness knows what—and Pantomime just faded out. I found myself looking down, not at a horse, but at the punctured and deflated remains of a highly ingenious balloon.'

*   *   *

'Not Pantomime but Pegasus.' Mrs Mutter offered this unexpected piece of classical learning with a brilliant smile.

'Quite so. The thieves' object, of course, had been to gain time. They managed to substitute their extraordinary contrivance for the real Pantomime just before Gunton came out in the dusk, locked the horse-box, and told Merry to drive off. The thing was tethered by no more than a nicely-calculated fraying cord, so that eventually it freed itself and simply soared up into the night. Probably it was designed that it should blow out to sea. Poor Merry and his lad were going to look very like the guilty parties—and while the trail was thus hopelessly confused at the start, the real Pantomime could be smuggled abroad.'

'And it was?'

'Certainly. The colt was discovered some months later in France. I believe there may be a good deal of litigation.'

Mutter, who had for some minutes been engaged in applying the friction of a silk handkerchief to his top-hat, paused from this important labour. 'Haven't you told us rather a *tall* story?'

Appleby nodded. I'm assured the false Pantomime may have gone to something like twenty thousand feet. So I suppose it *is* tall.'

'Perhaps you could say something about Pantomime's pedigree?'

This time it was Lady Appleby who spoke. 'By Airborne, without a doubt,' she said. 'And from Chimera.'

'Chimera? I don't believe there was ever any such—'

'No more do I.'

A DAY WITH THE TOFFS

by Geoff O'Hara

Readers of The Sporting Life, *Britain's famous daily paper for the horse racing fraternity, have for some years been enjoying a series of stories about a quick-witted and resourceful racing man named Brogan. In some 70 tales the author, Geoff O'Hara, has created a thoroughly believable character, wise in the ways of the Turf and those who frequent it—which is not altogether surprising when one learns that O'Hara was a bookmaker for thirty years.*

When Geoff O'Hara left school at 14, his ambition was to be a journalist, but his lack of education prevented him fulfilling this dream. Instead, he made his living as a bookmaker—all the time observing everything that went on around him. When at last he found himself with time on his hands, he decided to have a shot at writing, and the result was stories that were rich in humour, often based on events he had seen or anecdotes he had been told. When he sent a batch of four to The Sporting Life *they struck an immediate chord with the readers who promptly demanded more. So successful did Brogan become that a pilot film for a TV series has also been made, starring Julian Holloway.*

'A Day With The Toffs' is one of the most recent Brogan stories, an excellent example of the author's unique eye and ear for the world of racing.

* * *

I do not often favour British Rail with my travelling arrangements. But with the faithful Jaguar being off the road with a busted front end and sundry shortcomings due to an argument with a lorry in Holloway Road and none of my

friends having the wherewithal to furnish me with the
readies to hire a replacement, here I am sitting in a first class
compartment en route to Sancaster races.

Travelling first class is all down to larking, especially as I
only have a second class ticket. But travelling first with a
second class ticket is an art perfected with much practice
and is a decided improvement on travelling second class
with no ticket at all.

So, like I just now told you, I'm travelling to Sancaster by
rail and, judging by the scenery, it can't be bad, 'cos right
opposite me sits as lovely a piece of high-class pulchritude
as ever graced a finishing school. Oh yes, very classy, in fact
very top drawer. Pearls over a cashmere sweater, well-cut
skirt just above a well-sculptured knee leading the eye in
the direction of a nicely-muscled calf and thence to an ankle
combining strength with delicacy. In short, you'd have to
catch a lot of trains before finding yourself opposite a more
delectable travelling companion.

Being the gentleman I fondly imagine myself to be, I
quickly out with my Benson and Hedges and proffer the
soothing weed. 'Thank you no,' coos the classy one.
'Actually I don't use them and I would appreciate it if you
didn't: this compartment is a non-smoker.' Well that's a
right false start and no mistake. I mutter suitable apologies
and give it as my opinion that the lady is a bit of a judge.
'Matter of fact I'm on the point of giving 'em up myself: it's a
very anti-social habit.'

The proud beauty doesn't seem to be over-interested in
my personal habits or resolutions and proceeds to hide her
lovely features behind a copy of Dick Francis' *Banker*.

Having been suitably put in my place I take refuge behind
my copy of *The Sporting Life* and the train rattles on in the
direction of Sancaster. Not being easily put down, I make
several efforts to engage the lady in conversation, all to no
avail, and by the time the train pulls into the race course
sidings I have been handed a mitt so frozen we coulda been
at the North Pole.

The lady hastily leaves the train and I gather up belongings, binoculars, sandwiches (on account of race course
catering being a bit dodgy) and the Member's badge I just

happened to filch off Abe Zimmerman's desk when I went to see him about my account. An account which Abe, for some obscure reason, considers to be overdue. I am just about to step onto the platform when I notice that the lady has left her copy of *Banker* on the seat. So I scoop up the book and canter off in pursuit to return the book and perchance to enhance my standing.

By the time I've bustled through the barrier and flashed my badge I see my travelling companion being escorted towards the paddock by a right Hooray Henry. You've seen 'em, haven't you? Covert coat knee length, hard hitting trousers and chukka boots. Today's man in yesterday's threads. And of course, brown trilby set askew on the chinless head.

So I abandon further pursuit and flick open the copy of *Banker* and there on the fly-leaf is the identity of the lady. In a good class square hand is written 'Lavinia Strutworthy, The Grange, Long Knockington'. Talk about a turn-up! Lavinia Strutworthy just happens to be among the top flight of our lady riders. Furthermore and to boot, she is due to ride the favourite in the Sancaster Amateur Chase.

Well, it's gotta be my lucky day, hasn't it? I've only to return the book and Lavinia will feel duty bound to give me the good word about the chances of her mount, Kickalong. Not that I'll need a lot of encouragement. The horse looks good enough on past form, Lavinia is as good as most men and better than some I could mention at booting 'em home, and I'm a bit partial to backing favourites in three-mile chases. I cast a hasty glance round the paddock, but I fail to lamp Lavinia. Not to worry. The race does not come up for decision until three-fifteen. So I make tracks for Tatts and by the time the second heat has been decided I'm five and seventy to the good on account of the first two favourites having gone in with a bit in hand.

By now it has become a matter of some urgency to locate Lavinia and I finally run her to ground outside the Weighing Room. She is deep in conversation with the aforementioned Hooray Henry. The Hooray geezer is obviously giving her some hints on how to ride Kickalong.

He's making urgent whipping movements with his right hand and is rabbiting away fifty to the dozen. I'd have thought the riding could have been left to Lavinia but obviously he must know a thing or three because Lavinia is giving him all her attention.

Lavinia is now in her racing togs and right good she looks, too. Even better than on the train if that were possible. So I bowl across and proffer the book. 'Do excuse me, we travelled down together. I found this book after you left the carriage.'

Lavinia accepts the book and treats me to a medium-sized smile. 'Thank you, I really thought I'd lost it.'

'Very pleased to be of assistance and to make your aquaintance. I've admired your riding on many occasions. How do you rate your chances today?'

The Hooray Henry is now looking a trifle put out. It's fairly obvious he doesn't relish the lady taking up with race course riff-raff such as yours truly. 'Actually we don't think we've much to fear. The horse is well and he's been going frightfully well at home.'

All this from the Hooray Henry and nothing from Lavinia.

'Oh really, Roscoe,' offers Lavinia, 'don't sound too confident. You'll be causing this gentleman to have a very big bet which he otherwise wouldn't have.'

So it's Roscoe, is it? Well, it all fits together, as the jig-saw manufacturer said. This Hooray type is Roscoe Polkinghorne, man-about-town, permit holder and the owner-trainer of Kickalong.

Now how's that for a bit of mazzle? Not only have I met the rider, but I've met the trainer and he's telling me to have a tidy tickle. Who needs the advice of *The Sporting Life*, the headlines of which proclaim, 'Kickalong the danger to Ice Cube'? You don't need to be reading *The Sporting Life* when you're right among the heads, do you?

I make with a few hasty farewells, wish 'em the best of British and tell 'em I hope to come across them again. I don't think Lavinia or Roscoe are keen to endorse this sentiment, but who cares? I've got the horse, I've got the good word and all I gotta get now is a good bet. So I move into Tatts and get among the layers prior to making a few choice and easy pickings. Even money seems to be about the best offer for Kickalong so I hold my fire until I hear the stentorian voice of Jackie Bailer calling out eleven to ten. There's a rush for the price and Jackie Bailer lays five-and-a-half hundred to five hundred twice and a two-twenty to two. And still he offers it. So I'm in, aren't I? With both feet. 'A hundred and ten to a hundred, Brogan pays it,' says Bailer, copping for my century. But still he lays it, still eleven to ten when all around him even money is the top offer. He must be a right berk. But he doesn't know what I know, he's not in with the toffs, is he? It's not what you know, but who you know that brings home the bacon in the racing game!

I take up station on the stands and watch the contestants canter to the start. Kickalong goes down well, striding out and tossing his head as though he's only got a feather on his back. Lavinia Strutworthy looks a picture in her colours and appears well capable of delivering her mount first past the post with a little time to spare and thereby putting me well in the chips for tomorrow's card at Newbury. A quick glance through my bins shows me that Kickalong is now odds on everywhere bar with Jackie Bailer. He goes evens and is laying it.

But now the horses are under orders and I've no time to dwell on the seeming stupidity of J. Bailer. The field moves up to the tape, the starter sends them on their way and all I have to do is watch the race and collect. First time round it's anybody's race. No one seems to want to take the lead and the pace is far from killing. Over on the far side there are a couple of fallers and something refuses at the fence before the straight. With three fences to go I have no difficulty in focusing my bins on Kickalong. He's right up there with the leaders and Lavinia appears to have the affair well in hand; she's sitting very still with a double handful alongside Ice Cube and the pair of 'em are just to the rear of a thing called Hasty Taken. The jock on Hasty Taken goes for his whip, but to my experienced eyes he's no danger. After the second from home Hasty Taken shortens his stride and drops back. Kickalong and Ice Cube take over and they give it the ding-dong approaching the last. Ice Cube has the better of the junp, but Lavinia comes at him with whip flailing and it looks a cert for her to go by.

But it's not to be! Kickalong resents the whip and he hangs badly to the left. Ice Cube, ridden hands and heels, goes away and beats Kickalong to the line a length to the good.

So despite having travelled down with the rider, despite having had the good word from the trainer and despite having had a right good bet at the best odds, I've done it again. Well, that's racing. I guess Abe Zimmerman will just have to wait a little longer afore I settle the overdue account. I avoid the paddock bar and make for the refreshment room in Tatts. I know you meet a better class of person in the paddock bar, but I've had my fill of the better class of person. I'm just calling for a brandy and water when I'm joined at the bar by Sim Singleton. You know Sim. He's the floorman for Jackie Bailer. I'm in the chair so Sim opts for a scotch.

'Your guv'nor went down the sheet with that fav, didn't he, Sim? He was topping 'em all. Musta fancied the winner a bit strong, eh?'

'Oh yes,' laughs Sim, 'the boss gave the fav a right striping. Laid it right down the book and backed the winner. Had it well off he did. Mind you, the fav wasn't off a penn'orth, Brogan, and Jackie knew it!'

'Whaddya mean, "Not off"?' I say. 'I had it from the rider and the trainer. Know 'em well, I do. They told me to have a bet.'

'If you know 'em, Brogan, you don't know 'em well enough. Bet you didn't know that Jackie Bailer was once married to that Lavinia bird. He's still paying alimony and the only way she's sure of copping off Jackie is to let him know when there's a non-jigger in the offing. As soon as she went for the whip the writing was on the wall. Kickalong has to be ridden hands and heels, he stops if you show him the whip! And that Roscoe Polkinghorne geezer, he couldn't lie straight in bed, even with corsets on. He's pulled more horses than a dentist pulls teeth. My guv'nor has never looked back since he let Lavinia loose and she nipped between the sheets with the likes of Polkinghorne and a few other trainers. It's not all love talk between the sheets, you know. It was a lousy marriage, but a highly successful divorce. Have yerself a few quid on Connubial Bliss in the last, see yer.'

And Sim goes back to his guv'nor and leaves me thinking it's all down to travelling by British Rail. Mebbe I can sue 'em. If I'd had a roadworthy motor I wouldn't have met up with Lavinia Strutworthy and if I hadn't met up with her I would have heeded the advice of *The Sporting Life* and backed Ice Cube. But if pigs could fly we'd shoot for pork on a windy day. But I did back Connubial Bliss and it obliged at six to one. Not only did I back the last winner, but I hitched a lift back to town with Sim Singleton. You can have British Rail for me. You meet the wrong type of person when you travel first class.

OUTSIDE CHANCE

by John Welcome

*The name John Welcome is almost as familiar to lovers of horse
racing stories as Dick Francis, and indeed the two men are friends
and have co-edited two books,* Best Racing and Chasing Stories
and The Racing Man's Bedside Book. *John Welcome is actually
the pen-name of John Needham Brennan, an Irish solicitor whose
keen interest in racing has been demonstrated in a wide range of
both fiction and non-fiction works, including* The Cheltenham
Gold Cup: The Story of a Great Steeplechase *(1957),* Fred
Archer: His Life and Times *(1967), a biography of the famous
jockey, and, most recently,* A Light-Hearted Guide to British
Racing, *written with all the verve and wit of an insider.*

*In the following tale John Welcome takes us inside the world of
point-to-point and a case of confidence trickery that is both
ingenious and entertaining.*

* * *

'So you are going to ride your first point-to-point over here
tomorrow,' said my Uncle Rogerson, holding his port up to
the light from a Waterford chandelier and regarding its
ruby richness with a warm and appreciative eye.

My Uncle Rogerson is ninety years old, but his cheeks are
still as smooth as a baby's and the years have not dimmed
the sparkle in his eye. He has a mane of snowy white hair
and a carefully tended white moustache. In his youth he
had seen some service with a cavalry regiment—round
about the time of Majuba Hill I fancy, although the more
disrespectful of my young cousins referred to him as being

the last survivor of the Light Brigade—and he still preserved unimpaired in his walk the old-time cavalry
swagger.

It was, however, that look in his eye which explained to
me why I had heard him variously described as 'a bit of a
lad', 'a boyo', 'a holy terror' and other warmer if less
endearing expressions. Altogether he was a swashbuckling
old rogue and I liked him immensely.

Corbellin Hall, his home in Ireland, was kept up in
considerable state. The lawns were mown, the stables were
freshly painted and the gardens clean and trim and
weeded, all of which is rare enough even in the new
prosperity which has come to Irish country houses with the
influx of Americans and others—and their money. One
lived in comfort when one went to stay there, for there was
a flock of servants ruled over by an elderly butler called
Jeames who was nearly as old as my uncle and had been in
the house since the Dark Ages.

There had, I remembered as I sipped my port, been very
little money with the place when my uncle had come into it,
and there was some disreputable story, the details of which
the family had never been able to discover, about how he
had succeeded in finding enough money to put himself on
his feet. He certainly had found it, however, for he had later
set up the Corbellin Stud and prospered exceedingly.

He was still an enthusiastic supporter of the local hunt
and turned out regularly on an elderly cob, to the considerable worry of the Master and Secretary who daily expected
to have his corpse on their hands. He was well aware of this
and it gave him an impish delight to chirrup as he went
home at the end of a day: 'Still here, Master, still here. I'll
see some of ye young fellows out yet!'

Even he, however, had to admit that it was no longer
feasible for him to ride his own point-to-pointers. As he
liked to have a good horse or two running when the racing
came round he had to look about for someone to ride them
for him.

The previous year I had won my regimental race and a
couple of goodish nomination races on a horse he had
bought for me in Ireland, and I needn't mention how

thrilled I was when I received a wire telling me that he had a horse for me to ride in the County Corway point-to-point if I could get away. My Colonel had been sympathetic and that is how I came to be sitting at the old man's dinner table that spring evening.

The port decanter was enormous and I judged from the look in my uncle's eye that he had no intention of allowing me to rise from the table until it was finished. It did not seem to me to be the best preparation for riding a race the next day, but there was very little I could do about it.

'These modern point-to-points,' said my uncle, refilling his glass and giving the decanter a push along the mahogany towards me, 'they are only mock race courses. All made up fences an' flags and flat racin' rails at the finish, and if you put more than one turn in 'em some jumpin' jackanapes of a steeplechasin' fellah comes down and says the course is dangerous and he can't risk his valuable horses on it.

'Then the committee gets up in horror because if Mr Smellfer-Snooks and his valuable circus of travelling steeplechasers don't come the cars won't come, and if the cars don't come the hunt funds will go down. So they kick out the poor fellow who has designed the course and they straighten it out and they knock two feet off the fences and Mr Smellfer-Snooks comes down and gallops the legs off everyone with his broken-down, bandaged and propped-up steeplechasers and wins all the races and everyone goes home happy!'

My uncle may have been ninety but he knew a thing or two about modern point-to-pointing.

'Go away, Jeames,' my uncle said then, turning in his chair and scowling at the elderly butler who was hovering deprecatingly in the shadows. 'Mr Welcome and myself may be some little time. Besides, I want to tell him a story.' The butler faded into the shadows. A door closed.

'Help yourself to some port, me boy,' my uncle said, snapping the end off a cigar. 'And have a cigar, a small cigar! In the old days,' he went on, 'a point-to-point was a genuine race between hunters. When I was young all we did in the way of makin' up a fence was to cut the growth off the top of it and stick a flag in it. There was no nonsense then about whether the ditches were to you or away from you. We took 'em as they came. What is more we rode our own hunters, not badly schooled racehorses who'd never seen hounds. We pushed 'em around as fast as they would go to find out which of them and which of us was the best.

'In those days there were two country boys, by name of McHugh, brothers they were, who were great chaps to ride races. One of them was called Slippery Fippence and the other Jerry Jack Tom to distinguish him from his father Jerry Jack. Did you ever hear of them?'

I said I had not and I settled myself into my chair. We were evidently in for a sitting.

'Well,' said my uncle with a reminiscent chuckle, 'I'll tell you about them.

'They said of Slippery Fippence—and don't ask me why he was called Slippery Fippence because I don't know —that he was so crooked he could hide behind a corkscrew, and they said of Jerry Jack Tom that he couldn't go straight if he was shot out of a gun. So you see the sort they were. But ride? By the Lord Harry they could ride! There was very little between them in ability and it was said of each of them that he could bring home a donkey in front of the best.

'Sometimes the brothers would be the greatest friends; sometimes they would be at each other's throats. You never knew whether they were conniving together or against each other. A little matter of slipping the lead to a friend in the country who would be ready to return it as they came in didn't bother them at all, neither did the conspiring together to ride an unfortunate third party into a tree or a quarry or whatever happened to be handy round the course.

'Of course this was long before we became civilized and had INHSC representatives at our meetings to lay down the law and tell us to be good little boys. The two brothers were dangerous enemies whom no one liked very much to cross, so by and large they had things pretty well their own way.

But the fact that no one ever knew exactly how matters stood between them made it very difficult to bet.

'It made it difficult to ride against them, too, for you never knew whether they had the race fixed between themselves or whether they were trying to ride each other into the ground. The state of relations between them was a secret they kept to themselves, until one year, to the astonishment of everybody, they fell out and fell out openly.

'It seemed that the two of them had arranged for Slippery Fippence to win a certain race, but Slippery Fippence, unknown to his brother, had been getting on more and more intimate terms with a local bookie called Gentleman Jimmy Malone.

'He was called Gentleman Jimmy because he was very suave and cultivated and always wore a bowler-topper —that was a very smart hat in those days, you wouldn't remember it—and a grey covert coat, and had a most distinguished line of conversation. He had bought the bowler-topper and the covert coat at an auction of Lord Forth and Bargy's estate and effects, an auction brought about mainly by his own machinations. The devil himself knows where he got the line of conversation from, but that is by the way.

'Gentleman Jimmy had been, it appeared, for some time perturbed about the difficulty of making a book when he didn't know what the brothers were going to do. So he took to spoiling Slippery Fippence with little presents and to standing him half whiskies whenever they chanced to meet, which was much more often than usual although poor Slippery Fippence didn't realize this.

'At length, late one night in the smoky back room of Cassidy's public house, Slippery Fippence confided to Gentleman Jimmy that the next race they rode in the two of them had fixed it that he was going to win.

'It didn't take long for Gentleman Jimmy to see that if he could get Slippery Fippence to double-cross his brother the result would be exceedingly profitable for himself. He put this to Slippery Fippence; he put it strongly and backed up his arguments with certain cash promises so that it was not long before Slippery Fippence—about whom it was not said for nothing that he could hide behind a corkscrew —agreed to do as he wished.

'The brothers were artists in their own way. Even though they had a race fixed they liked to give the public the appearance at any rate of a run for their money. On this particular occasion the two of them were indulging in what looked like a whirlwind finish with Jerry Jack Tom just about half a length behind.

'Jerry Jack Tom, needless to say, had every intention of staying there when, three lengths from the finish, Slippery Fippence suddenly stopped riding, his horse stopped too, and Jerry Jack Tom shot out to the front and won by a neck. It was a pretty piece of work and Slippery Fippence profited enormously, but Jerry Jack Tom knew exactly what had happened and loud, long and public were his lamentations.

'"There is no honesty these days," he announced. "Ye can't even trust your own kith and kin!" And, "I've been stabbed in the back by me own brother!" he proclaimed over and over again in Cassidy's public house that night. He also announced that he would ride the living daylights out of Slippery Fippence if ever he dared to show his face against him on a race course again.

'The same evening Slippery Fippence and Gentleman Jimmy were celebrating their defeat in Julia Moran's, the rival public house, and it was not long before the news of Jerry Jack Tom's challenge travelled over there.

'"Tell him," Slippery Fippence said grandiloquently to the bearer of the news. "Tell him that if he comes agen me at Malane Races, he can ride his hardest and he can ride his best, an' he can ride harder than his hardest and better nor his best, and the only part of me he'll see is the back o' me jacket!"

'Cheers greeted this speech. Slippery Fippence waved a glass of whisky in his hand to round it off, Gentleman Jimmy raised his bowler-topper, bowed to the assembled company, and ordered another round. In a few hours the whole countryside had the news that there was going to be a right fight between the brothers at Malane.

'The brothers retired into great secrecy to prepare for the event. Both their houses became like training camps. Jerry Jack Tom had a great raw-boned bay called Red Heather that pulled like a train and Slippery Fippence a weedy chestnut thoroughbred called The Dandy, and each of them slept in a loft over his horse's box so as to be on the lookout for any interference.

'The countryside was divided, half of 'em rushing to back Red Heather, the other half going for The Dandy. There were other horses in the race but it was generally conceded that, now that the brothers were openly trying to beat each other, none of the rest had a chance. In fact there was a strong rumour that the other runners were withdrawing to leave the brothers free to fight it out between themselves.

'The only person to be worried about all this was Gentleman Jimmy and Gentleman Jimmy was very worried indeed, for if either of the brothers won he looked like losing a fortune. Gentleman Jimmy sat down and scanned the list of runners and wondered if there was any chance of a miracle happening and one of the outsiders winning.

'He took off his bowler-topper and he scratched his head and he put it on again and he furrowed his brow and while he was doing all this the door opened and the owner of one of the other runners walked in. He was no stranger to Jimmy and he bore the definite news that every one of the outsiders bar himself was withdrawing from the race. He himself had not quite made up his mind whether to run or not and before doing so he had a proposition to put to Jimmy.

'He put his proposition and the two of them sat down together and talked it out into the small hours. Finally they reached agreement about the financial side of the matter; a very satisfactory agreement, for it left each of them convinced that he had put it across the other. They then finished the whisky and parted.

'The next morning—and there were only two days before the race now—a grubby little boy pushed a note into Slippery Fippence's hand. This note was signed—as is usual, I believe, in such cases—A Well-wisher, and it told him that Jack Jerry Tom was backing his bets and had put a stack on The Dandy to win the race. Slippery Fippence ranted and swore when he got the note. He called down curses from heaven on dishonourable men. When he cooled down, however, he began to think and he thought exactly on the lines which Gentleman Jimmy and his friend had anticipated.

'He fetched from its hiding-place the roll of notes which represented his winnings on the recent race; then he paid a visit to Gentleman Jimmy and planked down the lot on Red Heather. No sooner had this been done than the same grubby little boy pushed a note into the hands of Jack Jerry Tom. This note informed Jerry Jack Tom that Slippery Fippence had just invested a large sum on the success of Red Heather. It too, oddly enough, was signed *A Well-wisher*.

'Jerry Jack Tom swore and his face set in more hatchet-like lines than ever. In half an hour's time he was knocking on the back door of Gentleman Jimmy's premises. He pushed a bundle of notes into the bookie's hand, told him to put the lot on The Dandy to win and took himself off muttering horrible things.

'I needn't tell you there was great excitement and tension on the day of the race. People walked and people went on outside cars and new-fangled motor-cars and every sort of conveyance to Malane Hill. There was the greatest crowd that had ever been seen and you couldn't turn round with the press of people on the hill. The three-card men and the trick-of-the-loop men and the hawkers and roulette wheels did a roaring trade.

'The crowd, of course, had come to see the race between the brothers. There were only three runners in it. Red Heather and The Dandy were at even money and you could get what you liked on the outsider. By this time the feeling between the rival supporters of Jerry Jack Tom and Slippery Fippence was running pretty high and people were backing their choice in anything from shillings to ten-pound notes. Gentleman Jimmy was standing there on an up-turned tea-chest in his bowler-topper and covert coat looking as benign as ever and raking in the bets.

'Malane Hill was a fine place for a race. It was a natural grandstand and there were only a couple of places on the course where the horses were hidden. It was a mile or so from the village of Malane. It's a flat part of the country there and the chapel spire in Malane is about the only other landmark and made one think of an old-time steeplechase.

'Red Heather and The Dandy both looked trained to a hair and fit to run for their lives. The brothers gripped their ash-plants and pulled down their caps and scowled at each other. No one could forecast which of them would win. All one could do was to back one's fancy—and hope.

'They went down to the start with Red Heather kicking and pulling and Jerry Jack Tom standing in his stirrups and cursing him. The crowd on the hill were quiet as they waited for the race of all time between the two brothers. The starter hadn't much trouble getting the three runners into line. He dropped his flag and off they went.

'The brothers were too experienced in the gentle art of losing races to start off at a snail's pace. They both got away well when the flag fell and went off at the steady hunting pace at which races were run in those days.

'There was nothing much to choose between the two of them. The third horse was lying handy about three lengths behind. They completed one circuit of the course like this and went off on their second. There was still no change in the order and all the horses were jumping perfectly. But the brothers were beginning to eye each other warily and to make surreptitious pulls on their horses' heads here and there and to go wide on corners so as to let the other fellow go ahead. The net result of all this was that neither of them succeeded in losing any ground but they slowed down the pace a bit.

'There was a dip in the ground about fifty yards from the last fence. This dip hid the riders from the crowd on the hill. By the time they came into it the scowls on the brothers' faces had deepened and Jerry Jack Tom had Red Heather's head back somewhere round his knees in an effort to hold him in.

'No sooner had the dip hidden them than Slippery Fippence drew his ash-plant from his left hand into his right and, leaning over, he hit Red Heather a real stinger across the quarters. Red Heather gave a snort and a bound, fought his head free from his rider's grip, and went for the last fence as if he was being ridden at it in a desperate finish. But Slippery Fippence, though he had set his rival going, soon found that he was not in much better case. In leaning over to strike Red Heather he had loosed his own hold on The Dandy's head.

'The Dandy was a fit horse and the gallop he had had round the course had scarcely made him blow. Seeing his old enemy galloping ahead he stretched out his head, got his legs under him and went after him. It looked to the rider of the third horse as if the brothers, despite themselves, were going to ride a finish, and in some agitation of mind he started to move up after them.

'When the horses came out of the dip, galloping like mad, Red Heather three lengths ahead and apparently all set to win, Gentleman Jimmy on his tea-chest was observed to turn slightly pale.

'He needn't have worried. Jerry Jack Tom couldn't stop Red Heather but there was something else that he could do. When Red Heather rose at the last fence he jabbed him hard in the mouth. Red Heather had had all sorts of things happen to him in his racing career, but this was a new one. He jumped big and he jumped bold and he liked to have his head free when he jumped, and this was something which hitherto his rider had always given to him.

'That jab in his mouth stopped him in mid-air. He hit the top of the fence and turned over into the next field. It was said by observers afterwards that as they went there was a smile of seraphic contentment on Jerry Jack Tom's face. Slippery Fippence was not much behind but, coming into the fence, he regained control of The Dandy.

'As his horse changed his feet on the top of the bank Slippery Fippence surveyed the *débâcle* below him. Red Heather lay stretched on his side; near his horse, spread-eagled like a star-fish and emitting the most artistic groans, was Jerry Jack Tom. It looked as if Slippery Fippence had the race at his mercy, which was exactly what Slippery Fippence did not want to have. No wonder his brother as he lay on the ground interrupted his series of groans with a chuckle of triumph. But Slippery Fippence was a man of resource. As he announced later—much later—the scene of woe beneath him struck him to the heart.

'"Bedad, me poor brother is kilt!" he exclaimed. "I must go for the priest!" And with that, gathering his horse together he abandoned the race and set off across country towards the chapel and the priest's house.

'Both the brothers had quite forgotten the third entrant who went on to win as he liked.'

My uncle finished speaking, drained his glass of port and lay back in his chair with a thin chuckle of ancient laughter.

'You are a wicked old reprobate,' I said to him—I cannot but think that the port which I had consumed had something to do with this outspokenness—for I had guessed for some little time back the identity of the third rider and I now knew the secret about which we had all wondered for so long. How big the bet was and how much he and Gentleman Jimmy had split between them were matters which I thought could well be left in oblivion.

'I'm surprised,' I went on, 'that Gentleman Jimmy didn't blackmail you.'

A faint cough sounded in the shadows and the elderly butler shuffled into the candlelight. He laid an ancient, claw-like hand on my uncle's shoulder.

''Tis long after ye should be in bed,' he quavered. 'An' keepin' the young gentleman up too and him with a race to ride tomorrow. Holy horrors, will ye look at the decanter! Don't you mind at all what Dr Morrissey told you about drinkin' port?'

'Bah! That old fool!' my uncle said. 'I've been tellin' Mr Welcome how we did the McHughs. They met their match when they met up with us, eh—Jeames?'

The butler's rheumy old eyes seemed to light up for a second.

'Oh, bedad, 'twas the gas of Cork, entirely,' he said with a cackle. ''Tis terrible hard on the nerves, that there book-makin', sir,' he here addressed himself to me. 'What with them crooked, thievin', connivin' blayguards the McHughs

I couldn't never balance me book right at all. 'Twas lucky for me when me poor nerves got too bad that your uncle was lookin' for someone to look after his house for him. I've had far greater peace of mind ever since, sir, and that's the truth of it.'

His claw-like hand tightened on my uncle's shoulder, and the creases on his face folded into what I can only describe as an unholy grin as he regarded my uncle with a look of mingled affection and domination.

'Indeed them was the times entirely, but lucky it was for me that your uncle had a place for me when I needed it. A friend in need is a grand thing, that's what I always do be sayin', sir.'

Then he looked me straight in the eyes. I had drunk too much port and his ancient face was wrinkled like old shoe-leather but I think, yes, I think, that he winked.

BREAKNECK

by Jon L. Breen

The final story brings this collection neatly full-circle, for it is a clever parody of the work of Dick Francis. American author Jon L. Breen is probably familiar to many readers as a writer of horse racing thrillers, and of one of these, Vicar's Roses, *English writer Peter Lovesey said recently, 'It is a glorious gallop over the whodunnit course—fast, funny and flouting most of the rules.'*

In introducing the following ingenious little story when it first appeared in Ellery Queen's Mystery Magazine, *Jon Breen admitted to a great admiration for Dick Francis' work and went on, 'At the time it was written he had never used a series character in his novels. Even now he has returned to a character only once, Sid Halley in* Odds Against *and* Whip Hand. *Ordinarily, the lack of a series character would seem to obviate the possibility of a parody. But Francis' heroes, always (at novel length) first-person narrators and often jockeys, have a style in common, as well as a tendency to undergo brutal beatings. And, of course, horse racing, usually steeplechasing, has figured to a greater or lesser degree in all of his novels.'*

I trust that Dick Francis—and other readers, too—will enjoy this last frisson of deadly odds as much as I did!

* * *

Lying in the mud, before the Colonel's chestnut clipped me with his right foreleg and knocked me senseless, I thought about Trudy Abbot's remark about small men always having to prove something. When I awoke in hospital, I had to pinch myself to prove I was alive. Moments later the arrows of pain in every fibre of my body made such a test unnecessary. I was alive and looking into Rud Mosby's scowling face.

I winced with the pain but got no sympathy.

'Wot happened?' he demanded.

'That gelding's no jumper, that's all.'

'Don't tell me that! I've been training jumpers thirty years, and that's a jumper.'

'Shadows he jumps, but fences are a bit of a sticky wicket for him. Did he come through all right?'

'He came through better than you. But we shot him anyway.'

'Oh. It was the Colonel's chestnut got me with his right fore.'

'I know. The jockey claimed interference against your bloody head.'

'Did the stewards allow it?'

'No, but you're suspended for a fortnight. And you'll never ride for me again, I can tell you.'

Trudy came later. 'Have to ride them, don't you?'

'It's my work.'

'A certified librarian, and you have to ride those damned jumpers. Little men always have to prove something. I fancy you fell off that horse and got kicked just so I'd come running and say I loved you. True, isn't it?'

'I wanted to stay on and win.'

'Huh! A lot you care about how I feel. And a certified librarian you are, too.'

'I can't be around books all day. I have a dust allergy.'

'You'll never change. Give us a little kiss.'

'I can't move. I'm in great pain.'

'Little men always have to prove something,' she said, and walked out.

At midnight after the night nurse had gone, three big blokes came into my room and beat me senseless with truncheons and riding crops. Nobody heard my screams and they found me in the morning. I was a bloody mess and a bit of an embarrassment to a tour going round the hospital.

At noon they discharged me, but I couldn't get any horses to ride at the Cleckheaton races. None of the trainers would talk to me. Soon I remembered I was inoperative for a fortnight and I went to fly my plane. I smashed up in a cornfield and the farmer chased me off with a pitchfork. I brought back the local bobby from the next town, riding on his crossbar, but all traces of my plane wreckage were gone. It made me a bit suspicious.

I went to see Trudy and told her things were not going well for me. She put me to work cataloguing her library. I had a sneezing fit. She said I was disgusting and told me to go away.

As soon as I stepped out of the door I saw the three blokes who'd beat me up. They took off in a Jaguar. I stole a horse from the stable and followed them to the farm where I'd crashed my plane.

I'd picked the horse at random, but he was more of a jumper than the crab that Rud Mosby had put me on the day before. He took the fences well but not too quietly. The three blokes saw me coming, and soon they came after me with their riding crops and truncheons, the farmer following closely with his pitchfork.

Knocked off my mount, I noticed his right fore hoof. It was the Colonel's chestnut. I should have recognized him before. Then Trudy knew the Colonel!

The chestnut helped me fight them off, flailing his hooves, as a good jumper will. I tied them all to the farmer's privy and took off for the Cleckheaton race course.

The trap was laid at the fourth fence. I could see them in the distance, the three crouched figures lurking behind the fence, hidden from the view of the riders and from the stands far in the distance.

I joined the field on the flat and surged to the front. The chestnut's ears twitched competitively. The stands were too far away for them to tell I was an interloper, though I had no silks on, only my flying togs. The other riders noticed, and shouted at me, but I pulled away from them. I had to reach that jump first.

The chestnut took the jump beautifully. At the height of

his soaring leap, just as he cleared the fence, I dived from his back and wrestled with the three hidden figures: Rud Mosby, the Colonel, Trudy Abbot.

'All in it together, were you?' I cried. 'Your horse betrayed you, Colonel, like a good jumper will.'

I threw them all in a pile, clear of the charging field, but as the seventeen of them cleared the fence, a big bay mare clipped me with her left fore and knocked me senseless.

Waking up in hospital, aching in every bone, I told a Scotland Yard man about the plot to end racing in Britain forever. He assured me Trudy, Mosby, and Colonel, the farmer, and the three blokes were all safely rounded up.

The Colonel's chestnut was cited by the Jockey Club for heroism.

I was warned off for life.

It gives me lots of time to fly.

ACKNOWLEDGMENTS

The Editor would particularly like to thank the following for their help and assistance in the assembling of this collection: Andrew Hewson, Michael Motley, Julian Symons, Robert Bloch, Bill Lofts and especially Ernest Hecht. He also wishes to acknowledge his gratitude to the following authors, their agents and publishers for permission to reprint copyright stories in this collection: John Johnson Ltd for 'The Day of the Losers' by Dick Francis and 'Outside Chance' by John Welcome; Macmillan & Co for 'The Broken Link Handicap' by Rudyard Kipling; Constable & Co Ltd for 'The Snatching of Bookie Bob' by Damon Runyon; The Bodley Head for 'The Race-Gang Racket' by Frank Johnston; Methuen & Co Ltd for 'The Ascot Tragedy' by H. C. Bailey and 'Horse of Death' by Ralph Straus; Mercury Publishing Co for 'Horseshoes for Luck' by Anthony Gilbert; Scott Meredith Literary Agency for 'Long Shot' by Ellery Queen; A. P. Watt Literary Agency for 'Jorkens Consults a Prophet' by Lord Dunsany; Hodder & Stoughton Ltd for 'The Owners' Handicap' from *The Brighter Buccaneer* by Leslie Charteris, copyright © 1933 by Simon Templar Limited; A. M. Heath Literary Agency for 'The Racing Robot' by Robert Bloch; Curtis Brown Ltd for 'The Grand National Case' by Julian Symons; Victor Gollancz Ltd for 'A Derby Horse' by Michael Innes; Michael Motley Ltd for 'A Day with the Toffs' by Geoff O'Hara; The Scarecrow Press Inc., for 'Breakneck' by Jon L. Breen.

The comments on Edgar Wallace by James Cameron are reprinted by permission of the *New Statesman*, in which magazine they first appeared; those by E. C. Bentley on Damon Runyon by permission of Constable & Co.